Off Locusts

and

Wild Honey

To my good Friend Phil — Thanks for the good times!

BRIAN BEATTIE

ISBN: 1449904254
ISBN-13: 9781449904258
LCCN: 2010901419

Printed in the United States of America.

Part One

$\mathcal{H}$e had a skiff hidden next to a pine tree near a bend in the river. On a Sunday in June, he made his way through the woods. He recognized a sporadic worn walkway. Where the canopy of trees spread out again farther on, the obviousness of a trail disappeared among the pine needle-covered, sunlight-spotted floor.

A full-lunged easiness underpinned his thoughts. Various birds chirped or flitted through the branches. The steady, quick percussion snare hammer of a woodpecker reminded him of the tavern. He saw the woodpecker by a dash of red up on ahead clinging to a dead bog tree rising from the water. That was past the point where the forest floor edged into marshy ooze. Spill-off from the river had stagnated to create that. He looked that way and walked along the edge. Some of the sapless, moss-laden bog trees were dotted with holes that resembled a shotgun blast before they ended in a craggy top. The holes in those hundreds of forlorn trees sticking up like empty husks reminded him of the barnacled pilings and torn planks of a blown-away pier, the remnants of a hurricane-battered structure he'd seen down on the coast when he'd been younger.

He didn't want anything to do with that marsh on his right. He'd seen reptile eyes in there before. Once he stumbled onto what he believed was a nest of alligator's eggs half buried in the mud. He'd had a mind that time to use his ax handle on the nest. But with a bit of awe at the discovery, he'd held back. Years ago, he'd taken the blade out of the ax handle. He carried the shaft as an aid for clearing brush or in case he needed it for protection.

The woods were more than five miles from town. Although it hadn't happened in the twenty years he'd been through there, a hungry predator might stir up enough courage.

He'd cussed himself for leaving those eggs. By allowing the gators to live and grow, he could've been instigating his own death. On his way back that time, he'd checked again on the nest. Some magpies were eating up the eggs. Despite his relief, he'd fought back an impulse to shoo away the scavengers. But he'd avoided that the same as he'd avoided taking the ax handle to the eggs.

So it worked out anyway, he'd told himself, like his cares did during the week when his kids or grandkids pulled on his patience, trying to avoid their daily tasks so they could go out and find their own play or trouble. Those cares would evaporate or at least become suspended for a while before they came back down on him heavily, somewhat depressively, and grippingly real on Mondays at his elementary school custodian job.

As he came to the large rock, resembling to him a distorted, half-smashed face, he knew to turn. He recognized a furrowed brow in the uneven wavy lines at the top of rock. That portion stuck out like a lumpy forehead. Below it was a jagged indenture that could be an eye socket. Then there was a crevice that could easily be mistaken for a mouth warped into a half smile down near where the rock ended in the ground.

In an uplifted mood, he greeted what he saw as the face of Bo Caine before turning toward the water. He could hear the river faintly now as a steady tapping on his eardrums. It sounded like someone dumping a bunch of marbles off a roof onto a concrete walkway, constantly tap, tap, tapping, until it all ran together in a steady rush of wet noise. The river sound came up out of the woods like a live creature drowning out the sound of the birds.

Where he would launch would be calm. He wouldn't have to fight it. He knew that if he got going past where you could see the first bridge his skiff couldn't handle it. If he got caught in that current, he might not stop until he was near downtown Mobile. The current got going too fast there. He remembered having to use all his arm power to pull over near the bridge and walk back carrying the skiff, which took most the day. He didn't want any part of that current. The gurgling laughter of the wide stream grew broader and deeper as the air got slightly cooler.

The tree came into view. Approaching it, he kicked at the brush underneath, connecting his toe with the hull of the skiff. Stepping around to the front of the brush, he felt for the rope, a black plastic rope he'd used to tie it up with. He pulled the rope taut so he could see where to grab the stern. Grabbing hold, he yanked the skiff out from the brush, breaking a few limbs in the process but leaving enough to camouflage again.

Light reflected off the water. He broke into a heavier sweat. He could smell and taste the water, humidly in the air, making him sleepy for a second. He entertained the thought of a nap. But to be back on time, he needed to keep going and get some fish before five. He was responsible from habit now. He only drank every month or so. With those grandkids to provide for, he'd straightened up and didn't fool around like some of the others.

He pulled the aged fiberglass skiff to the water. It had mildew stains across the bottom. On the side of the prow he could still read the outline of the formerly decaled black lettering marking it as his, *Snade's Skiff.* The smell of it was brash and sickening to him at first, but then turned familiar and full of promise of what the river might bring. The worn-out cover on the seat cushion gave off a heated-up plastic smell.

When he got to the water, he pulled his rubber boots out of the bag he'd carried with him and put them on. Then he took a scrub brush tied to the seat and scrubbed off some of the mildew, spreading a greenish tint to the sides. He went back to the brush and pulled out his cane pole. The shorter, cheap fishing rod with a mechanized reel, the one his wife gave him as a present eight Christmases ago, was already in the skiff. Today he'd prefer the more direct feel of the cane pole.

The bank came up at a gradual rise three feet off the water. It was a mixture of soft, muddy dirt splotched with lichen that fell off in loose pieces as he maneuvered the skiff. He slipped the skiff off the edge of the bank and out into the water. The rope still held the stern as he stepped into it carefully. He threw his bag with the hooks and bait in the back and slid the cane pole under the seat. He faced toward the woods as he gripped the rope with one hand and placed the other on the muddy bank, then eased himself into the skiff. For a slight moment, the utter solitude of the woods spooked him. There was a vast emptiness of human activity. Strong predators lurked there. He finished the routine of untying the stern and left the rope in a jaunty squiggle on the bank.

After he pushed off with his paddle, he brought the bag up and started working at a worm on the hook. As soon as he got it on, he put it into the water, and then set the pole under his leg. He paddled earnestly out into the broader part of the river. He knew the current enough now to know he couldn't slack at this point. He put some muscle into it. Steady beads of sweat ran from his black and gray hairline, dropping down his brown face. He wore a loose beige shirt with the top two catches unbuttoned. He pulled hard on both paddles that he'd locked in as oars to get him over by the pebbly sandbar that he knew was a favorite croaker locale. In the past, he'd even gotten bass there.

Moving steadily downstream, he got across at an angle. The gasoline colors on the water appeared. He'd traced the colors back before. They got thicker upriver where he'd seen some black sludge on the bank. He thought of the rock face back in the woods.

When he reached the sandbar, he didn't see any more gasoline or black sludge. But the gasoline sheen had spread closer than before. Those at the chemical plant said the water they used from the river went through filtered containers before it went back in, but he figured some of it must've been spilling. Ever since April, he'd been seeing more dead fish stinking on the sandbar. He landed, kicked off some dead croakers, and cast his line into the pool on the other side of the bar.

* * *

He'd responded to the fire along with the rest of those on duty. Under the forced silence of the sirens, he took stock. At six feet three and over two hundred thirty pounds, he was among the largest men in the department, and among those, he was the most fit. He wore his hair nearly skin short. His eyes were darker brown than his skin.

By the time they arrived, it was a two alarm. Nothing seemed salvageable. He presumed any people still inside were dead. The warehouse and residence were too far away for the fire to have been detected earlier. A neighbor had traced the smell, saw the smoke, and then called it in. Licks of flame still bled out the roof, and a thick, nacreous smoke billowed out in gray and black streaks. Although it was June, the winter smell of burning wood permeated the air. Charred two-by-fours stuck out where part of the roof had caved in and lay smoldering.

He could smell a less natural odor mixed in with the smoke and burnt wood. The smell was faint, but he recognized it as related to chemical explosions. He put on his breathing mask and took an ax.

After kicking in the front door, he proceeded cautiously through what appeared to be a living room. He backed up and knelt down because it was too hot to walk straight ahead, even in his suit. Pictures were twisted and warped on the walls. He crouched low and edged his way through the room then took a left down a hallway to check the bedrooms.

Through the heat and the mask, he heard something like a cat meowing, maybe multiple cats. He heard what sounded like a ceiling beam crack and fall toward the back of the dwelling nearer to the attached warehouse. He yelled through the mask's robotic transfer of his vocal cords for anyone to respond or answer. Moving quickly, he reached what he guessed was the master bedroom, a dark, plain room with black curtains. The whole room was burning.

Off Locusts and Wild Honey

One curtain had caught fire up toward the top of its rings. He called out and heard animal sounds again. The noise sounded farther away.

Back in the hall, he made his way into another bedroom. A plastic toy tricycle lay deformed from heat, burning in a corner. A child's bed was aflame. He overturned the bed quickly to look under it. He checked the closet where board games and dolls burned, sending out acrid odors of incinerating nylon and cotton.

He thought he heard a cat from behind. He glanced into another room from the hall. There was no bed there, and mildew clustered the walls. The terrible smell of the room invaded his mask just as the ceiling collapsed over it. His veteran heart motored faster, awestruck by real danger again. He considered this could be the ending moments. He thought he'd pinpointed the cat, but the sound was coming from the master bedroom. He hadn't checked the master bathroom. He scrambled toward it, thinking the delay could've been too much. He just wanted another thirty seconds.

He saw the kitten among six other apparently dead or passed out ones. But this was instantly surpassed by the sight of an unconscious little girl. She was slanted unnaturally on the tiled floor. Steam rose above her from the running water in the room that the heat was converting to its gaseous state. She'd have inhalation sickness at the least. The little girl's light orange halter-top and green skirt stretched underneath her. Gently, ever so gently now, he picked her up. Under the influence of adrenaline, she seemed too light, like she might easily slip out of his grip.

Part of the hall wall caved in. He looked at the bedroom window, but it seemed too high up. Limited options

7

appeared and were quickly discarded. He could hand her off, but no one could hear him.

He laid the girl down for a second then felt for a space between studs. He pulled his ax back and swung frantically to cut through the drywall. Kicking, punching, and hatcheting, he got through to daylight. His suited arm went through one side of the house. It must've looked strange and alien there sticking through, like the house itself was spawning disproportionately miniature limbs just as it was about to be consumed. The growing hole his arm had made brought a trickle of smoke with it.

He pulled his arm back in then put his boot through. There was a gap between the two studs. Two of the others held onto the limp girl he slid through the space. They grabbed her from his outstretched arm. He heard back and forth yelling. A hose was pointed on top of where the hole had formed in the side of the burning house.

He moved back to the bathroom, tucked the kitten against his side, and then rushed toward the space he was too big to fit through. He felt the studs holding him back and looked up to see a circular flame hole appearing in the ceiling. The roof was going to come down. He shouted out for them to move back. He hurried back to the entry of the bedroom and then ran shoulder down with everything. The studs and a section of wall gave way. Simultaneous to his exit, the roof fell inward where the two displaced vertical studs had been. In a mess of wood and drywall, he lay in uncut grass and weeds. He could feel others carrying him away. It got lighter then he lost consciousness.

* * *

He drove his Maiden County vehicle onto one of Caine's properties. A burnt-out hulk of a warehouse came into view. As he got closer to the wreckage, he could distinguish more clearly an adjoined residence, a smaller brick and wood structure. Half the roof was gone. The rest of the building was warped and covered in soot.

He'd heard the Caines bought the land originally to raise chickens to supply the nearby processing plant. That business plan altered once the developers and owner realized the business costs of separating the chickens from the machines by this much distance.

Once the chickens had been moved closer to the other industrial buildings along the river, the warehouse must've stood empty awhile. He'd heard that Caine had later leased it to a man who turned it into a machine shop focusing on engine repair and small welding jobs. Within five years that'd been abandoned. The Reynoldses moved in to use it primarily as a residence. Small machine repair continued there on an irregular basis.

He questioned why the drug activity had been allowed to go on for so long. After several months, they'd been on the verge of getting a warrant. An odd sense of vulnerability swept over him as his boots crunched through the ruins. Backup was a call away, but the radio had announced a traffic accident that would decrease response time. He didn't expect anyone besides the security guard, but he drew and took the safety off his firearm.

It was unclear whether Reynolds had left before or after the fire. Based on what was found, it pointed to a hasty exit. The other forensic detectives and federal agent

Mantle would handle more of this today. He scouted out the place to make sure nothing had been disturbed.

He conceptualized Reynolds again. Supposedly Reynolds had gotten the alias from throwing pitchforks into various farm animals as a kid and young teenager, revealing a cruel streak. None of that had been verified beyond word of mouth, but Reynolds did have a tattoo of the tool for baling hay on his forearm. He'd seen it when booking Reynolds into jail one night on misdemeanor charges for assault and possession.

Whether or not the farm bit was true or not, Reynolds had inherited tendencies. The mother had been a notorious drunk. Since she'd moved here, she'd spent half her life behind bars for her antics. He wasn't exactly sure where she'd moved from, New Jersey or New York. Wherever she came from, she'd inherited money and a mean alcoholic streak.

No one claimed to be Reynolds' father. He imagined the kids in school teasing and joking at Pitchfork's tall, lanky, awkward body, and at his quiet demeanor. Fertile ground for the makings of a psychopath. Reynolds had attended one of the local high schools before disappearing for a while during his twelfth-grade year.

They'd gotten to some in the network of criminals drawn in around Reynolds. That was how they'd almost been ready. The gun reassured him in case any of those vultures turned up.

The thought languidly occurred to him that this type of work—cleaning up a mess while gathering evidence—could as easily be done by a sanitation worker. An internal unsettling affected him. He calmed himself back into his rigid exterior as he convinced himself it was easy money.

As he nudged at a twisted, charred fragment with his boot, he looked to the dark indention that marked the wooded path going toward the shack nearer to the river. The shack was the only unburnt structure still standing.

He remembered the tattoo. Although it had faded somewhat and was a simple object, a stick with five or so prongs, it'd been done in great detail and shadow to add some dimension to it. The other mouthy criminals said Reynolds had stayed online most of the time, high on meth.

* * *

Reaching next to his nameplate, where he saw *Robert Mantle* marking the inner sanctum of his work, he turned to the bikers' lengthier federal files. Cat's Paw had beaten charges on murder two in Michigan, but had served three years on an arson conviction in Arizona and did some time for trafficking narcotics in California. There were twelve separate convictions for misdemeanor assaults and thefts dispersed across the country, with multiple other charges dismissed. Nothing apparently in this state yet. Muffler had served three years for the arson as well and had done a year and a day for assault with a tire iron. A possession with intent to sell had been dismissed in California.

He considered returning for another field search. They could tie Cat's Paw and Muffler to the property several times since they'd been watching them. Some of the agents suspected they were the ones who introduced Pitchfork to the meth business. To their knowledge, Reynolds wasn't an official Wraith but more of a business ally providing a safe house or a possible drop point. Some misshapen expired driver's licenses and the remnants of what looked like a laminated social security card turned up from the fire, but those didn't concern the bikers.

He wasn't sure yet where the girl fit into the picture, other than as an unlikely survivor. Her age was estimated at five or six years. There were no records of her, no birth certificate or other hospital records. She'd been moved to an orphanage and wasn't communicating. She could be Reynolds's daughter, but no tests to confirm this had been done yet.

They were given access without much interference by the state. They'd obtained a warrant before the fire, but they'd been waiting on the bikers' presence to execute it. The fire had destroyed most of what they'd expected and hoped to find there. A gnarled chunk of plastic had been discovered that they believed had been a laptop. Maybe a hard drive was still salvageable. Most metals had melted down in the intense heat.

He'd lost any good guess of where the bikers might be. They could be at their rumored enclave in Canada. They could probably last a year up there or at least through the summer. Their information and likenesses had been passed on to northern border patrol. He suspected they would be crossing through unmanned portions of the border given the tightened security and their criminal records.

* * *

He expected the people of the county knew Judge Aldruss obsessed over the Old Testament. Oftentimes verses from the text would come forth in Aldruss's speech, mostly in the form of admonishments. And he'd heard there'd been no hot water in the wood house little Jebediah grew up in on the outskirts of the city. Aldruss's family had to boil well water to get it hot. Despite the efficient spread of the computer to court administration, that inconvenient part of Aldruss's heritage must've led to his jaundiced eye toward and reluctant use of new technology.

He knew Aldruss's father Joseph had been employed by Caine's father Alcorn at the chicken farm before it morphed and expanded into the chicken processing plant. He could see the Aldrusses becoming linked with the Caines.

Alcorn had a reputation for shrewd bargaining. Based on an employment law case, he knew Alcorn paid according to when demands required movement of the chickens, not according to what Alcorn considered a welfare handout of minimum wage. The Great Depression must not have bothered the Caines as much as the Aldrusses.

Joseph must've managed to keep food on the table for his wife and five kids. He'd heard Alcorn would reward him excess hunting meat. While Joseph outwardly revered the Caines for the most part, he must've harbored a latent hatred for his dependence. At least if it'd been him, he could see thinking that way. He'd been told Joseph had taken out some of his frustration by whipping his oldest son Jebediah with a birch branch, many times for minor misbehaviors. Of all Joseph's children, Jebediah had received the strictest treatment, fasts and whippings for not concentrating on his studies enough or for engaging in childhood frolics on the weekends like stick ball, which Joseph must've considered unnecessary leisure. As soon as he was eleven, Jeb went to work at the chicken farm the same as his father.

Lore had it that while Jeb was still a teenager, Joseph joined a Pentecostal church. The congregation occasionally passed around strict nine based on the Bible passage in Mark sixteen. Joseph tried it himself a couple of times and forced Jeb to do it at the age of fifteen. Jeb's eye must've grown that fanatical gleam after tasting the snake poison.

After a few more years, Joseph had become disenchanted with the snake handlers and returned to the Southern Baptists. Jeb followed him but must've been permanently affected by the Pentecostals. Jeb had been described as reserved and deferential to most authority figures and others in the community, but he now had a confrontational aspect. Jeb had developed a way of saying something that could give a shock, occasionally causing uneasiness in his neighbors or the lawyers before him.

By the time Jeb had gotten into law school in the early seventies, that aspect must've served him well during contentious classes where he was reputed to have been a controversial student. His strictly conservative views nearly always outstripped everyone else even in a predominantly conservative school. From those early days of his career, he'd dedicated himself to promoting the return of the law to what many considered an archaic and cryptic place, where equality for race and gender were deemphasized. This must've led to his being chosen for many debates as a kind of unpopular whipping post. Although a good number considered themselves conservative in politics and culture, they must've feared Aldruss's views were too extremely backwards and counterproductive, especially considering what had happened in the previous decade.

After managing to graduate from law school, Jeb must've been unable to find anyone to hire him as an associate as he'd gone into practice for himself. Most of his clientele came from the Southern Baptists he'd attended services with and from the Pentecostals. Through writing and speech, Jeb continued to vehemently and publicly attack what he thought to be the misguided and ultimately evil direction the federal courts were taking the law. Jeb must've eked out a living for a while and found a wife at church that didn't say much to contradict him. They'd been unable to conceive children.

The most important factor in his run for county judge must've been his allegiance to Boesephius Caine, who must've recalled the long employment of Joseph Aldruss. He'd heard Bo had bankrolled the campaign indirectly. Jeb had leaned on those among his circles to donate the maximum allowed when the strictures on such donations were less often enforced. By the time the election came around, Jebediah Aldruss squeaked enough votes out to take the vacancy left by a retiring judge.

He'd heard through mutual acquaintances that Bo and Aldruss didn't meet often, but occasionally Bo would invite the judge to social functions. If Aldruss attended, they said he always seemed uncomfortable and out of place. Despite the awkwardness of their social interaction, Aldruss's rulings seemed to minimize, as much as they could, damage to Bo's interests. When the chicken processing plant had been sued by a maimed worker, Aldruss was quick to find among the facts the employee's negligent disregard of adequate safety measures in place.

Despite his partiality to Bo, he noticed Aldruss was careful enough to recuse himself in the more obvious conflicts where Bo's company or Bo himself was a party to the suit. But because of Bo's extensive interests in the community, Aldruss still sat on many cases that affected those interests. He figured Bo owned roughly fifteen percent of the county land and had influence in much of the business transacted thereon. On hearing criticism of his bias, he'd read where Aldruss bristled publicly in an editorial: *Find me another judge who grew up here that says they don't know Bo Caine or his family. I took an oath to be impartial and that's what I've done and continue to do.*

The maimed worker's case was summarily dismissed after Aldruss found that the man had assumed the risk by working in an area he'd been told to stay out of the day earlier. The man's supervisor had testified to that. The worker testified that he'd never been told that and pointed out a number of safety violations, including investigations done by the federal workplace safety agency that resulted in several citations being handed out.

The worker further testified he'd been walking the usual route to his place on the assembly line when a cord that hadn't been properly put away by the last shift caused him to trip. He fell into the part of the assembly line that chops up the chicken, causing him to lose an arm down to his forearm and two fingers of the other hand. Across the country, most other similar assembly lines had guards over the grinders to protect against these types of injuries. Despite Aldruss's ruling, over a year later his decision was overturned on appeal. Even though Aldruss had a good number of decisions overturned on appeal, he kept winning re-election as Bo and the Christian backers kept supporting him.

He'd learned from criminal matters that what made Aldruss more intolerable than usual wasn't the charge itself or that it'd been amended down, but the fact of a defense lawyer in front of him. The individual differences between defense lawyers must've blurred in Aldruss's mind into a concept of sleazy, untrustworthy, subversive creatures that he had to watch closely and engage in constant battle. To him they must've been a class of undesirables based on the sole fact of defending someone alleged to have committed a crime. He believed Aldruss secretly enjoyed berating them and coming down hard on their clients.

Most defense lawyers had heard this or unfortunately learned this from being in front of Aldruss. They avoided him however they could. Many used affidavits of prejudice and continuances to get away from him. He'd done so himself. Some of the less scrupulous ones had even made excuses of getting sick or making plans previous to getting Aldruss's permission for a continuance. Aldruss sanctioned those whose excuses weren't backed by written proof.

Despite Aldruss's general scorn of this whole class of lawyers, he did have a few names among them to whom he must've been obliged to dole out special treatment. They'd usually gotten that status through connections with Caine or Caine's interests or through consistently offering up their clients to Aldruss after entering a plea deal they knew he wouldn't follow. To Aldruss they must've seemed akin to subordinates in a culture where the high priest performs human sacrifice and rewards those who help prepare the ceremony. Those defense lawyers were the ones who rarely if ever went to trial. If they did, it was in a back-ended fashion as they gritted their teeth. They were the ones who could be heard talking how good a deal it was. They were careful to slip in, but de-emphasize, the caveat that the judge had the authority to give the maximum sentence.

* * *

At a local bar about a mile from the construction site, he questioned his co-worker, "And why should I care what Bo Caine owns?" When people got within earshot, silence irritated him. He'd fill it up quickly. Not receiving an answer, he continued, "I come up from Florida to work, and he's the one providin'. Florida was goin' gangbusters for a while, but people stopped buyin' the houses. It's overbuilt now. Put all yur Bo Caines together and they'd fit in a Florida tycoon's shoe. I for one am okay with Bubba Caine 'cause he ain't as greedy as I seen." He took a deep slug from his bottled domestic.

The co-worker, who he knew only as Louis, said he'd worked locally and in the surrounding counties for years, commuting down from near Montgomery. He noticed Louis had problems controlling one of his eyelids from blinking when he spoke. "Well, you ain't heard it all then. All you know is he pays a little 'bove the prevailin' wage and you get tail easier 'round here. No wonder you don't care. But when that dries up, whatcha gonna do?"

He innately found answers in this type of conversation. "Well, I got half a mind to go lay pipe in Miss'sippi. If it came down to it. Plenty of work over in Miss'sippi or N'awlins." He took another slug of beer.

Louis's wrinkled, stubbled, wry-looking face got irritated, a look full of bitterness. He thought it aged his co-worker by ten to twenty years depending on the light. He listened to tan-colored, receding-blond-haired Louis speak again. "Let me tell ya a little somethin' 'bout the man that employees you. I been hearin' 'bout Caine since I's a boy, 'bout Caine done this, Caine done that. Whenever I first heard 'bout him, it wasn't 'cause he was a pleasant guy. It's 'cause he sent the man that collected our rent when it was late. It was Bo Caine's daddy who was in charge of the land our apartment buildin' was on then, but then he turned it over to Bo. One time when a neighbor couldn't pay he found a lead pipe through his windshield the next day."

He was beginning to feel a buzz. He ventured to interrupt, "Zat all? Lemme ask you. How many kids you have runnin' 'round that apartment complex you grew up in? Couldn't it have been one of 'em? That ain't nothin' but chance. Even if it were true, a man's gotta pay his rent. I ain't sayin' it's right to bully, but hell, you gotta stay tough to keep yur money." He gestured to the plump-faced and gap-toothed woman bartender for another round.

Louis asked, "You hear that Pitchfork's his son?"

He felt his face features changing like someone had stuck a dart in his Adam's apple. He meant to give Louis a more guarded, scrutinizing look, listening to Louis go on, "Yeah, that meth head out in the boonies that started the fire. Where that girl was saved." He watched Louis take his look as a sign to speak on, "Yeah, they say he's Caine's bastard. His momma was a drunk. I heard she used to carry 'round vodka pints in 'er purse 'cause she couldn't stand to be away from 'er liquor cabinet very long.

"Rumor was she used to throw 'erself at Caine or made 'erself 'vailable whenever he pleased. He already had him a slew of women. She was from nawthurn money. She come down to Montevalla. Drank 'erself crazy. After school she settled in nearby here. Put all these paintin's up in 'er yard. I drove by once and seen one. Looked like someone swallowed some watercolor and puked it back up on a canvas. Thought to myself, why would anyone pay for that?

"She got worse and worse the longer she stayed. Must not have had anywhere to return to. People said 'er folks either 'bandoned 'er, disowned 'er, or had died. But someone must've left 'er money. She'd made a fool of 'erself in front of the Buck Points club people. Gave wild speeches that didn't make no sense. Once the paper said she was found downtown in the fountain asleep with 'er head restin' up against the concrete, where everybody could see through 'er clothes.

"They say one night Bo Caine was at the Buck Points and had him a bunch of fine scotch and high-priced wine. He got up from there. Left without anybody seein' him. But his car stayed in the parkin' lot. Someone at the club seen him come for it the next mornin', in the same dress clothes, all untucked and stained with muck. Pitchfork's momma lived a couple of miles from there. She had the little Pitchfork 'bout three seasons later. Those that've seen him say he's got his momma's face behind that hair. But his eyes are spittin' images of Bo Caine's. People got to sayin' Bo may've gone down there and sired that bastard. She was older by 'bout ten years. He must've been in rut. Or maybe he was only drunk and reckless enough to do it.

"Anyway, nobody had any hard proof 'sides 'em eyes and Bo's unexplained disappearance for the night. People spec'late that's why he never run Pitchfork and his momma off the property even when the law started sniffin' 'round there. People said it, you know, softened Caine to provide some basics for the bastard."

He roused himself from gloomy thoughts. "So he might of had a bastard son. It ain't unheard of these days. One could probably call my boy Chris a bastard if you're talkin' 'bout bein' born outta wedlock. Maybe I shouldn't of had so much bourbon after that Ole Miss game and forgot my rubbers. I didn't mind havin' a son. That dirty bitch left him to me to care for. You know, they can prove who's who all the way back to the pharaohs these days. Why don't they get a paternity on him?"

He watched tan-hided Louis lean back ponderously, his eye flickering. "Some wonder why. The momma had 'er trust fund monies to take 'er awhile, but she blew it on alcohol and some say cocaine 'em bikers started runnin' through 'er place. Some said she was plain out of 'er mind. That she didn't want to appear in court, and didn't really want Caine money. No one knows why Pitchfork don't push for the money."

He was agitated in having to tidy up the subject. "If he's Caine's son, I don't think he could get any money now 'less Bo Caine ain't written a will. Lawyers could do that for him. You ain't tole me nothin' impressive yet. I heard of tycoons down in Florida that'd charter a boat and have a party goin' 'round the Caribbean, with people fallin' overboard. They give away the hush money to keep those people acciden-tally drowned. And they sired as many bastards as a bull sea lion. But they don't pay no money 'cause the women on the islands don't know who they is."

He listened to blond-headed Louis wheeze a little while watching him light a cigarette. "That may be somethin', but talk 'bout a mean streak. You should've known the bachelor Caine 'fore he got married and had 'em kids. He used to run 'em cockfights. Once when he lost and the other guy said somethin' smart, he grabbed the other guy's rooster and twisted its neck till it broke. Then he threw it all limp and bleedin' in the dust.

"And he has a thing 'bout snakes. Used to chop 'em up. People that've been up in his mansion say he's got a bunch of snake skins up on the walls in one of the rooms. Boa constrictas, coral snakes, moccasins, yellow snakes from South 'merica I don't know the name of. Like he was worshippin' somethin'.

"And there was the contraversy when he was young. They went on a boar chase. One of the party was known to have strained tensions with him. Caine and he had words. Some say it was an intentional setup to invite him like that. The other guy was from a strong family. It was over who was to get credit for a boar they'd both shot.

"Caine had the type of high-powered rifle that'd blow a hole straight through any flesh and bone it hit. This boar had a hole the size of a half dollar in its guts, but it had a slug in its brain that matched the other guy's gun. Now the other guy's slug would've certainly kilt it. It may've been able to get on with the gut shot 'tributed to Caine. That may've 'ventually kilt it, but if Caine's'd come first, they'd aheard some squealin'. The less partial witnesses said there wasn't.

"When they came up on the dead boar, Caine looked over at his men and tole 'em to hoist it up on some poles and take it back to the truck. It was a big sucker, like two maybe three hundred pounds. The other guy wanted to claim it and stuff it. He's arguin' his bullet obviously kilt it, so by all rights the boar should be his. Caine ignored him and started to hoist up the carcass with his men. When the other guy put hands on him, he dropped the pole and they got into a fistfight. They punched each other, rolled next to the dead boar, and fell into the mud and leaves. When the others pulled 'em apart, it looked like one of the two's huntin' knives had fallen out on the ground. They got up and Caine laughed at him, suggestin' they go on 'nother hunt. They left the boar alone, leavin' a man and a dog to watch over it.

"Caine suggested they stalk the next one 'stead of shootin' it from the tree stands to see who's better. So when they saw 'nother smaller one, may've been one of the dead boar's youngin's, they got down from the stands, quiet as they could, and began creepin' toward where they'd seen it wander out of range. They heard some rustlin' and began chasin' lookin' for a clean shot. The others lagged behind 'em and lost sight, but could hear the other guy's voice yellin' out somethin' like, hold up! A shot cracked and echoed. The bullet tore a hole clean through the man's torso. Blowed right through his liver. Bled him to death 'fore the medics could make it back there.

"The county looked at a murder charge at first, but then dropped it down to manslaughter. 'Ventually the judge dismissed the case sayin' there wasn't 'nough proof for the jury to consider other than a huntin' accident. It was in the papers for a while, but then it died away."

He looked blankly at the shelves of hard liquor and ordered another beer.

* * *

He donned his black cassock. He wore it around town openly despite being visibly shunned by the more severe Baptists. He wrote his Jesuit friend residing in Mobile that he sometimes relished his less than popular role. He fondly remembered traveling to the Vatican together where they shared many good meals and a good deal of wine. He reviewed his most recent letter requesting donations to cover the utility bills of the rectory and school.

He signed and sealed the letter, leaving it on his desk. He hated to consider others who worshipped as Christians as possible enemies, but his conscience wouldn't accept giving into pressure to move or disband what he'd inherited five years ago. He was still young and resourceful, and they were a diligent flock.

A stubborn group had come up from Mobile years ago to settle on the parcel now off a main roadway that led to the interstate. Probably prompted by the preacher Douglas Abernathy and his Baptist congregation, Bo Caine had made attempts more than once to buy them out. Caine must've been irritated they were welcoming the Hispanic laborers.

The Latinos kept pouring in to work in the terrible conditions at the chemical plant. He'd recently added a Spanish interpreter in a side chapel to accommodate the growing numbers. It filled completely Sunday mornings at both masses. Those that got there after it filled went to the main congregation. He'd watched some respond to gestures they must've recognized. Others stared dumbfounded at times during the English mass.

* * *

By his thirty-eighth birthday, he believed most straight men in the county had married at least once by the time they were thirty-eight. It wasn't unheard of for some to remain single that long. He recounted multiple sexual escapades. There'd been drunken one-night stands. But those were becoming less and less as he aged. None had been sustainable. In lengthier trysts, he'd gotten bored or guilty and had then sabotaged it. Sometimes the woman he'd been chasing suddenly quit returning his attentions.

He remembered a law professor who had once announced that he'd known he was going to be a lawyer ever since he was a little child. He couldn't say the same thing for himself. He'd been an avid reader in his late teens and early twenties, but that hadn't revealed to him what he was headed toward becoming. After a liberal arts degree, he eventually sat for the law school entry test and did well enough to be accepted. Even then, he still didn't imagine himself going into criminal defense. Maybe it was the open-endedness that drew him in? An ability to cast doubt on a proposition? It could be a peculiar trait or instinct. Maybe it had corresponding effects on his personal relationships? Making him more cautious to commit to transitory ideas or feelings? Analyzing caused him to dismiss many behaviors as whimsical and unreliable. Maybe they'd been innocent flirtations or coyness?

The duty now had thirteen years of his life backing it, more than thin lip service of a promise to uphold high-sounding platitudes delivered at his swearing-in ceremony. The benefit of the trade-off wasn't always easy to see. It sometimes seemed to him an artificial and empty place invented by himself.

The thanks were uplifting, but so few and far between that they couldn't be relied upon to sustain him. After some time practicing, he received them with more frequency, but by then he internally deflected them almost as quickly as the many more criticisms he received. He'd become steeled against them both, just as he would steel himself against believing in a myth. The internal conflict was won day by disciplined day. It required an open-mindedness in accepting a rule maker who may be arbitrarily making rules, accepting a prosecutor who may be overzealously addicted to glory, accepting an unruly client who may be attacking him or themselves in the process, and accepting the unpredictable province of the public eye in the jury.

He recalled seeing a nature program describe salamanders living in fiery hot volcanically heated water. Another showed polar animals enduring vicissitudes of extreme wind and cold. He granted himself the luxury of recognizing he'd survived at least enough to make a name for himself.

It wasn't fortune, fame, or women hanging on both arms as some mythical style hound would've liked. There might be fortune one day, but he wasn't seeing an excess of it. Although on the outside his trappings would point toward an upper-middle-class lifestyle, it seemed more like hammering away on tough trade work. Using tools in the forms of motions and arguments brought a technical, though fleeting satisfaction.

What type of name had he built? Praises could be sung by many who he'd helped to go on with their lives after charges were dropped or they were acquitted at trial. His name could also be referred to in hatred by the unfortunate ones who'd gambled and landed in prison for long stretches.

He liked to think he'd built one of forthrightness and honesty among his peers that must've confounded those deadset against liking him. Those who spited him, like Aldruss, must not have been able to reconcile those traits with what they must've seen as an elusive ability to obscure or selectively present information in a persuasive way.

Developing reputation seemed more than glossy fame. He thought the concept more stolid than that, if that could ever be a fair description of a concept as amorphous and fluid as community opinion. Glossy fame would be more faddish, more subject to the winds of shallow values, a lighter vessel easily pushed around. Although some parts of the job required dealing with things in a quick and surface-y manner, putting stock in a steady, good reputation fit his character better than chasing after any illusory heights glossy fame might promise. Glossy fame, like cheap hard liquor, may take one higher faster, but a solid reputation wouldn't evaporate as quickly. It elevated one more gradually.

As he approached the courthouse and then went inside, he saw many women passing by. Some wore sharp outfits that seriously emphasized curvatures, livening his sense of producing things, making things happen. But the short daily fantasies inevitably died.

He suspected part of that precaution had been built into him early. The Catholic upbringing emphasizing taboo categories of conduct must've left a trace of babies' milk in his blood. But he'd never been able to resist purely on prohibition. He'd learned many times by misadventure. His internal bickering must've been meant to relieve a firmly set, overactive conscience. It was a seemingly resilient foundation, making it difficult for him to treat sex lightly, even against the pangs of hard-wired instincts writhing beneath it. He'd reasoned many times with that joy-killing voice to let those instincts run wild. For a time he would ignore the guilty pricks when the rush of pursuing and achieving became too pleasurable. In retaliation, or retrenchment, he suspected his conscience had set up an elaborate system, like a canal of locks, with high-walled ideals, roping analysis, fail safes, and booby traps, that typically doomed him from embarking on a relationship quickly after it got anywhere close to his hallowed ground. Any soft spots had become scarred places in the thicket of his curious inside.

* * *

He recalled scraping by two years at the traditionally black college washing dishes and eating cornbread mostly. Besides not discovering a major in those two years, he found he couldn't afford it. He left to join the navy, where he got his honorable discharge. Then there was a floating period of a few manual jobs.

He knew the city and the county and had a good idea of some of the surrounding counties. The military service must've honed his location memory. He knew the black Baptist Church community, where he ate, drank, and sang. He also knew where the crack houses were. He'd questioned prostitutes to find missing witnesses, and he had a concealed weapon's permit.

He preferred to dress casually most of the time. He often wore slacks or jeans and a short-sleeve button-down shirt. Having a shirt tucked in was about as dressy as he got in civilian mode. There were times when an investigation called for more formal wear, but he didn't really enjoy wearing suits. He felt unnatural and stuffy in them, which sometimes made his hands sweat.

His office had piles of papers strewn across the space of his furniture and the floor like a self-made island chain. The room was in a small corner above a downtown tavern. The disheveled aspect might've had something to do with his attention deficits. He realized he had them, but it also had something to do with the nature of his work in maintaining contact information, discarding leads, and accruing evidence and stories. Sometimes the light bill sunk its way into the sediment of his priorities.

Explaining why he didn't get an e-mail because his computer didn't have a power source when the electricity was shut off had become less of a worry. His wife made sure that the basics were attended to. Every couple of weeks, she'd check in on the office space. She cleaned up the coffee stains and cigar ash, among the other detritus left in his wake. Although she routinely stopped by when it came time to pay the overhead bills, she didn't move his papers, listen to his messages, or touch the computer. There'd been earlier arguments over this. Despite the apparent mess, he defended that he had it all synched. She would mock and chide him, but tolerated his habits. He'd come back from around the world and pursued her earnestly and sometimes clumsily. He looked at his light brown-skinned countenance in the wall mirror. Now he was a little less muscular. A pudgy gut was beginning to appear, but he was fit. He did all he could for her and the kids. She let him go on his private tangents, pursuing nothing sometimes, but getting paid for it.

* * *

Among some of the more suspicious, he suspected he had the reputation of a conjurer. Sometimes when he made public appearances during intense cases, the townspeople would visibly go out of their way to avoid him. At the beginning of his private practice, he'd feared he might be blacklisted. But based on the good number of not guilty verdicts he achieved, his services stayed in steady demand. Late night hour irrational fears of destitution were dispelled as the workday dawned where he discovered plenty of clients and problems to deal with.

Over the thirteen years he'd been practicing, he consistently talked himself out of thinking many flirtations had any chance of ripening. He remained open, waiting for someone that might dispel his doubts. But the high-profile cases took time and energy. By some fluke, he'd gotten through law school without finding someone to marry. Some of those temporary carousals had been torturous. There was the initial sense of accomplishment upon sleeping with the woman, but as that subsided in more sober moments, fears began to crowd in about an unwanted pregnancy or being tied to someone he didn't care much for besides satisfying that desire. Those occasions arose again and again. As his mid-thirties began, he became less likely to indulge.

Edging closer to forty, he realized he might have to accept permanent bachelorhood. At times he felt somewhat of a void that he suspected could be filled with a wife and kids. He was wary of what problems could arise in taking on the extra responsibility of raising kids. His was an occupation of controlled rebellion. How could he be an establishment of values when he was constantly working in rebellion? Or what appeared as rebellion?

These gloomier thoughts thumped along in his mind, like a dumpy hayseed on a pleasant summery Friday afternoon as he drove down to Mobile for a wedding. A friend of his from undergrad was finally getting married. He'd been asked to be a groomsman.

He arrived at the country club rehearsal party. It had all the warm finery of the comfortably well off. After a few hearty welcomes and a few strong drinks, he began to feel the intoxication of the evening swell into a buzzing night. A burst of confidence filled his mind as he gave snippets of stories to the guests, long ago friends, and strangers, listening, chiding, poking, and ridiculing by turns to achieve what he perceived to be maximum charming effects.

Eventually he began flirting with one of his friend's unmarried sisters. They stayed up late. He was highly drunk by then. She began wavering to flirt with another, a younger man he didn't know. The next day she smiled at him, but he sensed that any opportunity had passed, which he wasn't all that upset about. She was beginning to remind him too much of his friend, slightly stifling the attraction.

After the Saturday ceremony, as he was nursing a hangover back into the dissipation of more drinking, he ran into the golden-haired woman at the reception. He didn't remember seeing her at the rehearsal. She was with a group of women that knew the bride from somewhere. She'd been laughing as he came up to the table, showing a fine set of teeth through her tan complexion. He stood there not saying anything for a few seconds. Somehow he got their attention. He couldn't remember how he did things sometimes. It was more like emptying into an animal moment that could lead anywhere, perhaps disaster, and then he remembered being offered a seat and telling a story of a wedding where the groom's father had the ring stitched into his coat so he wouldn't forget it. But because the father was color blind, he wore the wrong coat, which not only clashed, but also didn't contain the ring.

She encouraged him with her smiling green eyes, listening even if there was no real point to his story besides exemplifying idiocy. She chatted with the other women for a while before she smiled again at him and left for the dance floor, which he normally would've avoided. But he recalled easing his way to her. He put his arms around her, and they danced to the blare of horns and saxophones. She had timely movements. He was attracted enough to mask his dancing mediocrity. More important to him were the eyes smiling with the gleam of interest. When she left, he felt the pull of her absence.

More informal toasts were made, and the women that'd surrounded her were beginning to peel away. They were left alone at a table and he was leaning close to her. With a slender but enticingly curved body, her breasts were accentuated by what she wore, suddenly seeming to demand that he place his hands on them. He was drinking in her tanned skin, mascaraed eyes, manicured nails, pearled neck, and honey golden hair. She put her hands on his arm, and then eventually she had his coat on. They were leaving for another bar where the celebration continued.

He expected she had to be younger, possibly much younger, but she seemed sophisticated enough. She scooted up next to him in a booth. They kissed openly. After a few minutes of cuddling and kissing, she looked across the bar and told him to wait. He felt the pull of her absence as she approached a bitter-looking male. His swirling mind flooded with acute jealously, and his heart rate increased, thudding like a demolition ball against the wall of his ribcage.

But she was coming back to him smiling, sliding back up next to him. There was a comfortable, good-smelling heat to her. She explained that the other guy, who'd turned away, was a past boyfriend. Eventually the other guy must've left, because he didn't worry about him or see him the rest of the night. Eventually she left too, with his coat, and he without her number, only the dream of her pending in his hungover mind.

After the wedding, he got an encouraging e-mail from her that Monday. Business cards had been in an inside pocket of his coat, which she promised to return. They exchanged several e-mails and arranged to meet again that next weekend for dinner.

On the next Saturday they met and nothing had diminished. There was a sense of exhilarating momentum. If anything, it blurred better as he didn't have to leave her that night as they booked a downtown hotel room.

They talked long hours at night during the following weeks. He began to look forward to driving to Mobile for the weekends. She was on the verge of turning thirty. On the phone, she by far dominated the time of possession of the discussion. He lent a patient ear and occasionally had to assuage some minor insecurities. She worked as a teacher at an elementary school. She'd talk about the kids, about having kids. She asked why he didn't ever marry. Eventually he had to upgrade the minutes on his personal phone plan.

It added new dimension. Hearing the sound of her voice became somewhat addicting. It had a high, lilting, melodic quality that gripped him inside with question-causing self-reflection. He opened up to her the best he could. She had a way of getting him to let down his guard. He spoke things he hadn't spoken to anyone else. It was as if a broken-down amusement that had lain dusty and dormant was shaking off its crust to work robustly again.

She'd been raised Catholic as he had. They began to attend mass together when he visited. During one of the services, a short, balding man sat in front of them wearing a worn suit. When the elder man turned around smiling vacantly in her direction, they saw a mouth full of straight teeth, too straight to be real at his age. He watched the elder man avidly sing the hymns, extending well past the notes, holding the tone so that he would emphasize the lyrics with a resounding whiplash inflection. Though lacking the proper cadence and tone, the elder man sang with the fervor of an opera performer. At first they couldn't tell whether he was mocking the songs. They couldn't help smiling.

Later he began to suspect the elder man suffered from some sort of derangement. The way the performance was directed added to his suspicion. The elder man wouldn't face the altar directly forward, but would turn to the side and sometimes even behind him. It seemed to depend on wherever the closest woman happened to be. It appeared the elder man was attempting to serenade them.

He watched the elder man turn to his left toward a young Hispanic woman accompanied by what looked to be her husband holding their infant child. During the Gloria the elder man would forcefully, with an intense, terribly furrowed brow, yell-sing, "Glory to God in the highESSTT!" And then he similarly emphasized, "EarTTHH!" and "WoRRD-DUH!" Obviously impressed with himself or the situation, the elder man flashed his oblivious smile.

He thought perhaps the elder man was experiencing his own personal epiphany. At times it seemed as if the elder man were preaching or dictating a lesson through the lyrics. He heard the man's Our Father express extreme "TrespassESSS!" and sinister "TemptationSSS!"

She slid her warm, slender-nailed hand into his and began to squeeze. He looked over. She was suppressing a giggle. He smiled at the grinning elder man to try and prevent from laughing.

The elder man noticed them and directed his smile to them. But the elder man didn't let up with the young Hispanic woman to his left, toward whom he'd taken a stance that seemed to be making her uncomfortable. In between music, when there was a pause after songs, it appeared the elder man was whispering or mouthing things to her. These were mostly unintelligible from his vantage point. It sounded like the elder man was commenting on the level the song had moved him, saying "that was a rise" or "that was a sign." Then the elder man burst out another long smile. It seemed to unnerve the young Hispanic woman.

As Sylvia commented that the elder man's serenading could be a reflection of their own relationship, he stifled a laugh.

After the mass, they approached the elder man and wished him a good day. He was all smiles saying, "The Lord has made a beautiful sign!"

He watched as the elder man tried to kiss Sylvia's hand. She pulled her hand back, but the elder man made the gesture anyway without making contact. They walked away in the other direction and laughed about it. Married women with uncomfortable husbands looked askance at the elder man. Mothers with children pleasantly smiled at him but remained distant, sometimes moving away farther down the pew.

As they were driving out from a parking space near the cathedral square, he saw the elder man walking down the sidewalk. The elder man had his head down, and his brow was wrinkled as if he were contemplating a complex problem. He'd pulled over at the cross street ahead of where the elder man was walking. He powered down the window and asked, "Do you need a lift somewhere, sir?" The elder man began smiling and making gestures. It looked like he was waving them off, but as he got nearer to the car, he began reaching for the back door, then let himself into the backseat.

"Where to?"

"The home."

"But which home, sir?"

The elder man smiled then engaged in a concentrated look. It became evident he was having memory problems. He drove him back to the cathedral to see if they could locate the priest who presided over mass. As they led the elder man back inside, she held the elder man's hand reassuringly, telling him he would find his way with the help of the priest. The priest seemed familiar with the elder man and thanked them for their help. Apparently the elder man lived only a few blocks away. As they drove off for lunch, she slid her hand comfortably into his again.

* * *

The nuns thought she might be Reynolds's daughter, but there was no documentation to confirm this. The nuns said she hadn't spoken at all, spending most days lying in bed. After several days of complete silence, in response to the nuns asking her name, she'd written *Spring* in a coloring book. Some of the orphans they could send to school with available funds, but there wasn't enough for everyone. Some had to be schooled at the orphanage itself. The girl didn't currently seem amenable to the social interaction demanded at school. The nuns told him they'd tried to get her to come down to eat, but she wouldn't. They'd brought her up bowls of oatmeal to no avail.

He arrived later that afternoon in his full-length cassock. He went up to her room with Sister Marie and found the girl curled up in a blanket with eyes peering out. She was sitting up on her new bed. Her light blond hair was scraggly from lying down.

They'd given her a separate room with a bed that had a used mattress. The iron bed frame had been painted canary yellow, but the paint had flaked off in a few pieces where dark iron could be seen underneath. The nuns said the girl stared at it for long periods of time. The air conditioner wasn't that powerful in the old building. Her room was hot and stuffy. The only other furniture in the room was a dresser made of cheap wood. One of the drawers didn't pull out. Some leftover stickers haphazardly adorned the sides and front of the dresser. They had been partially peeled off, leaving their paper glue backs.

"Hello there." He approached her carrying a small figurine in his hands, but she turned away. He placed the plastic doll from downstairs on the foot of her bed. "Do you like dolls?"

She didn't respond to the toy.

"We would like you to eat something. Would you like some cereal? How about some raisin bread?"

After staring at him and the bread he was holding out for almost a full minute, she stuck out her arm, pulled off a corner, and then ate it. Sister Marie let out a sigh of relief and exclaimed what a good girl she was. The girl didn't speak, but chewed slowly with her far-away stare.

After this, the nuns told him they'd followed a pattern of leaving a plate of raisin bread just inside her door along with a glass of water. When they stayed in the room, she wouldn't eat. They tried milk and orange juice, but she would only drink water. She didn't leave the room except to bathe herself.

She didn't show much interest in the toys and dolls they brought her, but she would watch videos on the black and white television, usually choosing cartoons. After nearly a month, the nuns were anxious to get her outside and into more social interaction.

He returned to help try to get her outside. The nuns had to physically pick her up to get her outdoors in the hot sun. She didn't resist but hung in their arms limply. One of the nuns went to get her some of the lemonade the other children were drinking. The girl wasn't saying anything. She covered her eyes. They looked around for sunglasses. Not finding any that fit her, they gave her a straw hat for shade. She didn't seem interested in the disks or balls left by the other children. The others were either at school or being taught inside by the volunteer teacher.

They walked with her toward the creek bordering a portion of the property. They passed solitary oaks interspersed with pines. She held his hand walking down the dirt trail while Sister Marie ambled close behind. The girl seemed less timid with him. As they got closer to the creek, the girl stopped abruptly to look at something in the grass. She looked up at him then pointed to what looked like an immobile insect.

After recognizing it, he let her know, "Yes, Spring. That's a beetle shell."

They continued walking until they reached the creek. Then they turned around and returned to the orphanage.

* * *

Next year was an election year. He'd been a classmate of Caine's back in elementary and high school. He'd done well in school, but back then he hadn't got much recognition among his peers. His coordination was lacking. Athletic prowess got much more attention. He accomplished enough through his grades to get a scholarship to the state university. After graduating there, he came back and entered construction management. He did well at it and made a name for himself in the business community.

The mayor he replaced in the eighties was an elder from Alcorn's time. He'd been conservative in a way that cast a suspicious eye toward the chemical plant located on the river. The prior mayor's mistake had been taking a lukewarm approach toward expansion there. That part of his platform hadn't fitted well with Bo's plans. Nor had it sat well with his construction outfit at the time. They'd already put in a bid in support of the plant deal.

From that seam, his platform arose and gained momentum. Bo backed him. With Bo's support and the guarantee of the construction firm to reinstate him should he not be elected, he'd entered the race.

In the year after he'd won the election, his former construction employer won the bid to construct the expansion of the chemical plant. He encouraged the city to lighten the ordinances and give tax incentives favorable to the pulp mill and chicken processing plant too. A long wave of business development brought increased revenues and new jobs. The city government depended more on the industrial revenues and development.

The majority of the dirtier and more dangerous jobs were filled by the minority population. Joust's seam had come from the discontent among those people. Now they had their first black city councilman. Joust's father had worked the local pulp mill for years. Two years after Joust's father had retired, the company declared it would have to end his pension because of increased costs. Many lifetime workers were bitter about the loss of pension. But their complaint wasn't organized enough. The local courts upheld the company's position. Joust's father had to take work as a janitor at the chemical plant. Then Joust's father had been diagnosed and was given a year to live. He figured that had something to do with why Joust was bitter.

* * *

In his Baptist pulpit, he expected himself to be confrontational. He occasionally referred to himself as a God warrior. Unlike that mealy-mouthed, cold-skinned priest McGowan, he wouldn't mince words when it came to rejecting Satan. Since he'd been an adolescent, he'd firmly believed human flaws could be corrected through vigilance and prayer. Heaven or a close approximate was possible on earth if only everyone would follow basic instructions. He did have a weak spot for barbeque. One of his flaws included a paunchy midsection. Looking in the mirror, his filmy, loose facial skin was the color of an unplucked chicken. He used to have dark hair silvered at the sides, but now it was all gray. He enjoyed bragging that he'd been married to the same woman for twenty-five years.

At barbeques and other social functions, he sometimes relaxed, showing what he considered a more jovial and affable side. But in the pulpit, he was an earnest and serious Bible enthusiast. He could hear his own voice resounding on Sunday through the refurbished white wooden and brick Baptist church. He enjoyed pointing out it was the largest church in the county.

He accepted meals and money from his followers. Occasionally his conscience rang his own words back in his mind causing him to lie in bed awake struggling and torturing himself over hypocritical thoughts. But what had already been worded couldn't be reworded, nor could things that had already been done be undone.

Then there were the lustful thoughts that plagued him. He could take such a natural thought, without having taken action on it, and scourge himself with it. But in the light of dawn he would tell himself that those with sensitive and superlative consciences were burdened with such internal struggles. God made them that way because they were able to harness a strong drive in proportion. Once he heard what he perceived to be the clarion call of his conscience telling him the difference between a right and wrong choice, he would employ every weapon he had against the wrong.

The fracture of Christian religion upset him. He believed that dilution of his church was an insidious plot of a very personalized Devil, who still demonstrated his persistent sway in a world prone to evil left by itself. Through attacking the organizations that were meant to worship and honor, the Devil was making the organizations look hypocritical and weak, causing them to become shunned, ridiculed, and flung apart like the various tongues in Babel. This led him to organize and support the Christian Unification Discussion Group.

One thing he particularly despised was the pomp, icon worship, and excesses of the Catholic Church. He believed God was slowly revealing their need to repent by exposing those pedophile priests preying on innocent children. With disdain he observed that some of the priests, despite their vows of poverty, lived an upper-middle-class lifestyle with their comfortable rectories, servants, and SUVs paid for by their parishioners. He attributed his own comfortable home to his attitude toward God.

The Catholics seemed unusually susceptible to corruption. They were bent too much on the routine. They were less engaged on displaying social action. He found their ceremonies uninspiring. He was suspicious of McGowan. What he'd heard from others stoked his concerns of having a pedophile in their midst. He was disturbed by the priest's attention to the young children at the orphanage. He wouldn't hesitate to expose any pedophile. The meetings let him keep a close eye on McGowan, giving him opportunity to ask pointed questions to see if McGowan squirmed any.

Now he was in the midst of raising his boys in the ways of God and was having a tough time with his eldest son. He suspected his son had gone astray into the terrible world of illicit drugs. He feared his son wouldn't amount to much, which would be equivalent to one of the worst possible outcomes he could encounter in raising them. He couldn't understand why his son would be that wasteful.

His firstborn was the same age as Bo's son. He'd encouraged them to befriend one another and go hunting. Could Seth be a bad influence? When weighing Bo's position, he quickly silenced such protests. He told himself it would be foolish not to cultivate a friendship with the Caines. They'd been in the community so long, and they were integral to so many. To not seek that out would be a dark error.

* * *

He recollected being hit with baseball bats, lead pipes, and bike chains. He'd been knifed twice, once in the gut that nearly killed him, but the hospital was close enough to sew him up. He'd been shot once through the shoulder. There was a scar down the left side of his face where he'd been slashed by a beer bottle that split his cheek open. Stitches had been delayed because he didn't think the cut deep enough to warrant hospice. It'd left two marks that some of the brethren said looked like he'd got into it with a cougar, leading to his moniker. The name stuck while working construction sites as a laborer. He imprinted the tool representing his namesake on his unshot shoulder.

He'd traveled most of the country on his chopped hog. He knew the bike in minute detail. He kept it well tuned. He could rig it when he had to. Once when the throttle mechanism acted up, he'd used some fishing line tied to his finger to accelerate, pulling on it like he was working a puppet. When he was on the open road, with the sun burning down on him, and there was a long stretch ahead, he'd sink into that unencumbered spot. Even if there were complications behind him, they'd all fade in the rumble of his cycle with the elements and pinched air coursing by. He didn't feel the need to reflect as he was usually moving in some way on the inside, whether it was riding out a waning, angry coke buzz, dealing with a high-octane hangover, or carelessly staying zoned out on weed.

Being told what to do by some other prick got in under him. It automatically irritated him so that he would often do the opposite or take action to disrupt or defy. When the cops came nosing around, although he did have more than one conviction for resisting arrest and obstruction, he wasn't stupid enough to get himself thrown in jail every time. He'd get quiet usually and wait for the irritation to pass. He'd do the same if it were elements he was having a hard time riding in. It interfered with that unobstructed vision he sought on those open stretches, distorting it like an out-of-place billboard. What man or woman had authority to tell him what he could or couldn't do? Then his thoughts turned back to beer, cocaine, bar floozies, and various combinations of battle.

He'd been in the Wraiths for almost two decades. His thick, curly black beard had some white visible in it. On the crown of his head a small bald spot was forming. He assured himself he'd never gone soft. When he became suspicious that he may be losing it, he made sure to double his edge in business dealings.

Since the turn of the millennium, more of his peers and elders had been incarcerated in the federal pens scattered across the country. Interclub murder by gun, blade, or odd diner fork jabbed in the jugular had depleted their numbers too, as well as heavy drinking or drugging that'd caught up with others in heart attacks or strokes. Even though he never cared for rising too high up in the brethren, he'd moved up by default.

He remembered joining the laborer's union when he was twenty. At that time, he was getting closer to his patch in his first club and had to find a way to maintain his enhanced hog. And he'd wanted some space to take his bartender girl at the time. The wages allowed him to pay for the place, which she'd called his shithole.

He didn't like going into the hall to wait for a job. That interfered with the unencumbered notion. But it beat jail, and once he got used to it, it fit well with his unpredictable schedule. After a couple of years in, he became a journeyman. He came and went as he pleased. He discovered other bikers there too, including Muffler.

He did the heavy construction projects. He had loops on his worn and blasted work jeans for his hammer and his namesake, the only tools he carried. He'd jackhammer poorly poured concrete pilings, tear up wood scaffolding, and throw garbage from high distances. He occasionally enjoyed it. But ultimately it was an agreement to be a slave. He wouldn't last long at one place.

The end usually began by getting into it with his foreman or supervisor. After receiving instructions he didn't want to hear, he'd ring off some choice expletives, leading to the occasional brawl. He'd been banned from a couple of northeast locals in Pennsylvania and Ohio. But the union always took him back because of his strength and his ability to put in a full day, even with a full hangover. There were times when he'd been sweating out the prior night's debaucheries. He'd stink something foul as he hadn't bothered to bathe. Others wore dust masks if they were required to work near him.

After he'd been initiated into the Wraiths, he relied less on the union. More exhilarating work had become available. Through test after test, he'd become reliable to the elders. Unlike other prick bosses, he could follow their authority. He saw it differently because he saw himself in them. They'd fought, been through orgies, and stayed high together.

Muffler usually went along with him. The two had run together over twenty years. The time had been interrupted by jail stretches, hospital stays, separations while keeping away from the cops, and once because of an unfortunate Mexican donkey. In the last instance, occurring over fifteen years ago, they'd both been stoned on weed, high on speed, and drunk on tequila after leaving their favorite Mexican brothel. Muffler missed a turn back to their lodgings. When Muffler turned around to get back on the next highway, he'd told him later he'd lost his way. After guessing a direction, Muffler'd come to a small hamlet. People and animal traffic crowded the road. At nearly thirty miles per hour, before Muffler had time to slow down, he'd ran smack head-on into a donkey, which threw him a good ways and eventually killed the animal.

Muffler explained he'd gotten up to examine his scrapes. He was still functioning. After inspection, his bike was not. The front tire had mashed in, warping the rim. There was serious frame damage and a thrown chain. There was no way to drive it out of there. Muffler had enough cash on him from an exchange they'd made earlier to grease the squeaky peasant discontent growing around him. He paid for the dead animal so the *policia* weren't called.

Muffler had decided to fix the bike rather than abandon it. Muffler had walked or hitchhiked to larger towns to find welding tools and parts and worked on the bike during the scorching, dry day then found a local to pay to store it. In the cooler evenings, Muffler had found his way back to the brothel, where he'd gotten in good with one of the whores. Muffler had stayed cheap while drinking tequila and doing speed. Eventually Muffler fixed the bike and made his way back to Arizona.

Unlike so many of their other relationships, the bond never really strained to a breaking point as both knew the other one was willing to give an expletive-laced *sianara* and go a separate way, which usually happened a couple of times a year. They could stand one another's company just slightly better than their desire to be left alone, unencumbered by anyone else's influence on their decisions of what to do and when to do it. The other Wraiths had it too. That common tendency to stand apart somehow brought them tighter together. The two gravitated toward one another partly because of self-interest, and partly because of the oath in joining the Wraiths.

The first job they'd done involved getting money from a delinquent drug dealer who owed an elder eight thousand for a coke debt. They hadn't said much as they rode toward the address of the dealer. From the first job, he'd been the more talkative of the two. When Muffler spoke, it many times came out in a garbled string of expletives, which many found to be unintelligible, influencing his given alias. Later, Muffler reinforced his moniker by improvising on whatever dulled or muffled gunshots or explosions.

When they got to the address of the first job, he rang the buzzer while Muffler stood beside him holding a tire iron. The delinquent dealer let them in and offered them a seat on the couch before backing away toward his kitchen. They recognized the gaunt, paranoid look of someone who'd decided to snort much more of the product than he'd sold. As Muffler approached him, the dealer tried pulling a gun. Being shot at didn't mean Muffler was automatically going to run away. He'd been shot at before, leading to the scar on his forearm. Instead of running, Muffler threw the tire iron he'd been carrying. Then Muffler charged the guy, tackling him before he could get an accurate shot off. The bullet plunked into a pleather couch.

Muffler proceeded to apply the tire iron to the dealer's ribs, legs, and face until his fury had been spent. The man lay unconscious, bloody, and broken. They took whatever value was out in the open. Because of the gunfire, they were in a hurry. They scooped up a couple of grand on top of a bedroom dresser next to some nudie mags. Muffler held up keys to the dealer's rental car, hinting that they could sell it for scrap. He'd shaken that off. He didn't want to drag something into it that might be easier to trace. Any payoff wouldn't be worth that risk. He'd let the beaten man's fear work without bringing other unnecessary attention to the matter. They let the dealer know that they'd confiscated a late fee. The debt had been paid in full four weeks later.

There'd been situations where the job went bad. There was the fire in Arizona. They'd used the tavern as a way station, dropping off or exchanging goods or information. Eventually they'd heard a rumor that the guy who owned the place had been pressured into becoming a government informant. People had become leery of going there. They were so pissed off that they'd personally volunteered to torch the place. After getting the go ahead from the elders, they'd filled the back of an old truck with five-gallon tanks of gasoline. The place was near about dead that night at a quarter before four a.m. except for one patron from a rival club who would later describe two madmen driving a truck through the front door before getting out to pour gasoline over everything. By dawn, the tavern and the truck had burned to the ground. The Wraiths had better lawyers back in the eighties. They'd each entered a deal to serve three years.

* * *

Looking up from the federal case files on the bikers, he remembered originally being assigned to shadow one of the prominent agents in the mafia division. He wasn't a field agent at the time, spending most of his hours at the computer reviewing evidence and analyzing data. It hadn't been glamorous. The prominent agent he shadowed assured him the work was part of paying his dues. He'd already gone through a rigorous training, navigating through the secretive, convoluted, and sometimes baffling application process. He had the brains for the job and a curious, almost instinctual, tracking capability. He suspected he may have inherited this from his mother, who had many times unraveled his juvenile plots. She'd told him she could smell it in the tone of his voice and read it in his body language.

After becoming a field agent, he'd been assigned to the investigation of outlaw motorcycle clubs. After a few years of this, he was assigned special emphasis on a particularly gnarly, rootless sect, the Wraiths. For the past three years, he'd been watching Cat's Paw and Muffler. He knew they were in the upper middle echelon of the club's hierarchy. They weren't handling the riskier activities anymore, leaving that for the dwindling younger ones. Of late, the two had mostly been involved in moving stolen parts and drug trafficking, which sometimes led to assaults. They were still homicidal, but they'd become less conspicuous.

He saw these outlaws as manufacturing their own oppression. They were free to pursue whatever legal happiness pleased them, free as any people had ever been. But they insisted on claiming they were oppressed by law enforcement in going about their illegal activities. Rebellions could be forthright, but the perverse nature of any criminal urban or biker gangs had inherited only the negative and destructive energy without a higher purpose. These outlaw clubs weren't organized in some principled fight for the sake of new ideas or a better way of life. They were despotic organizations seeking control and plunder. Like a plague on the continent, they infected the roads of interstate commerce. Some among them were psychotic killers. He firmly believed these societal cancers needed to be cut out.

* * *

He'd seen glaring errors of government covered and glossed over by arrogance and cruelty. His distrust caused a growing, uncertain bubble within him. During these periods, he would have to summon all his mental resources to remember that he shouldn't take his employment for granted and that there could be worse outcomes. Thinking of it as just his employment, he speculated outwards, wondering whether others were more satisfied.

In his younger years he'd been too unpolished, too apt to question, and not quickly given to following orders and structure without testing its merit first. At the time, other money-prone tracks looked like a pointless accumulation of trinkets and status symbols that didn't quite motivate him. He enjoyed the finer things with his burgeoning success, but those things were wardrobe and scenery. He'd never been overly materialistic. He could live modestly, even spartanly.

All these conjectures seemed submerged in the wake of what he did. The calling, or employment in his down days, hadn't come as an epiphany. The entry into law wasn't about greed for him. He'd determined that early on in public defense. He'd paid off his loans and had a skill to help others. Even when facing derision, whether from a prosecutor, a client, an officer, a judge, a co-worker, or a random question from a relative or friend, he'd found something to do which satisfied. It wasn't about a collection of accolades, but about a livelihood that piqued his interest, gave him enough to explore and sustain himself. In the swirl of the myriad pressures of the legal system, he'd become a contention.

* * *

After he signed *D. Abernathy* beneath his written sermon for the week, he relaxed while his Baptist brain indulged a piece of historical reconstruction he entitled *Know Thy*

Enemy. The Catholics had come up from Mobile. Maybe New Orleans first, but whichever, they'd arrived on the continent like a plague of frogs and settled on the coastline, burrowing into the mud. They built up their palaces to simulate worship of a king. Mankind's kings haven't fared well now that there was atomic weapons and such. If he was to draw their progression on a map, they'd spread up like a horn out of Louisiana. Like the horn of a horned toad, and right about here would be the spear tip.

They'd spread their churches through Slidell, Biloxi, Pascagoula, and Pensacola. It was the French and the Spaniards. Those Spaniards down in Florida shot all through the Caribbean with its volatile heat and uprisings in unstable governments. Both of them had contributed to make this horned toad. They infested the area with their magical intonations. With all their extra water rituals, they'd eaten up the crops to feed themselves and their large families. They'd carried baggage from Europe: their wars, their Inquisition, and their mindless devotion to habit. They'd brought obsessions and compulsions, standing, kneeling, and sitting. And they'd brought their squirmy, guilt-ridden consciences. Their leaders tried to repress the natural urge to procreate, which had led to wars and sexual atrocities.

Didn't biblical figures have wives? Having those priests go without women stored up poison in their minds. They got away with it for years until all the settlements started cascading down. Served the fools right for trying to suppress nature. Poison heavy ones were still there, but they'd probably burrowed down deeper to silence the noise in their frog ears. They'd repeat the lie to themselves that their church was the one true one.

It must've been built into their frog structure. Some straightforward people had had enough of this. They'd seen the corruption of its edifice, with its hieroglyphics and stained glass. They weren't any different from a group of sorcerers emptily recanting. What easier medium for the Devil to come through?

And those upright Baptists had broken away, calling foolishness what it was, realizing they were men ruled by men, not god-men dressed like kings. They'd refused to worship them like kings. The ones that had reformed didn't believe in buying their way into heaven. Those courageous and wise ones had determined to follow the Bible more closely. They wouldn't be fooled by these latest incarnations of glamour that rang and smelled of the Devil. Those good people had come across the ocean. Their culture grew southward and westward to meet the toad. The frogs already had a hold on the coast.

The good Baptists had gone about town by town building simpler houses of worship. They'd tended livestock and lived on simpler terms. Some had gone into the larger cities like Mobile and New Orleans to compete with the Romans, to turn the tide against mysticism. They'd pointed out and decried the corroded morality that allowed one to be absolved by only attending an hour service involving a series of slow calisthenics to gothic-sounding music. They'd proclaimed that you had to get in and do some legwork on sin.

Closer to the coast the wealth of frogs may one day cause those cities to slip into the Gulf. The toads want to keep expanding their lost ideas. The papists are trying to get a hold of the country by the backdoor. They realize we've found plentiful bounty that harmonizes God and nature. Once they'd seen some profit in it, they sent their social machinations. If one could see behind their glossy exteriors, there'd be sulfurous hell fire belching forth those poisonous men.

* * *

He stopped by whenever the tavern featured some local blues players. His wife allowed for it some Fridays as long as he didn't come home too drunk. It was located off a main street in a less affluent part of town near the railroad tracks, among a group of brick buildings. A barbershop occupied the space on one side of the tavern. An auto mechanic's garage occupied the space on the other side.

The tavern had been there as long as he could remember. When he was a kid, he got his haircut at that barbershop. He remembered the aftershave smell and the seriousness of the black barbers that had worked there. They'd worked quickly and talked in few-word comments on whatever the client brought up. They'd seemed like some kind of doctors to him with their matching white coats and their shelves of bottles with different colored liquids and lathers, clippers and scissors in various shapes. Like traveling doctors he'd seen in pictures or on television going out west. Those doctors would've sawed your leg off if they had to. They'd pour some whisky on your wound to keep it from getting infected. They had jars of leeches to suck the bad blood out, ginseng root for longevity, and wormwood to numb pain.

Brother and Daddy would sit on some cheap plastic-covered cushioned chairs and flip through the magazines.

Those barbers weren't the singing kind like he'd sometimes seen, four in harmony, but one wore a mustache like they could've been. The peppermint candy-colored pole twisted out front while their shears snipped the time.

They'd let him into the tavern at eighteen. He'd been drawn right away into the place. Later he understood it was the blues, whether live or coming out of a jukebox. Early on, he remembered seeing one of the performers, through the smell of smoke and beer, lit up on stage in an unearthly light. The performer would cringe then twang his instrument, sweating, telling about how bad things looked. He'd clap along with the crowd and cheer as the older man in a suit sitting on a chair explained how his girl didn't tell him she done found another man, and how he'd lost his job 'cause beer was too friendly. The older man's lip had twitched a little as he'd go on about how his dog wouldn't even greet him no more. That instrument had been steely sounding. The performer made it whine to emphasize what he was saying. A bass player and drummer backed the older man up.

Then he'd seen what the electric guitar could do. It filled up the place so everything felt like it was vibrating. The walls seemed to be breathing, and the ceiling rattled like loose change. It enveloped him, reaching down into a pit core of his guts, buzzing there. He'd get up and join the others hollering and dancing to the music, jerking, juking, grooving, improvising rhythm to the lead guitarist's picking as he'd slide back and forth hitting high notes on a riff then go back to the main rhythm.

Before he'd been married, more than once he'd found himself a woman there. They'd go out to some woods nearby to kiss and do whatever he could get her to do. More than once he'd gotten underwear off. He was usually drunk by that time. Sometimes he felt regret the next day. Once he'd taken a woman much larger than he was back to the woods. He wasn't too proud of it the next day knowing that he would've probably left her alone but for all that beer. He worried about it until he saw her a couple of months later and seen he hadn't gotten her pregnant.

His wife didn't get jealous that often. She'd gone with him and seen it was the love of the blues that brought him in. Besides that, most of the girls there now wouldn't want anything to do with the granddaddy he'd become. He sat alone most of the time at a table or at the bar sipping his foamy beer and sometimes tapping a bottle cap to the beat. Sometimes friends would join him at the table, but they met up less and less. Some had passed away. Some had given up drinking. Some had just stopped going. He had gray in his hair now, and he was a little rheumy in the knees so he usually wouldn't get up to dance. Once and a while, he'd be overcome by memory and with a big grin he'd get up.

He got home sometimes after midnight. He'd get in his warm bed next to his wife. She sometimes yelled at him, like the time he almost pissed the bedroom floor. He was in trouble for that for a long time. She almost completely forbade him from going back. But she'd relented. She let him go there about once a month 'cause she knew he loved the place just like he loved his fishing. Without one or the other, he couldn't cope.

* * *

He'd been suffering from vivid dreams at night. He remembered wearing a tuxedo at a barn speaking event and casual clothes at a more formal event. He thought it might signify something, but groggily tried washing it away by splashing water in his face. He worked his way into shaving his stubble.

He remembered a girlfriend from college who analyzed dreams frequently and obsessively, but he never took that seriously. He would wash them away in the morning water and set about his tasks for the day. His vision longed to return to more pragmatic thoughts.

In college he'd gotten into discussions with professors about how the black man needed to have better representation in state government given their respective population. Besides federal representatives, they needed black leaders in the state congress, in the city councils, as mayors, and even governors. The disproportion wouldn't correct itself on its own. It had to be righted by standing up to the decrepit structure still clinging on for white men only. They'd seen it succeed in larger population centers in the South. But one didn't see this phenomenon as often in the smaller cities and towns. It disturbed him because nearly forty percent of the citizens of his county were black. Yet rarely did you see a local black man or woman rising up to the share in the leadership.

As he started into politics, he believed that the trend could take hold here where he'd grown up. There had never been a black mayor or even a black candidate for mayor. While thinking along these lines, he sometimes experienced a tingling in his mind. He liked to think this was foreshadowing a surge of confidence in realizing his potential. On his down days, he dismissed it as high blood pressure, a possible prelude to early death from a stroke.

His city had developed deplorable trends. The white leadership had let their land be abused for profit and disregarded the by-product waste. They'd let their citizens be poisoned. With Bo Caine running things through his puppet mayor more blacks would die prematurely and negligently as they had been for centuries.

He could see this as well as he could see his glassed dome head in the mirror as he splashed water on his face to get the shaving cream he'd missed on the side of his jaw. Because the heat from the hot water caused his glasses to fog slightly, he removed them to wipe them off. He had a sense that somewhere in that tingling outer body sense that he couldn't see, there was already—and always had been—a conflict. As he returned his glasses to his face, he thought about the cowards or ignorant ones that worked Caine's machines for him. He would need good, solid people to have any chance.

He left to visit Eric Brandy in the hospital. He meant to display genuine respect and care, but he was insightful enough to recognize an agenda orchestrating his actions. He had a political tact he believed comparable to what directors or producers might see. He couldn't define it well, or plumb its depths, but whatever it was, it seemed at work as he visited the firefighter suffering from smoke inhalation. He envisioned a good picture of them together at a charitable event.

He saw Eric awake now wearing a hospital gown sitting up in bed. Eric's muscular brown arms were folded across his chest and a remote sat in his lap. Eric was watching the television bolted to a corner up above. Eric's face displayed a half-asleep, listless look, until it alighted on him as he entered. Eric seemed glad to see him and said he expected to be up and going again within two days. It had been boring for Eric being laid up, but he described a good number of visitors. Even the town paper had been by for an interview. His inner ear perked up. "Have you heard about the girl you saved?"

"Yeah, I heard they moved her to the orphanage with them nuns. Anything new?"

"Doctor says she wasn't exposed to the heaviest smoke. Must've been low to the ground. Doctor says her and her kitten check out okay."

Eric seemed relieved to hear it. Other than some chest pain, Eric felt healed up. The doctors wanted to make sure that his lungs were clear.

He gave Eric what he meant to be a querulous look that must've been emphasized by a glare in his glasses. "You know the council is considering a police and firefighter ordinance that could be used to update better equipment for you guys. But money's real short. Those damn industries on the river siphon off their profits. Only people gettin' rich off of it are the industries and the Caines."

Eric angled his eyes toward him. Through his self-concept reflected in Eric's eyes, he saw his own shaved head and glasses. He wondered about this ability. Being able to see himself through others' expressions and responses must've been due to an acutely developed sense of empathy or emotive depth perception. A flashbulb of a smile could ephemerally light his own features, alternating between joy and an earnest look. The glasses must've emphasized a more intellectual or professorial look. His large head drew attention to itself, and he could feel the resulting magnetism causing others to listen closely to whatever might burst forth from his mouth.

He knew he was an imposing figure, over six feet and well over two hundred pounds. Unlike Eric, a greater proportion of his weight was due to fat rather than well-toned muscle. He had the beginnings of a paunch belly showing behind his tucked-in shirt. Eric was talking about his itch to get back to the gym and a daily workout routine.

Most knew he loved seeing himself in the news, and that he could live up to the scrutiny of spontaneous public exposure. In those unscripted moments, he spun around answering questions, saying things that seemed to originate from nowhere but had a way of sticking in one's mind afterwards. In a private situation like this, he seemed an ordinary man with unpolished speech. A stutter here, with a long pause there, sometimes seemingly in a calculating manner as if he were picking over his words to deliver the best ones possible. Eric laughed as words must have seemed to spout and explode in the air from his brown-glassed dome of a head.

Sensing an opportunity to rally one of his strong supporters, he felt comfortable enough expounding again on what he called "the Second Reconstruction of the South." The first Reconstruction came from outside pressure of the federal government. The change was resisted by the old guard as fiercely as a natural body would resist a foreign substance. To those unrepentant slave enthusiasts, the new social apparatus put inflexible benchmarks of equality in place. Expectations hung above them like ominous iron girders as cranes boomed above their places of power dismantling the archaic architecture there. The Southerners had received a transplant of ideals.

Smoldering anger and indignation remained. To the mostly vitriolic sentiment of the defeated and tired Southern white hierarchy, the first pioneer black politicians were called to stand firm even if their constituents were unsupportive and undermining. Caught between those forces in a stifling band of tension, they'd been hamstrung from the beginning.

He told Eric the first Reconstruction had been doomed to failure as the pendulum had swung too quickly in a clock wound up too tightly. They'd been in the age of mechanical industry, not rockets. The black pioneers had been made into federal congressmen, but the districts they represented were broke and the remedies they sought called for too much time and money. It was a topsy-turvy blip on the historical suppression of their heritage. Subversive tactics were carried out to reestablish what had been lost legally and symbolically in the war. The pioneers were either thrown from their pedestals or the pedestals toppled over. Within a couple of decades, the old guard had returned and whites regained complete control of its representatives. The blip had been only a mirage of validation. They were prevented from voting or meaningfully participating in the political process. They remained or went into the homes of the whites for work, to cook, to clean, to nurse the white children.

The regression continued for nearly another eighty-odd years until the second civil war got underway. This time it arose internally. Even though the federal government arrived again to back up the movement and keep the peace, that was more of a symptom to the internal pressure. In the aftermath, the second Reconstruction commenced.

It continued through setbacks. The new leaders had to be vigilant. The complacent could easily be overcome by the constant impulses to subjugate another. They were still in the heat of it. Would they submit to the predominantly white-controlled economy dwarfing that of the black communities' economy? He warned him that their prosperity wouldn't come by politely waiting for the future to crawl comfortably into their laps.

* * *

He soaked up the elation and reassured himself. The representative of the public eye had deliberated for about an hour and a half before acquitting his client. He saw again the ability within himself to find holes, to cast a general pall of doubt about the proceeding, to eventually take the case over completely. He cautioned himself against delusions of grandeur that he'd seen others susceptible to. Although he might have been able to overcome negative stereotypes some of the time in the courtroom, outside of it he was often a lightning rod for society's scorn.

He cautioned himself as well on being destroyed by the negativity of the peculiar ability. It had to be respected and used only when needed. He wouldn't shirk the oath to represent unpopular people and causes. If called upon, he would use the ability for dissection and dissolution of the government's case.

The elation was fine, but by the next day, any delusions of being overly secure, overly skilled, or indestructible had deflated. The many knotted up and tense situations demanding his attention swarmed back from the deferred time needed to perform in trial. He'd seen men and women his age chase after the delusions. Most of them were talkers who never produced exactly what was promised. He realized this wasn't easy to do. He'd avoided promising as often as possible. Maybe that difference in the eagerness to promise supported the skill.

Too many times he'd seen promises lead to overextension, conflicting commitments, and inevitable disappointment of someone's expectations. Actually, he got a thrill out of pleasantly surprising. This may have led to his slightly perverse practice of outlining the worst possible outcome in solemn detail when in all likelihood it wouldn't happen that badly. But he'd seen how things could go wrong quickly in the courtroom. This had deepened his natural caution. The important thing was to let them know upfront and not to smooth talk them into a rosy false reality.

The client had been a college baseball player from a family with money so the media picked up on the case. The young man was profusely thankful for the outcome. He'd cautioned him that it could've easily gone the other way and to be more selective in what he did. The young man's breeding in the upper middle class of Birmingham would've hit a severe shock in being introduced to prison. On cross-examination, he'd gleaned from the woman accuser that she'd taken roofies for pleasure before, that she did use cocaine frequently at clubs, and that she and the young man did have sex before the alleged rape. The case began to collapse into shambles as another patron Prentice was able to locate came to testify that he'd seen her that very night taking pills voluntarily from another man at the bar.

He'd been on the news about the case, and he'd made some brief comments. He preferred to be less of a spectacle as it added to the delusions, which could undermine the slow, methodical work of investigation, analysis, and preparation for performance before an unknown audience. He tried keeping a moderate distance from those he believed twisted with delusion. Some had hinted at their joining forces to make more money or to gain more attention. He'd worked with some in his past life as a public defender and on co-defendant cases where he'd seen some of them operate at a severe delusional deficit. Some were so far in debt they had to amplify their delusions and accelerate them faster and faster to keep postponing the realization of their ordinariness.

* * *

His primary residence contained over twenty rooms. It sat on the edge of a short hill overlooking the city. He'd built it on his land over twenty years ago. Some of the rooms had been added ten years later. In one of the main chambers, which he loosely referred to as the living room, there hung several mounted animal trophies, mostly deer. This was where he liked to sit and watch the large screen plasma. Occasionally his kids came to join him, but as they grew older, that happened less frequently. He'd usually smoked outside, but he'd become less concerned. A cigarette sat in the tray next to him as he drank whisky and ice while watching a news story about a lawsuit against Dynomi. Then there was that goddamn uppity Levi Joust commenting where he had no business. A curse lurked in his throat, waiting for some physical object to be spat on. The mood subsided as he began thinking of his golf game with Hanslow scheduled for mid-morning Friday. He could ask him what the lawyers thought about it.

As the kids were mostly grown now, he and Shelia had gotten used to their own domains within the mansion. She usually stayed in a separate wing of the house. Sometimes they'd go days without seeing one another. He had his other women to keep him company. She made her rounds on the local circuit of wealthy wives. The servants would pick up after them both.

He knew some of the townspeople and even some of his staff referred to it as his fortress. The edge of the property was gated. The house stood at the end of a long drive. Part of the front lawn was enclosed with a second barrier, a black wrought iron fence. The back acreage was maintained for a couple of acres before reaching another barrier that marked the undeveloped woods. Some of his supporters had told him the estate was a pinnacle of local strength of character and good taste.

Despite these manifestations of great wealth, he had moments where uncertainty lurked and he couldn't quite put a finger on what it was he needed in order to eliminate the doubt. He'd sometimes go to the display room to console himself. He'd go in and rub the skins of the dead reptiles. He couldn't give a reasoned explanation why he ordered things the way he did. It pleased him to have things arranged this way.

When he entered the room, it could be a comforting retreat into oblivious thought, especially when his normal comforts weren't bringing him enough satisfaction. The closed door to this room was a personal barrier. The house staff knew that he wasn't to be disturbed when he was in the display room. Not even if Shelia was calling. Not even for emergencies. Maybe it was by virtue of his worldly success that those in closest proximity to him didn't disturb him when the door was closed. While it remained clean, the maids didn't spend much time in there. The discomfort or anxiety it seemed to engender among them wasn't discussed.

When he went in and locked the door, every one of the staff stayed away as if in mass obedience to some unknown force. He imagined them sitting absently like unwound clockwork. If any were curious about what sounded like his voice, they told themselves he was having a moment to compose himself. Those with good noses entering the room would be able to detect the faint scent of oranges. He used the juicer with a skull on the end of its handle to mix drinks.

After watching the news, he locked the door to the display room. He went to a desk at one end of the room and pulled open a drawer, slid back a false bottom, and retrieved a key that would open another lower drawer in the desk. In that drawer he retrieved a document. He looked at the deed to identify it then he sat down and turned on the desk lamp. After re-reading its contents, he placed the deed back in the drawer with the lock. After he put the key back and closed the drawer, he walked over to a mamba skin and caressed it before leaving the room.

* * *

On Tuesday, his mood alternated between annoyance with himself and dissatisfaction with his local community. He used Tuesdays to prepare a homily for the next Sunday's mass. This week's readings focused on the ubiquitous theme of faith. It was already afternoon, and nothing had been written. Millions of pages had already been filled with the topic. He was leaning toward recycling an old homily. Amongst his flickering hopes for the day—that were nearly blotted out by thick clouds of doubt—he attempted to reassure himself. Creation was constantly evolving and changing. Perhaps there was more to say.

He'd been educated. He wasn't a strict interpreter of the Bible. He could live with reconciling most scientific theories and the creation story. He consoled himself with the idea that man had a limited and feeble understanding of the Godhead and the mystery and power contained there. He didn't believe religion should require humanity to abandon the search for understanding its surroundings and its ultimate physical fate.

The fate of the child Spring occurred to him as a recent personal example. He thought of incorporating her into the homily but reconsidered. Her story was still too fresh and uncharted. He wasn't sure how it would turn out. He decided to wait to talk after seeing more. It didn't keep him from wondering how she'd come through unscathed among the filth and danger of a known meth house. Had she been born addicted to meth? The doctor said she was fine health wise. Were there lingering psychological effects not yet discovered? She was exceedingly shy. The nuns had been able to get her to look at picture books with them. She participated in school though she rarely spoke. How had such a hapless creature grown amongst the scattered thorns and weeds she'd been thrown into?

He felt himself reenergized. What were his worries anyway? His shelter and food were provided. He had more comfort than a good number of poorer parishioners. A recent influx of Latino workers lived in squalor among a community of trailer parks and shacks. He'd visited them and seen their poverty exported from whatever destitution they'd tried to flee from. But it had followed them and taken root where they landed. What did he have to do but come up with some thoughts on the vehicle of human progress?

There were differing degrees. Some had faith in the ultimate salvation of their soul and all its toil through the world in the flesh experience. Other more practical men and women had faith in their own abilities, even to the point of being godless or anti-religious at least. The phenomenon was an incredible force. He reasoned it could be used to build a city where no city had been built before. But it could also be used to demand unquestioning allegiance to cruel warlords conducting genocide. Blind following could be dangerous, but how was blind faith in salvation any different?

He believed pursuit of faith mustn't be used as an excuse to think one was justified in shirking religious duty. It was also important to realize that piety by itself didn't translate directly into faith. Piety was more of a potential rather than a kinetic energy. Piety could be coldly gained and stored by attending to a predictable script, a certain set of actions that had become habit. He would concede piety might help where faith was absent. The ceremony and choreography of the services might imprint one's body and mind with a reminder of it.

* * *

He had an office in the ten-story city center building, the tallest building in the downtown area. The building's commercial real estate was divided between various government employees and two floors leased to private companies. Caine held a large shareholder interest in one of the construction companies leasing space there, and Caine's influence permeated every floor of the building, including the top floor where the mayor and some of the city councilmen had their offices.

He and another councilman, Bolter, were considered juniors because of their shorter span of service. They received less office space down on the fourth floor. Bolter was a young, conservative Baptist. He detected a naivete in him that might not have been noticed by some of his constituents as Bolter cloaked it with an amicable and enthusiastic manner, combining religious talk with rhetoric aimed at stimulating fearful impulses.

Despite Bolter's base, he occasionally backed proposals aimed at helping the disenfranchised. When Bolter happened to do so, he usually quoted a passage from the Bible then hammered on the duty of the city not to ignore the poor. He was surprised to hear what came out of Bolter's double-edged mouth sometimes.

The three elder councilmen had offices on the top floor near the mayor. Usually they voted in unison. One of the three would occasionally break ranks to vote with him on some of his more mainstream proposals. That elder had been accused earlier in his career of leaning toward socialistic tendencies. But having been relatively free from scandal during his twenty-two years of public service, that elder was still popular enough to maintain his seat.

The other two elder councilmen, who never voted with him, cried continually that his measures would bankrupt the city. They pointed to one proposal aimed at giving incentives for teachers in black school districts. Because revenues from business taxes were low, they complained the budget would run redder than ever.

The revenues from the industrial business taxes had increased slightly given the multiple millions the companies were making. Despite increased net profit, Caine lobbied for lower tax rates. The rates went even lower than the original low rate set decades ago as an incentive to lure companies to locate there. Even the elder councilmen and mayor were contemplating raising the rates, something they must've been afraid to suggest to Caine. How else were they going to get the money for the operating budget and the new projects that had passed based on the three votes? They could declare funds unavailable, but he could use this against them in next year's elections.

He remembered Bolter contacting him. He'd been out in the community a good deal of the time, but Bolter must've learned he was in that day. Bolter had approached him apprehensively. Upon shaking hands, he detected a small bit of moisture in Bolter's palm. They exchange pleasantries for a few moments. Bolter became more at ease. He recounted to Bolter how he'd visited one of the poorest schools in the city yesterday. The principal of that school in a rundown part of the city was hopeful they might be able to afford more current books. Additionally, the heating system there was spotty at best. During the coldest part of the winter, some of the mothers kept their kids home rather than send them to what they referred to as the ice-box of learning. He spoke his mind to Bolter, "Financial beatings can hurt worse than physical ones. A person who takes a beating usually heals up within a couple of weeks, but a person oppressed financially is crippled for life. Death becomes a salve for that person."

As he described his encounter with fervor, Bolter appeared more and more downcast, averting his eyes. Bolter had an incredulous look on his face as he'd responded, "Why look at yourself, Levi. You've risen to an outstanding position and you're a minority."

"One man may be a blip on the frequency of history. If he's impressive enough, he could cause a lasting imprint that may shift the frequency just a little. I'm not one of those great men, but I do know that what I've done is not attributable to any great changes in Southern society. Yes, some doors were opened that would've been completely closed to me in the past, but I had to fight for this position at least as hard as any person aspiring to be a politician would."

Bolter had seemed visibly upset. "But I don't see why you insist that things haven't improved?"

"Look at the fact of why you came to see me in the first place, as an extension of the old guard trying to switch my vote and suppress my ideas."

* * *

Relatively, if he counted all people, he was still young. But he was no longer young in the sense of most marriage-minded American women. He wasn't thrilled with the potential complications of being a second or third spouse to someone. There could be an ex-husband, possible step-children, and layers of in-laws and ex-in-laws that might still have hooks in the woman. Considering this, bachelorhood didn't seem all that bad. He had the ability to cook basic meals, clean occasionally, and generally care for himself. After the conflict of the day, he could enjoy time alone. If he wasn't enjoying that time alone, he had an above-average tolerance for loneliness. He'd grown used to being independent and flexible. He imagined the prospect of being bound to any degree by another's schedule and priorities would be as difficult as overcoming a force of gravity that accelerated the more accustomed he grew to his independence.

There was his work to consider. It was work he enjoyed, even excelled at, but at times he felt precariously close to the edge of some procedural or performance-related precipice. He had his doubts about sustaining a relationship through these trials. Whether that inclination was self-protective or selfless, he didn't want to start a marriage that would end inevitably in divorce, turning him into another weekend parent if kids were involved.

His analytical mind had narrowed the acceptable field substantially. By now almost all the girls from high school that he'd heard about were married or had been married. Same with friends from college for the most part, although he'd heard less from them. The meetings and experiences had been more transitory in the less structured world of the university. He hadn't stayed in touch with any of the women he'd known from there. He was repelled from joining any singles groups, which he perceived as filled with desperate and ultimately risk averse, uninspiring persons.

There could be unmarried women from law school, as their careers, like his, dominated their existence. But they would be competitive like him. He didn't think marrying another lawyer was a good idea. A few exceptions came to mind that involved judges and their lawyer spouses, but the number that didn't work out was much higher.

He questioned whether his analytical training may have put him permanently at odds with handling the emotional nature of a relationship. It may have cut off that possibility for him completely. Nearing the end of his negative reflections on the topic, he saw his chances as poor to dismal in meeting an available woman that navigated through all these failsafes in an over-protective mind.

Across that cold landscape of his comfortable but icy and isolated bachelorhood, he imagined swollen summer sun-rays evaporating freezing waters and encouraging birds to return. It was a tremendous change of season. It had happened so swiftly that it left him somewhat awestruck and euphoric at his great fortune.

She was affable, conscientious, younger, and seemed fuller of hope than he felt. And he believed her appearances were sincere. Then there was her physical attractiveness, the green eyes, the well-shaped breasts, golden hair braided about her head sometimes with queenly effect on more formal occasions. Other times she wore it in mild curls with wavy ends that were a wispy cascade about her head. She had a thin waistline and well-sculpted legs.

The skepticism that had served him so well in his livelihood but so poorly in relationships blew back for a moment against the heat. It cautioned that this was an ephemeral dash of luck that would dissipate as all luck eventually did. She had the power to attract many others. The trouble with finding such a beauty was trying to keep her entertained and satisfied. Besides the presence of drinks, her presence was intoxicating. His attentions took the form of gifts, dinners, and social functions in a swirl of fine scenery about them.

Her parents had stayed together until her father died a few years ago, suddenly. She happened to be rising back from that gloomy chapter of her life with what he guessed were a few tiny more creases under her eyes and a little more striking gravity in the shining green orbs above them. He imagined it had added more strength and experience to her beauty, which made her more attractive. It may also have made her more accessible despite their age difference.

She retained her friends from college and high school and now spent time with other teachers from work. She and her mother had their differences occasionally, but the death of her father had diminished the amount of meaningless conflict of opinion or fruitless attempts to control one another.

He sensed the mother was wary of him. She hadn't seem thrilled with the concept of a defense attorney dating her daughter even if he had been raised Catholic. He'd grown accustomed to this presumption of dislike. He tried to dispel it in amusing ways as if he were on trial, which wasn't far from the truth. Although her mother remained cautious and sometimes said things that seemed overly bitter or misplaced on an emotionally reactive level, she seemed to be warming to him.

He felt a surge in his chest, a boon of confidence that seemed to expand his lungs and make everything clearer. Her body was compelling as fragrant earth. He felt as if a great barrier had been torn away, spilling some built-up, gnawing pressure. It was an incredible boost to his energy. He slept less and bore tasks more easily. Work became a series of light impediments between the last time he saw her and his anticipation of the next.

* * *

Through what he'd gathered from his practice and what he'd studied of local history, he knew the town had grown up near the river in the eighteen twenties. There'd been plantation houses scattered about the area, but no commercial hub. The plantations had been there before statehood. The settlers that established those plantations and other hamlets in the area were a mixture of westbound men out of Georgia and northbound men out of Mobile, Louisiana, and Florida.

The beginnings could be traced to a carved-out square, a plaza used to market different kinds of crops. It was nothing but a group of loosely connected plantations at first. The local plantation owners were drawn into bartering with one another for their own household needs then selling the rest in bulk. The river provided an outlet for the goods down to Mobile and from there to New Orleans or wherever. Cotton and soybeans curled back up north or went to the Caribbean and across the Atlantic.

Eventually a blacksmith and a tanner settled on the plaza. Then a tavern was introduced. Not long thereafter,

a church went up nearby. Then another of a different de-
nomination. Some of the plantation owners were spread
so far out that even neighboring farms were unknown to
them except for a wooded border described in a deed. The
plaza provided a basic site for culture to develop as the
owners or their surrogates began to find out more about
their neighbors.

The first Caine arrived from the east, the decade the
war was looming. After a brief boom during the beginning
of the war, the town suffered miserably. It nearly dissolved
as each plantation owner retreated into a self-sufficient,
protective mode. Many were ruined by mostly Confederate
troops commandeering their crops.

That first one, Smitty Caine, had established a farm
before the war. A story of uncertain veracity passed down
later. It was shortly before Sherman's march. A group of
shoeless men in tattered gray uniforms were camped out
in one of Smitty's fields taking corn off the stalk to either
eat directly or cook quickly over the fire to make cornmeal
mash. One of Smitty's last remaining field hands had seen
their fire. On receiving the high-pitched, anxious message,
he misinterpreted it as a Northern advance to force him
out. Smitty put his boots on, grabbed his rifle, and gave the
field hand a pistol.

The field hand went up first in the crops near the
intruders. On seeing the color of their uniforms, Smitty
suspected they were deserters. Between the four of them,
there were two pistols and a rifle. When Smitty got within
firing distance, he sent a shot high above them. On hearing the shot, they went for their guns. Before they could
grab their weapons, the field hand was shakingly holding a

pistol aimed at one of them. Smitty reloaded his weapon. Seeing they were Confederates, he asked what the hell they were doing on his land. One of the soldiers yelled back through a mouth of missing teeth that the generals had given permission to live off the land. Smitty told them they'd have to get somewhere else or he'd finish them off. He kept the guns on them until they began packing up their ragged, meager belongings.

Smitty had supported the war because he relied on slavery. He told his sons not to have any sympathy for a man or a people that wouldn't stand up for themselves in a recognizable way. If it was a whole race, Smitty didn't care either. But these crop snatchers had been annoying the countryside like a plague of starved crows. Large parts of his fields had already fallen into disrepair, growing wild bastard corn and other produce he couldn't protect from the roving scavengers. He'd run off those four from one of the only good patches left.

As stray soldiers laid waste to the edges of his land, Smitty's economic interest was driven toward the town plaza, specifically a stretch of undeveloped forest to the north. He'd discovered it belonged to a plantation owner who'd fled his house to live with relatives upstate. Smitty put up fences around a sizable chunk. About five years after the war, relatives of the previous owner came back and tried to fight for the land in the courts. Smitty paid a lawyer to confirm his adverse possession.

The town's growth remained sluggish. Smitty passed on his land to his son Marshall. The town plaza grew to the point where the horse trails were cobbled over with stones and then streets of brick, which were later repaved with money from the industrial boom. Merchants and other professions moved in, providing a broader supply of goods and services. The citizens built houses radiating out from the hub.

Marshall, Bo's grandfather, entered into the insurance business, providing another source of income to keep them apace with the upper echelon of the town's occupants. Most of the wealthiest still lived on their farms or in their antebellum plantation houses, but more and more owned some interest in town. The town grew healthy enough to survive the Great Depression. During the Second World War, it grew back what it'd lost.

After the war, with the rise of industry, different sections of town developed. The wage workers lived in a section sprinkled with used car lots, drab government agency buildings, the VFW building, a railroad depot, thrift stores, and junk yards. Another section grew out of the southwest into a suburb. The interstate was built a good forty miles away. There wasn't as much passing traffic as some of the other small towns directly along the interstate. Those towns had sprung up like fungi, surviving on the nutrients of gas-starved and irritably hungry motorists.

The industries had steadily churned out a higher percentage of profits each year. He'd read a promotion piece saying if the city had a backbone, then the succession of Caines were its vertebrae. Smitty was buried where they'd made a portion of the Caine land into a family cemetery. The paper had said the Caines had more than just an interest in the town's growth. It was as if they were joined to it biologically.

After Alcorn's deals had been struck, the forests on the Caine land were cut to clear sections for the mill and the chicken processing plant. Secondarily, it provided wood for the paper pulp mills.

Bo hadn't seen nearly the lean times of his father or grandfather, but he'd inherited from them an obsessive drive for profit. Bo could probably have run the city as a mayor if no one else had shown an interest to run, but the Caines didn't really seem drawn to overt public service. Probably didn't want the scrutiny. Bo preferred controlling the men better suited to dealing with the public and media.

Not holding an official public position must've given Bo better cover to deal with problems that got in the way of promoting industry. The evidence of higher cancer rates and dead fish must've been only subtractions on the equation at a base in Bo's mind where the weak die off and the tougher or cunning ones live. The flexibility Caine enjoyed in carrying out his agenda would've been more complicated if he were mayor. Those roles and titles must not have meant much to him.

Bo complained through the papers that the environmentalists wanted a paralytic lifestyle of always worrying and checking for bureaucratic red tape and inspectors. Without the industries, Bo's supporters cried, the city wouldn't be nothing more than a cluster of houses around a plaza, a lackluster village in the middle of nothing important.

* * *

He and Muffler were on the way back through the Tijuana border. They'd provided extra protection for an exchange of weed and meth between a cartel dealer and the American contact who'd hired them. These protection jobs were more common now. Their days of running any substantial amount of drugs through the border had dwindled. They usually met tight scrutiny at the border. Looking over at Muffler's disheveled appearance and recognizing his own lack of attention to hygiene, he expected they would be searched.

The security detail proved to be easy money as the contact already had a small group of personal bodyguards. He suspected they'd been added as an intimidation factor. From prior dealings, the contact must've trusted them enough to witness what transpired. If not, the contact had a catalogue of crimes that could be pinned on them if they ever betrayed him.

Crossing borders always made him apprehensive. The lanes pinched up traffic like tollbooths, raising a natural aversion in him. The felonies on their records prevented them from getting into Canada through the front door, but they still managed to get in and out of Mexico. The process put a squeeze on his mind, making him irritable and uncomfortable. Maybe it was part of that thing in him that really didn't care for a group of people's assumed authority over him to tell him where he could and couldn't go. He didn't care for artificial and temporary man-made boundaries.

They eased up on their bikes slowly, bearded and unwashed, stinking of their glut on pleasure. In their off time, they'd spent some of their upfront money at a brothel, staying drunk and high with their favorite Mexican prostitutes. He tried ignoring his throbbing tequila hangover. The tranquilizers he'd popped hadn't kicked in yet. As they approached the border, they were directed over to a barely moving line.

They showed their identification and were directed to put their bikes to the side and park them. He assented to the commands but grumbled at the inevitable search. The dogs barked loudly at them but didn't alert on the bikes.

They had to be more careful than in the past. There wasn't so much as a joint in either of their pockets. It wasn't the actual time they'd get for such a small amount, but more the hassle of going through the whole charade. It'd be a hassle of time and money that wouldn't be worth a personal supply. They could be reunited with one soon at the clubhouse. The patrol patted them down for weapons. Those had been left in Mexico with the American contact. Not finding any contraband, the patrol finally allowed them to get back on their bikes. The crossing took over three hours.

Back at the clubhouse, he called his escrow, whose phone was temporarily out of service. They'd come through hot summer daylight, and he'd wanted to crash for at least a day. But he didn't like the unresponsive escrow. Only one quarter had been paid up front. Fighting off sleep, they went straight to see him.

The escrow ran a tavern on the outskirts of Phoenix. They were dusty and sweat soaked again by the time they arrived. Sitting down over a drink, the escrow gave them the other eighteen hundred in cash. The escrow mentioned there'd been a fed nosing around asking about Alabama. After returning to the clubhouse, they popped some speed, grabbed a few items, and headed north. They traveled at night and slept the next day in a non-descript, family-owned motel. It was ratty with mattresses he suspected were lice filled. He instinctively didn't want to stand out right now.

* * *

In California, he discovered he'd arrived at the border two days after they'd crossed. When questioning the patrol supervisor and viewing the security check logs, he saw their legal names had been run. He pulled up surveillance and saw them. He figured they would be at the Phoenix clubhouse by now.

Bolstered by two federal marshals, he stopped by the Phoenix tavern again to question the owner if they'd come through. The owner couldn't remember the last time he'd seen them. He pressed the owner, threatening him with obstruction, and got the owner to admit that he'd seen them recently, but didn't know where they might be headed.

After explaining he was on assignment from the Alabama office, the Phoenix federal branch lent him some temporary working space, where he pinned up a field map. He narrowed the potential stops to places in North Dakota, Washington state, and Oklahoma. He estimated they would be headed for the cooler air of either North Dakota or Washington.

He had limited resources to track them. He'd been waiting for a basis to chase them down and get them incarcerated for as long as possible. With their prior history, the prosecutor might be able to get fifteen to twenty for trafficking. He wasn't sure how reliable a snitch Reynolds might be, or even if he would be one at all.

He believed the bikers were beyond reform. If their blatant barbarian criminal element couldn't be reformed, then it needed to be put behind a barrier. He suspected they were as committed to their lifestyle as he was to his. Theirs led more often to losing circumstances: loss of money due to demoralizing habits, loss of liberty for crimes committed, and loss of life sooner on average. They were only popular and respected within a small section of other losers. They'd chosen a painful and tortured path, but he was devoid of sympathy. It was their choice. He would hunt them down regardless of their stupidity or lack of judgment.

His vehicle churned more as he climbed uphill toward Flagstaff. The air had been cooling and there was an alpine tint to it as sturdier dark green trees shot up. He hadn't slept much the night before. In between his alert anxiety as to their direction, he experienced moments of delirium interspersed with euphoria as the oppressive summer heat began lifting slightly. He pulled over for more coffee.

He headed toward a cabin used by the Wraiths in the southern hills of Colorado. This intelligence had been gained by an informant from a rival club. The informant had purloined the information from a defecting Wraith who'd been later found dead.

* * *

They arrived at the cabin late at night. He hoped to stay a few days, maybe a week, and live off burning meat over the fire. They parked their bikes near the end of the trail, dismounted, and approached where the one-room cabin was hid from view.

As they got close, an overwhelming smell of something rotten hit him. They approached slowly, in case an animal might've lodged in there. As they were going in, he saw Muffler pointing out scraped markings on the door.

Although it looked like a few had tried, no animal was inside. The smell came from the freezer that had stopped working. No one had replaced the battery per the usual cycle. They placed the rotting meat outside. Without good meat, they decided not to stay more than a day and leave that night.

It was just before five a.m. He noticed a shift in the color of the sky to a lighter blue. The summer dawn was coming. He fell asleep to the sound of a few birds whistling.

He woke in the afternoon to the foul odor mixed in with the fresh smell of pine. He stretched and growled. They worked quickly on getting rid of the rotting deer meat piled outside. Some of it had been gnawed on by an unknown creature. They dumped the rest down by the stream.

By the time they were done, the sun was disappearing. Darker blue settled in as a few white specks flickered. After eating some candy bars, they drank down some cold well water.

* * *

When he got to the trailhead the next day, he saw obvious signs of activity. He drew his gun. He believed he could strike before they did. Besides that questionable reassurance, he hadn't seen their bikes. He saw four separate singular tracks in the dirt and gravel.

He tried the door to the shack, but it appeared to be jimmied shut. He didn't put it past the bastards to booby trap the place somehow. He went to a window and peered in. It was a single room containing a couple of mattresses and what looked like a freezer in one corner. He tried to pull up the window, but it was nailed shut. He went back to the wooden front door and tried again. It seemed bolted shut.

He called the nearest federal office over two hours away to let them know his whereabouts and what he was about to attempt to do. There could be something inside that might tell him which way they were headed.

As he was about to break in, he thought they might have concocted a way to situate him where they could kill him easily. But if they intended to use guns, they probably would've shot him by now. He decided to do a perimeter check first. Finding nothing, he went back to the cabin's door.

He kicked until he broke through the door. Looking around, he didn't see anything of use. There were a few candy bar wrappers next to the mattresses. Probably attracted by the lingering smell of rotting meat, some flies had gotten in. An unpleasant air filled the inside. He wondered how the two could have endured the smell. There were no other maps or any paper indication of which way they were headed. He took the candy wrappers for possible prints.

There was a possible stopping point, a cycle parts store previously linked with receiving and passing stolen goods in northern Colorado. It could be a path for either route. It had an attached garage where they could potentially hide. He wasn't sure they'd contact the place. It was contested territory.

He notified the state patrol of his persons of interest. He suspected they would be taking back highways instead of the more visible interstates. It was unlikely word had gotten around to all the local sheriffs and their deputies on patrol or to all the city cops. He held back from notifying neighboring states.

He suspected they would have no trouble getting through the mountain passes this time of year if they were headed west. It was possible they hadn't crossed out of Colorado's boundaries yet. He estimated maximum mileages as he continued farther north toward the parts store.

* * *

The night before, they'd made a long stretch. In upper Utah, they scouted out a place off the highway to make a bed. They'd gotten some materials in Denver earlier, mostly from a clothes dumping area around a salvation store. Rummaging through the darkness, he'd found a couple of pallets and broke off some wood about three feet long. There'd been some sheets and clothes they bagged up along with some folded up cardboard. They'd tied these miscellaneously discarded items to the back of their bikes.

They'd pulled over near dawn. He saw what appeared to be endless desert wasteland interspersed with weirdly shaped geographic features. They headed toward a mesa in the distance. Compared to the mountains and forests of upper Arizona and Colorado, it was as if they'd ridden onto another planet.

After finding a suitable place to crash, they rode their bikes from the view of the road. Using some rocks to hold the wood from the pallets in place, they erected two separate ramshackle tents. Bed sheets formed a canopy. Some of the clothes and cardboard were spread over the top to keep the sheets in place and absorb the unrelenting blaze of sunlight. The rest of the clothes were spread underneath to sleep on. He'd managed to grab a stained pillow that propped up his head. Muffler balled up a sweater to lay his head on.

* * *

He extended his coffee-drenched delirium. When he arrived, the parts store was closed. He debated back at the motel whether to go back for more information or to head north. As he lay in bed, he realized he'd taken a substantial risk at the cabin. He was trained in hand to hand combat well enough to reassure himself he could take both down by force if necessary, but he shouldn't have gone out there without further backup. His tactics had departed substantially from agency protocol. Outnumbered two to one wasn't a safe ratio.

As his exhaustion brought him closer to unconsciousness, his mind filled with combat scenarios. He vaguely sensed a psychological advantage of having them on the retreat. If they had their running mode turned on and paranoia filled their minds, then their fears and subsequent caution would be amplified. They would have no way of knowing whether a small army of marshals pursued them.

Was it Washington or North Dakota? He was leaning toward Washington. There were more Wraiths in Washington. There was a stronghold in North Dakota that could function as a lower-level bunker, but there would be more creature comforts in Washington. They'd potentially stand out less there among more people and more derelicts.

* * *

After waking near dusk on the hard ground in upper Utah, he shook off what drowsiness he could. Even with the stained pillow, he hadn't slept much. It'd been more of a twisted power shutdown. Although he'd pushed extremes before, there was limit to how long he could go without falling asleep, possibly while riding, then laying a bike down. It had happened to others. Gravity seemed increased three fold. Simpler movements took more effort.

He was especially pissed at only getting a glimpse of convalescent rapid eye movement before being jerked straight awake into a hostile reality, outlined in red hues. His nerves felt askew and jangled. Hypochondriac thoughts whistled through his usually thick-skinned mind like nettling enemies, whispering that maybe he'd blown a disk in his back or damaged his spinal column.

Despite his grouchiness, he was satisfied they'd accomplished what they needed to. By dawn they could reach Idaho or the top of California. His years of experience had taught him not to flinch or fade away from pain or discomfort. But as he'd aged, sometimes a sharp craving for basic creature comforts crept up on him, especially with the recent debauchery of Mexico fresh in the pleasure center of his brain.

After an hour or so of rousing themselves, wiping off the sandy dust, drinking water, and eating some beef jerky they'd bought earlier at a rundown gas station, they got back on their bikes. He re-energized on the bike. A visual connection to the environment whirred past, cutting through the extra gravity weighing on him. He could still feel it pulling on him, like the tension of a taut fish line. Riding again eased off the murderous thoughts floating through his consciousness. They were moving again towards a better bed. He estimated it'd take at least two more nights, perhaps three more, before they arrived north of Seattle. There wasn't much life out here in the deserted area they were leaving.

* * *

The next morning, he got a call on his cell. They wanted him back in Alabama on the Reynolds's investigation. He was ordered to return immediately unless he was within certain striking distance of the bikers. Despite his fatigue, a jerk of disappointment pumped a rush of thoughts through his head. When questioned, he admitted there were no significant leads. If need be, the investigation could be taken up again with warrants and more force. He hung up and drove south to Denver.

* * *

For indigent criminal cases, the county relied on paying individual attorneys a modest sum. Any attorney who'd passed the bar and wasn't in a suspended status could get on the assignment list. Most were young lawyers eager to gain experience and some form of compensation as they struggled to pay off the increasing size of their school loans. Occasionally this became a launching pad for some distinguished legal careers. But he'd seen or heard of a number of inept legal disasters as the inexperienced took on more than they could handle, sometimes leading to valid ineffective assistance claims.

He knew some lawyers in the county were more conscious of the constitutional guarantee of effective assistance of counsel regardless of income. Some of these lawyers realized an obligation to take on these non-profitable cases, even if it were only one per annum. There was no consistent enforcement mechanism. Occasionally the judges would appoint randomly from the bench.

He'd been on the list since he entered private practice. The local method of assigned counsel disgusted him, but he felt he would overextend himself trying to spearhead an overhaul of the system. He saw it as a failure of government to make sure everyone got a decent or at least an adequate lawyer when charged with something as far-reaching and potentially devastating as a crime. At some jail calendars he saw the right to counsel thrown away as easily as a used tissue.

He'd seen Aldruss take guilty pleas without much discussion whatsoever about the right to an attorney, much less the waiver of that right. And he watched some of the unadvised with a sense of vicarious dismay as they were surprised to find out that pleading guilty didn't mean they would be getting out of jail. Instead, it often ensured they would be staying there for a while. Some didn't seem to know what they were pleading to. It may have been a reflexive action to the stern, condemning eyes of Aldruss, who seemed to have some mystical ability to conjure up guilt, even out of innocuous situations.

Although the federal public defender system was still overworked and had short resources, it had been much more organized. While learning his craft there, he hadn't seen as much of the blatant abuse as on the county side. Because of the paying cases it would displace, staying on the county assignment list was a hindrance to him. Nonetheless, he stayed on the list, consistently taking whatever case was thrown his way.

He knew there was a mechanism in place for the assigned lawyer to decline based on conflict of interests, lack of experience on the particular charge, or scheduling hardship. More rarely permitted was the exception for certain crimes and persons so offensive to the lawyer's beliefs that the lawyer couldn't effectively represent them. When certain undesirable cases came into the queue to be assigned, this provision had been cited as a way out.

When it came time to assign the recently jailed Edward Reynolds a lawyer, as no one knew whether he had any income source or how to access it, this clause out was frequently cited. Although there were more atrocious allegations at the time than meth manufacturing, Reynolds was known to be borderline competent. Besides this, there was the alleged aggravating factor that a six-year-old girl had been nearly killed and effectively orphaned as a result of his meth operations. He reasoned by the time the administrators had run down the list of many lawyers opting out, there were only a few left before his name came up.

* * *

As June became July, the temperature outside rose from uncomfortably hot to unbearably sweltering. Despite his black cassock and sweaty face, he'd been anticipating the visit. Through the heat, his mind danced with saints who'd suffered as martyrs, whether by arrows or upside down crosses, but he especially focused on those who'd died through burning. The thought of the torture of being roasted alive with temperatures triple, quadruple, ten times the day's heat index of one hundred ten degrees, with the resulting burning flesh and suffocation, seemed beyond comprehension. He saw shimmering off the street. The blacktop seemed to be rippling. He took a swig from the bottle of water he'd brought for his walk. As he arrived at his destination, he contemplated ancient journeys through the heat of Jerusalem, heat that had reoccurred for centuries burning down on mankind. He felt purposefully engaged in man's plight.

Closer to the jail, he tried to imagine how others viewed him. He tried to remain indifferent to those speculative judgments. He walked in his full black cloak. He must've been a striking presence to the retina on this blistering Sunday afternoon. The onlookers undoubtedly believed he sweated. The disproportionate amount of clothing for the environment had drawn attention to him, which some of the more superstitious townspeople might've imagined as an unearthly presence seeming to draw in the air around him, making him more distinct. The purposeful way in which he walked likely added to that impression.

People who knew he visited the jail about once a month had no doubt gotten used to seeing him on this path. But even knowing this, seeing him display the absence of color in his dress combined with firm militaristic steps, they must have been struck by an alien bearing. To see such a presence in the heated streets seemed unnatural even though they probably assured themselves it was something they should've come to expect by now. He knew he'd acquired insulting nicknames.

As he approached the jail, driven by something he told himself was the charitable impulse of following the beatitudes, he acknowledged his ongoing sense of curiosity. Where had the undocumented girl originated? How had she sustained herself? Besides the occupants of the house and the transients who'd tramped through there, no one had known about her until the fire.

The cycle of degradation and poverty occurred to him. From what he'd gathered from snippets of undeniably known facts co-mingled with town gossip, there was the northern mother, an heiress who became a wasted and bloated pariah living in squalor until she died in jail. Whatever virtuous qualities she might have inherited from a family able to amass a fortune, they'd reversed in her as she went on raving drunk binges in a town foreign to her, further ostracizing herself. But he couldn't assume that virtuous qualities had amassed her family's fortune. It could just as easily have been greed, twisted motives, and other moral compromises.

He'd seen other children spoilt like this. Given so much opportunity and financial security turns them to the negative. The recipient becomes a hapless forager in a murky bog, depleted of any initiative or moral steadfastness. Such recipients would try striking the same golden angle as their parents. Being unwilling to understand that success doesn't always come as quickly or as easily as merely thinking it due to them, they become frustrated and misdirected. The wastrel recipients often cloud out disappointment with a certain vice, or a multitude of vices. With a diversion of their attentions, they decrease the chances of ever coming close to reaching the level of their parents, much less exceeding them. The cycle enters full circle as the need to escape from themselves expands in the face of realizing that they're either incapable of being pathologically driven or horribly inept. Depression or any manner of psychological defects ensue, confounding the recipient, until the cycle comes round like a severe familial market correction, turning the once affluent into the impoverished. The man labeled Pitchfork was an offshoot in the decline of his mother. He imagined Edward Reynolds as the family's true bottom.

This was in line with his biblical thinking. The wisdom he believed the book imparted gave him a sense of security. It allowed for returns to decency, even greatness. All he could hope or want for the girl was a return to decency. Despite the latent optimism in him that arose from evidence she was improving, he had a more critical and cynical voice that reined in his hopes, telling him it was much too soon to think of such strides now. There was still the strong possibility she'd been permanently damaged.

They were assuming that she was Reynolds's offspring, but one couldn't tell really whether they favored one another from his mug shot. Given his sores, the rotted teeth, the matted, disheveled hair, the disfigured face, no one could tell what he really looked like. For a second, he thought of Reynolds as a modern day leper. But instead of being innocently stricken with disease, Reynolds had chosen to be one.

Was Reynolds any less culpable because of the cycle? Although he'd heard and taken part in many discussions on addiction, he still found the response that an individual was predestined to be addicted with nothing to stop it a lame and unsatisfyingly hopeless plea. He reasoned catching leprosy or the ebola virus could happen from ignorance or bad hygiene. But willfully snorting a controlled substance in a conscious effort, a pleasure, perhaps a guilty pleasure depending on the individual brought into play more culpability. Even though he'd seen and heard of chronic alcoholics literally drinking themselves to death, he believed the majority of persons played the main role in making decisions that led to their destruction. Nobody was eating ebola on purpose for a rush, or joining a leper colony for a guilty pleasure. It was as much a lack of spiritual strength and insight into one's self that would drive people to try and destroy their body and mind as they had no drive for anything else. They certainly were more culpable than the Third World country citizens born with acquired immune deficiency virus, those inheriting lethal dysentery from polluted water, those contracting salmonella or ebola from bad meat, or those living as a host for other true medical conditions that hooked into innocent populations, depleting them at will in wildfire fast numbers.

He believed these tendencies to distinguish addictions and diseases seemed a luxury of the affluent. Their mentality was easy prey for abuse by those that sought refuge from responsibility for their own conscious decisions. It would be easy to mimic or masquerade as an addicted personality with no way of uncovering the fraud or self-deception.

He supposed the results of those espousing such a calamity in a larger than warranted percentage of the population could have a net positive impact. But there was a suspect lack of integrity in identifying and analyzing who was truly, unwittingly addicted, which he believed to be a much smaller number, and those who'd consciously or complacently chosen to destroy themselves. Indulging in suicide wasn't a disease; it was more of a control issue with God. It could begin with one not understanding or divining the point of one's existence. Then all the pain, sadness, and ennui that seems so prevalent in a moment overwhelms the individual, and he or she decides to take the decision encrypted in his or her body's natural mortality, ending it earlier than one's allotted time.

His thoughts turned to how the girl had progressed in the last few weeks. Spring had begun talking more, even with other children. Though the nuns described it as not more than a few words usually involving exchange of a toy, she was interacting. When the television went on, they reported she became glued to it. They figured she'd spent a lot of time watching it at the burned down house. The nuns made an effort to cut down her time in front of it, usually by taking her outside. She cried softly sometimes at this movement away from whatever children's program she was watching intently. But when outside, she showed an affinity for the outdoors as well, chasing birds and insects to the outskirts of the play area and inspecting plant life throughout the grounds.

He visited at least once a week believing he provided a male role model for the orphan children. He tried spreading time out as evenly as possible between all the children, but paid special attention to her as she adjusted to her new environs. The nuns accompanied them both for walks that meandered through trails leading to the river. On one of these walks she began to question the location of Uncle Rey-Rey. Her avuncular labeling of Reynolds caused him to question the girl's paternity again.

He got closer to the entry door of what he believed could reasonably be considered a box holding tormented souls in hell. In a homily sounding voice in his brain, he contemplated modern society with its wide gulch between the rich and the poor. There was also the commitment to on-demand self-gratification with the ability to order online anything that might fill an incompatible feeling one might have, leading to overabundant consumption, with an increasingly frenetic pace for everything, along with the maddening drive to become the best or be nothing. He believed these phenomena had a substantial effect in creating bad ideals, especially in those whose minds could easily be overcome.

Perhaps Reynolds was another casualty of this societal disintegration? He couldn't see this as an excuse for Reynolds to shift responsibility for his own actions, but it may be an explanation. The societal mentality to promote all those selfish incentives then to lock away those acting according to the stimuli of fast food, fast money, and fast drugs seemed to encourage a mixed message of moral confusion. Like some of those excessively glamorous and successful, weren't some of these people in jail striving to be excellently selfish with their destructive, anti-social habits?

He approached the visitor sign-in counter. A line of various jail workers, medical staff, and a few in sports coats that looked like lawyers were all waiting in a single file line before the vacuous rectangular portal of a metal detector, which he couldn't help imagining as a Dantean gate leading downward.

Behind bulletproof glass, a guard sat at the desk to the side of the metal detector. The guard's countenance gave him the sharp and bitter impression of a man who's made a deal to sacrifice any semblance of enjoyment at his work in order to gather some weekly dollar amount that others indicated was necessary to be acceptable. He didn't know what had driven the man to make the deal. He suspected having a second wife and some older children to support could drive one to it. He imagined the guard many times saying he didn't care what others thought about his employment. But in fact, his whole existence had been chosen or conceded to because he cared what others thought about his ability to accumulate money and how he would use it to buy a house and raise children.

He imagined the identity of those nameless others judging the guard wouldn't be discernible, but the pressure had to have been real. That vague source would torment the guard, speckling his gloomy mindcast with malevolence and self-loathing. Had the exact terms of the deal been advertised or announced? Perhaps the man had fallen into some unseen trap. More likely, no thought of this kind was put into it. Why would he think about things the way a priest would? It could simply be a way to make a living.

The guard may actually have been in his forties, but most passersby seeing his sour grimace would think him to be in his sixties. On hearing his rigid barking of commands and reprisals, they might suspect he had cynically and caustically entered his seventies.

He greeted the guard briefly as he signed in on the visitor sheet then went through the detector. He'd discovered some of the background and tendencies of the guard during uncomfortable delays that forced small talk with others in the fortress. Without the delays, the guard refrained from any non-essential talk. The guard seemed fidgety, indicating it was nearly time for him to indulge in one of the few pleasures left to him in life, smoking outside. The guard indifferently left, causing the impatient line to grow longer and more anxious to pass through. He suspected the guard relished the spread of misery.

After being buzzed through the heavy steel, electrically controlled door, he walked down a corridor to the elevator. The unwashed smell hit him. These were probably the underprivileged mostly. They'd sealed their underprivileged fates by acting how those with wealth and power expected, with inappropriate displays of protest and selfishness that could be criminalized and used as a basis to keep them working perpetually in slavery-like conditions. That assumed they would even be able to get a legitimate job with their records.

Despite the label of a correctional building, he didn't observe much correction being accomplished based on the recidivism rate. He could even see it channeling and encouraging criminal behavior as the inmates stewed together planning more ways to subvert and disrupt. This ran consistent with what he reasoned was his obligation to visit the incarcerated. When he talked to inmates, he explained his thoughts and then offered some reasons why they might want to break the cycle. He had small successes, usually with persons who'd been raised Catholic and who must've recognized his garb with some latent respect. He saw some of those actually rehabilitate to build productive lives, but that was rarely maintained. Once they'd fallen into the sludge, it was difficult to pull themselves out of it and wash it off.

Beforehand, he'd talked to Reynolds's lawyer, M.L. Sheet. He knew the case had garnered media attention. He didn't want to interfere with the legalities. Sheet had approved of the visit.

As he rode the large and slow-moving compartment up, like riding in a freight elevator, he concluded the failings of interacting with other individuals was directly related to one's own failings. Counteracting the ills of society was within the individual's power. It boiled down to self-control. Something that the weaker minded, the ignorant poor, the mentally ill, or the desperate didn't often have in great measure.

Ever since the door had locked behind him, the cruel and brutal seriousness of confinement assaulted his sensitive, airy reflections. Once off on the higher floor, he was buzzed through another layer of locking, thick metal doors, which clanged shut behind him ominously. He proceeded down the corridor to Clem Payne's office. The jail chaplain would escort him to Three East.

Section Three East contained the mentally ill and especially dangerous inmates. They were kept locked up twenty-three hours a day except for psychological evaluations or visits to the medical doctor. They were given a one-hour break a day to walk around or exercise in the common area while being watched by at least two guards. An additional guard viewed by camera.

He gathered the jail guards considered it a punishment to be sent to Three East. They'd told him they tried to make the best of it among the bizarre, repulsive, and sometimes inhumane behavior they witnessed, not only from the inmates, but also from their co-workers. Sometimes the tedium and the environment got to them. Stirring up or manufacturing trouble kept the day moving. They stuck together so the inmates were blamed and reported.

At the end of the corridor was another door to buzz through. He pushed the button, but nothing happened. After waiting for a few minutes, he began to get anxious, pushing the buzzer again. Clem's room was just on the other side of this barrier. The curtailing of his movement increased the discomfort brewing within him. He anticipated the goal of his visit, meeting with the inmate. This was a meaningless delay. Eventually he pushed the button underneath the small pattern of holes on the metal paneling that marked the radio. Someone crackled abruptly from the other end that he needed to wait until they were done moving prisoners. Looking through a rectangular, face-sized plexiglass window in the door, he didn't see anyone on the other side. Five minutes later, a buzz unlocked the door, unleashing within him a deep-seated response of relief and gratitude.

The stench steadily increased. It smelled of unwashed things. It was unpleasant, sickening, and not a place he would think of eating. Several years before, during his initial visits, he had been taken aback so far that he'd choked on it and felt waves of nausea. Now it had grown more familiar as the smell of the condemned, the dying, and the homeless. He summarized it as the palpable odor of sin pervading the whole institution of forced punishment and cruelty. The remorseless degradation stunk of caged animals, some dangerous enough to be corralled by the electrified lash of a taser's tongs, others unpredictable enough to require tranquilizers after being forcefully subdued.

Clem was a chubby, bald, quiet man that didn't seem bothered in the least by his somewhat medieval environment. The two were acquainted from his earlier visits to other inmates. They greeted each other briefly. He sensed his words sounded anxious to get somewhere else, that he didn't mean them and that he couldn't hide he didn't want to take part in small talk. Clem seemed used to it or ignored it and directed his comments toward locating the one being visited.

While waiting for the door to Three East to open, he listened to Clem describe Reynolds's entry into the jail. "He was coming off meth or worse, and he couldn't even walk without the guards supporting him. He retched in the elevator, and he banged into the walls. I could hear him as he went by. They had him in waist shackles and leg irons because of his thrashing around. Two guards on each arm, and a third dragging him about by the center circular link connected to the waist. He had unkempt long hair and was covered in sores. The guards wore gloves and masks over their mouths.

"Medical checked him out first. The doctor described Reynolds as a highly toxic walking disaster. After checking his vitals, they shuffled him into Three East to detox. The guards told me they could hear him wailing and weeping between angry outbursts. They'd see him sprawled out in a disheveled mass on the floor, lying in puddles of his vomit. His jail uniform was stained with urine and defecation. The unlucky guard with the least clout had the job of cleaning him up every other day. After they pulled him out of his cell, the guard splashed a bucket of water and disinfectant throughout the cell, then squeegeed out the resulting sludge.

"His hair was still a clotted mass. Some clumps had dreaded up as he apparently had no familiarity with a comb for an incalculable time. The guards were concerned about lice or other organisms living in it, besides the repulsive stench it'd collected from his rolling around on his cell floor or sinking it into toilet water when he kneeled before the latrine, caking it with vomit and other bodily functions. It was ordered cut.

"The jail barber only attempted this after Reynolds had been given some heavy anti-psychotic sedatives prescribed by the jail doctor. Even with this chemical restraint and the chains and handcuffs physically restraining him to the barber's chair, the barber had a hard time as Reynolds gnashed his teeth and turned his head to defy the cutting.

"The barber told me he'd worn plastic gloves and sterilized his utensils. First he'd used shears to cut through some of the clumps so the clippers wouldn't have too much trouble with the rest. He watched as bugs crawled or jumped off after the hair hit the floor. He said it might've turned his stomach when he was younger, but by now he went about his work mechanically. He said it was one of the worst cases he'd seen, worse than a wild, rabid dog. At one point, they had to put a spit mask on Reynolds to continue.

"When the barber turned the clippers on and got close to the nape of Reynolds's neck, Reynolds started whirling his head in a disruptive manner. Another jail guard was called in to physically hold Reynolds's head in place. After a couple of minutes of this, the clipper cut was done. They'd nixed the planned razor shave because of the difficulty in holding Reynolds's head still. They'd doused his head with anti-lice liquid. The newly shaved Reynolds was led back to his cell. The barber contemplated throwing the shears and clippers away after it was over. But he'd decided against it, letting the tools soak in the most stringent solution he could find."

After a few moments of strained quiet, the door buzzed. Turning to leave, Clem bid him God's grace in dealing with his visit. He'd been up to Three East before. He knew it was a convocation of lunacy, a floor full of deranged and delusional inmates. When entering, he heard a cacophony of noise and conversation pinging wildly off the walls.

He went through the corridor past a surveillance booth and came to what he knew was the last door before entering the common area. To his left, he saw a jail guard sitting behind a table panel with several video screens before him. Through the rectangular window in the door, he could see another guard coming toward him. The final door opened and the guard gruffly informed him to follow. The common area contained a few hard metal tables in between the cells. The cells lined both sides of two floors. Stairs led up to a grated walkway on the second floor where another guard stood watch.

The stench of the room became stronger, as if he'd hit upon the nauseating source of it. He correlated it with the destruction of civilization while imagining what a dark vigil the guards of this floor kept. It had to be a grind bolstered by the blackest of cynicisms and placated by coffee and cigarettes. He imagined such a war post would even warp the minds of those ordered to watch through the protective distance of a video screen. They would watch for long periods of time with nothing between but the deteriorating and slovenly dissension of inmates interrupted occasionally by a sudden outbreak of unpredictable, panic-filled violence. Perhaps it would be spurred on by violence some of the more sadistic guards had created. The guards' attempts at humoring him bubbled up to the surface of a murky bog, popping in shallow ways. He tried to avoid condoning this by stating facts, whether or not those facts seemed obvious. Responses to the factual statements were often inarticulate grunts or the oafish delayed reaction of a numbed mind.

He believed many of the souls of the prisoners of this floor were similarly numbed by chemicals through a variety of medications and tranquilizers. Some were adjusting to their regimen, which could cause alternating periods of lethargic oversleeping followed by wide-eyed insomnia. He'd heard of unfortunate situations where someone would be taken in and their meds left behind in the medicine cabinet wherever they'd been living. They would go off their cycle and be unable to proceed competently in court. Some sat in cells or stared out in catatonic stupors; others made noise in manic nonsensical outbursts. Eventually those that readjusted might be reintroduced to the general population of the jail, but according to Clem Payne, the initial designation to this floor tended to stick.

A majority of the inmates in Three East had been diagnosed as schizoaffective to various degrees. Many refused to take their medications. When pressed, they spouted out a series of objections often laced with obscenities. He could hear some yelling on paranoid topics about brain control.

He watched a squat, elderly jail nurse push a cart with a tabletop. She wore a generic white outfit and plastic gloves.

Different sized bottles filled the top of the cart, mostly brownish-orange prescription bottles. He could see her dispensing contents from a prescription bottle into a cuplike paper container. She did this with slow deliberation even as the loudest protests came from the cell she was nearest. She was accused of maniacal power control tendencies. Viewing the frumpy, simple-minded looking older woman, he thought of her more as a slow wheel in the institution, a mechanical creature lacking any diabolical intent. She merely carried out preconceived orders based on the jail doctor's review of the records or evaluations from the state mental hospital. She carried on with benign deliberation in the face of these insults and accusations.

For the more difficult inmates, a guard helped her administer the doses by opening the individual cell door and handing it to the mouthy inmates. For the more dangerous ones, the guard braced against the cell door while cracking it open to leave the medicine on the floor.

He noticed someone he'd previously visited. The inmate was a deranged ex-soldier who'd become chronically homeless, a repeat trespasser. The shaggy-haired and bearded man didn't speak often. If he did, it was mostly unintelligible. The ex-soldier sat on the floor in the corner of his cell. The guards had warned that the man was known to defecate on the floor and to consume his own body fluids. He watched the guard slant open the ex-soldier's door, slide in the day's paper cup on the floor, then push the door firmly closed to lock it.

The nurse and guard would watch the inmate swallow the medicine to make sure no stockpiling occurred. While a good number refused to take the medications, some eagerly greeted the daily dispensation, thanking the jail nurse profusely as she came by. The rest were indifferently tranquil, mechanically popping the pills handed to them.

He remembered Clem's warning that some of the guards had become tainted by the environment. They'd fallen into temptations of sexually interacting with some of the more desperate inmates. The male guards complained or warned that the women inmates could be manipulating. Every year or so, a scandal broke out. Someone would be fired or disciplined depending on the severity. Then things settled back to the way they were before. Favorites developed and some inmates figured out how to receive more comfortable treatment or to at least avoid being treated harshly.

The guard came to Reynolds's cell and unlocked it. A distinct stench wafted out. He attributed it to Reynolds not washing, not washing for days. Then he saw what looked to be puddles of dried vomit on the floor. The guard, seeing the direction of his gaze, commented, "Heez been havin' strong withdrawals. Ain't got 'round to cleanin' up yet. Seemz like evar time we open, we get a new surprise. Second day he shat his bed. No one wanted to take that one."

Reynolds joined the conversation, repeating with different inflections the phrase indicating he'd defecated on himself. First Reynolds used a high-pitched questioning voice then switched to exaggerated and mocking ones. He wondered if Reynolds was having some kind of reflective stuttering fit in his head, like a funhouse mirror demonstrating the fractured remnants of his drug-shattered mind.

Physically he saw a different person than he'd expected from the mug shot in the paper. Instead of a long mane of unruly and tangled hair, the creature before him had a close-shaved head. Reynolds's eyes were black bulbs of fury, reflecting what dim light was available. He'd seen eyes like that somewhere before, but he couldn't exactly pinpoint whose, probably another inmate. These eyes were less stable, though. There was a jittery, unstable quality to Reynolds's whole eye area. They moved around constantly searching for something, perhaps rolling about on inward tangents. The volatility of the inmate's upper face made him think of imminent disasters or physical attacks, possibly an internal combustion like a heart attack.

Reynolds was bound by waist chains and leg irons over his navy blue jail uniform. There were unidentified stains on the front of the uniform. What looked like dandruff covered the shoulders and front. A strong odor of urine permeated the cell. The latrine looked unflushed. As he gagged, he took a handkerchief out of his pocket to cover his mouth and nose.

The logistics of transporting Reynolds had already been discussed. Three guards were required to move him. Even then, it was difficult to get Reynolds going in a direction they wanted him to go. He had offered to meet Reynolds privately in his cell if there were adequate safeguards in place. He saw Reynolds had been chained to a railing on the wall. He sat down on a stool close to the door of the cell. The guard stood outside the slightly cracked, unlocked door within easy calling distance.

He lowered his handkerchief and greeted Reynolds by asking if he were alright. Reynolds burst into hysterical laughter then switched suddenly to an uneven, spastic voice, "No, no, man. Yur alright. Me, me, they got my molars wired. Was fine till they shaved my head this mornin'. Think it's to make room for the electrocution. They won't want any burnin' hair. It would stink too bad in their little room. They want a clean current scramblin' right through my brain."

He looked toward the dried vomit. "Are you still feeling sick?"

Reynolds snapped, "What're you here for? Nobody here will believe in yur spells anyway."

More hysterical laughter was aimed like spit at his face. Chains jingled as Reynolds switched positions, straining against them and yelling, "Angels and devils are all 'round. Which are you?"

"I'm only a man with good and bad traits. I come to visit here once a month."

"Are you on shortwave? Where's the antenna yur car-ryin'?"

"I deliberately chose to visit you because of a five- or six-year-old little blond girl. She was found at your house the night of the fire."

Reynolds seemed to register an inner revulsion. His head slanted down for a second. Then he put his hand up as if he were trying to ward off some premonition. He heard Reynolds rambling about the noise in his mouth getting louder. "They're tryin' to insert a television frequency now. Tryin' to project images on the wall of my cheek. And on the roof of my mouth through a back molar. She, she, didn't do nothin'."

"She's recovering well from the fire and is staying at the orphanage until we find her a home."

Reynolds snapped his head up, yelling and spitting, "No, no, we can't let the devils get to her now. They'll feed her all the consumption shit with the poisoned germs. She's too good for that."

"The nuns and I wanted to let you know she is well taken care of. She was very quiet at first, but she seems to be more outgoing now."

Reynolds looked suddenly sullen and burst out, "Take this molester away!" He became incomprehensible at that point, growling and spitting more.

He thought of leaving, but beneath the symptoms of Reynolds's withdrawal from drugs and probable mental illness, there was the chance of learning more of the origins of Spring. He saw open areas of skin where Reynolds must've scratched himself bloody.

After the outburst, Reynolds rubbed and scratched his arms with the limited movement the restraints allowed him. Reynolds grinned wildly and began pulling at his restraints before returning to genuine interest in her well-being. Smiling a grisly-toothed smile, Reynolds asked, "Do you think I'll be able to take care of her when I get out?"

He uttered a small prayer hoping that the girl hadn't been abused. He couldn't help but look downward and shake his head. He'd been trying to be as diplomatic as possible with this volatile man, but he wouldn't be misleading. "They say you're looking at a lot of jail time here. If you get out, I'm not sure that the Department of Human Resources will let you act as her guardian because of things that've happened."

Reynolds mumbled, "Why, why?"

He watched Reynolds curl up with his head down around his knees. He tried to engage Reynolds in conversation, but Reynolds wouldn't acknowledge his presence. Reynolds would sporadically look up, staring at the wall, speaking rapidly about subjects out of sequence. It reminded him of someone holding down a channel changing remote button for television. Reynolds's thoughts seemed to flip again and again, paralyzing him in a separate dimension where connected thought was a luxury.

After about fifteen minutes of this, he began to doubt whether they could communicate. Even his prayers on the subject began to annoy him. They seemed like unsatisfying, aimless attempts to get around his frustration. He wondered whether he should even bother with this man, who appeared to have destroyed his mind. Based on lack of resemblance, he began to doubt the possibility of a direct parental link between Reynolds and Spring.

After Reynolds calmed somewhat, he ventured a question. "Who are the girl's parents?"

Reynolds looked point-blank at him. "Hell if I know. All I knew was her mother. That fat pregnant bitch."

"How did you know her mother?"

"What do I have to tell the informers for, they should already know it. I know you got an eight ball camera eyeballin' me or a tape recorder wired somewhere, probably in yur collar."

"Is she your child?"

Reynolds laughed hysterically then switched serious as if he were contemplating whether it was possible. Then Reynolds slowly shook his head. "No, no. Her momma came pregnant to the house, I didn't cause that girl."

"Did she say who the father was?"

"How many ticks does it take to get down to it? I ain't yur source of information, man. Yur part of the great machine chain, the inhuman slaughter festival." Raising his voice, "She came pregnant to the house and then left, goddammit. She came there and did meth, and then she stopped, then she did it again, and then she left. Alright, it's all a simple pattern, is that 'nuff for you? The girl ain't 'cause of me!"

* * *

Upon the appointment, he opened a file with the client's name, last name first, on the outside. He debated whether to send Prentice over to talk to Reynolds first. Sometimes he did this as a kind of reconnaissance as he prepared his approach. Other times it was imperative for Prentice to go collect evidence that might quickly disappear, usually in the form of cuts or bruises that should be photographed.

Early on, it would be important to establish with Reynolds who he was for consistency's sake. He wanted to avoid any confusion or any adverse reaction by sending his investigator. He'd heard from the priest the man was talking in elliptical gibberish yesterday. The day after he was appointed, he scheduled a visit. Reynolds had been in custody over two weeks before the appointment. It irked him that Reynolds had to sit there that long without counsel, but he was responding as soon as it was feasible. Aldruss had set bail sixteen days earlier at two hundred and fifty thousand.

He carried a briefcase of seasoned dark brown leather. He expected Reynolds's new slender file inside to one day grow larger than a briefcase could hold because of the potential mental health paperwork. He was familiar with the jail. He could deal with the unpleasantness, the odors, and the slow-moving guards even when they were irate and miserable to deal with.

Each time he went reminded him of his federal public defender days when he frequently had in custody clients. He hadn't lost sight of the depravation, the loss of self-respect, the loss of freedom to move about, the overwhelming sense of condemnation and defeat, the general hopelessness pervading the institution, with madness lurking and seeping through the cinderblock walls and iron bar cages. He'd grown accustomed to it and adjusted his expectations accordingly. The strangeness had slightly worn off. He didn't find himself overwhelmed or at a loss of how to accomplish things there.

As time went by going through those locked steel doors, he toughened and became more adept at reaching through multiple delusions to reach the jewels of his job. Many proclaimed their innocence without offering an adequate explanation. He could get through occasionally to some shreds of reality with these erratic minds by showing how their stories were blatantly flawed. He'd tell them they'd have problems getting an acquittal on all charges. A significant category of repeat offenders refused to see anything but persecution despite a long list of crimes and convictions. Some alleged he wasn't fighting for them.

The most recalcitrant were often among those. They'd given up on any semblance of society or civility, falling off the radar of anything redeemable. They'd degenerated into an animalistic existence, living nomadically from institution to institution. He'd come to believe that the hopeless were inevitable. They were the ones who couldn't break the cycle: the toothless, degenerate crack heads, the zombie-tranced pill heads, the heroin addicts reeking of bad chemical reactions, becoming edgy and antagonistic as their dope or methadone wore off.

Perhaps they'd been victims once. They may have been sexually abused by a parent, a relative, or someone else. They may have been physically beaten into a ferocious state. They would take out their hatred with all their being on others who even hinted there was a comfortable norm to enjoy in life. They would take it out on the jail guards, on themselves, on the walls.

Then there were the severely mentally ill. Some had self-induced psychosis while others were born with unlucky genetic permutations causing them crippling societal disadvantages. Collectively they were the condemned, their bodies like uninhabitable, broken-down buildings slated for demolition because of the danger they posed.

By his estimates, this was true for a good number inside. But not all were correctly there. There were too many that shouldn't be there. Innocents got herded into this societal slaughter pen by over-eager, sloppy, or corrupt law enforcement. Rookies with quick triggering minds made mistakes based on personal bias or even malicious bias to those that showed any hint of disrespect. Some of those being incorrectly held had been there before. They'd donned the dark mantle of the condemned so long that it was nearly impossible for law enforcement to distinguish anything other than a guilty constant. Other times there was a high-profile crime that law enforcement believed required them to hold someone even if there was no solid case. He'd seen instances where professional standards of detective work bowed to public scorn.

Worse examples were the child-minded men and women with mental deficiencies that prevented them from understanding. He'd even seen one young woman with down syndrome sit it out for a while waiting for the state mental hospital to opine she was incompetent to stand trial. These hapless ones had no business being corralled with the ones who made conscious adult decisions, whether slick or stupid, the conscious ones who dedicated themselves to criminal decisions.

His early perceptions of holding facilities had gradually evolved from slightly shocking and jarring on the senses to not allowing himself to flinch easily in the face of this clinical dissection of freedom to move about and live on one's own clock and agenda. Early on there may have been some hesitations or missteps, but not long after he began, he walked right into the common areas between cell block walls. He was among many street-hardened men and women. Maybe on the outside they could've been intimidating and dangerous. But on the inside, at least to him, who was free to exit, it seemed to be a lot of bluffing and pomp. It was the braggadocio of recounting the number of fights or kills, of throwing gang signals, of tattoos worn like elegant gowns, of bowing up, showing off scars, comparing bicep size, all the miscellanea of material street wealth.

In turn, he wasn't a serious threat to their evaluation system. He had an inside view on the main thing many of them were concerned about. That commanded respect if handled properly. Of course, there were those who harassed him, cursed him, accused him of being an informant, a public pretender, but most of these squawkings came around eventually to reckon with him on finding a release date.

Some of the homeless saw it as a decent living when the streets were cold. Three square meals a day and shelter against the winter. By differing degrees it wasn't as bad as some of the highly sensitive ones made it out to be as long as one was willing to sacrifice a certain degree of self-respect. He wouldn't minimize the danger. Even one who kept quietly to himself, ignoring the pressured struggle to gain street credibility, could at anytime be threatened with a shive or be forced upon by a more hungry criminal appetite. That risk could lead to paranoia and lack of a good night's sleep.

He remembered being asked why and how he could deal with what must be depressing work. He acknowledged a long and protracted focus on negativity might eventually submerge him or take something vital from him. He'd seen other lawyers engage in reprehensible behavior because of it, uncontrollable gluttony, sexual promiscuity, drugs and alcohol abuse, or corruption through selling out their clients or becoming criminals themselves. Analyzing himself, he could possibly be accused of the promiscuity, but then again he wasn't married, and he'd been faithful to Sylvia. He drank more moderately, but some hungover days questioned whether he might've damaged his liver when he was younger.

The rigors of the job didn't leave him wilting away in depression. There were moments when he'd rather not be implicated in someone else's public embarrassment or downfall, but it was ultimately their ass on the line. He would do his best to give them the competent and zealous lawyer they were entitled to constitutionally, but if it didn't work out, no matter how emotionally invested in the outcome he was, he wasn't the one that had to do time. All the rancor between the government and the defendant, with the forces pressing down on him to get his client to bend and take it for the good of society, could weigh leadenly on him, but it didn't overcome him with despair. The competitiveness that led to acquittals or dismissals uplifted him.

The jail could be a depressing place, but so could a high school gym weight room with its pent-up hormone denials. Some good might rise out of both in the end, although it was easier to expect that from a high school weight room. The athletes became stronger there, theoretically enabling themselves to perform better on the field. While an inmate was more likely to hone anti-social and destructive behaviors, he'd witnessed a few who corrected themselves upon release.

Those pissed off by his questions and his successes would complain he promoted mayhem and anarchy through his employ as a tricky salesman of sorts, craftily working illusions on gullible jurors. Even though it might seem to the standard eye he was engaged in a deplorable, unpopular business similar to working at a dump, the work required his full intellect and soul.

Whatever doubts he held about his employ's affect on society, he believed that if nobody else did the job, there would be worse consequences. He saw himself as a deterrent to government mistakes, mistakes that he'd witnessed through the government's imperfect human implementations. They were just as susceptible to malaise, callousness, arbitrariness, laziness, and corruption.

There were times he contemplated terrible, abrupt solutions when he felt trapped by the rules, the politics, or the expectations of his clients. There'd been situations where he had waived an argument that might have gained ground, an argument that he shouldn't have waived in hindsight. Sometimes an objection had lain silent where the evidence could've stayed out and might have made a difference in a juror's mind. The abrupt solutions were whimsical gasps for relief, a type of mutilated prayer to stop his self-flagellation. Even that got choked up on shame and self-hatred, accelerated by a severe loneliness in defending a losing cause. In those situations, it seemed he was a defiant island in a sea of pressure, with the sea pressing in slowly to eventually submerge and drown the effort for good.

His casual mentors had groomed and trained him for those moments, the times when he contemplated quitting on a variety of levels. He would be tempted to find something else to do or to end things in melodramatic ways that hadn't seriously allured him since his teens and young twenties. But he could only do so much with the facts and the clients he had. There were certain persuasive measures he could take, but there were real limits. His years in public defense had been filled with impossible odds at times. It'd seemed as if others were winning more, somehow eking out victories on limited resources, bad facts, and unruly clients. Some were quicker on evidence rules, others wrote better than him, others still had better political connections or knew how to read the judges better. This could send him into self-doubting spirals, turning his guts into anxious knots, wondering whether he was really in the same league as these people. He then would have to remind himself that he'd prevailed before, he'd gotten not guilties, hung juries, and dismissals. He'd gotten the innocent cleared even though sometimes the innocent got convicted.

To endure, he'd made an unspoken compact with himself not to drag anyone else into this ride careening through fear, intimidation, greed, and lust for power. At least until some stability emerged. He came close to reneging a couple of times for the soft comforts of a marital home with kids on the horizon, but those few women had faded away. A crisp, bright future was burning again, a future engendered and enlarged through Sylvia. But before he got intoxicatingly lost in chasing it, he thought back. It seemed now that the extra caution had been justified. He'd shown he could maintain a practice and even be successful at it. Sufficient time had passed to prove this. He was getting older. They laughed together. He thought the financial stability was always subject to change, but his doubts had lessened as he'd become more sought after. The loans for his education, car, and part of his home had been paid off.

A sublime joy had begun animating his actions. The gruff judge couldn't smother it, the unyielding prosecutor couldn't squelch it, and the ungrateful and verbally abusive client couldn't undermine it. It rose up like a plain, grassy, peaceful hill drinking in sunlight, invigorating him as he approached the jail.

Most of his experiences with mentally problematic clients came from his public defender days, but there'd been a handful since he joined the county appointment list.

When he arrived at Three East, he knew what to expect. His adrenaline rose a little as he heard a different combination of moaning, yelling, and whimpering. The jail guard spoke loudly like a field commander under fire, "It does get quiet sometimes. They'll go off into their own little worlds talkin' to 'emselves."

The guard led him to Reynolds's cell. Through the face-sized, rectangular-barred opening in the heavy door, he saw a human figure curled up on his jail bed, which consisted of a thin cushion on a concrete box spring, an extension of the cinderblock wall. The guard beat on the door, yelling, "Reynolds. Wake up! It's your lawyer."

The guard opened the door, but Reynolds stayed in a curled position. The guard went over to make sure Reynolds's restraints were in place. Reynolds sat up and looked around groggily. His head was shaved. The guard left them alone with the door unlocked.

What looked like turnip greens had been slopped and smeared on Reynolds's white cinderblock walls. It looked like Reynolds had been trying to write a message or draw something.

He stood looking directly at his eyes. "I'm Mark Lyle Sheet, your assigned lawyer on charges of manufacturing methamphetamine and reckless endangerment. Do you understand why I'm here?"

Reynolds stared at him suspiciously.

He sat down in the chair near the door. "I'm your assigned lawyer."

He heard Reynolds mumble incoherently.

"What was that?"

"Yur a mouthpiece."

"You could say that. I'll be speaking for you in court, but I'll also be your legal advisor."

Reynolds snarled in a low sarcastic voice, "Use'ta have a toy when I's little. It had a microphone to sing into. It'd project voices. It could also record voices. So that's what it is. It's all rigged. Yur a recordin' device. Yur job is to get me to plead guilty."

"No, that's wrong. I'm here to defend you the best I can. We'll go over the evidence they have against you. That will take some thinking and require you to weigh your options. It may remind you of some things you don't want to be reminded of or don't want to hear. But that's part of my job too."

"Yur a different race."

"What do you mean? I'm the same as you."

"I've seen the courts, all rigged up. Yur like angels and fallen angels battlin' 'fore the judge who plays God."

"Do you understand that I'm your lawyer?"

"I won't be forced to plead. You can't railroad me!"

"Why do you think I'll railroad you?"

"I've seen it and know how it goes. Yur all railroad men. I don't have to sleep on yur railcars."

"Okay. Let's talk about why you're here for a second."

"There's no good reason I'm here."

"There was an explosion and fire at your residence, right?"

"Were they watchin' me with their eight ball camera in the ceilin'? Don't you know 'bout the gov'mint division in charge of holographic reality shows? Don't you know that the people on those shows are gov'mint experiments? They try new products and drugs on 'em. They give 'em steroids, shoot their peckers and faces up with dewrinklers. They give 'em suppositories that shorten their lifespans."

"No, I wasn't aware of that. But if we're going to accomplish anything today, we need to start discussing your case. You don't seem to be following me."

"It's okay to put me on a magazine rack in a convenient store. I won't steal the hotdogs or the slush drinks. I'll sit there quiet and listen while watchin'. Be careful that they don't see yur eyes move on camera."

"What is it, do you think, you're being charged with?"

"Charged? Charged!" Reynolds sneered sarcastically. "I've been charged all my life since they first charged me with livin' in a drunk whore's dream. I've been charged with criminal trespass from the day I's born! They've their cameras all over the world in every city, town, or house to make sure of it."

"But what about your meth lab?"

Reynolds laughed, wildly rattling his restraints before speaking again. "They came and put cuffs on me and dragged me back up here. It was a terrible ride. I kept askin' why were they takin' me? And they tightened the cuffs and beat me. The cuffs cut into my wrists." Reynolds held up his chained hands, which showed red and pink healing scabs.

He figured those had just as likely occurred in Reynolds's flailing and being dragged about since he'd been in custody, "What do you remember happening the night of the fire?"

"Which one?"

"The fire that—"

Reynolds interrupted, "There's many people in jail. Murderers, rapists, thieves. Maybe the gov'mint castrated or fondled us all when we were young. Maybe that's why we all meet up here now 'cause we're all criminally trespassed once we came out the womb."

"But what about the fire, Edward? Do you remember anything about it?"

"The lass fourth of July I heard was a good one. Sparklers, M-sixties, blackcat bottle rockets, and then big ballbuster cannons all bought on the outskirts, where the Indians were sent. Tell 'em those things can start fires too. Hell, there's sacrificial barbeque pits that can catch the whole damn woods on fire!"

"Do you think you're ready to stand trial?"

"Who, me? I didn't criminally trespass intentionally. They put the cuffs on tighter, and it's all part of their game to make me an arsonist, rapist, murderer, weirdo."

"So you recognize part of this charge involves fire?"

Reynolds adopted a mockingly serious tone, "It may involve many things." Then he resumed a high-pitched rant, "Ain't that what I'm suppost to say? How do I keep 'em from consecratin' me in here? You give off bad recordin' wavelengths, man. Bad feedback. How much do they pay you to be an informant?"

He stood up for emphasis. "I'm not sure whether you're faking mental illness or not. But if you don't start making more sense, I'm going to recommend a mental health evaluation."

"Oh yeah? That's right. Send me down to the state hospital where they'll shoot me full of drugs. Threaten their guinea pig chemical experiments. We're cheap test subjects for yur chemical empires."

"You're exhibiting paranoia. I'm not sure we're ready to go forward with defending this case."

"Just send me down to get shot up so I come back and bend over for y'all. I know what yur doin'."

"What I'm doing is leaving for today."

As he pushed open the door, Reynolds yelled, "I'm not yur goddamn guinea pig! Guards, take this man away!"

The guard shook his head, yelling, "Christ, Reynolds! Keep it down."

He wondered if there might be some malingering to mimic symptoms to avoid a trial. He wasn't sure how familiar Reynolds was with the process, but Reynolds had been in before. If an incompetent defendant wasn't found to be a grave risk, then the defendant wouldn't be civilly committed. He'd seen others try to fake symptoms and fail.

First, he'd call the jail mental health staff for their opinion. When he got back to the office, he faxed the standard letter asking for their opinion on Reynolds's mental state. There was a chance Reynolds hadn't fully detoxified yet. Sore-ridden Reynolds had fidgeted and scratched his arms as far as he could with his limited mobility.

He went about other business that'd been piling up. He reviewed his phone messages. An investigative reporter for the local newspaper had called about Reynolds. Louise told him the story had even reached Montgomery, mentioned briefly in one television broadcast. He decided not to call the reporter back.

He expected the attention would blow over after a few weeks or a few months at the most. It was one case among many other heinous alleged acts and scandals. Although the chemical analysis could get complicated, the charges were relatively straightforward. Sometimes they delayed filing on the manufacturing cases to make sure they had solid evidence from the labs. But because of the fire, they'd filed charges immediately and got a warrant when Reynolds didn't show. They'd found him in Mobile.

He'd received written police reports and an initial lab report. The lab analysts detailed samples from what the state burn recognition experts determined to be the blaze's source, a charred mass of metal and glass with glass fragments scattered throughout where the warehouse had once stood. Residue was found on some of these fragments, which were carefully stored and catalogued. Whitish sludge had been found in a drain nearby. Somehow packets of ephedrine and pseudo-ephedrine, although partially burned, had been preserved through the fire. Containers believed to contain lye and solvents, and other products commonly associated with manufacturing, had been blown apart or twisted almost beyond recognition.

* * *

The morning of the competency hearing, he'd gotten a call from the jail mental health professional who'd met with Reynolds. She reiterated what he'd seen and recommended further evaluation. As he approached court, he went through a mental picture of what could happen. Reynolds could come shouting disruptive obscenities or he could be in one of his withdrawn, silent moods.

On his way inside, he noticed a television camera in the hallway. There was a journalist he recognized sitting in the back of the courtroom. Normally he'd be surprised by this much attention in a manufacturing case. Even where something blew up, it might get some negative publicity initially, but then it would pass. It must be the girl's rescue.

Feld hadn't gotten there yet. There were some others dispersed through the gallery. Curious observers, he guessed. Reynolds didn't have any family left that he knew about.

He heard some muffled sounds of doors closing indicating an inmate had arrived in the court holding cell adjacent to the courtroom. But after opening the heavy door separating the rooms, he saw an empty holding cell.

He went back to ask the clerk about it. She told him they were having some problems transporting him through the tunnel from the jail. She wasn't sure of the details. He exchanged pleasantries with her aimlessly and then went out to get a newspaper. He returned and sat in the front bench of the courtroom scanning it. All his paperwork had already been submitted. Normally he would sit in the hallway, but with the camera out there he decided against it. He saw nothing to be gained at this point in making comments on the case.

Ten minutes later, he distinctly heard a door clang. He heard some yelling through the thick door. When he pushed open the door to the holding cell area, he found Reynolds being held down by two guards with a third standing ready in an aggressive stance.

"What's the problem here?"

"Sir, just step back for a second. The inmate is unstable and dangerous."

Reynolds was baring his teeth, twisting his chains and arms, screaming, "Let me go!"

"Reynolds, what's wrong? You've got to calm down for the judge."

He got his attention. The struggle with the guards subsided.

"Yur the double agent, right? Edward the confessor. Recordin' my confession to play it to every other conspirator in there. I don't want what you call yur services anymore. You just want to have me shot up with drugs so then, so then—"

"I'm going to be representing you in there. The judge is going to order you evaluated for sure."

He went back in to let the clerk know to call the prosecutor. A few minutes later Feld arrived. The clerk announced the judge, and Judge Miller came out onto the bench. He greeted the parties then turned to the guards, "Bring him in."

As the door to the court opened, some yelling ensued. The two guards had to struggle with dragging Reynolds over to counsel's table. They held Reynolds standing. Miller had already received a motion and order of evaluation that had been signed by both parties. He was grateful Aldruss wasn't handling this. Aldruss may've forced them to continue toward trial.

He glanced over at Reynolds, who was still being held standing. Although Reynolds had quieted down, he seemed to be struggling with something internally. Reynolds rocked back and forth jingling his chains with his black eyes fixated on the judge.

Miller addressed his client, "Mr. Reynolds, do you understand that you're charged with a felony and a misdemeanor?"

Reynolds muttered while moving his body back and forth more aggressively.

"What are you saying?"

"By whose authority?"

"Mr. Reynolds, the state has charged you with crimes in this authorized court of law."

Reynolds raised his voice, "And you work for the same people. I'm gettin' feedback from yur implant. There must be direct interference at this range."

"What are you referring to?"

"You know which one. Don't play dumb with me."

"I assure you, Mr. Reynolds. This is no game I'm playing with you. We're here to decide something that will have an important and real effect on your life. We're here to determine whether you understand the nature of the proceedings and can assist in your own defense. Now I'm going to ask you some questions that may seem obvious, but you need to answer in all seriousness. Do you know what you're charge with?"

"I assert my right to silence."

"Mr. Reynolds, I'm not asking you to testify against yourself. I'm asking whether you know what charges you are facing?"

"They sayed I was makin' meth and the house caught on fire so I guess that's equivalent to second-degree murder."

"Do you know who I am?"

"Yur the one askin' questions. You know 'bout the cabal 'cause you wear a black dress, but you haven't gotten into the higher circle yet." He began sputtering, "Ya, yur not gettin' into—"

Miller cut him off, "Do you know who the man sitting next to you is?"

"He works for you. He's been comin' to see me to get info so he can get his pay."

"Do you know the man sitting at the table across from you, to your left?"

"Never met him."

Pointing back at him, "How are you working with this man here?"

"I don't work for him. We're enemies. He says he's a lawyer for me, which is confidential code for informant. I want to fire him."

"If he's your lawyer, why would you want to fire him?"

"He only tries to take things from me. You know people like that. I mean I had a home with things once."

He leaned over to remind Reynolds what he said was being recorded. Reynolds turned to snap at him, "I don't care. You gonna let me finish?"

The judge spoke, "I don't want to hear anything about the facts of the case."

"What case?"

"You are currently charged with manufacturing methamphetamine and reckless endangerment on a date in June. Now remember, I don't want to hear about the facts of the case. Do you know what the maximum penalties are for these charges?"

"Those charges have already been dismissed."

"No, they haven't. You are currently charged. Mr. Reynolds, I think you're not fully understanding what you're up against."

"What's not to know? You want to shoot me up with drugs."

"Mr. Reynolds, it's not about what I want to do. It's about whether you understand what's going on."

"I know a railroadin' when I smell it."

"I'm inclined to sign this order directing the state hospital to evaluate whether you are competent to stand trial. That means someone from the hospital will come to visit with you and ask you questions, and then write a report. Your attorney and the prosecutor have signed it. Is there anything else you would like to tell me?"

"Why, yes there is." He watched Reynolds grimace for a second. He suddenly became aware of a sharp, sickeningly acrid smell. Another jail guard was coming near. A puddle had formed at Reynolds's feet around the jail issued sandals.

He objectively noted that the public deterioration of Reynolds stood in stark contrast to the formal trappings and environment that surrounded them. The elevated wooden structure where Miller sat in his black robe looking down gave the primary sense of this. Where the court clerk and the court reporter sat lodged in lower wooden stations supported the impression. The room had a high ceiling, making it somewhat cavernous. The resulting acoustics could amplify voices, turning whispers into slightly audible speech and turning loud voices into booming ones. Behind the judge stood the regalia of the state and federal flags and a plaque hung with the state insignia. Besides the bailiff, there were uniformed guards to keep peace in court. From somewhere, perfume and cologne wafted in the air together, charging the air with some supposedly dignified purpose, lending participants in the occasion a visceral uplift.

He thought an observer might enter this civic room feeling a broader license to act than if he or she had entered a house of religious worship. However, once accused in this civic house, all the fury and guilt that could be raised in a religious ceremony, the finger pointing and the potential ostracizing, would be palpable. Latent threats promised cold exile for violations of the communal taboo. That sense of impending catastrophe would be amplified just as voices were by the acoustics of the room. In the hard-pressed moments of trial, the follies and mistakes of the accused individual that might have been overlooked inside a religious house of worship could become unacceptable flaws in the formerly more accepting civic house.

He imagined that enthusiasts of the phenomenon might ask how else could the law be respected? Behavior deemed outside the acceptable bounds of the majority had been agreed upon by the duly elected representatives, theoretically coming from various religious and moral perspectives. The players involved either knew or thought or intuited the question on a subconscious level. If there were no enforcement of what the legislature had proscribed as criminal, then how would the will of the people be realized?

And now Reynolds had just pissed himself in the hallowed halls, leaving a puddle on the floor, just as any un-housebroken dog might. After an initial reaction of disgust, Miller announced he'd seen enough and ordered Reynolds out of the courtroom. The urine smell began to overwhelm the formerly intoxicating and suddenly cloying smell of any perfume or cologne, clashing with any noble and upstanding visions those present might've been enjoying, crashing their thoughts onto less desirable sides of life. The guards soberly came out with disinfectant and paper towels.

He watched Reynolds talk briefly in atonement before laughing hysterically, doing nothing consistent. Reynolds's mind changed directions indiscriminately, not reacting to matter and gravity in his time and space, cut loose into ongoing hallucination. He grimly looked on as Reynolds was dragged out. Feld shook his head with a look of disdain. He imagined Feld would likely resolve to punish meth users worse than before. He saw the live feed of the news camera couldn't angle to get the puddle, but Reynolds had a wet jail garb from the waist down as he was dragged back to the holding cell.

Miller had signed the order. Reynolds would be evaluated within the next weeks. They were given a return date to court in approximately a month. The newspapers would write about it and the public would know. He thought of prospective jurors and made no comment as he left.

* * *

After he returned to Alabama, he and the other federal agents took custody of anything believed to be connected to the bikers. The demolition crew had arrived before the fire investigation had ceased. He'd watched County Detective Deputy Jones turn the crew back more than once. After a month, the crew had been let in to tear the rest down and truck it off to the nearest dump two miles away. Evidence of burnt remnants of flasks and containers with residue and sludge from the grate would be returned to the county sheriff's office after it had been tested at the federal lab.

Gregory Crease had frequently appeared at the site as the investigation continued. He'd watched the deputies repeatedly tell Crease to step back from the crime scene. Throughout years of working around construction developments, Crease must've developed, utilized, and relied on his thick drawl—emphasized through a bad set of teeth often covered in chewing tobacco—to get results more effectively. He'd heard Crease complain about his gums bleeding. Short in stature, Crease's face was weather worn, mildly improving an already bad complexion. But nothing seemed to improve the misshapen appearance of Crease's reddish, bulbous, and vein-y nose.

He'd watched something akin to trench warfare develop between Crease and law enforcement. Crease began working right up to the boundaries of their caution tape. After announcing they wanted to recheck the rest of the property including the shack by the river, he'd heard Crease confront them more sharply than before, "Yur takin' too goddamn lawn. How much lawner this goin' awn?"

His agents and the deputies told Crease it would take as long as it needed to. Crease had asked, "Y'all got a wharint to surch evarwire?"

He'd turned what was meant to be an incredulous look on him. He thought he'd heard a more conciliatory note in Crease's voice. "Jest wanna get the crew started. Had 'em lined up more than a week now. Could be makin' other money."

His agents had explored an area toward the river covered with brush and trees. They'd found a clearing and the remnants of a campfire. Underneath some of the brush they'd found a gray wooden box containing some blankets, old coats, a canteen, some matches, and a worn-down bowie knife. There was a book of matches from the tavern in Arizona where he'd tracked Cat's Paw and Muffler to. The clearing was over three hundred yards into the woods on the back of the property and couldn't be seen from the house.

After informing Crease they'd completed their investigation, he watched a track hoe back down from the wide-load trailer bed used to transport it. By the end of that day, the track hoe had knocked down the charred walls, crumbling what was left of the structure into a black wooden pile. After a week, he'd returned to see if they'd finished. The dump truck hauled off the last of the wreckage, and the foundation was scraped clean. A chain link fence had been raised around the dirt and gravel road entrance. Crease had cut off the water. He must've been trying to deter squatters or maybe slow down potential looters from stealing tools or hotwiring the machines. A few dark spots on the foundation were all that remained to remind anyone of the fire. The rest of the yard had already started to grow. The foundation had become an indented, rectangular island surrounded by thick grass.

* * *

He skipped over the narrative to the conclusion in bold lettering. After further observation, the psychologist concluded Reynolds wasn't competent to stand trial. He then skimmed through the narrative. *The following history is self-reported and its accuracy is wholly dependent on the subject's reliability. This information was gathered in conjunction from an earlier report on Mr. Reynolds for a previous assault charge. He was incommunicative during portions of this interview.*

He skipped to the personal history: *Edward Reynolds is a thirty-four-year-old male. Mr. Reynolds grew up in the same town he was born in. His mother was a severe alcoholic who eventually died in jail through complications of her alcohol abuse. Although her income was sporadic as she was a self-employed painter and sculptor, she and her son were guaranteed an amount of money held in trust for her and her offspring from her family in New York. Mr. Reynolds reported previously this was enough to live on and support both of them until her death. There is no indication of who his father is.*

Mr. Reynolds reported not finishing high school. He went through eleventh grade before dropping out. He indicated he did not enjoy himself there, saying that there was nothing there for him. He worked a number of unsteady jobs during his late teens and twenties at fastfood restaurants, landscaping, and some labor and construction projects. He reported that a majority of his time was spent on the property his mother rented. His main activities other than substance abuse included watching television, playing video games, and surfing the internet.

He reported his first drug use occurred around age twelve or thirteen with marijuana. He tried hallucinogens for the first time around age sixteen. At the same time he also tried inhalants, primarily gasoline and freon. At seventeen he used cocaine for the first time and continued use into his twenties. He drank during these periods, but preferred the effects of narcotics. In his early twenties he tried crystal methamphetamine. He snorted it for a few years. He began smoking it around age twenty-seven, and then began injecting it a few years after. He has steadily used the drug for at least a decade at the time of this evaluation.

Mr. Reynolds's criminal history reveals ten convictions with more than double that in number of arrests. The convictions are mostly misdemeanors, including multiple possession of narcotics, criminal trespass, resisting arrest, and assault charges. There is one drug possession felony conviction. On a prior assault charge, he was referred to this state hospital for evaluation. It was determined at the time he was not competent to stand trial and involuntary restoration was authorized. With a medication regimen, Mr. Reynolds was restored and returned to the courts. The charge resulted in a conviction after a change in plea.

The prior diagnosis was chemically induced schizoaffective disorder, with bipolar disorder and personality disorder to be ruled out. The previous evaluator found there were high chances of restoration through chemical replacement therapy. Without medication supplementing his imbalanced neural function, the chances of reoccurrence of symptoms were determined to be very high to inevitable given Mr. Reynolds's history.

He skipped to the observations. *At the jail, Mr. Reynolds's physical appearance was unkempt. He was malodorous. His arms and face were covered in scabs apparently due to late stage methamphetamine addiction. His mouth exhibited significant decay, including missing and rotting teeth. He was constrained in waist shackles and leg irons. He was fidgety, non-cooperative, belligerent at times, and had difficulty tracking. He appeared unable to focus, and seemed to be battling thought insertion. Because of his hostility and being unamenable to an in-person interview with this evaluator, Mr. Reynolds was transported from the county jail to the state hospital to undergo further evaluation.*

He skipped to Reynolds's ability to understand the nature of the offense: *After Mr. Reynolds was transported for fuller observation, communication continued to be strained. He would not respond to questioning, and seemed to be responding to internal stimuli. Occasionally, Mr. Reynolds would stay on topic when talking about the court system. He related delusional beliefs concerning what roles the parties played. He explained persecutorial delusions, referring to lawyers and judges as supernatural beings.*

After one session where twenty minutes was spent trying to communicate, Mr. Reynolds began yelling expletives while violently shaking against his restraints. He refused to answer any more questions. The interview was terminated at that point.

The next day during another interview, Mr. Reynolds was disoriented. Presenting a pronounced labile effect, Mr. Reynolds also hesitated many times when speaking. While Mr. Reynolds seemed less physically agitated during this session, he still responded to internal stimuli. He would not answer questions freely. During most of this interview, he maintained a vacant stare and was non-responsive. After termination of this interview, Mr. Reynolds was monitored to sleep for an extended period of time, over sixteen hours.

Through multiple interviews and attempts to interview, Mr. Reynolds exhibited dramatic mood swings. Based on the interviews and his prior documented history, it is apparent that he is suffering from a serious mental illness which could be the result of multiple disorders. The most prominent of which is a schizoaffective chemical imbalance. Based on earlier reports, it can reasonably be inferred that this has been exacerbated by Mr. Reynolds's continued use of controlled substances, in particular, methamphetamine and any of its derivatives. He seems to lack any insight into his severe mental health issues.

He skipped to Reynolds's ability to assist in his own defense. *It is highly unlikely that any attorney would be able to effectively communicate with Mr. Reynolds while he is in this untreated state. There is a high probability that he would be disruptive to any legal proceedings given his random, tangential remarks, his belligerent outbursts, and his inability to sit still for long periods of time when there are others present. It is the opinion of this evaluator that Mr. Reynolds is not competent to stand trial at this time.*

He glanced over the standard language requesting authority to administer involuntary medication then skipped to the dangerousness assessment. *In his current state, Mr. Reynolds poses a high risk of future criminal activity. Based on static factors, sex as male, age young to mid thirties, lack of support network, no home or stable community group, Mr. Reynolds is more likely to reoffend. Given a documented history of substance abuse, a number of criminal convictions involving drugs, with one conviction for assault, and the current alleged charges, his aggressive stances and required chains, Mr. Reynolds poses a high risk of dangerousness to himself or others if left untreated.*

* * *

Before meeting her, he'd often speculated it wasn't meant for him now, that his approach or style must've been locked away in some other time, somewhere when there was reason to call it pursuit. Now the lazier had the option of ordering their mates online. It was as simple as going to the grocery store to buy a certain brand of eggs and milk. But somewhere down the line, whatever one discovered this way might be as easily auctioned off. The humanity and socialization had been substantially whittled out of it.

Besides his own doubts of contrived matching, he imagined questions of prospective children. It would be similar to explaining how replication can be established in a lab, a purposeless endorsement of instinct that would leave the young ones with bland and characterless ideas about pursuit.

There was no execution of a plan to chase, to capture, or to conquer. The chase was part of the build-up of tension, the anxiety over whether it was mutual, the fluctuations of emotion that better reflected how a longer-term relationship would be, a new entity with its own expansions and contractions. The more computerized approach was a pre-designed cold blueprint that may look fine on paper. That way would be easier to manipulate.

He reasoned the manner in which one earned a romantic relationship would give it significance and meaning. It could be the secret pride of accomplishing something one didn't openly discuss. Either way, the manner in which it'd been obtained worked on the inner coils of one's mind, in structural, basic ways. If shaken or threatened, that pride could carry shockwaves of doubt, fear, and shame throughout one's being. One's faith and loyalty could career into an abyss of worry and negative reflections. But on returning to mutual reaffirmation, brilliant bursts of pleasure returned as scenery and characters became bright and meaningful again. Even the lowly and sour parts became tragically beautiful in sharp and clear pigments. Maybe the easy to click mate would reduce these extremes, but at the same time, the upside could reciprocally seem stale and antiseptic. The initial selfishness, lack of ambition, and passiveness in courting a screen was rendering pursuit a nullity. It was only a mutual admission of sexual and companionship needs to address. The whole prospect seemed slated for ultimate failure or the death of something.

The jail front desk informed him Reynolds had arrived back yesterday. If he were to see him before the hearing tomorrow, it would have to be this afternoon.

The usual glum smells of the jail added to the weight of the air. The blandness reminded him of a picture he'd seen of communist communities, gray and forlorn with no hint of color, the citizens plodding along in a sluggish lack of identity or individualism. The guards were slow as usual. Getting to Three East took over fifteen minutes.

He found Reynolds in a manic mode, speaking of things difficult to comprehend. "Shoot me full of drugs? I tole you that would be illegal. They're goin' to give me the newest version of the plague. I won't volunteer as their little guinea pig!"

"They're going to give you medication that will get you through this so you can understand the court and legal proceedings. If you don't take it, they'll have authority from the court to inject it."

"They probably already know 'bout the locusts then."

"What are you referring to?"

Reynolds screamed, "You know! You have to!"

"I'm sorry, Edward, but I'm not following you. See you in court tomorrow morning. I'll note your objection, but the judge is probably going to sign it anyway. Do you remember going through this before? You got better. Remember?"

"Shoot me full of drugs! That's all they want to do. To get me to sign."

* * *

As he sat at counsel's table the next day, he heard yelling and rattling from the other side of the holding cell door. One of the guards appeared, walked over to him, and informed him quietly that Reynolds was demanding to talk to his lawyer. He followed the guard to the holding cell.

Reynolds sat physically restrained by the guards against the cinderblock wall. He yelled intermittently, "They can't contain my ever livin' soul by shootin' me full of drugs without me speakin' to my lawyer! There he is. Now see."

"Calm down. Stop struggling with the guards. That'll only make the situation worse."

Reynolds cried, "I knew you were in it with 'em!" He thrashed about some more before becoming still. A vacant stare crossed his face. The guards then led him into the courtroom as he followed. Reynolds's resistance had suddenly disappeared. The guards led Reynolds to sit down.

He watched Reynolds's demeanor alternate between openly hostile and catatonically anti-social. He waited for Reynolds to settle for a second then reviewed a copy of the competency restoration order before handing it to the clerk. The standard boxes were checked.

The guards had been prepared for the worst. Reynolds's chair had been covered with a towel. On his way in, he'd noticed the media had another camera waiting in the hall. The newspaper journalist was in the back of the court again. Almost a month had passed since the last hearing, and no updates in the case had been announced. He figured the media must be hungry to squeeze more intrigue out of this. As he watched Miller come out, he perceived a high degree of anticipation in the onlookers of what would happen next. Whatever Reynolds did, he was sure the procedural result of the day's hearing would be anticlimactic.

He listened to Miller begin, "On the record now. An order has been presented to the court, and I've reviewed it. Would the state like to address it?"

Feld answered, "The state defers to the evaluator and the court."

Miller turned to him. "Defense?"

"Your Honor, my client would object to the forced medication. He argues that he shouldn't be forced against his will to take medication based on these charges."

Miller shifted to look at Reynolds, "Mr. Reynolds, do you think you're ready to stand trial?" Reynolds wasn't looking at the judge. "How are you doing then, Mr. Reynolds?" After receiving no answer, Miller asked, "What do you think about this order?" Pausing for another period of silence, a sharper tone inflected Miller's voice, "Mr. Reynolds, if you don't say anything to tell me different than this report, then you're going to be forcefully medicated. Do you understand?"

Reynolds exploded, standing up, stooped over by his chains. On seeing the movement and hearing the jangle, the guards physically restrained him. The cords of Reynolds's neck muscles and his jugular stood out as he yelled, "Yur goin' to shoot me full of drugs! I know all this!" Gesturing toward him, "He's in on it! Some law!" He watched Reynolds break off his tantrum and quit struggling. Reynolds remained standing in a stooped posture.

With equanimity Miller inquired, "Mr. Reynolds, do you remember going through this type of process before on another charge?"

"They've been makin' me into a lab rat ever since they got the new mind jelly invented. They've been fillin' my brain with it at night."

"Mr. Reynolds, the court is not interested in performing experiments on you."

During this interaction, he'd been gesturing for Reynolds to sit. Reynolds ignored him, screaming, "I want a jury trial. A box full of labrats!"

Miller spoke with finality, "Okay, Mr. Reynolds, I'm finding that you're not competent to stand trial at this time, that you're charged with serious offenses, and that the government has a strong enough interest in bringing you to trial. The state hospital is authorized to use the least intrusive measures, including forced medication, to attempt to restore you to competency. I note your objection, but I'm signing the order."

Reynolds clenched his teeth, tensing up again, screaming, "They're goin' to shoot me full of drugs!" The last of this was muffled as Reynolds was awkwardly led away by the guards. He heard more struggling and yelling as the door closed behind them. He wouldn't try to predict the timescale for this one. He expected it to be one of the many unpredictable phenomena his career had conjured up.

Because it was an appointment case, a sense of unbalance mildly irked him. But he recalled where he'd worked himself up from. He'd take whatever case they handed him, whether it took a day or a year's work. As it was, he already had plenty of referrals and business. There were some DUIs he needed to attend to. Deadlines in the second-degree murder case were approaching. As he left the court back into the hot sun, his thoughts returned to Sylvia.

* * *

He knew Freight had once been involved in the transfer of illegals across the Pacific in shipping containers. Although that activity had ceased shortly after the turn of the millennium due mainly to an increase in cargo inspections, Freight was still known to be exceptionally adept in the logistics of moving things. Once they arrived at one of Freight's places, he was their primary contact by throw away cell phones. They worked on their bikes in Freight's garage.

The residential garage was located in an unassuming spiral of urban sprawl. The inconspicuous suburb had camouflaged them for the last month and a half. He'd shaved off some of his beard. In the past week, he'd set up two labor jobs over the phone. They were quick paychecks, not longer than a day's work at a time.

He'd known the labor dispatcher for years. Though it'd become more complicated and uncertain, he could still occasionally land jobs like this in an anonymous manner. Taking any job longer than a week would require paperwork and more scrutiny. These smaller ones could be done under the table with cash. Most regulars at the hall didn't want to fool with a short job. They weren't official union jobs. They paid less, sometimes by as much as half. Many times these employers didn't follow regulations, but times were low for the laborers' union. He'd heard these piece meal odd jobs were popping up more often, even tempting some long timers from holding out for a sweeter full-time setup. Because of his connection, he didn't have to go into the hall to wait for the jobs. He wasn't sure if the feds knew he worked around the union. He kept conversation to the essentials.

Muffler'd done a couple of minor drug deals to keep the cash coming in to help pay for their food. Although Muffler probably could've gone out on these labor jobs with him to see if they needed an extra hand, they'd figured it would be better to stay separate publicly for the time being.

Freight had gone on an extended road trip, leaving the place to them for a couple of months. Freight owned the house, but several of the brethren had stayed there for extended periods of time. It was understood they were responsible for paying him back by making mortgage payments and paying the utility bills. The four-bedroom house wasn't known for its hygiene. Some of the rooms were a squalor of beer cans, full ashtrays, and stained carpets.

He'd settled into a routine. When not occupied with gaining cash, they'd stayed close to the house getting drunk, watching the tube, and working on their bikes. They'd reluctantly refrained from riding, taking alternate transportation by bus or car. There was an old sedan at the place for situations like this.

After a few more weeks, he'd loosened up to the idea of going out. There was a dive bar nearby they'd frequented on weekend nights to get out of the house and try to pick up some women. On the third time out, he'd been playing pool. He'd drunk several pitchers of beer with Muffler when he first noticed Cheryl. She'd been hanging at the bar steadily drinking, looking over at him. He'd gone up to her and got her to come over. She was overweight with big breasts and wearing a lot of mascara. He'd pat and pinch on her as they were playing, and she'd knock his hand away playfully in a mock, coy kind of way. Although he'd begun to get loaded, he didn't want to bring her back to the house. He made sure Muffler knew this.

He'd left with her. They'd gone to a motel nearby. He'd paid thirty-five dollars for the room, thirty-five dollars that he didn't really have. Being this close to getting her into bed, he hadn't cared. He'd find some way to replace the money.

After having his way with her, he'd passed out for a few hours. He'd regained consciousness around five thirty according to the clock. He'd roused himself, quietly got his clothes on, then headed out. The light blue dawn had reminded him of that early morning sky in Utah. The house was within a mile of the bar. He'd walked it. There might've been some cops patrolling on the main road at that hour so he'd taken the neighborhood streets to make it back.

* * *

August arrived fully robust. As if summer were showing off its chest, the season strutted with heat. Wavy mirage pools on the roadways played before his eyes. He saw straw hats worn by elders working outside. Central air conditioners, along with leaking, less efficient window units, chugged along, keeping a droning, laconic pace with their adversary, the natural heat of the climate.

He had a ceiling fan in his office. Classical music filled up the heat-tinged, heavy air, which he turned up a bit while taking a break from writing a motion to suppress. Several cases were weighing down on him since he last dealt with Reynolds. He turned to scan through the evaluator's report. *For the last five days, Mr. Reynolds has been taking medication orally. He presents with a stutter. Delays in responses and processing have shortened. Mr. Reynolds answered questions similar to the second session, but with more rapidity. His appearance has improved and he seems to understand his legal situation.*

The arrival of Reynolds back to the jail from the state mental hospital had diminished in importance for the moment. He languidly recognized it was evening time. The birds outside had quieted down as they got ready to rest. The temperature had dropped to a more pleasant eighty degrees as the sun was setting. He remembered the priest and decided to give McGowan a call. Prentice was too busy getting ready for the second-degree murder trial, finalizing witness interviews, and dealing with other cases.

* * *

When he approached the cell the next morning, Clem Payne informed him that it was rumored they may move Reynolds to the jail's general population given his improvement. They'd still keep Reynolds on extra restraints.

He found Reynolds reading a newspaper. The shock of this gesture at urbanity kept him from commenting for a moment. Reynolds looked up and grimaced a little then looked back at the paper. He greeted Reynolds, but Reynolds didn't respond.

"You look much better, your skin has cleared up."

Reynolds kept looking at his newspaper, ignoring him.

"Would you rather talk to your lawyer at this point?"

148

Reynolds looked up. "Wha-what does it ma-matter to you? Y-yur not one."

"Thought you might like to talk to someone from the outside. Doesn't it get pretty cramped in here?"

"Y-Yeah, it does. Wha-what do you want from m-me anyway? I'm not Ca-Catholic. I'm not relij-j-jez. Evarthin 'bout m-me's been opposite of that. Wh-Why don't you go hang with others m-more like yurself?"

"That's fine. I'm not here to judge you or to sell you anything. Just write the chaplain if you want to talk about the girl at the orphanage."

Reynolds glared, "G-Get outta h-here!"

* * *

Over the phone, he listened to McGowan report Reynolds had improved, but the priest suggested he might not be the best-suited emissary. Two days remained before the next scheduled hearing. That morning before visiting, he reviewed the competency restoration report again. He was pleased to read that Reynolds's hygiene had improved considerably, with many of the scabs disappearing. Reynolds was less combative for the most part and had fewer delusional, tangential outbursts. The report did contain observations of occasional lapses into anti-social behavior that the evaluator speculated might be part of Reynolds's base personality. There also appeared to be slight physical side effects from the medications, most evident of which were a delay in speech and a stutter.

The psychiatrist noted that this followed the pattern of the earlier competency restoration Reynolds had gone through. Reynolds's condition was highly treatable with regular doses of medication that would supplant the neurotransmitter deficiency he appeared to be suffering from, but the psychiatrist cautioned Reynolds must refrain from alcohol or other controlled substances while taking these powerful anti-psychotics.

The report typified what he'd seen before. He was concerned whether the side effects might affect Reynolds's ability to testify. He wanted at least the option of putting Reynolds up there on the stand.

As he entered the jail, he reflected on what men and women did to allow other men and women to put them into locked pens and cages, treating them as dangerous animals. Many of them were actually predatory and dangerous. It was easy to see why they'd ended up here. Others were defective humans. Many had brain defects or mental illness. Several suffered from not being very bright. There were a few on the wrong side of politics. In Reynolds's case, it looked like he'd brought it on himself.

He appreciated the importance of deterrence, but excessive punishment could take someone, especially a younger one that could become productive, and mold him or her into a permanent hopeless reprobate. He recognized the large majority inside lacked good decision-making ability. There were ways of avoiding being locked up. Having money to bail was one way. The poor were especially susceptible to being caged.

He made his way again to Reynolds's cell. Reynolds was let out, and they were allowed to meet at one of the tables in the common area between the rows of cells. "Remember who I am?"

"Y-yes. I m-might as well get it over and pl-plead guilty, r-right? I've been readin' the papers."

"Hold on a sec, let's take one step at a time. We haven't even gone over what the police reports say yet. It doesn't look good, but the manufacturing charge carries anywhere from five to twenty years in prison based on your history depending on what level. It'd be worthwhile to go over everything first. Now you seem much more aware than last time we talked."

"I only r-remember bits and p-pieces."

"Are you taking your meds now?"

"Y-yes."

"If you fall off into mental health problems again, they may try to keep you down at the state hospital for a while."

"I don't want to go ba-back. Dr-droolers and bra-brainless, brain-dead z-zombies. And the wa-ones that yell or try to t-touch you."

"You're not able to post bail, are you?"

"N-no. Ca-can't afford nothin'. Evar-th-thin's gone. Money ma-may be tied up in a ba-bank somewhere. M-my inheritance. D-don't know if I ca-can access it."

"Well, we can look into it. It would be better to have you preparing for trial on the outside if possible."

"But wh-where would I live?"

"Not sure. Maybe you'd have enough for an apartment?"

"D-don't know."

"We'll have to fill out paperwork for you to give me or someone from your family access to transfer the money. It will also depend on whether your bank will even allow this."

"I d-don't have any other fa-family."

He began going over Detective Deputy Jared Jones's investigative report. On June second, there'd been a call in to emergency. A fire crew responded to the scene. After the blaze was controlled for the most part, the fire chief called the sheriff's office as he suspected a meth lab was the source.

When Jones arrived, the suspect material was still smoldering. Jones took a sample of sludge from a drainage gutter in the foundation. Jones tested it with his narcotics kit. The color it turned indicated meth. The area was officially designated a crime scene from that point forward. More specialists were called in to collect evidence, including a fire reconstruction expert.

A few hours after the county detectives had arrived, fed agents arrived to discuss with the county investigators inclusion of this evidence in cases they were building against two bikers known to associate with the residents of this dwelling. Their more advanced lab could be used to analyze the materials. Burnt cans, half-melted flasks, warped plastics, and shards of glass were bagged and identified. Jones examined some garbage cans on the side of the house. The detectives went through the garbage, finding syringes and other materials more identifiable and intact than the burnt materials.

Many digital photos had been taken by the detectives. After he read through it, Reynolds looked at the reports. A preliminary fed report had come back positive for precursors commonly used to make meth through the red phosphorus method. He let Reynolds know, "The case doesn't look good for trial. Do you want me to try and negotiate a plea deal?"

"I guess so. I m-mean the c-cops have all the evidence."

"It doesn't look good for a manufacturing charge. Why don't we talk about it some more after the next hearing? Meanwhile, I want you to make an appointment with the jail dentist to get your teeth in better shape in case we're forced to go to trial."

* * *

Two days later he appeared for the hearing as scheduled. He noticed the media. They must've been expecting some more unpredictable outbursts. Reynolds's security escorts inside the courtroom had been downgraded from three to two. There was no loud or awkward arrival or shouts from the holding cell. Noticeably more relaxed, Reynolds walked in quietly. Miller asked the parties to be seated and then began discussing the competency restoration report. "Now, Mr. Reynolds, I don't want you to talk about the facts of the case. It appears you're doing better than the last time I saw you in court. How are you feeling?"

"B-better."

"Do you know why we're here?"

"B-because I have to understand wha-what's goin' on."

"And do you know who your attorney is?"

"Y-yes, he's right here. Em El Sheet."

"And can you work with him?"

"Y-yes."

"Do you know what a trial is?"

"Y-yes. I know it's when a j-judge or a jury decide if I'm guilty or n-not."

"Do you have any questions?"

"N-no."

"Based on the report, and his responses, I'm inclined to find that he's been restored to competency to stand trial. I would note for the record a remarkable improvement in his hygiene and demeanor. Does either side have any comments or objections?"

Feld had nothing to add.

"Your Honor, I agree generally with the conclusions of the report; however, I would raise one issue should we end up in a trial on this case. There's case law on the side effects of competency restoration and whether it will later impede a defendant's ability to present their defense or testify. Because of his stutter it's a concern. We would object on that basis should the side effects detract from him testifying."

"Alright, Counsel. Your objection is noted at this time, but I'm not sure what that would lead to in the alternative. I'm finding Mr. Reynolds has been restored to competency in agreement with the expert's report. I'm also finding at this time that the side effects appear to be minimal. I'm not sure that he didn't have a slight stutter before this, but in any event, defense will have to show something substantial for me not to accept this method of restoration. We'll see you in three weeks for the pre-trial hearing."

Before the guards came to lead Reynolds away to the holding cell, he leaned over to whisper, "I'll see if we can get a better offer. The last I heard it was twelve years."

As he left, the cameras and reporter swooped down on him. He thought of a flock of gulls begging for crumbs. He declined any comment.

* * *

He awoke to a call from Father McGowan. He'd been out the night before with Sylvia. It was coming back to him slowly. They'd gone to dinner. He drank too many scotches then added multiple beers at the house party afterwards. She'd been driving so he could drink as much as he wanted. Now in the sickening dawn of a Saturday hangover, he thought how the pleasure of drinking to his heart's content might be inversely proportional to his stomach and mind's discomfort. He remembered her giggling at him. They were kissing on his couch and then groping, but she'd inexplicably left. Maybe he forgot the reason. He couldn't remember drinking that much in a while. His body ached with a sickly throb, nauseating him. He wasn't sure he could hold anything down yet.

There'd been a white tablecloth at their table. He gazed at her for long periods of time complimenting her, trying to amuse her. She occasionally smiled back while putting a hand up to one of her dangling earrings and fingering it ponderously. Her laughter sparked victory after victory of drinking bouts. That's when he downed the three scotches. They went down easy, at first heightening his awareness and joy, bathing everything in a goldish hue. But now it was a reversal of perspective, a clouded prism ladening his sight with painful complication.

He wasn't in school anymore. His body would need the full day to recover. During the week, the pressured moments of the job wouldn't allow for this. He'd cut back the alcohol intake quite a bit since his college and law school days. But on occasion, usually involving chasing a woman or a wedding, he would revert to his old ways.

He walked out into the warmth of his backyard, a half-acre expanse with a chain link fence separating woods at the back. He thought he saw a bird flying off seemingly blend into the sky and disappear. His thoughts were erratic and strained by overtaxed nerves.

She must've helped him into bed because his dress clothes were hung up and his shoes were sitting neatly beside the closet door. Why had he drunk the beer? They'd kept offering, and he hadn't seen any downside. He'd been ecstatic. There was the pleasure and laughing that seemed to only get brighter. This new wondrous lady he would be marrying was supplanting numerous stag situations he'd suffered through. It had him reliving younger, more fool-hardy decisions.

When he began talking to McGowan, he imagined a brain scan would show blunted activity. The priest asked, "Would it be okay to approach Edward one more time to give a message from the girl? After explaining to Spring where Edward was and that he may not be coming out for a while, she told me she wanted to go see him. I told her they wouldn't allow that. When her insistence didn't prevail over me, she modified her request to giving Edward a message. I promised to do it. Thought I would check with you first."

"Don't see any problem with it."

He hung up and rolled back into his bed to try and sleep it off. Monday seemed far enough away for him to get back in shape. He'd worry about things then. His empty prone mind slowly lapsed back into unconsciousness by degrees.

* * *

At the jail, he found a more receptive Reynolds. "Spring wanted me to tell you it was okay about the fire because the kittens are in heaven now, and she still has one of their sisters." Reynolds looked at him dazedly. "She's got some new coloring books now. But she's been drawing some disturbing pictures in them."

"Of wh-what?"

"I was hoping you might help explain it. I've seen boys older than her draw guns and knives and other acts of violence, but never from a girl this young."

"It c-could be from some of the m-movies we use'ta wa-watch. She'd be in b-bed most t-times, but m-must've seen some of 'em."

"Then there's many insect drawings. She seems particularly fascinated by them. I haven't seen a girl that young distinguish between so many different bugs."

"She's b-better off with you g-guys now. She has a fa-fair chance of not bein' scr-screwed up."

"She's not your daughter?"

"No. Not fa-physically. There was a m-methhead that had h-her and then went back to sh-shootin' and sk-skipped town."

"I have to let you know that DHR is going to try to terminate any parental rights you might have."

"I never had any to b-begin with. Won't I at l-least get to see h-her?"

"I'm not sure. Her legal guardian or future ones may push for a restraining order against you."

He watched fury flare up, distorting Reynolds's face for a moment as if something had laboriously stirred to wake after lying dormant for a while. He was amazed to see the face slowly relaxing to become placid again. As he was leaving, he remembered the heavy medications Reynolds was on.

* * *

As Reynolds's pre-trial hearing approached, he negotiated with Feld. Feld regularly handled high-profile cases. Although this was a lower-scale felony compared to rapes and murders, the media attention surrounding the girl had ramped up the status. He'd worked with Feld before. They knew one another, but he would've described their professional relationship as strained.

The original offer had been twelve years to manufacturing in the first degree. Initially, the lowest he could get Feld to go was seven years to manufacturing in the second. He was able to talk him down to converting some of the seven years to least restrictive alternatives. If Reynolds went to trial and lost, he could get the twenty years maximum, plus one year extra for the reckless endangerment. The lowest Feld would go was five years of prison. Reynolds would serve three with good time counted. After release from incarceration, he'd either have to be on home detention or work release for two years minus a third for good time with regular urinalysis testing. Probation would last the maximum amount of time possible. Under the current plea offer, the second count of reckless endangerment would be dismissed. Feld was less concerned about wrangling over the misdemeanor.

The amount of jail time on the table was more than Reynolds had ever served by more than thirty-three months. Nonetheless, he stopped worrying about the case given Reynolds would probably be looking at three times as much on a charge that didn't have much chance at trial. Reynolds had indicated that he'd take five years or less. Additional lab results had arrived showing the presence of more precursors of meth. He felt confident they'd be able to ink a deal.

* * *

He wondered why the girl hadn't been questioned thoroughly yet. After initial excitement, the agency's enthusiasm on linking the bikers was beginning to wane. They could put them at Reynolds's residence, but that didn't put them there selling or possessing contraband. Everything had burned in the main buildings. The things found in the shack were incidental. There was debate about talking to Reynolds to see if he would turn evidence.

She was six years old. Even if she had useful information, she might not have the capacity to testify. But even if she didn't testify, she might have some other useful information.

When he got to the orphanage and rang the doorbell, one of the nuns pushed open the screen door and greeted him on the porch. He let her know he was the one who'd called earlier. She led him to the girl in her room. Spring was sitting on her bed with a blanket wrapped around her. She looked up at him silently with what seemed like serious contemplation. He told her, "I'm Robert Mantle, an FBI agent, a policeman for the federal government. I wanted to ask you some questions about the house you used to live in."

The nun encouraged her, "It's okay to talk to this man. You won't get in trouble for speaking with him."

The girl had a lithe voice. "Will Uncle Rey-Rey have to go to jail longer?"

He thought she seemed more aware than what he expected from a six-year-old. "Edward is looking at a lot of trouble and possible jail time. How much trouble depends on what the truth is. Did you ever see other men come by the house?"

"Un-hunh."

"Who were they?"

"I don't know all of 'em. Too many to count. Lots of people. Sometimes girls did too. Sometimes they only came one time. Sometimes they stayed with us."

"Do you remember what any of them looked like?"

"One was skinny. He and Uncle Rey-Rey used to yell. Before he started yellin', he tole me to go back. Back in my room. They'd stay up way past bedtime."

"Do you remember anyone else?"

"There were all kinds and lots of people."

"Did any of them have beards like this?" He showed her an older photo of Cat's Paw.

"Un-hunh. When they came I could hear their motorbikes."

"Did you see them when they came inside?"

"Not always. Uncle Rey-Rey sayed for me to go to my room sometimes when they come over. I could see 'em come on their motorbikes from my window. They would get off their motorbikes. They had black shirts and coats and blue jeans. I's scared of 'em. But they came inside when I's there playin' with the momma cat. One of the uncles sayed to me hello little kitten. He was smilin'. Then he picked me up in the air and ast me if I wanted to walk on the ceilin'. Then he turnt me upside down. My feet were on the ceilin'. I laughed 'cause it made my feet and my tummy tickle. I wasn't so scared of the uncles after that."

"Do you remember what their names were?"

"They were Uncle Cat Paw and Uncle Muffler. They always made loud noise."

"Did you ever see them take anything from the house?"

"I don't know. They would stay sometimes for a long time. And make campfires."

"How long would they stay back there?"

"Too many days for me to count. Sometimes not so long."

"Did they bring things with them?"

"They brought me a doll once. And they brought me cuhlorin' books."

He noticed drawings nearby. Some depicted scenes of crude violence. "What are these pictures about?"

"That's the locust tree."

"What's that?"

"Uncle Rey-Rey used to go talk to 'em."

"What do you mean?"

"He used to go out in the back yard and talk to one of the locust trees."

"What would he be saying to them?"

"He wouldn't let me go near. He'd only do it sometimes when he was mad. Sometimes he'd been stayin' up. I'd hear him bang on the wall. Then I'd go look out to the back door and he'd be standing by the locust tree. One time he got mad with Uncle Cat Paw and pointed at the ground."

"Why do you call it the locust tree?"

"'Cause the locust tree had shells on it. Well, it use'ta, but one of the lower shells was kinda torn off. There's more than one. But that one had three on it just where the woods started." He watched her hold up three miniature fingers.

"If we went there, do you think you could show me?"

"Un-hunh."

He went to his vehicle to request another search warrant. While waiting, he decided to visit the property first to see if he might get permission. When he got out there, no one was visible. Construction equipment lay inert. A backhoe sat next to the stripped-down foundation. There was a chain link fence around the entrance. He entertained going in by himself for a look, but thought better of it on the off chance he discovered something of value that might later be compromised by his actions.

As he was looking onto the property from the street, he noticed some movement that materialized into someone coming his way in drab clothing. It must've been the security guard. The man came up with a drawn weapon. "What the hell you doin' here?"

He flashed his credentials and told him to lower his weapon immediately. He guessed the man was probably in his fifties. The man wore a mustache on his slumped, reddish face. Facial skin draped down around the mustache.

"A'right. You got a wharint?"

"Not yet, but I'll have one soon enough. Thought I'd come out here to see if the owner might let me on."

"Ain't nobody got permission to come on here. Got my orders from the owner."

"Is he paying you as security?"

"That's me and his business. Somebody's gotta look out here for equipment. A kid could come in and run it inta the river. Weese on direct orders to let no one atall in."

"You say we? Is there another person here?"

"Naw. Just me back in the trailer."

"I got a little girl that's going to help me look for something here."

"Not without no wharint."

A few hours later, he returned in his work-issued SUV with the warrant, the priest, one of the nuns, a marshal, and the girl. The nuns had been reluctant at first to remind her of the traumatic event. After seeing the warrant, the security guard stepped back and got on the phone for a second before relenting and undoing part of the fence that was padlocked.

The six of them headed back toward the wooded area. When they got close to the edge of the woods, he turned to the girl. "Now which one was that locust tree?"

He watched her walk silently holding the nun's hand. On hearing the question, she shied away behind the bulk of the nun. The nun urged her on, "Go ahead, honey."

The group followed the two along the tree line. Eventually the girl pointed out a healthy adult pine. He saw the locust husks she'd been talking about on a chunk of bark. There were remnants and discoloration where one of the husks must've been ripped away. A couple more husks clung on above it.

"Where'd you say Uncle Rey-Rey pointed to the ground?"

She pointed to an area on the edge of the unkempt lawn that receded to crabgrass and dirt closer to the tree.

"Did you ever see Uncle Rey-Rey dig around here?"

"Ont-unh."

He looked at the ground. It seemed hard packed. He turned to the security guard, "You got a pick?"

"Now I ain't lendin' you nothin'. That's yur job."

"Alright."

He and the marshal went back to the car. He took out a shovel. Handing the marshal the keys, he told him to go buy them a pick.

He went back to where the group was standing around near where the girl had pointed. He tried starting a hole with the shovel. The ground was harder-packed nearer the pine. It got a little easier the farther away he moved.

The security guard spat then predicted, "Yur gonna waken all 'em sleepin' grubs."

While he worked, the priest and nun went to walk along the river with the girl. By the time he'd cleared a good squarish section of surface grass and soil, the marshal returned with a pick. He handed the shovel to the marshal and took the pick. He slammed the pick to break up some of the harder ground closer to the tree. Even though it was October, it was warm, and he began to sweat. The air had a heavy, full soil scent. He appreciated being outdoors working with his hands. After several swings, he and the marshal traded tools again. The marshal pounded the earth with the pick, breaking up the soil in chunks. The swoosh of the shovel cleared the dirt. They continued for two hours.

Irate and ruddy faced, the security guard returned yelling objections, citing he'd just gotten off the phone with the property owner. He waved the security guard off, explaining they had a warrant. While they were arguing, the metallic whistle and thud of the pick stopped. The marshal cried out that he had something. On the tip of the pick was a humanoid-looking skull devoid of flesh.

Within a couple of hours, he watched the property fill again with the frantic buzz of law enforcement. Within a couple of hours of that, he watched newspersons line the chain link fence.

Some of the investigators were incredulous. He explained it over and over again as a forthright follow-up of their conversation at the orphanage. He'd been looking for a stash of meth or cash that could be traced to the bikers. There was nothing magical about it. From his perspective, which he didn't share vocally, the inexplicable part was the failure of the state detectives to interview the girl.

* * *

He realized his hopes for a plea deal to seven years on the manufacturing charge evaporated the moment the pick hit that skull. Law enforcement was now excavating the entire premises. After a couple of days searching, no other remains had been found. The sheriff had begun dredging the river abutting the property.

The bones were sent to the fed lab to identity. He'd heard there was some stringy gray material strung about what had once been flesh. The initial estimate placed the remains between ten and twenty years old.

He expected additional charges as soon as the next hearing. He anticipated Feld would want to lock in higher bail. The scope of his appointment could expand significantly. He struggled with whether he should opt out if additional charges were filed. His usual approach on appointment cases had been to help the assigned individual through whatever came up during that appointment related to criminal law. Sometimes that led to lengthy commitments. But this was in keeping with remembering where he'd started. He prided himself on being able to handle any criminal legal matter that might surface. So far, he hadn't turned down anything that came up during these assignment cases.

He was due to be married within the next year. A case like this could demand many hours of extra discovery, expert evaluations, possibly culminating in an elongated trial. It occurred to him that no one had stepped up to take the meth charge to begin with. He doubted anyone would be willing to take on more. The thought of professionally abandoning someone irked him.

When he arrived at Three East, he found Reynolds in the common area reading a newspaper. He would've figured stricter security since the news broke yesterday. Maybe the guards hadn't ratcheted it up before official charges were filed. He was able to walk right up and sit across the table from Reynolds.

"Did you hear what they found on your property?"

"I d-did."

"What's going on with it?"

"Ca-can't say."

"Look, if I'm going to be your lawyer you've got to be honest with me. Do you know anything about these remains?"

"Ca-can't say."

"You know whatever you tell me is protected by privilege, right?"

"Ca-can't say."

"Well, I guess you're implicated somehow?"

"No. I just ca-can't say."

"How would the girl know about it?"

"D-don't know."

"You better think about it. If they charge you with more serious crimes, I'm not sure how long I'll be able to afford to stay on your case. I'm not quitting, but if there are hundreds of hours involved in defending you on this new information, I may not have the kind of time to do the best job. I've got other things going on, you know."

"I ca-can't say."

He raised his voice sarcastically, "What ca-can't you say?"

"I d-didn't do it."

"Okay, that's a start. Are you saying you're innocent of knowing that skeleton was there?"

"Ca-can't say."

"Now remember, I'm your lawyer. I'm not the investigator they'll probably be sending over shortly to discuss this with you. By the way, if they do send people like that over, you'll want to ask for your lawyer to be present or just don't say anything at all, not even what you've been repeating to me just now. You should demand to have your lawyer present. Do you understand?"

"Y-yes." He watched Reynolds's head nod before his gaze dropped down to the paper again.

He left feeling more frustrated than when he'd arrived. If Reynolds had made a convincing explanation, it would've been easier for him to decide not to decline the case. He didn't want to deal with any more surprises from Reynolds. He wanted to know what he might be up against and what his client's story would be.

Back at the office, he checked his e-mail. He saw one from Feld with Reynolds in the subject line. On opening it, he read a succinct statement that all deals were off because of the new evidence. Self-preserving instinct told him not to get entangled. It told him to resist being pulled into some unknown chasm where he wasn't sure what could happen. After a few moments, his sense of equilibrium returned. He faced the squirming doubts running through him. He called Feld, who wasn't in. He left a voice mail.

About an hour into composing a motion brief, Feld called. "You probably knew this was coming, but we're going to charge Reynolds. They estimate the body has been there between ten and fifteen years. Until we hear otherwise, he's going to be charged with murder one at his next hearing. We're going to have to re-discuss the situation on the meth case."

"Have they identified the body yet? Or when do you expect them to?"

"We should get some results within a couple of months. The feds are processing it."

"Why are you rushing to charge?"

"It's on his property, for God's sakes. He's been there the entire time. Just on the face of it we can convict. Look, you know that people want answers for this, and we're going to be filing."

They hung up. He took a dissatisfactory moment to review his calendar. He'd have to request a continuance. He realized they were doing this to increase bail so there was no chance Reynolds would get out before the murder charge anchored him to the local holding facility.

* * *

By the time of the pre-trial hearing, Reynolds's skin had healed considerably and his hair had been shaved short again. By the time the media came in, Reynolds was seated at counsel's table in his restraints. There was no ruckus, no outbursts.

Feld addressed Miller, "Your Honor, new circumstances have come to light. The state will be asking the court to arraign the defendant on another crime today. Based on the probable cause statement that's already been given to Mr. Sheet, the state charges Mr. Reynolds with murder in the first degree of a john doe found on the property of his former residence."

He acknowledged receipt of the complaint and entered a plea of not guilty.

Feld continued, "Yesterday we filed a probable cause statement and indicated we would be asking for one million dollars in bail. The defendant has already been shown to be a flight risk. The seriousness and dangerousness of the charge easily justifies the amount requested."

In addressing bail, he knew full well that Miller would probably follow the prosecutor's recommendation, but reminded the judge that, "Your Honor, restraint before conviction should be the lowest amount to ensure appearance. Given my client's limited resources, a much smaller amount would be appropriate at this stage of mere allegation."

He had looked into transferring funds from Reynolds's checking account for bail, but there was no way it would cover an increase like this. The account received automatic deposits monthly, but it would be years before it would even approach a bond on ten percent of the requested amount. Reynolds had no collateral even close to covering the remainder.

Miller entered bail in the amount of seven hundred fifty thousand bondable.

Feld then moved to join the trials of the manufacturing case and the new murder case. He strenuously objected, "There is too much prejudice here talking about making meth and burning a house down, and an alleged murder that no one can point to with much specificity. The charges can be expected to involve many different witnesses, and combining the two would impede a fair trial."

Miller declined to join them at the time. "It's too early at this point to talk of joining trials. I don't think there's enough evidence before the court showing a common nexus at the time of the alleged crimes. I'll leave it open for later briefing and argument if there's more discovered that would address this concern. Until then, they'll remain separate. Mr. Sheet, will you be representing Mr. Reynolds on both cases?"

"Yes, Your Honor. Subject to confirming this with the assignment panel."

He'd decided that morning he was going to take the additional assignment all the way through its completion. Surely it would've been tough for Reynolds to find another lawyer if the others had balked on the meth charges. It would be an uncalculated increase in work and more publicity. Since there was no longer a plea offer on the meth case, he moved to continue both for further investigation. Feld was happy to agree to this, as the state hadn't even gotten a full lab report back yet on the murder charge.

In waiting for the lab results, he expected a tremendous amount of speculation as to the identity of the remains. Some thought it might be a rival of Reynolds in the drug trade. Others thought it could be a transient meth head. Still others brought up the disappearance of a councilman that had occurred eleven years earlier.

Reynolds's routine didn't change much. He remained at Three East. Any plans for releasing him to general population were scuttled. There was a jail recovery program that he signed up for that might allow him to attend Narcotics and Alcoholics Anonymous meetings held in the jail. He'd heard the jail staff debate on whether to allow Reynolds to attend these. Until a decision could be reached on the substance abuse meetings, Reynolds would only be allowed to talk with the mental health counselor and his lawyer about his substance abuse.

* * *

He suspected they were in the Northwest now. He pushed for an arrest warrant based on both the trafficking and the new murder charge. After Reynolds had been arraigned and bail had been set, he applied to a federal judge who signed an arrest warrant. His superiors granted him permission to travel. Two agents located in Seattle would be assigned to him.

When he arrived in Seattle, he met the agents assigned to him. Rotund Agent Camphon had a lethargic sounding voice. In person, Camphon didn't appear very agile. Agent Snodgrass was a decent, younger type that had already begun searching before he got there. Snodgrass's report led him to believe Cat's Paw was in the area. Camphon, who he came to find out had glandular issues, thought the two bikers had split up.

He set up in a hotel near field operation headquarters. He was given basic accommodations and per diem for two weeks to bring them in, subject to further developments. He sent Camphon to surveil a biker hang-out in Tacoma where several Wraiths were thought to be living in a run-down house.

Snodgrass had marked a few biker hotspots, including a dive bar north of Seattle. A bartender there had given a description sounding like Cat's Paw. The bartender had seen someone matching Cat's Paw's description picking up and leaving with one of the regular floozies.

He sent Snodgrass north to the bar. After a couple of days, Snodgrass reported he'd located the woman the bartender had described. Through the bartender, Snodgrass arranged to meet her. The prostitute known as Cheryl described the cat's paw tattoo on his shoulder that had faded into a darkish blue. After leaving her, Snodgrass called in to have the motel investigated. Back at the office, he drew a schematic of where Cat's Paw could have traveled by foot at that hour within reasonable distance. There were apartment dwellings and residential homes nearby. Snodgrass was leaning toward an apartment dwelling, but hadn't ruled out other residences within a one-mile radius. Within this geometric circle, they ran names, aliases, and addresses of all Wraiths and their associates from the area. He hit upon an alias about a mile from the dive bar.

Within an hour they were knocking on the door. No one answered. He and two marshals drew their guns. Instead of kicking in the door, he decided to have some of the local police help them execute their arrest warrant. That way a more dangerous shoot out might be averted.

Within a few hours, they were inside the dwelling. The cops were left standing in a minimally furnished, nondescript, clean suburban house that appeared either unoccupied or up for sale. If they'd been there, they could be quite a distance away by now.

* * *

He'd grown more comfortable not having to slink around. He even entertained the thought of making some side deliveries to increase the cash flow. The under the table jackhammer jobs enabled him just enough to pay rent and deal with necessities.

Although he could live in filth and act as a slob for extended periods of time, he had an innate sense of how to cover up tracks. He often questioned whether staying at

Freight's house might've been too risky. Eventually, he split from Muffler, and they rented apartments. Before they'd left, they scrounged together money for maid service to clean the place. The maids must've been appalled with the amount of work in front of them because Freight let him know they'd tried charging extra afterwards.

Just east of downtown, he'd moved into a Capitol Hill apartment, signing a lease under a viable alias. The studio apartment was three hundred square feet, larger by far than most jail cells. He knew the neighborhood was a good fit. He was more likely to be ignored than noticed. He paid his landlord in cash through a tenant manager, who seemed to be on the run from something himself. Nobody asked him many questions on the hill.

As October proceeded, a chill crept into the air. He started his beard back to cover up the scar on his cheek. He landed a longer gig jackhammering internal flooring on a barge being transformed into a trash hauler. He wore plaid and other worn-out shirts covering his tattoos. He caught the bus down to the industrial part of the harbor. He came home and drank beer until passing out. He'd leave the next morning for the dull thud of work. The job would run another month or two, and he would see where to go from there. The lack of action was beginning to bind up in his blood. Some nights he itched for that unencumbered-ness and for that expanse of business affairs that knew no boundaries, state or federal. An inartificial need born out of a more primal supply and demand.

* * *

After splitting from Cat's Paw, he'd gone down to Tacoma to work under the table there as a longshoreman's grunt. He lamented some of the changes to the longshoremen over the past couple of decades. When he was in his early twenties, all you needed was the right contact. It was like you were a union member. But things had changed. The bureaucrats had put their greedy hands into it, skimming and slicing off money, throwing down regs and laws to prevent any under the table competition. He was among a dying breed, which his contact reminded him of every time he called.

Just this last time, the dispatcher had told him, "Look, Muffler, I know you're hurting for work, but we can't do things that way anymore. You'll have to sign on as an apprentice. I'll make sure you're protected. We have apprentices come and go all the time. They won't notice one bogus application."

He tried arguing for another way, but his contact forbade it. Not in a real position to negotiate, he grudgingly went to work under the guise of apprenticeship. Even as an apprentice, he was making almost as much as Cat's Paw did under the table as a laborer.

Lodging was cheaper down here. He'd gotten a studio apartment in a rundown part of the city near downtown where he could walk or take the bus to the docks.

While burke barring crates to fit inside transport containers, those moments were beckoning again to him, loud as the goddamned seagulls clattering and crying out an impotent mocking of power. He heard it as loud as a gull would hear the cry of its flock mates.

During some of his longer hours, he became delirious, imagining life as a gull. *There's a position up there on that light post or water rock, and I'm gonna beat you to it. There's food scraps there, easier to make us bigger and warmer than the slimy sea crud we're sometimes forced to eat to survive. There's flight now to demonstrate what we can do as we ride the currents of air and handle water landings.*

He didn't really feel any affinity for the gulls and their white shit droppings. He probably would've twisted the birds' necks off if he managed to catch some barehanded. The flight and noise had him thinking of taking off again.

* * *

He was on probation for not passing his physicals. Although Snodgrass made his weight a running joke at the office, he kept eating an inordinate amount of pastries. This problem would prevent him from advancing. He moved slowly and sweated easily, but his mental detection capacities were decent to above average among the agents. As Mantle had instructed him, he methodically went through possible biker club contacts in Tacoma.

Over the next couple of days, he pulled binoculars out and tracked a few of the known Wraiths or close affiliates at random, not seeing much. He saw movement from bike stores to bike bars to flophouses where they slept and drank and rolled in debauchery. He didn't even witness substantial criminal activity that might be used as leverage. A few times he nodded off while looking through his binocs.

Despite his bad diet, his poor health habits, and his lethargy, he was strongly motivated in his limited prescient moments of digging something up. He thought he'd go through some of their trash.

He waited until the trash men came early in the morning to one of the flophouses. He was counting on the bikers being passed out drunk at seven a.m. so that he wouldn't be noticed. As the backman was about to dump several foul-smelling cans, he approached. The flophouse denizens hadn't used trash bags. The refuse had been dumped directly in the plastic and aluminum containers. He sauntered up to him before he had a chance to brace for the lift and offered fifty dollars to pour it in his bags.

After conspiratorially eyeing him for a second, the backman took the fifty-dollar bill. He put his bag over the top of one of the de-lidded containers. It took about five minutes of rushing. By the time he'd gotten six bags out of the three containers, he was sweating profusely.

After a squeaking release of brakes, he watched the garbage truck pull away. He anxiously took the filthy, squishy bags over to his car across the street. He then put them into containers in his sedan's trunk. There was only room for two at a time. He wasn't going to put these dirty bombs in his back seat. He was already fighting the urge to vomit. He'd planned to move them to a warehouse about ten blocks away that he knew was unoccupied. He moved them two at a time. Thirty minutes later, he arrived with the last two in a heated relief as his pulse calmed down.

When he poured the refuse out, he was unpleasantly reminded of the time he watched while some fisherman split open a shark's belly on a pier. He'd brought a mask and an apron with him, both of which he donned before searching the refuse thoroughly. It still smelled terrible, causing him to sweat more in withstanding the odor.

He separated rotting fruit and torn-up underwear with a rake. Sludgy beer ash, among other unidentified liquids, spilled across the warehouse floor in a horrid, funky heap. Despite his choking revulsion, his training had him particularly attentive to any documents floating among the foul debris. He located receipts for food, beer, cigarettes, and bike parts, but that was about it. Standing disgusted in his grimy apron, he began sorely regretting the decision to search their trash.

He left the warehouse in a terrible mood. When he got back to the cheap motel where he'd set up, he felt like puking. But he lay on the bed and held it in instead.

He must've fallen asleep. He roused himself with a shower. He remembered a backup plan he'd contemplated earlier of hitting a dive bar.

He wore an untucked, faded button-down shirt and some jeans that would be baggy on a good number of agents, but fit his legs snugly. He knew that some of the affiliates of the Wraiths sometimes hung out at the dive bar. Maybe he'd get a lucky lead. After he entered and sat at the bar, he ordered a cheap draft and chatted with the extensively tattooed bartender, who had several renderings on his face. The bartender talked to him a bit, but he was generally ignored as his gullet filled with suds.

After about five of these, he was on his way to a strong buzz. In his haze, he got into a pool game with some out of work bar flies, no one he recognized connected to the Wraiths. They ended up taking some money from him.

After he napped off his buzz back at the motel, he decided to go speak with some of the local state detectives. He called from his cell. They hadn't seen much activity from the Wraiths lately. They'd been more focused on the city gangs. They suspected there might be some pawnshop fencing operations the bikers were tied up in, but they hadn't gotten enough proof to go public yet.

He went back to surveilling the Wraiths he knew about as the days moved by in an oppressive oblivion. His two weeks had been extended to a third by Mantle, but he wasn't finding anything new. He'd volunteered for this special assignment to counteract some of the negativity his reputation had suffered at the office. But the unfruitfulness of the venture only drove him to watch more television and to eat worse than ever.

As he sat watching a flophouse, he read the local newspaper. He saw an article about port security clamping down harder on scabs. It mentioned how many of the under the table workers were either in the country illegally or had criminal records. While eating a cinnamon danish with white icing on top, he read how criminal members of outlaw biker clubs were reputed to be among those who'd infiltrated the unions for several years and had become ingrained in the system. He sat for a few more annoyed moments. Then, after partially wiping crumbs from his khakis, he phoned someone in the port security office and got confirmation of what the article detailed.

He began scoping out different union halls. He stopped by the laborer and ironworker locals. He sat around reading the paper appearing like he was waiting for work. He talked to the dispatchers through barred windows. Nothing stood out to him. When the regulars began giving him suspicious looks, he moved on.

He tried the longshoremen's hall. It had the smell of a building holding things in trust, like a bank or a library with everything officially stored in papers. As he was running out of time for the assignment, he tried a more direct tactic. After informing the longshoremen dispatcher who he was, he arranged to meet with him behind the front window. The dispatcher didn't seem flustered and answered his questions directly, "No, I don't know the guy in the photo with the beard, but we have apprentices come in all the time. I don't know if I'd recognize all the new ones."

"Where are the apprentices currently working?"

"All over the docks. Once they get sent out, they get turned over to the foreman and could be anywhere."

"I'll go take a look then."

"I'll give them a call to let the foreman know what's going on. Otherwise they may not be very receptive toward you."

He'd knew the port security in connection with national security, and the labor division of his agency had tapped the line already. They'd be able to catch any advance warning sent out. He listened to the dispatcher announce into the phone, "Hey, I got a federal agent here coming down to talk to you and look things over. Big guy named Camphon with a federal badge. Just answer his questions. Call me if any problems develop." The dispatcher turned to him. "You know how to get down there?"

He got up to leave. "Yeah, I got a map."

He had a map, but by the time he got down there, the entryways were closed. It took him almost an hour before he found the foreman. He saw guys walking out to their cars. He saw a trailer indicating where the managers were located. He walked into the foreman's office.

He addressed the grisled foreman, "I'm the agent the dispatcher called about."

"You got some credentials?"

He showed him his badge and then a picture. "Have you seen this guy?"

"No, not with a beard like that. Can't tell what that person would look like."

"How about with less beard?" He showed him another photo from a booking of Cat's Paw.

"Don't know if I'd recognize him."

Showing him another, "Lanky fellow in this picture, you seen him?"

"He looks more familiar. Without the beard, looks like a new recruit, but I suspended him two days ago for getting into it with a crane operator. He might be back tomorrow. Kind of had a wild look to him. That type doesn't stay in one place for long."

"Do you know where he lives?"

"No idea. Don't think he drove into work as far as I could tell."

"Anybody else might know where he lives?"

"Most of those guys've already left for the day. It's a three o'clock shift. You'd have to ask around from the second shift or come back in the morning."

When he got back to the motel, he called Mantle. As hopes of extending his longevity with his employer ensued, he couldn't suppress excitement from creeping into his voice.

* * *

At six a.m. the next morning, he was at the dispatcher's office asking for records regarding the recently hired dockworker fitting the description of Muffler. Upon writing down a street address, he abruptly left and called Camphon, who'd been waiting at the docks for the past two hours without any sign of Muffler.

They arrived at the apartment complex, walked through the unlocked front door, and found the landlord's room. After a thirty-second delay, the landlord answered his door with a stained undershirt too small for his belly. He watched yellow teeth click behind a fat face of stubble. Once the landlord found out they had an arrest warrant, his unalert countenance changed to worried obsequiousness, relenting to their entry. He looked at the picture they held up and led them to a room.

They entered a room with a mattress on the floor, an old television in the corner, some nudie mags strewn about, a couple of half-empty bottles of whisky, some full ashtrays, and an open street-level window. The landlord shuffled his feet, offering up an explanation, "Must be down't work. Usually comes home in the evenings. Stays to hisself mostly."

"When did he move in?"

Camphon joined the questioning. "Did he have a vehicle?"

The landlord's eyes jerked around like they were houseflies being swatted at. He tried to deflect the scrutiny. "He paid in cash!" He squeamishly whined, "How's I to know he'd be a most wanted? Must've cleared out."

* * *

In the meekly lit dark, he tried the buzzer to Cat's Paw's address he had on a scrap. After many tries, he wasn't getting any response. He walked back to a bus stop and headed for another area of town. There were some rundown motels off Aurora. He'd saved some cash. He could go for about three weeks or so in motels.

* * *

Ignoring the ringing buzzer, he'd slept off the half case of beer he'd drunk the night before. He vaguely remembered waving in the air at some distant noise then rolling back over.

As he entered the next sour morning, he cooked an egg, ate it with some toast, and drank some coffee. He headed down to work.

He was walking under the viaduct, about to cross the railroad tracks near the water, when he saw Muffler. "What the hell are you doing? You trying to get us seen in the open?"

"It's the feds. They came within a day of catching me."

"What are you bringing them to me for? Am I supposed to quit now and run?"

"I think they've been leaning on the unions hard. They may get one to turn on you."

He grinned, thinking of that itch to break out of straight, boring pay. "I don't feel too much like going in anyway. I think we'd better get out. Where'd you stay last night?"

"Motel on Aurora. Paid in cash. They'll have a hard time tracking that."

"You know the north route we slipped through?"

* * *

By day's end, they'd searched many areas on the waterfront looking for information on dockworkers or other jobs near the water. The television Muffler left in the room had a sticker on it traced to a donation store in Seattle. They scanned the Seattle waterfront too.

In coordination, port security came forward. Among those brought in was the laborers' dispatcher. They grilled him about call-in jobs until he revealed the under the table work on the barge. It was evening by then, and there was no activity on the hulking, floating metal husk.

The next morning, he and his agents were on the barge where they learned Cat's Paw had been jackhammering up the floor the day before yesterday. The foreman on the barge project identified Cat's Paw by photo. "He didn't show for work yesterday. Didn't call or leave any info."

"Do you know where he lived?"

"No. But another of the workers seen him walking toward the hill. I think he said he seen him go into an apartment there."

He let Camphon interview the other barge worker, a somewhat withered but wiry older Asian man who swept up debris after it'd been broken apart by the jackhammer. He didn't speak English that well. They called the language line to get a Chinese interpreter.

Between several guttural rasps and pauses the interpreter answered, "Yes, he know the big man who work the jackhammer. His cousin own a small convenient store on Capitol Hill. He been walking up there after work one day and see the man going same direction. Then he see him go into apartment building there."

He had the Chinese worker lead them to the location. He listened through the language line again, "He think it one of these two apartment buildings, but he not sure. He stay far behind when he notice him."

Both buildings were on a generally rundown street interspersed with posters of redevelopment. Several different apartment buildings lined the street for a couple of blocks. The two buildings the Chinese sweeper focused on were side by side. Camphon informed him the house across the street was a halfway house for the heavily medicated just released from various psych wards. By the time he tried the buzzer of the first building, it was almost noon. According to the tenant manager, no one fit the description in the photos.

Moving to the next building, a dreary voice message indicated the tenant manager was at work for the day. He knew it was common for tenant managers to be comped room for doing the gritty work of actually dealing with problems in older buildings like these. Such a person would still have to get a second job to eat, but it was upsetting that he hadn't left any type of contact information. He asked a group of people trying to get into the building if they'd seen the man in the picture. Three of the four ignored his inquiry, but the fourth identified Cat's Paw as a solitary neighbor of his.

He knocked on the door the neighbor had indicated. Not hearing anything, they drew weapons and tried the doorknob. It was locked at the handle, but didn't seem dead bolted. He broke in through a series of hard kicks. Anticipating a warm, hostile body, they arrived in a cold, empty, and desolate studio room. Next to a mattress were some torn-up couch cushions that looked like a makeshift mattress on the floor. He recalled they'd passed a couch on the street that seemed to match the cushions. Some dishes and coffee grains stagnated in the sink. There was a used television with rabbit ears on the floor. No papers were evident.

What he lacked in paper, he got in a live witness at one p.m. The Mexican carpenter had been working on the redesign of a building across the street next to the halfway house. The carpenter described two large guys heading out earlier in the day around eight or nineish. The carpenter had seen them get onto bus number forty-one heading north.

* * *

He and Muffler had left the waterfront for a dive bar they knew opened early in the morning to serve breakfast. He believed he could make a phone call there without detection. They were going to need the bikes back for the voyage north through B.C. They had a small stronghold set up in Saskatchewan. Many sucked down weed to endure the harsh winters, waiting for proof of their various crimes to grow stale.

He'd learned the bikes would be ready once they got up there tomorrow morning. Freight, who was now living out of a rental where the bikes were stored, had undertaken a task that required him to commute out for the night. Freight would unlock the garage and leave their keys inside on a shelf.

There was something nagging him still. He wasn't as sure about the border. Some foreboding scenes played through his mind before he convinced himself to dismiss the fear with an obscenity.

They'd arrived back at his apartment in the afternoon with a case of beer. They'd drunk through the evening. As they were on the verge of passing out, they'd gurgled and chuckled remembering all types of stressed circumstances. He had a puffed-out chest feeling about getting back into the jeans and leather on their bikes.

He wanted his own space to sleep. There was only a single mattress. The one productive thing he saw Muffler accomplish that day was to take some cushions from the old abandoned couch sitting in front of a nearby apartment complex with a hand-scrawled "free" sign on it. He watched Muffler bunch the cushions under his arms as he headed back up. By eleven p.m. he must've fallen unconscious.

He awoke just before seven. Finding himself in one sore piece, he went to the small fridge and looked in on eggs, buttermilk, and a few leftover beers. The only other food in the place was half a loaf of stale bread, one microwave meal in the freezer, and a couple of canned foods in one of the cabinets. He'd get rid of those in the dumpster out back before they left. He made some eggs and coffee. While waiting for the coffee to brew and the pan to heat, he kicked at the still body that was Muffler until he heard a grunt of life and a cuss directed to whoever's foot that was.

After a few trips to the dumpster, they'd been ready to catch the bus north. The streets were active with the hum of morning traffic before he heard the steady rhythm of construction across the street. He was numb with hangover, but some of the thrill of drunkenness still flared in warm arcs through his aching stomach and mind. With these short flashes of disregard toward being injured, he'd been less concerned about being seen.

They boarded the forty-one bus at eight forty a.m. Just over twenty-five minutes later, they got up to the park n' ride where they caught the next bus north to Snohomish County. Freight had left their clothes and colors near the bikes in the garage. After retrieving the key, he let them into Freight's rental. They smoked a bowl. They put on their riding jeans and leather then got back onto their bikes, storing their colors in the back. After reconnecting back to the rotating world and their place on it, they rumbled off headed for highway two.

* * *

He tracked down the bus driver of forty-one by calling in an emergency stop. They interviewed him and verified a match. Within walking distance of where they'd gotten off, there were two buses going north from the park n' ride and a couple going east. The soonest wait time would've been the one traveling to South Everett. The rest of the routes were over thirty-minute waits. He decided this was the most likely path and scanned the dropped off point for known biker residences.

While Snodgrass ran the search, the bus driver of the second suspected route confirmed another match. Snodgrass located a rental under the alias of a known affiliate in South Everett. The ten-minute wait for the bus route they were focusing on would've dropped them off within four blocks of there around quarter to ten. Three hours had elapsed from the time he left Cat's Paw's abandoned apartment before they found the house in Everett where a large tattooed Chinese man sporting a goatee was passed out on the couch. After being tapped awake, despite his protests about a warrant, he was placed under arrest for rendering criminal assistance and possession of marijuana.

He saw more than one set of tracks in the gravel driveway. He called in an APB on the two bikers. He suspected they were back on their bikes and advised as such. Their most likely route came to him abruptly with a slick, nauseating, anticipatory lining that he would have to hurry. They could be trying to slip through to Canada, where it was rumored they had enclaves. Their likenesses had already been distributed to the border patrol. He calculated the bikers had at most a four- or five- hour head start.

* * *

The mountain passes were clear and cold, but didn't have much snow yet. He'd run this route dozens of times. Every time he started climbing into the alpines with its Douglas firs and evergreen, the colder wind invigorated him. He was still high even after the weed wore off as they crested through the Cascades.

The road was fairly empty. They saw a few truckers on the way out and then some activity near the ski resort. There was some mild traffic through Leavenworth. Fortunately no state patrol or local cops were visible. He'd contemplated taking the longer route through the Cascades Highway, but they were in a hurry. Except for the steady rumbling acceleration of their motors, the trip had been quiet.

The next stop would be up north of Wenatchee, probably in Orondo. They would take two across the Columbia then head up north on ninety-seven. Ninety-seven would take them straight up through the border. They wouldn't cross on ninety-seven. It'd be too conspicuous. They would take the less traveled older highway that jogged west to Loomis then follow the Sinlahelain north around Palmer lake. After Nighthawk, they would leave the developed roads altogether, going along the river through the forest to cross and pick up the highway just short of highway three on the other side.

He knew the area was sometimes patrolled for drug smuggling, but now more attention and resources were being diverted to the heavier traveled crossings. More contraband could be easily moved through a false door in a truck bed than through whatever method might be devised through this undeveloped, hilly, desert-looking terrain, interrupted with thick forests. Some rudimentary trails existed, but many of these had disappeared or wound to no end from lack of use. It was a labor-intensive passage that must be made lightly.

He and Muffler had gotten through the Nighthawk crossing before with small amounts of drugs. Now the economics of scale dictated driving through in larger carriers, whether by truck, van, tractor-trailer, boat, or helicopter. Sliding through with a kilo strapped to a special compartment built on the side of a gas tank was no longer that competitive.

He planned to reach Nighthawk by late evening and bed down. They could wake up near dawn to cross. One of the problems with getting the cycles across would be the noise and a short wire border fence. There were some trails, but there'd be a mile and a half stretch where they'd have to walk the bikes with the motors off, which he expected to be a pain in the ass. The fence was broken down in many parts. He had some cutters in case they needed to improvise. Once they were sufficiently across to the trail leading up from the river, they could fire the bikes up again to head north before heading east.

In Orondo they gassed up and bought some food, enough to last two nights. He checked his packed blanket tied to the back of his seat. Muffler left for town to find one for himself.

* * *

His APB had gone out live across a wide band of law enforcement frequencies. He scrambled to get in contact with the various border stations. Two white bikers, possibly armed and dangerous, were wanted, and must not be allowed to cross. He suspected they knew to avoid the more obvious like the Peace Arch in Blaine. He'd studied them before and had heard vaguely of crossings in Okanogan County. There were two or three suspected places, directly through Oroville, through Molson, or near Nighthawk. He contacted Wenatchee and Okanogan law enforcement.

An hour later, as he was putting up schematics on a board in a frenzy, he got the call. A Chelan County deputy had seen a pair of biker types cross the dam prior to hearing the APB. He estimated he'd seen them about forty-five minutes ago.

He wasted no time in securing a helicopter. He alerted the border patrol. The patrols in the area happened to be thin that day. The crossing above Nighthawk had the minimum couple of guards present with no backup in the vicinity.

The helicopter took off from Boeing Field headed east. The evening was beginning to twilight. He estimated they could be near Omak by now. Although he preferred not to rely on patrolmen he'd never met, he was hopeful the call out would keep the two held up or possibly caught before he got there.

* * *

Even though he hadn't physically seen law enforcement around them, there was something inherent in the crossing that made his blood pressure rise. He wanted to get it over with. But he relented to Muffler's request to search for a pillow.

They were about twenty miles from Nighthawk. It was becoming darker. They turned on their headlamps. The road was pretty deserted, and the temperature was dropping. He hadn't thought they'd freeze, but he was beginning to have some doubts. They'd just have to survive one night in it. No cops were seen as they pulled through Nighthawk.

They headed off the mapped roadways and looked for a place to bed down. After a few miles, they found a grassy area near a rock face where they could hide the bikes under some trees. The rock also blocked some of the wind. They laid out their makeshift bedding materials. He ate a little bit then tried to go to sleep.

He was drifting off when he heard the motor of another vehicle. It sounded stronger than a cycle engine. When he realized it was a copter, he roused Muffler. Then they were running, scrambling for more cover.

They moved closer into the cover of trees. A searchlight beam illuminated near but not on them. He worried that some of the bedding or the cycles would be exposed. Then the copter sounded off to the north, becoming fainter. He whispered about whether they should attempt to cross now. It was cold and dark, but he figured they could follow the river. Then again, he wasn't sure they'd been seen. It could've been routine patrol looking for drug runners randomly.

It was getting on toward midnight. They were tired and decided to bed down. They would rise up around four a.m. so they might have the aid of some dawn light. It was severely dark. The star-filled sky above might've inspired things on any other night, but now it was somehow menacing, a mocking beauty. They'd need more light. He didn't want to use the headlamps.

They lay down again, this time closer to the trees. Muffler went out first and began breathing steadily. They hadn't ridden in a while and the full day had worn them out. But he couldn't fall into much sleep. He jarred himself awake from momentary dreams of violence and capture, calls to action where he was frozen. After four hours of this, he heard the first dog.

* * *

He'd organized what he could swiftly. He would've liked more border control collaborating, but there were only seven men at the moment to cover twenty miles of crossing points in wild terrain. There were the regulars at the station crossings. Two more were called in from farther east on an emergency basis. He'd wanted the Okanogan sheriff's K-nine units there during the fly over, but there were only two K-nine units available, one of which was clear across the county. The first unit was estimated to be there between two and four a.m.

When the first K-nine unit arrived at three thirty, he directed them near the main crossing of ninety-seven. He believed this was the most likely crossing point although they could veer off to the sides. Crossing at Molson hadn't looked likely when viewing it by copter. They would fly over again but save the dogs for above Nighthawk.

Landing near the ninety-seven crossing, he checked to make sure the searchers were alert and in order. He had marshals on the way, but they wouldn't get there until the morning. He wasn't sure they'd have enough time. He decided to send the dog in. He'd brought pieces of the mattress and couch cushion coverings to give the dogs a scent.

For about an hour, he didn't hear anything. The border patrol agents began to patrol on foot near the line. There was a lot of terrain to cover considering they had to leave some presence at the patrol stations. He was coffeed up, waiting at the ninety-seven crossing to hear something. The second dog would get there around five a.m.

* * *

When he became conscious of a dog barking, a sickening thought ran through his head. Unwanted pressure was suddenly surrounding him, closing in, suffocating him. He'd underestimated the reaction time of the feds to catch up with them.

They'd brought pistols from Freight's place. They got ready to move and took the weapons out. He waited for his eyes to adjust better to the dark. Prison loomed in his thoughts. Killing and even suicide became familiar reoccurrences. The dog was yelping closer. It was a hoarse-sounding bark. Only one bark, not many. This perception soothed a little in the overarching annoyance. The darkess seemed to be inching toward dawn.

They tried moving with the cycles, but it was too much noise. The bark was getting louder. The trees grew tighter together, impeding their movement as they tried to weave through. Turning toward Muffler, he let out a frustrated whisper, "We gotta do something about that damned dog!"

He realized it wasn't going to work with the bikes. He hoped that the dog was unattached. Killing an officer could at best result in life in prison with their records.

* * *

The second dog arrived before the breaking of dawn. The German shepherd was held in abeyance despite his whining instinct to join the yelping bloodhound. He gave the handler a piece of the cushion, and then he was in the air again.

* * *

By the time the dog reached where they'd bedded down, he saw Muffler had a thick limb from a fallen tree. Knocking the dog out this way would make less noise. They'd piled up some beef jerky left over as bait. The bloodhound stopped to sniff it. Muffler must've thought the dog was eating, but he could see the dog was only obtaining a scent. He watched Muffler miss the dog's head, whacking the dog instead on the back and side. The bloodhound yelped then bore its teeth. Muffler put a boot in its nose. The dog bit onto his boot and started thrashing, which threw him off balance. On the ground, Muffler pulled out his pistol and shot it point blank in the head. He watched the dog slump into a heap next to the beef jerky. Then he heard the low, steady rumbling of the copter again.

After shooting the bloodhound, he watched Muffler run to his bike. They started walking them again through the woods. He scolded him in a light voice, "They had to have heard that."

Muffler defiantly whispered, "Damn dog got a hold of my boot. Tried knocking it out. Was all I could do to get it off me."

They stepped through, crouching at times on the frosty forest floor. Dark still hung over everything, but the first sure blue of dawn was beginning to tone it down. He knew the passage through the woods. He'd been through it at least a dozen times. All the other times had been on foot with rides arranged on either end, carrying duffle bags or other cargo. He knew how to get through, but it'd been awhile. Sometimes it'd been cloudy, but never as dark as this. They had to go slowly to keep the bikes away from drop-offs. The bikes clinked as they waddled with them through the trees. By the time dawn was breaking, he estimated they were within a mile of the border. He'd been running out of breath. He let Muffler know, "Probably an hour more of this and we'll be across."

Soon after he said this, he heard the distinct barking of another dog. The faint sound of the copter had gotten louder. He looked up from taking a breather then began walking as fast as he could with the bike.

* * *

He'd narrowed down the diameter to a two-and-a-half mile swath in the area from where the handler had radioed in. He informed the seven border patrol agents by radio. The two farthest in toward the river were still getting into position as dawn broke. It was clear enough for them to see without artificial light. On the southside position, three Okanogan deputies, including the second handler, moved north toward the first handler's position. By the time dawn had fully broken, they'd reached the first handler. He heard the first handler radio in his bloodhound was dead. He directed the pilot to hover overhead, but he couldn't see very well through the tight rows of evergreen firs.

* * *

He turned to look back for Muffler, who'd been struggling a bit, lagging behind. They both had broken into a reeking sweat as they struggled to keep the bikes. He estimated they were three-quarters of a mile from the border. He led them to a path near the river. He knew things were passable enough there. He thought it would be the only chance to get across with the bikes. He hated to leave the bikes. He estimated they were about half a mile away. He heard a gruff, wooden bark now, probably less than a football field away. He looked at Muffler, who wore a blank stare, as if he wasn't sure whether to throw his bike down or to start his motor and risk driving through the tangle of trees.

He put his bike down on its side. He took his gun and his blanket then started running north toward the river. He looked back to see Muffler running a little farther behind him. He heard the dog accelerating close, racing up. He must've been let loose like the bloodhound. He heard gunfire, but it must've missed or grazed the dog. He got behind cover of a tree and turned to see the dog had a hold of Muffler's arm now, wrenching back and forth. Struggling to get the dog off, Muffler fell to the ground. The dog began mauling him. He watched Muffler kick and punch the dog's body until Muffler got another chance to shoot. He saw the dog limping away, leaving blood from its shoulder. He could see the deputies running past the limping dog. They pointed their weapons. Muffler's arm was a tangled, bloody mess of shredded flesh. His face had been torn apart. He watched Muffler limp behind his fallen bike then lay on the ground.

Running would just delay getting caught on the other side. Then they'd be shipped back for a long stretch in prison. He heard the cops calling for them to give it up. The copter loomed overhead. He saw Muffler standing up to fire in the direction of their pursuers. The first shot hit Muffler in the torso and turned him around. Two more hit him in the back before he fell. Some bullets ricocheted off the bike with a ping.

He ran then walked swiftly toward what he knew was the river. He could smell it through the cooler air. He hadn't reached the same point of self-abandonment. Canada was close. He only had to find an effective way to transport himself. But leaving his bike behind had been like leaving a leg behind.

He heard renewed barking. He could hear the river as well. He saw a rock outcropping. He climbed onto it. He figured the dog would be able to smell him, but he'd have a height advantage. He was more exposed to the copter now as there were fewer trees on the rock. Before he got up there, he found a sturdy dead tree limb.

He saw the German shepherd running toward him. He crouched on the side of the boulder swinging the limb at the dog, trying to knock it out to keep it from barking. He could hear radios. Then the copter was overhead. If he shot the dog, they'd pinpoint him by the noise. If they saw him with a drawn gun, he expected to be shot to death.

A self-destructive impulse rose up, but by some inexplicable twist, perhaps because he hadn't been mauled by dogs, he didn't relent to it. Instead he raised his hands up. He had a sick feeling that he might be shot anyway. Two bikers shot dead in the wilderness. Then he heard an amplified announcement, like he was playing in some movie. The bloody dog still growled and bared its teeth. With a weapon drawn on him, the handler reattached the dog's leash.

After laying the dead limb next to him on the boulder, he raised his arms. The voice from the copter informed him not to move. He followed instructions to get down on his knees. Three cops found their way onto the rock. He was handcuffed and dragged down by his cuffs accompanied with sharp cusses. Numb to it at this point, he let himself be led back through the woods. Somewhere under the numbness was the bitter estimate that he'd been within a quarter mile of Canada.

When they came to where the bikes were abandoned, he could see some black birds around a still, unnaturally twisted body. Muffler's bike was on its side, dead and useless.

It took at least an hour and a half of walking until they got back to the main road in Nighthawk. By now it was a clear, late October morning approaching noon.

The cops transported him to the Okanogan County jail. He was told extradition to a federal detention center in Alabama was being arranged.

No one came to talk to him for the brief time he was held in Okanogan. He understood the brethren would want to avoid any implication. Expecting a long stint, he settled into a deep sleep.

* * *

He debriefed his supervisor in the Alabama office. The supervisor had been listening to casualties and costs with a pacified, thoughtful lean and rock in his ergonomically correct chair. He didn't sense any objection to him continuing his monologue summary of the chase and capture.

Leaving the debriefing meeting, he relived the dull satisfaction of having met a clear checkpoint in his overarching mission to dismantle or cripple the Wraiths. He'd taken down two of the higher aides-de-camp.

* * *

During transport, he stayed to himself. There was no reason to say anything. Most of the time, he contemplated whether it would've been better to go out like Muffler. There was relief to no longer be on the run. He'd been shackled and tagged, but there was no more being chased. Even though waking up in jail periodically through the night was not refreshing, the constant push to be in motion had come to rest.

He was transported by van in heavy chains from Okanogan to the SeaTac federal detention center. From there, the marshals arranged to put him on a plane back through Atlanta and then on to the Alabama detention center. During this gray period of movement and dead time, he thought of how to get in touch with the brethren. His movements were so constrained that he had no way to contact the outside world. Not even by letter.

Led by chains one way or another, he went where they moved him. What was left of his imagination was all he had to comfort him. Muffler had earned his way out. He made them kill him rather than be reduced back to the caged dog scene.

He knew the trick of the guards trying to level with him. Admitting some of their own failings and crimes in hopes he would speak of his. He heard stories of wild gun battling, whore banging, and drug busting times. He smelled some as put-ons and exaggerations to gain his confidence. He wouldn't talk to them. He could be silent. The tedium wouldn't break him. He knew that only by volunteering for them could they use his statements against him.

When he'd fallen asleep on the plane, he sometimes dreamed of talking against his will, revealing too many secrets. He'd wake up with a sick, betrayed feeling. But when he came back to his senses, it was the same staring match into a vast void.

He wouldn't put up with a mediocre, half-assed attorney. He wondered whether the brethren might hire one, but then thought it'd be too much exposure. Besides money being tight, they were being watched closely by the feds. He'd reject the public defender if he or she were a clown.

During his struggle to remain solid in front of his captors, some deep down uncertainty he couldn't name or get a hold of started plaguing him. As he groped at it, it seemed to grow larger. He tried shaking it off, telling himself that it was all meat and bullshit inside. It couldn't be regret or remorse. He'd been the way he'd been for decades now.

Any turning back seemed pointless or a waste in a sort of way. He got money under the table for that reputation. He felt certain he would be spoiling something if he gave into or acknowledged whatever that alien recognition might be. He stifled it. He assumed internally what he'd been displaying externally for some time now, callous indifference. But he couldn't fool his inside completely. It was still there like heartburn or an upset stomach, gnawing at him and driving him slightly insane on the plane to Atlanta.

These guards weren't his people. He didn't trust them enough to even start small talk. He hated small talk anyway. It didn't really sit well with the idea of being unencumbered. He'd done away with participating in unnecessary constraints at an early age. This five-hour flight through the clouds in a belly of tin would vanish by.

Part Two

*B*y November, he began to publicly remark on his ambitions. Most of the comments reiterated positions he'd voiced on the city council. He turned up criticism of the current leadership. He called for greater oversight of local industry, citing its record of pollution. He sensed less resistance to his opinions. He organized the black leaders of the community, including the Baptist preacher Melvin Kincaid, the fireman Eric Brandy, and even the scatterbrained Prentice Pomice.

He reached into his drawer to reread the transcript of Kincaid's sermon, *That individual who leads is subject to be a target for all those malevolent factors in the universe, those forces that would steal or poison or kill. That individual stands up not only to the indifferent elements that sap one's energy, that drive one to shelter, but also stands against those of his own make and model that turn against him. That individual bears the most to show the others that they can bear a little more. Without that initial individual acting, the crowd scatters and can bear nothing, not even their own skin as they shiver in fearful and lonely decisions. There is much to lose by being a lightning rod. But if the individual bears it long enough then that potential energy is liable to be tapped. The wheel will start, carrying with it all the hopes and dreams of a whipped and spat upon people.*

* * *

Although he resumed his monthly visits to the jail, he hadn't visited Reynolds for several months after their last encounter. Spring continued to express a desire to go see

Reynolds, but the real possibility of Spring being a witness made him reluctant to enter any more discussions. On one occasion she'd even cried when he'd confirmed the nuns' refusal. He thought of how innocent this child was, crying for a meth addict charged with murder, a man who'd burned down their house almost killing her. He likened it to unconditional love, at times illogical, baffling, and otherworldly. But this was a vulnerable and naïve creature capable of injuring herself because of her gullibility.

Spring had enrolled that fall in kindergarten. The books and supplies she needed had been paid for out of charity. Uniforms weren't required. Her clothes had been donated. The nuns reported she was quiet mostly and did her work, scoring good points with the teachers.

There was talk of finding her a foster family. The nuns admitted they wanted to raise her themselves. They praised her sweet disposition, adorableness, and inklings of brightness. It would be hard for them to let her go to allow someone else to mold her potential. But the other children required them to divide their attentions.

One November afternoon before dinner, he saw Mantle and another unknown man with the nuns walking behind them. The men were dressed in collared shirts and khakis. They'd called him ahead of time to request another interview with the girl. He called Spring in from playing outside.

The six of them sat in a room that functioned as an office at the orphanage. This was the same room where he and the nuns talked to prospective parents who wanted to adopt. Other times, less frequently, unmarried mothers talked tearfully of giving their babies up. The spare woodenness of the room seemed to bear some of the sadness and disappointment of reality. Those scenes seemed to have somehow loosened the boards of the structure. The impression flowed through the cushions on the upright chairs and leather couch, lending them a pliable and submissive comfort. He imagined the slouchy furniture giving way from witnessing overwhelming grief.

The bright colors the agents and Spring wore contrasted with the solemnity of the room. He tried to lighten the room by asking Spring about school and playing outside. But the gravity was reaching for and pushing them to get past lighthearted pleasantries. The girl seemed to sense this and didn't respond to small talk. With a smile and a firm manner, Mantle began. She described Reynolds's drug habit as medicine.

Mantle asked, "What type of medicine would your Uncle Rey-Rey take?"

"It was white. When I's thirsty one time and got up to get some water, he was sniffin' it up his nose. And in his bathroom he had needles. He was kinda mad when I saw him sniffin' his medicine, but then he got real happy all a'sudden and tole me to go back to bed. He got me some water and he was talkin' and walkin' 'round real fast."

"Did he ever do anything to you when he got upset?"

"Not really much. He'd just tell me to go to bed. If I cried, he'd sometimes cry too. And one time he broke a chair 'cause he was mad and then threw it up at the wall."

"Have you talked to anyone else about the fire?"

"For a little bit once. It was a policeman like you. He had real police clothes on."

"I wanted to talk to you about something other than the fire. You remember saying you saw your uncles yelling by the locust tree?"

"Un-hunh. Sometimes Uncle Cat Paw and Uncle Muffler would stay with us for a long time. They'd live back near the river. They'd catch fish and let me watch. They'd drink lots of beer."

"Did you ever see them dig any near the locust tree?"

"Ont-unh."

"Were there other people around in your house?"

"Lots. Different people. Aunt Cherie and Aunt Linda would stay with me sometimes when Uncle Rey-Rey wasn't doin' good. Sometimes he'd go out near the trees and look all 'round. Listenin' to the birds I guess."

"Who were Aunt Cherie and Aunt Linda?"

"Aunt Cherie was Uncle Rey-Rey's friend who stayed with us. She made me two birthday cakes. One when I's four and one when I turned five. She braided my hair and let me braid hers. She had pretty brown hair. Her face was pretty too, but it got messed up sometimes. She sayed it was 'cause of the medicine. She and Uncle Rey-Rey yelled at each other and one time she left."

"Did they get in fights?"

"When Uncle Rey-Rey broke the chair up on the wall, she left. I's in my room, but I heard. There was a hole in the wall and the chair was broke. Aunt Cherie didn't come back. She would bring us home grossries from the store. Aunt Cherie and Uncle Rey-Rey were like a momma and daddy sometimes. They slept together in the same bed. I's really sad after she left."

"What about Aunt Linda?"

"Aunt Linda showed up like Uncle Cat Paw and Uncle Muffler. She's bigger than Aunt Cherie. She had red hair. Her and Uncle Cat Paw stayed together. She didn't sniff the white medicine, but she drank a lot of beer. She had a real loud voice. She'd yell at Uncle Rey-Rey to clean up. She'd sometimes put on music and sing. She was funny. After she got done bein' sick from drinkin', she'd leave for a while. Sometimes she'd stay and clean up and buy grossries. She says she changed my diapers."

"Where would your aunts go?"

"Aunt Cherie talked 'bout the beach. She'd get real tan 'fore she'd start takin' the medicine. Sometimes she'd go to the river and lay there in the sun and get tan again. Aunt Linda sayed she was goin' to Mobile. She'd bring me Mardy Graw beads. She tole me she was goin' to take me one year."

"Did you ever leave the house?"

"Wasn't 'llowed to. I could go play outside though."

"You remember anybody else coming through the house?"

"A man who sayed he was sick and they took him away. I stayed in my room mostly. Aunt Cherie played with me. She made Uncle Rey-Rey buy me new dresses and clothes. Those all got burnt up in the fire."

"Did Uncle Rey-Rey ever dig anywhere near the locust tree?"

"Not that I seen. I seen him that time he was yellin' at Uncle Cat Paw and pointin' at the ground."

"Anything else you want to tell us about Uncle Rey-Rey?"

"He'd tell me evarthin's fine. And there weren't no such thing as bad guys in the woods that would want to snatch me out of bed. He'd read me stories but would tell me don't worry 'bout the make believe. He bought us a pumpkin one Hallaween where I could light the candle and it had hot orange pumpkin smells. We fried the pumpkin seeds and Aunt Linda put salt on 'em. They were kinda hard in places, but I ate some."

"Did any other kids come over?"

"Chris. He was older than me. He showed me how to play hide n' seek. He was a lot better at it than me. He could climb trees and find places where I didn't think of lookin'. And he'd always catch me real quick. He was faster than me."

"Did Chris come over by himself?"

"Chris came with his dad."

"Do you know Chris's last name?"

"Un-hunh. Screed."

"Did you and Chris ever talk about the locust tree?"

"Sometimes we'd use it as home base when we were playin'. He showed me the locust shells. I thought he's goin' to pull one off, but he just stared at it real close."

"Do you know where Chris and his dad are now?"

"They's goin' to New Arlens. He sayed it was like a hundred tornadoes in a trailer park hit 'cause of all the wind and floodin'. They'd go to Florida too. Chris tole me 'bout playin' at the beach and how one day I should go with him. He sayed it was better than the river. The big waves come splashin' down and you can hear it from far away and the sand was hot and soft. He says evarone wore bathin' suits. You go in the water and you can ride the waves in."

"Did you hear Chris's dad talk about the locust tree?"

"I can't remember. He'd tell me and Chris stories real fast."

"And you never left the house?"

"Not far back as I can remember."

"Did you ever go to school?"

"Ont-anh. Aunt Cherie would teach me on an old speak n' spell and the computer. She taught me the a-b-c's. Sometimes Uncle Rey-Rey tried to teach me. But a lot of times I couldn't understand him 'cause he talked too fast. Aunt Cherie would read me books too. When Aunt Linda wasn't drinkin' too much, she'd sometimes draw with me."

"Anybody else that you would've talked about the locust tree with?"

"Uncle Rey-Rey sayed not to talk 'bout that tree 'cause it liked to make him cuss. That's how he sayed it. I ast how a tree could make him cuss. He sayed the seventeen-year locust lived underneath it. He tole me not to talk 'bout it or the locust might hear me and wake up."

"Anything else we should know about your Uncle Rey-Rey?"

"Once I tole him he was the only thing closest to a daddy I had and Aunt Cherie was closest thing to a momma before she left. Then his eyes started waterin'. He was smilin' and the tears were comin' down his scratchy hairy face 'cause he ain't shaved. Even though he was cryin' he was smilin'. I thought 'bout when the sun is shinin' but it's rainin' at the same time."

"Do you know the difference between telling a lie and telling the truth? You're not trying to get us to go easy on your uncles are you?"

"Ont-anh. It's not make believe or nicenin' things up. Aunt Cherie tole me the truth was like rain and dirt and usin' the bathroom. Lyin' was like tryin' to nicen things up."

Mantle looked up at him and indicated he was done. He stood up. Spring left the room with the nuns. The agents remained sitting. Mantle addressed him, "I would like to ask you a few follow-up questions."

He sat back down. "Certainly."

"You've taken care of the girl since the night after the fire?"

"She was placed in the orphanage after the fire. The nuns deal with the day to day management of raising the orphans until we can hopefully find placement for them."

"When did Spring get here?"

"It was within days after the fire. After she'd been cleared and released from the hospital. I'm not sure exactly how long she stayed there. Probably within three or four days."

"And she has stayed here continuously?"

"She has. She began kindergarten this fall."

"How long until you expect to place her?"

"We're in the process of taking applications for foster parents. We do the best we can with limited resources. It's really a shabby substitute for the structural reinforcement and attention a family unit and home can provide a child. There are several dozen children and only three of us running things. We look for responsible placement as soon as possible."

"Any prospects on who her new parents will be?"

"We've got a few going through the application process. It's confidential at this stage. A non-profit handles the screening process, which can take months. They do a thorough background check."

"I'm curious about her ability to remember things and her honesty. Any issues?"

"Not that I can tell. She's usually very taciturn, especially when she first arrived here. For a while she wouldn't talk to anyone. We thought she might still be in a state of shock. She has improved quite a bit. She does seem to stand apart from the other children at times."

"Do you think that could cause her to invent things?"

"She'd probably speak more if she was doing that sort of thing. As it is, she doesn't speak much. I've never known her to lie and the nuns haven't reported any such behavior to me."

"Did she tell you anything about the tree before we found out about it?"

"Nothing specific. She's fascinated by insects. It seemed a normal fascination for a child to have."

"Does she have any trouble sleeping? Ever complain of nightmares?"

"You probably would want to ask the nuns those sorts of questions since they live here on a permanent basis and can closely observe her sleeping cycles. I meet her occasionally during the day and haven't been around much at night. When she first got here, there were some transitional issues. I think there were some bad dreams and some screaming episodes. We were worried by her silence and lack of social engagement in the beginning. When she began opening up, some of the other odd behaviors were easily forgotten. After about a month's time, she seemed to have a normal sleep schedule. She was in bed around eight or nine and waking up around six."

"Could I talk to Sister Laverne?"

"Certainly. I'll go get her."

He led Sister Laverne in. She wore plain clothes, having done away with the full habit years ago. He thought she had somewhat of a harried look to her, probably from dealing with a constant swarm of problems.

Mantle asked her, "Have you taken prime responsibility for the girl since she's been here?"

"Yes, I've been her primary caretaker. But you must understand that we share the burdens around here. Sister Marie has watched over her many times when I wasn't available. Early on I gave Spring a lot of attention."

"Did she have problems adjusting?"

"Definitely. At first, the cat made more noise than she did. We were worried for a while that there might be some serious long-term damage. There may be things that surface later, but she seems to be a relatively normal little girl now."

"How does she do in school?"

"She learns very quickly, especially considering the lack of any prior structured education. Who knows what terrible habits she could've been poisoned with? It's a miracle she can spell and has begun to read. She does seem very smart."

"Does she have any physical impairments that you're aware of?"

"She's healthy as far as I know. She's had a cold and a fever since she came out of her shell a little. It was a normal flu bug."

"What problems did she have initially?"

"She was so withdrawn and skinny. She wouldn't eat. And I think she may've been feverish at that time too. She would sometimes sweat in bed at night. The doctor checked

216

her out and prescribed over the counter pain relief, which was difficult to get her to take. After she recovered from the fire, the doctor couldn't find much physically wrong with her. He said it could be ongoing shock from a traumatic experience. She had problems sleeping initially, and she had nightmares."

"Did you stay with her at night?"

"Actually that was Sister Marie. She would have more on that. A few times I remember being woken up and having to go up to comfort her. I remember her holding her kitten once and looking out the window shaking. I led her back to bed. It was disruptive to the other children. For a while we thought we may have to move her to a more intensive care place."

"Do you know when this stopped?"

"After about a month, she got more stable at night."

"What type of imagination does she have?"

"That's hard to say. She is still relatively quiet."

"Does she ever make up stories?"

"Not that I've heard. She keeps more to herself. Anytime she talks it seems to be sincere. She isn't given to talking frivolously."

"Did she ever talk to you about a locust tree?"

"No. At least not before the discovery of the body. She showed an avid interest in insects. It must've been because of those events, which made a mark on her."

"What type of interest did she show?"

"She'd inspect them closely if she could get near them. She'd chase after crickets and try to capture them in a clear plastic cup. If she did, then she'd observe them for a while before letting them go."

"Did she ever do anything harmful to the insects she captured?"

"No. She is such a sweet creature. Who knows, maybe she'll grow into a biologist. Think of what a miracle she could be! It may be too early to be hopeful, but I'm already so proud of her."

"Is the other sister available?"

"Yes, she is. I'll go get her."

A few minutes later, Sister Marie entered the room where the agents had sat in near preternatural silence. Marie was slighter, more angular, and older than Sister Laverne. She wore the same inexpensive, casual clothing. She greeted them in her Irish tinted accent, "Good afternoon."

"Thank you for meeting with us. We understand you work the late shift here?"

"I usually stay up till ten here, then retire. There's a hired caretaker that keeps watch overnight and alerts me if there's a problem."

"Have there been any problems with Spring?"

"I awoke etch night for about a wake when she first arrived. There were some incidents over the first month. We were very worried."

"Did she talk about what was bothering her?"

"No, not relly. She had some screming fits, and when we found her she would be standing up, holding her kitten, looking out the window. She was such a shy one that she didn't talk for nerly a month. She didn't et much the first couple of wakes."

"Any indications as to why she was having these screaming fits?

"I think it's directly because of that horrible tyranny she was coming from. She was coming out of it, and it was a shock to her system. And she still has bean adjusting to a larger and more complicated world."

"Anything specific she would say?"

"It was more screming than anything. It was disruptive to the house. Save for those piercin' outbursts, she was mute during those first wakes. We thought about other options. The doctors clared her and eventually she settled down."

"Did she or has she mentioned anything to you about seeing an Uncle Cat Paw or Uncle Muffler or bikers on the property she used to live on?"

"She doesn't say much about before. Honestly, I'd like her to put those events behind her as far as possible. They all seem so negative."

"You tell her bedtime stories, right?"

"When I can."

"Does she ever make up stories?"

"She usually remains quiet when I'm reding her those stories. She sometimes asks what if questions about the stories, but I've not known her to fabricate."

"Has she told you things about her past?"

"There was mention of a playmate by the name of Chris. There was also mention of aunts and a grammie."

"What is this about a grammie?"

"I think she was referring to Reynolds's mother."

"Do you know about her?"

"We've heard some things. Men were rumored to frequent her place. A horrible drinker. She'd spend half the yer in jail. She died a yer or so ago in jail."

"Has she ever said anything specific about Grammie?"

"She talked about Grammie's things in the attic. Paintin's and what not that are all burned up now."

"Has she mentioned anything about talking to Grammie about digging, shovels, burying, or anything related to the body?"

"Not that I remember. She once described Chris's father and Edward Reynolds having a rel wild argument with their shirts off. And he yelled at them both for playing hide n' go sek around the locust tree."

Mantle ceased following up. Marie got up to leave. He leaned back in his chair.

He stood up with them. "Any more questions?"

Mantle extended his hand. "Not today."

* * *

He'd received Charles Dustin's case two weeks prior. At the first hearing, the federal judge set bail at five hundred thousand bondable given the details of Dustin's flight and near entry into Canada combined with his prior history. The investigative reports alleged trafficking and violation of RICO.

He knew Sheet. He'd seen several of his former co-workers go into private practice, but to him, none were as talented as M.L. Mark was able to handle the higher profile matters and make a living doing it. The potential peril he saw with others running a practice gave him pause. He made a middle-range income and had enough to shelter, raise, and feed his young.

Why was he contemplating getting out again? He couldn't seriously consider it anymore. He'd slid into that decision too long ago. Things were too dependent now. Was it the case? Occasionally, when feeling squeezed, he sought refuge in the hope of not being stuck with impossible to win situations. Then he would remember that was part of the trade-off: security for doing some of the less desirable work. Dustin was demanding that everything the feds were trying to pin on him be litigated to the fullest extent, especially anything to do with the alleged murder. He suspected an innate intelligence lurked somewhere underneath Dustin's sedimentary layers of misdeeds and substance abuse.

The feds were hinting about their own murder charges while letting the state focus on Reynolds. He expected they wanted to cause friction between Dustin and Reynolds. He might find himself having to work against M.L. If it came down to it, a reasonable defense would be to blame Reynolds to keep Dustin from getting convicted.

The current offer of thirty years would likely keep Dustin in federal prison for life. Dustin would be well over seventy if he lived that long. Even if there'd been a decent offer, it wouldn't have made much difference as Dustin's demands rang again in his mind's ear, "No deals!"

He'd take umbrage at the suggestion he was afraid of trial. He estimated he'd conducted close to two hundred by this point. But unnecessarily committing legal suicide or watching someone else do it didn't really appeal to him. The severity of being convicted on just one of these charges promised a heavy prison sentence. The uneasiness must've been acknowledging and committing to the mental preparation required. That effort to get mentally ready to handle what was to come had been futilely triggered in him so many times before. The initial flood of anticipation and problem spotting came with an underside of doubt of whether he could handle another.

As the day got longer and his prior experiences began congealing into hardness within him again, he began to get organized. He systematically went over his files, picking through the duties rising out of them. As he realized Dustin was making it easy to decide what to do, a firm self-concept sank in again. Some defendants would talk tough initially then crumble later under pressure from the evidence against them or from the confinement they potentially faced. Others lost interest. But he couldn't count on weakness or ambivalence manifesting itself later.

He got his head around the idea that a trial would be set. They had Dustin in the state several times over a period of years for visits of limited duration, but no drugs had been found on him. Although Reynolds may be a sketchy contact, and he wasn't sure what Reynolds might say, could they make the assumption that Dustin must've been doing something? There was ample room to attack that assumption. What would Reynolds say? He called M.L. and arranged lunch at the café.

* * *

Since arriving in custody, he maintained his indifference. The guards left him alone in his cell. He read a few books to pass stagnant time. The books he read during those first few weeks involved brainless plots of over-exaggerated valor and romance. Sap like *the steamy passion between the two was exponentially enhanced by his successful crossing of the ravine* passed through the registry of his mind unchecked. They brought him a newspaper every once and a while but not every day. He hadn't read so much on the outside. He more often had been on the move. But in the clink, there was a limit to how long he could look at the walls and how many push-ups he could do.

Although his current charges were much less violent than others on his floor, he'd been placed in the highest security level. Most on his floor were facing murder or armed robbery charges. There were a few other mouthy, disruptive ones being disciplined.

* * *

The DNA test was still pending, but he'd gotten a copy of the exhumation report and the autopsy. The body was estimated to have been buried eleven years ago. The cause of death appeared to be a gunshot, a stab wound, or a combination of the two. A bullet was found with the remains. One thing he didn't do was react to the media attention. The reporters had come to him for comments. He ignored them.

He'd visited Reynolds to go over Spring's potential testimony. "Did you and the bikers get into an argument that the girl was describing?"

"I th-think so." His stutter had been slighter, but still noticeable.

"Did it happen like she described?"

"If it was the t-time I'm thinkin' of."

"Were you high on anything at the time?"

"I's usually on m-meth, but I may've been c-comin' down a little."

"What was it about?"

"I'd rather n-not say."

"Come on now, we've been through this. How am I going to represent you?"

"It's n-not tha-that."

"What else could it be? Are you covering up for the bikers?"

"N-not really."

"Who else would you be covering for?"

"L-look, I don't wa-want to get into it, j-just defend me. H-how can they prove it wa-was m-me?"

"I am defending you, but you're not letting me. I need to know everything in order to anticipate how to proceed. If you're hiding something it could sabotage you."

"It's n-not so m-much what I know. I d-don't want to 'cuse the wrong p-people."

"So it must be the Wraiths that will come after you?"

"I d-didn't say that! L-look, why ca-can't it just show that w-we were sta-standin' 'round w-workin' in my ba-back-yard?"

He'd narrowed his eyes skeptically. "Who do you expect to believe that? They found the body in your backyard. The bikers were there, but it was where you lived and the jury will consider that critical. You're the one that'll have some explaining to do, and I'm trying to find out if there is another way than putting you on the stand. Recovering meth addicts with criminal records aren't usually deemed the most credible. There are multiple authorities investigating this now. There shouldn't be anything unusual that escapes their detection. If people are being bribed or threatened then they should find out. Has someone been threatening you in here?"

"N-no. I'm isolated. I don't interact m-much with others. But if I w-were in gen-general population somethin' m-might've happened to me."

"What is it that's giving you this scare?"

"N-nothin'. I just know th-they could r-retaliate to k-keep that hidden."

"Are you having some residual delusions? Is the medication lapsing?"

"N-no. I know what I'm 'bout. I ca-can tell you tha-that other people w-were alive when that b-body was p-put there."

"Why are you being so elusive? Come out and say it! Now's the time!"

"M-momma."

"So your mother did it?"

"I d-didn't say tha-that!"

"Good, because now she can't say anything to the contrary."

"B-but sh-she was alive then. I th-think she knew it was b-buried there."

"Did she ever tell you who was buried in her yard?"

"N-no. I d-don't even know who it is. Can y-you t-tell 'em?"

"They'll have a better idea or know soon enough as the lab tests come back. The identity of the body could no longer be an issue by the time of trial. You can tell the jury on the stand if you like. Now again, I have to be going soon, are you going to tell me what you know about how the body got there?"

"I d-don't know. B-bikers c-could've buried it there. It c-could've b-been a time when I's g-gone to M-Mobile or

N-New Arlens. B-but I didn't w-witness what happened or who p-put it there."

"But you knew it was there?"

"I's t-tole 'ventually."

"And what were the bikers doing there that time you pointed at the ground?"

"Th-they were blackmailin' m-me. I'd tole 'em I had to ra-raise the price of m-meth. Th-they thought I's gettin' greedy. So th-they threatened they would dig up the b-body and l-leave it in the open."

"Wouldn't you have gotten rid of it though?"

"Y-yeah. Probably. B-but it was more proof th-they knew somethin' 'gainst m-me. I d-didn't want to see it and d-didn't want to have to throw it in the r-river. If I uncovered it, th-then I w-would've known f-firsthand."

"So you knew secondhand of a body, but decided to let it sit there?"

"I d-didn't see it. I'd j-just heard 'bout it."

"From who?"

"Sh-she tole me one t-time when sh-she was drunk. B-but then the b-bikers knew too. Sh-she splattered a ca-can of Na-Natch Light 'gainst the wa-wall. Sh-she'd call 'em and screamed 'bout sh-she shouldn't have let h-him do it. H-he was a goddam d-devil's ma-man. Sh-she w-went and pulled down h-her pa-paintin's from the wall in h-her workroom and gazed at it all w-wild eyed. I thought sh-she was goin' to put a h-hole through it. B-but sh-she held it up and y-yelled. Sh-she moaned and la-laughed on the floor awhile. Then la-later on I'd get that the b-bikers knew. Th-they and h-her was in on somethin' I d-didn't know. 'Specially when I's high and pa-paranoid. Th-they'd say things 'bout what was out in the yard r-right before the p-pines started. I'd g-get to thinkin' so m-much 'bout it I even 'magined I m-might of k-kilt someone and b-buried 'em there. Th-they used to mess with m-me just to see how I'd act. If it evar c-come up, then I'd b-be blamed too."

* * *

He'd gained very little information from his meetings with Dustin. No admissions or explanations, just "No deals!" Maybe lunch with M.L. would help him get a wedge into Dustin's mind. They met at the familiar café in Montgomery where they'd gone many times as public defenders. The wood floors were well worn. Open windows helped circulate grilled food smells and the tinge of smoke.

M.L. arrived and they ordered. They'd eaten many of the hot-pressed sandwiches. After the sandwiches were run through the steam press, they were soft and chewy. While waiting for the food, there were some pauses then some comments interjected about football that had nothing to do with finding out more about each other's client.

The talk turned a little more personal. Because of the distance between the two, he hadn't talked to M.L. since the engagement. He tried congratulating him, "So you're finally getting married?"

"I am. You know the average age to marry here must be in the twenties somewhere. At least for the first time. For a while there, thought I might be becoming one of those stuffy and arrogantly aloof bachelors that no one knows what to do with."

"You've been showing signs of that since as long as I've known you at least."

Smiling back, "Well at least I've identified it. Maybe I can do something?"

"Why change? You've had a good run so far."

"Sylvia's a real beauty. Doesn't let me get away with too much. I may actually be settling into becoming a family man." Smiling, "How are your wife and kids?"

"They're alright. Tom junior is going through elementary school. The little girl is about to enter kindergarten. If you ever get to having kids, beware about how much school costs if you try sending them private. Then again you're making the big money."

"We'll see if that continues. It's not always that stable on the private side. We're planning to have the wedding next June. Taking on cases like Reynolds may drain whatever is left in my bank account."

"How is the Reynolds case handling?"

"He had to stabilize on his meds. There's a residual stutter, but otherwise he's making a lot more sense."

Their sandwiches were brought out. They paused to eat for a few minutes, commenting only on what he perceived as safer subjects. There seemed to be an unspoken agreement to defer talking about the case until they were through eating.

Once they were done, M.L. got to it. "How's the biker doing?"

"He's holding up well. So what's Reynolds saying about the corpse?"

"Can't really say for sure at this point. He's denying any part in putting it there."

"Usually a frame job is a little more subtle than that."

Smiling, "He's probably going to implicate Dustin with knowledge of the body."

"Okay."

"What about Dustin? What's he going to say?"

"Won't talk to me. So we're getting ready for trial."

"How's the evidence?"

"Not that strong. They're leveraging everything with the discovery of the body and anybody within proximity of it. Including Dustin's relationship to your client and the almost proven fact that your client was a meth manufacturer. They're trying to pit us against one another."

"Does your guy plan on taking the stand? They both have credibility issues. If we go to trial on the murder, I'm thinking Reynolds will take it."

"Dustin is a stone wall at this point."

"There's the issue of the body's identity."

"It could be a transient possibly. Even if Reynolds or my guy didn't have a hand in it, one or the other will get stuck with it."

"He's given me an explanation. It may have to come out on cross. It's still too early to talk about beyond the denials."

"So when the prosecutors come at each of us with plea deals in exchange for testimony against the other, which one of us is going to buckle?"

"It's up to our clients, don't you think?"

"We still have to advise them."

"Are you suggesting a unified front?"

"More of an agreement to no ambushes. The prosecutors will likely try to put the screws to our clients to divide us."

"Fair enough."

He stood up, wiping some bread crumbs off his pants. "As long as we understand that some things are demands of the client."

M.L. stood with him and shook his hand. "Good to see you, my friend."

* * *

Recently, he'd started reading the Bible. The concepts seemed like entering a foreign country or a place he'd been exiled from. A string of morals was discussed that had long been abandoned in any part of his thinking. He focused mainly on the older readings, believing those stories better reflected the wrath, violence, and sudden death of his world. He developed a routine of exercising in his cell, reading the Bible, eating, exercising in his cell some more, eating again, and then sleeping. He'd heard some of the jail guards joking they had a fundamentalist on their hands.

He'd been a public school kid. Before thirteen, he'd done alright. His family had been mildly religious. His mother and stepfather had attended a church, he couldn't remember which kind, and took him, his brother, and his sister. Memories of this flashed back into his consciousness as from an abyss. By twelve, he'd begun to shun the ideas there as weak and out of touch.

Eventually he dismissed it all. He'd been more docile at first. When he felt others were trying to pry into or irritate his more private side, he'd closed them out. He dropped out around the same time he'd gotten into bikes. It wasn't only the bikes that drew him in. It was the unencumbered-ness. He found in himself and developed a natural penchant for violence.

The high school he dropped out of was the third his embarrassed parents had moved him to. He was expelled from the first school for weed on his person. Then he was expelled from the second because of a parking lot brawl, when he'd beaten that snotnose into the hospital.

His stepfather would complain about how Charlie had the size to be a powerful athlete, but Charlie wasted his talents on drugs, booze, fighting, and hanging out with losers. He hadn't been involved much in team sports. He'd tried to join as an early teenager, but it seemed some false optimism incongruent to reality was being forced upon him. He hadn't needed those pseudo versions of fighting. After he dropped out from the third school, his stepfather, with his mother's consent, kicked him out of the house.

He'd stayed homeless awhile, traveling about the country on his bike. Despite all the bitterness lurking in him toward his foolish family, one thing he could appreciate his stepfather instilling in him was a work ethic. It'd been useful to him.

He'd gotten on as a prospect in one of the clubs outside Seattle. The club gave him a place to stay in exchange for some collection work and a few small-scale drug runs. He had enough to eat, drink, smoke, or snort to get by. After a few years on the West Coast, he'd run into a couple of the Wraiths. The more nomadic group eventually convinced him to switch clubs.

He'd naturally moved up the Wraiths's hierarchical structure—if one could be consistently identified. He was known to have above-average intelligence and to be a good brawler. He wasn't quite in the leader's circle, but he'd become a higher up within the club. Doing serious time was expected of a higher up now and again.

After two months in the clink this time, he'd received a letter. The letter stated in short, coded terms they couldn't bail him. They were getting hammered by the feds on multiple fronts. Some had retreated to Canada. A number were in prison. Some were dead like Muffler. A few had just disappeared. Most of the other higher ups had been forced into some quiet suburb to suffer through a menial job.

Now these ancient stories were bursting back from before adolescence and the onslaught of his hormones had placed him at odds with the world. The wholesome stories cut through some of the armor he'd built up over the years to deal with the harsh realities he'd perceived. Although he hadn't loosened his hold with regard to his legal troubles, he sensed changes on a visceral and tetonic level. He had returned to somewhere he thought he'd abandoned forever in the pursuit of the unencumbered. But in his cell, where he was completely encumbered by cinderblocks, daily regimens, chains, cuffs, buffoons with lightning sticks and rubber bullets to torment him if he stepped out of their line, he could still access that childhood world of comfort.

* * *

He wasn't completely shocked to read the report from the lab the evening before the news broke publicly. Prentice had been telling him his best guess for the last couple of weeks.

Up until his disappearance, Craig Spindle had been known as a dedicated family man type of politician with four children. The youngest, who'd been just a toddler at the time, was now sixteen years old. The oldest was twenty-four. At the time of his disappearance, Spindle had been in the middle of controversial reformatory efforts that the city council had been fighting over for months.

When Spindle disappeared, there was speculation into some scandals, but no mistresses or corruption had been revealed. After he'd been gone a year, his widow Julie moved the family up to Birmingham, where she'd grown up. Prentice had gone up to talk to her before the identification news and reported she still seemed upset. She'd told Prentice that Craig had done fifth-grade homework the night before with the second oldest. Craig had grilled them a steak family dinner that night. There had been no reason for him to leave.

Although Prentice could be disorganized at times in his retellings, he believed in Prentice's instincts. When the lab report proved Prentice right, he felt less affected than Whaley had sounded over the phone. He heard Prentice's enthusiastic laughter, "I told you, man. That wasn't any random transient."

He saw the complexion of the case changing. A transient buried in the backyard wouldn't have boded well. The possibilities had increased. But he wasn't giddy. There was still the nearly indomitable fact of the body's location.

The announcement had been printed between Thanksgiving and Christmas. Dental records hadn't worked in reviewing a match because the skull discovered had no teeth in it. Part of the skull appeared damaged where sharp, specific blows were suspected to have dislodged the teeth. The skull had splintered from the hole where the federal marshal's pick had entered. The mandible was smashed. The lab had matched DNA samples collected from Spindle's brother and two of his children to confirm a match with an undoubtable degree of certainty.

People were sensitively preoccupied with holidays and family. Extra horror and attention had been paid to the discovery. He couldn't expect to get level-headed jurors at the time. Based on the new evidence, additional investigation was needed. They continued the case into the new year.

* * *

He tried adapting his theories to how this implicated Cat's Paw. There was an obstinate strain in the sheriff's office that stuck to Reynolds being the murderer with no need to go further. Some of the federal agents adopted the same approach, but he thought that was myopic. His supervisor had ordered him to investigate completely.

They'd traveled to find the owner of the chemical processing plant, Winston Hanslow, who was often in Atlanta. After he was located, they arranged to meet with him in the lounge of a luxury hotel. Wide-open spaces greeted them, as well as fragrant plants in the moist air, an environment of ease that beckoned one to vacation.

He learned Hanslow had been in Atlanta for the last three weeks brokering an extension for operations in Alabama. Amid a contentious period with the scrutiny regarding pollution, Hanslow preferred staying away in Atlanta. He was dressed down casually for this meeting as if he'd just finished playing a round of golf. Although Hanslow was an Alabama native, he suspected the man was more comfortable now staying in a pseudo world of maximized leisure. Hanslow had straight, conservatively parted black hair, a slightly pockmarked complexion, and deep circles under his eyes. Hanslow's eyes and his adjustments in his chair conveyed an intelligence of sorts or at least a calculating and crafty manner. He was on the chunky side, with an undented tan.

"How many plants do you own?"

"There's the plant on the outskirts of the city. One in northeast Alabama and one down in Baldwin County. Three outright. I own parts in Georgia and Mississippi too."

"The business has been profitable to you?

Something in Hanslow's raspy voice reminded him of a blade churning into wood. "Undoubtedly. Even were things to go completely sour in these current negotiations, which I don't think they will, we have a bright outlook for all the companies. That is if the govenmint does what's right and lets us keep operatin' costs at a reasonable level. But why talk 'bout my interests? Don't you want to ask me if I murdered the councilman eleven years ago?"

"Did you?"

"I don't think I'd be so calm and comfortable talkin' 'bout it if I'd the slightest idea what happened to that poor boy. I couldn't live with myself if I had."

He found himself revolted by Hanslow's fat neck that bulged at the sides when he spoke. He expected Hanslow's neck would eventually fill in more in the front, giving him a prominent double chin. Hanslow's distended gullet suggested the capacity to swallow large objects, making his oily pronouncements seem disingenuous. "They found him on a drug attic's property? Seems case closed to me. But you guys have to write it all up. I understand."

"Wouldn't you have been motivated to see him dead?"

"Dead? Well, that's goin' too far." He thought Hanslow's neck suggested otherwise. "We've a right to our own views. Just 'cause we disagreed doesn't mean I'd have anything to do with wantin' him dead."

"Did you talk to anyone that might've?"

"I heard a lot of people complain 'bout and even cuss him. But we're all civilized men. We may try to out negotiate you or be properly represented in govenmint, but we're certainly not interested in the messy underworld of contract killin'!" Hanslow's neck jiggled a little.

"You think it was Reynolds then?"

"In the lass couple of weeks, I's watchin' a program on that methafetamean use. That's one mean sucker. It'll rot your teeth and your brain. No tellin' what a fool'd do on that stuff. He does seem to be implicated just by the geography of the thing."

"Did you ever know Craig Spindle to hang out with meth addicts?"

Hanslow paused for a second, then a smile sliced across his face revealing a twisted front tooth. He thought Hanslow seemed pleased in being given an opportunity to say something. "Not really a reason for a person like the councilman to visit a person such as Pitchfork, is there? But he was known to go and inspect the river from time to time. He'd check it for pollution. He could've strayed onto the place while Pitchfork was in a drug rage 'nuff to kilt him. Seems perfectly plausible to me."

"Do you think it's possible Bo Caine was involved?"

Hanslow's neck pulsated as he chuckled a bit. "Why would Mr. Caine go and do a thing like that? Bo is one of, if not the strongest man in that county. Why would he have to murder anyone?"

"Because it would eat into your profits, which would then eat into his profits."

"Well, that might make an emotional appeal to those less intelligent who like to hear 'bout mudslingin' and scandal, but you've gotta give Caine more credit for brains than that. He'd 'nuff money by then to switch into any business. Why would he care even if that councilman outlawed us? Which he wasn't goin' to do anyway. He was only goin' to curtail us a bit and raise our operation costs. I might understand that you're wantin' a better explanation than a methafetamean attic that hung out with transients murdered the councilman eleven years ago, but that's what the true headline should read. Sometimes people look for too complex an answer when it's really simply right in front of their faces. Now if Caine really wanted to do it right, why would he leave the body buried? Why not dump it in the river or incinerate it?"

"Can you tell us why those things didn't happen?"

"No, I can't, but it shows that this was more primitive, less thought out. If Caine were to go 'bout it, he'd of probably burned those bones to ash in an incinerator. It's unfortunate someone would stoop to murderin' another, but I work in a civilized occupation. Murderin' someone to protect my civil affairs would undercut some basic principles I operate on. The business is there to provide jobs so men aren't drawn into that sort of thing. If the business goes under, then so be it. Other ways to make money can be discovered."

"Does Caine have easy access to an incinerator?"

"Hell if I know. He's got access to most of what he wants, though. And if he wanted to find out a way to do it, he could've, or easily paid for it."

"You've thought about this a bit, haven't you?"

"It's intriguin'. I've known 'bout that sorry meth attic Pitchfork for as long as he's been alive. Don't know him personally. Just by reputation and what I'd heard 'bout the bad stock he come from."

"What do you mean by that?"

He watched Hanslow pause a moment while his eyes seemed to refocus or recoil. Hanslow's neck lagged in coming to rest after his facial features readjusted. A crimson blush ran up Hanslow's neck into his cheeks, "I's referrin' to his momma. The drunk whore from up north, which she was. She died in jail a couple of years ago. No wonder the kid was so screwed up. She rode in like a blight upon the land. Hopefully now that'll end when Pitchfork gets convicted of this murder and we don't have to let 'em eat away at our society anymore."

"Did you ever meet his mother?"

"Not that I remember. Not personally at least. Think I saw her in the town square once all ragged out and shoutin' crazy. They called the police on her and halled her off to jail as they should've. Now if you gentlemen will excuse me. I need to be goin'." Hanslow stood and abruptly walked off across the white-tiled floor.

When they got back to Alabama, they stopped by to talk to local law enforcement, who mostly praised Caine. The chief sheriff, Baisley, defended who he called Maiden county's most successful citizen, "Caine's been given a well-off inheritance. Instead of spoilin', he put it to use to make the city profitable. He was able to sustain us growin'. We wouldn't be as big as we are without him. Of course, when you get bigger you can attract some of the undasyables. The people that need to be removed. You know 'bout this. It's on a nashenal level for y'all. You probably feel the same way 'bout those bikers as we do 'bout some of the scum that settle in here. If they don't want to play by the rules and they endanger us, then we ain't gonna cut 'em any slack. We're tired of the meth epademic. If we can show others what not to do through the example we make of him, then the law'll be workin'."

"Have you considered that others might be involved?"

"We've considered it. There's no evidence to show anybody else in the vicinity but the transients that would've come through there. That includes your biker. Someone like him might be involved."

"Do you think some of those in local industry could've set the body there to make it look like Reynolds had done it?"

"S'pose it's possible, but I don't believe it for one second. I think the councilman just stumbled into the wrong place as he was takin' a look at the river. Same as if he took a step into a nest of moccasins. They kilt him 'cause the undasyables are bred that way. The guys with the money always found a way to make their money without murderin'. Why would they risk it? Spindle may've caused 'em some loss or setbacks, but Spindle was way too speclatev a threat. There was still five votes on the council with two or three friendly to industry. It's not like they'd be shut out by him."

"Doesn't Caine own the property?"

"He'd been leasin' it to that family for years."

"Do you know if he made any personal visits?"

Baisley looked curiously at him for a moment, but then seemed to shake off whatever stalled him. "You mean whether he would stop by to check out the property in person? No. No evidence of that. I think his property manager would've handled that."

"Do you know Caine personally?"

"Yes, I do. I don't see him that often, but he's hard to miss."

"Do you know him to have a temper?"

"Temper? Well, I wouldn't say he'd have any more temper than anyone else with as much drive as what he's accomplished would have. Sure he can get fired up, but I've only heard 'bout it."

"Anyone ever called the cops on him?"

Baisley looked askance for a moment. "Ah, not that I remember too well. He may've gotten into a bar fight once in a while when he was younger."

"Did your friendship with him or his family influence decisions on whether to file charges against him?"

"Well, no. I's only involved once when I's just startin' as a deputy. At the time I didn't really have what I'd call a friendship with him. I knew him. But we didn't cut nobody no breaks. The evidence probably wasn't there. A drunken bar fight situation. We didn't cut him no speshial favors."

"Have you ever told a deputy not to file a charge on him?"

"I've tole deputies not to file reports for charges when there's no good evidence to support the charge or when it doesn't seem like the public would be served by filin'. I don't remember any specifics 'bout Caine. Do you guys have somethin' on Caine I don't know 'bout?"

"We're investigating like you are."

"'Cause I don't see why I'm the one bein' examined when there's no other evidence linkin' Caine to that body 'sides that he owns that land and was rentin' it to 'em."

"Don't you expect your deputies and detectives to be cross-examined?"

"'Ventually."

* * *

He thought of Sylvia as he got in line for another visit to Reynolds. The wedding was six months away in June. Back stepping through his memory, he tried to remember years as a bachelor that had proceeded in a lackadaisical fashion. There'd been weekends he slept longer and engaged in more aimless diversion. Now a structure had been imposed, but certainly he was less lonesome.

The attractiveness and assurance that Sylvia brought to mind shone brightly in his conscious again, lighting up and sparking new sources of energy and drive. His work burden appeared lighter. He imagined he required less sleep and food. Even if they went out during the week, he'd work just as tirelessly and thoroughly the next day. Some of the negativity he'd been prey to seemed to have been banished to a diminishing polar cap in the wake of a massive sun. Any sacrifice of freedom was an easy decision.

Whatever difficulty his analytical impulses had in defining her sway, he couldn't deny, discount, or blunt its effects. Some courtroom participants had noticed and commented on his added enthusiasm. He imagined the others with the sharp, unfriendly looks probably thought he must be experiencing a blinding optimism. They'd preferred to kill it and disabuse anyone of being tempted to believe in such false hope. But to their further disappointment, whatever he had a hold of seemingly made him immune to their attempts to drag him down into any feeling less than the active and moving winning of something.

The internal brightness contrasted again with these cages of frozen spite and hatred choking the stale jail air. When he got to Reynolds, he had to struggle to put the gladness down. He didn't want to appear out of sync with the gravity of Reynolds's situation. Recognition of a bizarre and wondrous occupation zipped through his mind. "Now there's been rumors of this. Do you know whether Bo Caine might've had relations with your mother?"

"I d-don't know."

"By putting you up in a house on a substantial property, do you think he was easing his conscious?"

"H-his property manager dealt with us mostly. M-momma had m-money from the inheritance. Sh-she used it to pay rent and then I used it to pa-pay rent."

"Did the rent increase or decrease when you took over payments?"

"D-didn't change from what I know."

"If Bo Caine were your father, then that could explain why he let you stay on that property. He could've probably put it to use in more profitable ways?"

"Y-yes."

* * *

He approached the federal detention center with a nagging, nauseating loss of hope. He'd been dwelling on the negativity that permeated his day-to-day practice when focusing on superficial matters. Although he'd gone through all that school, passed all those mentally straining tests, and gotten under those staggering loans, some cops with high school diplomas made about the same as he did. It was too late to change career tracks. He had the kids and a house payment. There was the beginning rebellion of his teenager. His wife wasn't satisfied with what they had. She said she was happy with whatever he could bring in. But he sensed she didn't mean it. He believed the sharp tones and complaints toward him were caused by that underlying friction.

He stopped himself. What was he doing? It had to be Dustin's case. The negativity was radiating out from it, renewing a familiar, depressive track of well-worn concerns. Recognizing it helped him summon up the remedy to it or at least a partial one. It didn't make him feel instantly better, but it'd gotten him through before.

He recalled a list with militaristic discipline. He had been given responsibility for challenging cases that any lawyer would find hardship and stress with. His wife did support him and she'd never abandoned him on the important matters. He'd given his kids much more than what he'd seen in a lot of clients' lives. They had as good a chance as any to turn out fine. He didn't make as much as a private attorney could, but he made enough to get things done. He did have equity in a home with a family. But repeating these thoughts didn't do much to ease his mood.

He was allowed to meet Dustin privately in a visitation room as long as Dustin's legs were chained. The religious turnabout had surprised him. Dustin carried the Bible with him now to their meetings. Dustin read, or at least hunched over, the book. Occasionally Dustin would cite an obscure, cryptic-sounding verse. Dustin wouldn't respond to direct questions involving his visits to the property. A rendition of questions bounded off the walls of the clinical and antiseptically white visitation room with an unclean air.

From what he'd heard, the guards weren't having many problems with Dustin. Dustin remained on high-security detail because of his prior fugitive status, but he hadn't been violent inside. Dustin's arms were allowed to remain free during the visit. There was a call button for help.

After news of the body's identity broke, he included questions on the councilman. Dustin presented the same stare with arms crossed. Occasionally Dustin would issue a quote from the book of Proverbs or Jeremiah and then return to more stiff silence. In court, Dustin didn't object to requests for continuances.

He'd become concerned the judge might lose patience without any visible progress soon. An opportunity had presented itself through the liaison of the local Baptist preacher Wilcox. In his occasional visits to the federal detention center, Wilcox had happened upon Dustin. He and Wilcox met with Dustin the next day and started talking Bible.

During the visit, Dustin showed a look he remembered seeing in some fervent congregations. It was a look full of emotional, ostentatious, almost violent worship. He wasn't sure he'd be able to reach anywhere behind that gleam. Dustin turned that gleam on him, "I'd found some others to run with, but they were a dying breed. What's left of them had to go on living. These cinderblocks and metal keeping me penned in here are manmade limits that don't really compute on the eternal scale. The chains don't matter. Man can't get over it sometimes. They got to lock you up to show their power. To show they got a patch here that they got control over."

* * *

In February, due to the expanding amount of business being referred to him, he advertised for an associate position. After screening a hundred applications, conducting fifteen first interviews and four second interviews, he decided on Latanya Drake. She was considered one of the brightest in the federal prosecutor's office in Montgomery. They'd met working against one another.

She would be expected to handle some of his less serious cases, misdemeanors and lower level felonies. She expressed a desire to sit second chair in Reynolds's case if it should go to trial. Soon after hiring her, she helped him draft a motion to compel a DNA sample from Bo Caine.

At the in camera motion hearing, Miller questioned, "What about the man's privacy?"

He'd expected resistance. "Your Honor, privacy is outweighed in this case by the important interest of my client in demonstrating to the trier of fact that the true owner of the property where the body was found is brought before them to face our questioning. It is part of the confrontation right and essential to our theory of the case."

"Do you have more than speculation? We can't get into taking everyone's DNA in the off chance they might be implicated. Shouldn't law enforcement be having these discussions and not you?"

"Understood, Your Honor. But the man we're seeking DNA from owned the actual property where the body was found. Mr. Caine is known to have had major disagreements with the deceased. He's implicated by motive in the councilman's death. Caine had something to lose in stature if a familial connection to Reynolds was revealed."

"Well, there are several persons in town who may have disliked the politics of the deceased. Are we to take all of their DNAs too?"

"No, Your Honor. Caine is tied to the case in a peculiar manner. I have set forth his connection. He owns the property, he's possibly the father of Reynolds, his well-known antagonism, and his motive based on financial gain."

"What's the state's position?"

"What important relevance does this have to the case? The defense hasn't shown that, even if this were true, how this would get past inadmissible other suspect evidence. It is too speculative to implicate Caine just by virtue of a blood relation."

"And Mr. Caine's counsel?"

"We object wholeheartedly. This would be a gross invasion of privacy instigated by a desperate and crude attempt to deflect blame and draw an innocent, law abiding, upstanding citizen into this morass of misery for the county. They've shown no credible connection. At best this is a flimsy, speculative theory which my client's privacy interest outweighs."

"Anything else from defense?"

"It's our main theory of the case, Your Honor."

246

"Based on what's before me today, I don't see enough to order a DNA test."

* * *

The idea came to him as he put on clothes that day, a casual outfit composed of an untucked, loudly colored, tropical button-down and a pair of jeans. His wife was still asleep. The clothes were still slightly wrinkled. He thought he detected a faint odor to them, but nothing intolerable.

He'd already showered and was looking in the mirror, checking himself out, swabbing his ears when he thought of it. For several days now, he'd spent odd hours trying to track Caine. His target stayed holed up in his mansion most days. When Caine did come out for lunches or meals, they were at sporadic and random times. The man usually dined at one of three high-end restaurants.

He couldn't get into one of the three because he didn't have membership to the country club. He did have a suit that might pass muster in the other two places.

That afternoon, he observed Caine leave his office in the SUV. He tailed him to a pro shop. He learned the sandwich guy had overheard Caine's later dinner plans. He followed Caine to make sure that he did in fact stop at the restaurant then he left to change clothes. He figured he had about thirty minutes.

He returned in his suit. As he went into the restaurant, he was stopped at the entry and asked aggressively about how many he'd be dining with. He answered two. The hostess told him without reservations he'd have to wait for a table. He kept out of sight in the lobby as best he could. If

Caine or one of his hanger-ons came through, they would probably recognize him in connection with M.L. He kept the brim of his hat low and tried reading some papers. He'd expected a wait in the lobby, but it'd been five minutes longer than even his longest estimates.

Finally, two tables opened around the same time. On his request, the hostess led him to one on the other side of the restaurant from where Caine was seated. He maintained a visual of Caine. He ordered water. Now he experienced a reversal of anxiety in wanting Caine to leave so he wouldn't find himself in the awkward situation of not being able to afford a high-priced meal. He would have to stall somehow.

After stretching the bread and water fifteen more minutes, he watched Caine get up to leave. An obsequious troop of restaurant men came to give Caine his coat and escort him out while profusely thanking him.

He got up from his table and walked as naturally as he could. As he got close to the other table, his peripheral vision saw Caine turning back from his exit into the lobby. He adjusted quickly, going around several tables in a zigzag fashion then took a right down the hall to the restrooms as Caine and another of his party returned to the table.

He watched from the edge of the hall to the bathroom. He saw the man holding up a pair of leather gloves to Caine. If they turned around, he would be easily seen. As he watched them talk, he could see the busser clearing napkins and glasses off the table. The items were mixed together with others from the party. He lost confidence in getting a good sample. He thought of bribing the busser, but he only had a little cash. He wouldn't want such an attempt to backfire so he made his way slowly back to his seat.

After they'd been gone a few minutes, he informed the nonplussed waiter that it looked like he'd been stood up. After receiving a condescending and incredulous stare, he left him a five-dollar bill. In an awkward exit, he uncomfortably realized that he might be unable to repeat this performance again.

Another week elapsed. That morning he looked through the clothing hanging is his closet then donned a faded polo shirt and a pair of wrinkled khakis. Despite Caine's erratic schedule, Caine did go to the golf course on a regular basis. Caine alternated between playing at the country club on the weekends and playing at a public course closer to his office during the week. The traffic on the public course was stifling on the weekends. But on the weekdays, it was typically fluid. Caine usually went on Tuesdays. After adjusting his ball cap, he headed to Caine's office.

Around ten, he saw Caine leave. He followed him to the course. He waited in his car until he could see Caine and three others drive their two carts up to the driving range near the starting hole. He positioned himself in a way that overlooked the driving range. He brought up his small binoculars to focus on the bag Caine had strapped into the back of the cart he drove. He got a close look at the design of a towel. It looked attached to the bag. He didn't think he'd be able to get away with snatching that.

He glanced at the type of clubs Caine was using. Those grips would work although Caine was wearing a glove on one hand. Those clubs would most likely be staying close to Caine. His idea distinguished itself as he dialed in on the tees Caine was using. He couldn't see the specific type of tee. From where he was sitting, even through his binocs, they looked like white splinters thumb-tacked into the ground. Two of the others were using white tees as well. He dismissed the problem for the moment and hurried to get registered for a round. M.L. had always covered him.

As he observed Caine's party line up at the front nine, he thought of a possible hitch in getting behind Caine. Sometimes they would alternate persons between starting on the front or back greens. He made sure he played the front nine first, offering an explanation that he played those better and that he might be called away on a personal emergency. He paid in advance for nine holes and a cart.

He stalled on driving his cart over until he saw they were well out onto the fairway of the second hole and getting ready for what looked like approach shots. He'd been unable to see the type of ball Caine was using. It looked like Caine bent over to pick up his tee from the second hole driving area. He teed up his shot on the first hole. There was no one in between them.

He knew how to get the ball out there, but his accuracy wasn't great. For the first couple of holes, he was chasing his ball on and off the fairway. This allowed him to stay a safe distance back from the foursome. At each tee-off area, he examined for discarded tees. He found a couple of broken ones and placed them in a plastic bag he'd brought with him. He couldn't be sure which ones were whose. His break came at the par three fourth hole. The distance to the fifth hole was shorter than previous holes.

With his binocs, he was able to discern Caine going to his bag and unzipping a side pouch, pulling out a square, bulky item. He watched Caine produce a bag of tees. They didn't appear as white as the other tees, some off-white color. Caine drove his ball on the fifth then pulled up his tee. After they'd moved to the sixth, he surveyed the tee area. He only saw purely white or brightly colored tees either flung in splinters or driven like nails into the ground. He was sure these weren't the ones he'd seen Caine using.

He watched as Caine prepared for his drive on the sixth hole by deliberately pushing one of his tees into the ground with an ungloved thumb. After driving, Caine didn't reach down to pick up this tee. He tried to eyeball how close Caine was to the edge of the tee area to narrow off the vicinity. He waited for them to clear the hole.

When he arrived to the sixth tee area, he went to where he estimated Caine had hit from. He found a wood-colored tee snapped in half a little ahead of where he thought Caine had teed off.

He collected it with a pair of tweezers. He didn't want to rely exclusively on it so he continued to trail them. The seventh hole was another par three. He didn't see Caine use a tee there. On the eighth he found another wooden tee driven into the ground. This one had a monogrammed green *C* on its side. Then on the ninth, he got another tee chipped in half on the top, but relatively intact. He put these in a separate bag then slowly sauntered his way through the ninth. He saw the foursome enter the clubhouse. After they disappeared inside, he quickly parked his cart, gave the key to one of the kid attendants running the carts then hurriedly made his exit.

As he was about to enter the parking lot, he was startled by someone yelling, "Sir! Sir!" in his direction. Not wanting any attention, he ignored these calls and kept walking with his beat-up golf bag toward his car. The voice behind him was persistent and gaining ground. A wave of tingling anxiety coursed through him. As he was leaning over to pop his trunk, he heard the person much closer so he turned around. He was facing the cart attendant. "Sir, I didn't want you to forget this." The attendant handed him his binoculars. With adrenaline high, he thanked him and drove off.

* * *

He listened to Prentice rightfully boast of ingenuity in obtaining the samples. He wasn't sure if the private labs were strong enough to detect what might be small trace amounts, but he'd submit the samples anyway. They talked about other angles on the case. He'd been wondering about Judith Reynolds. Her date of death had been confirmed by the records department. There were no other persons locally who knew her that well.

He wanted to track down John and Chris Screed, but they had such flimsy information on them. It wasn't certain those two would have helpful testimony. There were many contractors in both New Orleans and Florida. He couldn't spare Prentice to go chasing around the coast.

They had a capacity and competency hearing coming up mid-month to address whether Spring could testify. It sounded like she'd recovered from whatever she needed to recover from.

To further the certainty of a jury trial, Feld had been taking a non-negotiable stance. Reynolds would have to plead to the murder to avoid it. There'd been a hint that some of the charges surrounding the drug fire might be lowered or possibly even dropped, but either way, they were seeking life without parole, and the manufacturing charge was staying. He found Feld simply unwilling to discuss anything but murder for the body. He'd expected at least an offer of murder two given their theory of a rage killing. There was no reason for him not to prepare for trial.

The separate federal and state forensics teams were coming to their own conclusions. Both had found a bullet with the skeleton and what little material remained of the decayed flesh. Both determined what type of bullet was found with the skeleton, but neither had a way of pinpointing the gun. The bullet would fit a pistol. The bullet's location in the upper torso was not typical of a self-inflicted wound. Suicide had been ruled out. Other trauma such as flesh wounds or contusions had long since disappeared.

He read divergent reports over the missing jaw components. What was left of the lower jaw had broken to pieces. The upper jaw was toothless as well and fragmented. The state expert opined a shovel likely caused this damage. By reconstructing and matching the curvature of the remaining skull with the normal impact of a shoe or boot driving down a normally sharp shovel, the state expert found similar and consistent forces had fractured the upper jaw. Smooth arcs marked where the teeth had been.

The fed expert came to the slightly different conclusion that the blunt object could've been any number of things. She believed the skull would've been less intact had a shovel been used.

Both agreed it was inconclusive as to when the teeth were removed. It was possible that the jaws were altered contemporaneously with the death. The state expert believed that all of the teeth could've been dislodged by a shovel. The fed expert opined that a pair of pliers or a wrench may have been used to get out some of the back molars.

As far as timing, the fed expert estimated the blunt object had been applied after the bullet entered the body, possibly much later. She reasoned that a person alive or conscious couldn't withstand the pain to keep from thrashing about as the teeth were removed.

After making their separate but similar investigations, they both concluded the same thing as to cause of death. Most likely death by gunshot wound to the torso, probably rupturing the aorta or the heart. He set down the reports. The conclusions from the different labs tended to support the theory of whom they were trying to convict.

* * *

He continued to capitalize. He imagined the stench of corruption wafting heavily through public opinion as he indirectly stoked the idea that Spindle had been killed while standing up to local industrial powers. Sentiment against the inordinately wealthy in the community found its way into influencing discussions, shaping them, even redirecting words and gestures with a distinct disgust toward how things were proceeding in the city's government. He described how local industry had become an entrenched foe of the people. Even in more mainstream camps, given the turmoil and potential scandal, his remarks didn't appear as offensive as they might once have.

He had the support of the crooked-tooth poor with their tin roofs on the outskirts. Some of those would barely be able to read enough of the ballot to distinguish one from the other. Educated elite supporting the incumbent joked that they better have a picture ballot for these illiterates. But the outliers knew his name and were going to vote for him.

Brandy was one of his stronger, more moderate allies, who was also connected peripherally to law enforcement. Brandy'd made news through another generous example in foster parenting the girl saved from the fire. He imagined wondrously positive energy in a dark cloud of negativity, forming like a lightning bolt. Whatever positive ripples flowed out from the fireman joining him, his bid gained traction.

He saw the incumbent receding further inward and backward, becoming more misshapen and vague, seemingly absent from public view. He was charged up, but he knew that the opponents, his enemies, would be tenacious. They were deeply rooted in the community. His movement could be like a breeze to it. With their money, they could reconfigure and swat him down in a week's time.

* * *

He'd spent the winter carrying out his liturgical duties and making an earnest effort at self-improvement. At moments, he'd reflected wryly that this undying, reoccurring need to cleanse or improve himself might be better categorized as an ailment. More guilt attached to that thought, leading to a circular winding of internal discomfort. Most times, it was nothing completely unbearable.

But when it seemed so, he'd pace, drink wine, or exercise to chase away specters of failure and meaninglessness. His pattern of identify, pray, and release worked out most details, but the release part seldom came full force like he'd seen the Pentecostal televangelists claim as saved ones fell back in writhing ecstasies. Those moments when he felt like a non-believing fraud living off of charity or guilt, he'd sinned like all the others. What difference did degree really make?

Self-flagellating moments reliably returned after he'd given into less than worthy thoughts and actions. He'd compare himself to some of the prisoners he visited or parishioners whose confessions he'd heard. After slogging through the painful sadness, he imagined looking forward with an undistracted conscience. Then he'd be thankful for the ability and opportunity to scrub his inviolable set of scruples clean with meticulous scrutiny.

He maintained his jail visits, but he refrained from seeing Reynolds. Now, weighed with the uplifting news of the fireman's foster parenting of the girl, he felt responsible for letting Reynolds know her fate. He found himself again on the way to the jail, this time with a long black trench coat covering his cassock. His dress and appearance didn't contrast with the cold and sprinkling weather as much as it had during the past summer.

When he saw Reynolds, the sores were gone with only a few scars left to remember them by. Reynolds must've had some dental work down as well. Gaps and rotted teeth weren't as noticeable. Reynolds's hair remained short, just above a buzzed level. Not only did Reynolds physically appear better, but his eyes seemed more cognizant and alert. Reynolds's features bore the light of a sane man.

After telling him he looked much better, Reynolds was more receptive than last time. "Th-they've been 'llowin' me into the common area to r-read the papers. Most of the t-time they're a day b-behind. I seen 'bout the body and wh-who it was."

He brushed this off. "Talk to your lawyer about it. I'm not sure we should discuss the case. I'm not sure what's privileged. I don't want to be put in a position of becoming a witness."

Reynolds blurted out, "I don't know wh-who my fa-father is."

Although Reynolds had led a reprehensible life, he couldn't prevent a fleeting moment of pity for the man. Reynolds had been given a less than adequate mother and father figure and had become a scarred drug addict. But Reynolds was clean now, sitting in jail with his mental deficiencies medicated. He began to stagger in his thoughts at a new concept emerging, but it wasn't quite visible to him yet. It reminded him of watching light rise up on eastern peaks at dawn, not giving a full glance yet of the source.

"I came here to tell you that Spring is going to be placed with a family soon. The fireman who saved her has a family and home for her. Their application to be foster parents has been approved."

"Tha-that's good." He watched Reynolds look down for a second. "H-her momma started sh-shootin' meth again 'bout a year after h-her birth. Then she took off l-leavin'."

He let pass by what struck him as a slight unsavory flavor of mawkish melodrama. He tried not to judge this creature expressing a foreign reality. And through the stutters, he began to see what was trying to be communicated. Her presence must've transfigured the negatives, even for the bikers, drawing positives out of them as they played good-naturedly with the girl, lifting her into the air by her armpits in a sunny back yard. It could've been gleeful in that light-filled moment as she giggled, a yellow-haired jewel shining through the prickly, vicious thorns of misfits. And that band of shunned outcasts must've been thankful for that one redemption, almost solemn about it, as it would've been one of the only sanctified areas they all remained dedicated to preserving. They must've tried to keep her from losing her precious, virtuous qualities that they lacked words for in their barbaric tongues.

He recognized what he couldn't distinguish a moment ago over those distant, dark, cold peaks in his mind's eye. Those peaks represented the assuredness of Reynolds's guilt, mountains of evidence that couldn't be moved. He realized how automatically skeptical he'd been at any demonstration of innocence by Reynolds and how quickly he would've cast a guilty vote had he been chosen to judge. And now the light that was rising up was the concept that this pitifully twisted and fragmented man may not have murdered.

* * *

He'd been in touch with thick-glassed Wilcox. The preacher had been impressed by Dustin's familiarity with the Bible. Through the winter, Dustin's body had hardened, and his mind had apparently cleared. They'd been able to go over the details of transporting meth. He was prepared to go to trial on it, but the more serious implications of Spindle's bones still loomed over them.

A few days after Wilcox's last visit, he went again to the detention center. He found a serious Dustin sitting in a plastic chair in his jail clothes, with folded arms, staring. It'd been over four months since he'd been assigned the case. For the first time, Dustin told what he knew of the body.

* * *

The murder trial was scheduled for April, only a month away. Whaley had called him that morning and scheduled lunch the next day. He figured Dustin must've revealed something. Otherwise Whaley wouldn't have wasted time calling his cell. He was used to Whaley understating most things. He cancelled another appointment and scheduled to meet Whaley.

He arrived at the same café in Montgomery. Whaley was smiling. After they ordered, Whaley explained, "Dustin says Caine's the one. And that he had nothing to do with the murder."

"Bo Caine?"

"Yes. He says that Reynolds's mother told him."

"He's had access to papers, right? So he's had time to think this over and come up with a story. Besides her being dead."

"All good anticipation of what the prosecutor will cross about."

"It'll have to be obvious before the state office will charge Caine. The feds might charge him, but the state won't do it based only on what you've told me. I can see Feld brushing it off now as a long-delayed explanation. Caine's practically immune locally. There's some honest deputies that might have the integrity to stand up against it, but the ones higher up are loyal to him."

* * *

He'd entered the final stages of preparation. The methamphetamine case had been pushed back.

But in April, after the recently revealed fact of a ninety percent similarity in DNA between Bo Caine and Reynolds, Alcorn Caine passed away in a Birmingham hospital due to liver and heart complications. Prentice hadn't been able to obtain a sample from Alcorn while he'd been dying. There'd been a security guard at Alcorn's Birmingham hospital room.

According to their theory of Bo Caine's involvement, owning the property where the body was discovered, the profit motive, and the increased familial link, he'd prevailed this time over the prosecutor's and Caine's attorney's objection. He'd been able to convince Miller to allow him to obtain a DNA sample from Alcorn's corpse. This caused another delay in the trial.

* * *

He'd discussed whether to bring Caine in for more questioning once he'd heard about the initial link. He knew Caine had money, but Caine was tied to the land and had all his political connections. It would be difficult for Caine to leave those behind.

After seeing results showing a paternal match between Alcorn Caine and Edward Reynolds, he grew more frustrated. He'd never wanted Caine, but now he was discovering an obligation after the fact. But just on the cusp of gathering enough to seriously pursue the suspect, Caine slipped across borders on a plane.

Something could have been done, something to block Caine, but he was left like a gawking motorist in a vehicle passing the carnage of a roadway accident that could've been averted. On an internal ledger stored somewhere in the basement of his consciousness things weren't reckoning up correctly. Even with all his perceptibility and the regalia of past accomplishments, letting Caine escape seemed to leave a soft spot where there should've been marble. The immovable failure drained him.

* * *

Because the murder trial and the wedding were now both scheduled in June, he and Sylvia decided to postpone the wedding until August before she finalized the planning. He suspected the heavy load of his cases might be taking a toll on their relationship. He took her to the finest restaurants he could find. She expressed to him at one of those dinners that she couldn't fully comprehend why he spent so much time on a case that wasn't paying him for all the extra work and stress.

They'd gotten into a few arguments over whom to invite. There weren't many from his side. His father was dead. Sylvia got along with his mother, but she didn't care for some of his lawyer friends. He relented to whatever was required to appease her. Beautiful and eight years younger, she could be one of his last chances. While he told himself he trusted her, doubts had festered. Her slow response to a phone call or a text could cause him to conjure up scenarios of why it couldn't work and why he should get it over with. But after wrestling with it and becoming exhausted by it, she would contact him as if there'd never been anything to worry about. He became convinced that his line of work made him neurotic. He wasn't sure if it was reversible. The neuroses helped him to be diligent and effective, but he'd seen that inclination wreak havoc in others' personal relationships.

Sometimes there were no issues to identify. It was only his well-honed mind working overtime. Those mental hunts would come up empty because the issues were self-created, deriving from powerful fears. They were self-defeating, turning in to answer themselves. He couldn't make it into a game, something competitive with tallies capable of being measured. It wasn't to be a shrewd negotiation. There were exchanges that heightened it and kept it thriving, but these were less definable and more lackadaisical, casual, and independent of a strict time line of captured months together. He could try to rationalize it and make it linear, but he was beginning to realize or at least suspect that it defied such constraints.

He believed he had a high tolerance for uncomfortable or painful situations. In her presence, worries and concerns of the previous day would disappear and become inconsequential, demonstrating the transitory nature of his overactive mind. There would be plenty of legitimate issues or differences for them to compromise on without his mind creating more to work on. He told her he was confident the case would be done by summer's end.

* * *

Marshals had picked up John Screed from a contracting job in New Orleans. Bail had been set for charges of trafficking in narcotics and contracting without a license. Thinking of leverage on Cat's Paw, he met Screed and his assigned counsel in the interview room.

"Did you ever run across a tree with locusts on it?"

"My son got him mad one day for foolin' 'round there. Pitchfork was high on speed and hollered at him. We thought he was a little psycho from the speed. I don't remember it too much. Like I sayed, we'd stay high there a good bit. Sometimes it got crazy and I'd get ready to leave. They'd get 'bout where I thought they'd claw our throats out."

"What we're looking for is a witness. Are you going to testify?"

"What do you want with me anyways? I's tryin' to make a livin'. He sold stuff. I saw Cat's Paw and Muffler come through there. They'd get shipments from him. They were the ones involved in movin' meth, is that what you want me to say? I just stopped there 'cause I could and I'd get high with 'em. But I wouldn't sell none of it. I could do 'nuff busy work to keep Chris and me fed."

"Did Edward Reynolds ever talk about a murder?"

"Not an actual one I remember, but we'd talk 'bout other people gettin' kilt."

"What about on his property? Did he say whether any-body ever got killed there?"

"Not that I remember hearin' him talk 'bout directly. I seen now in the news they found a body 'neath that tree with the locust."

"You wouldn't try to be covering for him now, would you?"

"Wouldn't evar try that. I know this here is serious fed-eral shit I'm in now. Can't say if he had anythin' to do with it bein' there."

* * *

After getting word, he went quickly to examine Screed. Right away the man struck him as a kind of bumbling tramp, probably harmless most times. Screed seemed like an unscrupulous and opportunistic weasel ready to turn with whatever kept him out of trouble or gained some benefit for him. His profession brought him into contact with this class of men, or what he would more accurately think of as a kind of spineless invertebrate. This specimen seemed able to mimic the traits of an able-bodied man with his construction know-how and his ability to fix or put to-gether things mechanically. But Screed's shiftlessness and lack of gumption eventually would reveal themselves, and Screed would be whisked along by other random and im-pulsive currents with little in the way of a rudder to steer him.

He figured that somewhere along the line, Screed must've lost his moral direction. Maybe he was born with-out it, or maybe he didn't get raised correctly. This degen-erate half-man could vocalize and possibly retain useful information, but the trouble was getting a true reading of any such information from the refractions through the opaque glass of Screed's self-interested mind. Being able to separate what was useful and credible might be difficult, but it was the only lens he had besides Reynolds and Dustin.

The assigned lawyer, Breedlove, appeared for his interview of Screed. Young Breedlove seemed timid and deferential. "Where's your son?"

"Chris? Still down in N'awlins lass I know of. Probably at one of 'em shelters or sleepin' in a half-built house."

"But isn't he eight or nine years old?"

"Just turned nine. I ain't worried 'bout him, though. Chris knows how to take care of hisself. I taught him how to survive real good. Hell, he's probably found him a nice setup by now."

"Aren't you worried about finding him?"

"Naw. He'll be able to find me. We got a few places where we can meet up. He could go back and find my parents in Miss'sippi too."

"How often have you stopped by Reynolds's place since you've known them?"

"I met Judy first. I's 'bout twenty years old and didn't have Chris yet. It must've been a little over fifteen years ago. Stopped through there 'bout once a winter or spring season on the way to the coast, and then once on the way back through to Miss'sippi in late summer. Probably went through there twice a year."

"I take it you don't want to talk about what you guys did as far as drugs?"

Screed looked over at Breedlove who nodded in a complacent manner then whispered something in Screed's ear. Screed answered, "We drank a lot. Judy'd out-drink me, though. She'd have 'bout three cases of Natch Light stored up in her fridge. She must've paid a beer 'stributor to swing by once a week to stock the fridge 'cause she never really liked goin' out in public unless she was wasted. We'd get lit up and sometimes fall 'sleep in the yard 'neath the stars and wake up achin'."

"Did Reynolds ever tell you anything about a body on the property?"

"Well, no, he didn't come right out and say anythin' direct. But I knowed somethin' was buried."

"How'd you know it?"

"His momma sayed somethin' 'bout it once. I don't remember keenly. 'Bout somethin' bein' hid 'neath the ground."

"Did you try looking for anything?"

"Yeah. One summer day I woke up with a mean hang-over. I knowed she'd come from money and thought she'd been talkin' 'bout some type of valu'bles. I's broke and wanted to take just a little to tide me over till next summer. I dug 'round the yard. Judy came up in one of her furies. Didn't find nothin' but earthworms."

"Did they ever pay you to fix things around there?"

"Naw. I'd just do it for 'em when I got bored of sittin' 'round drinkin' beer. They housed and fed me so I tried to help 'em out."

"Did they ever mention anything about Bo Caine?"

"Yeah. I think I remember Judy usin' that name like she were puttin' a hex on someone. She'd cuss his name."

"Did she make you think Reynolds had put the body there?"

"Naw, I didn't know nothin' 'bout an actual body till I come back from N'awlins. I don't keep up much with the news 'cept the hurricanes. Don't know if they'd picked up on it down there. I seen 'bout it on the way back up here."

"But you knew something was buried there?"

"I thought somethin' was buried there on 'count of what Judy sayed."

"Did Judy talk about that more than once?"

"Naw. She was wasted that time."

"What type of work did you do for them?"

"I worked on patchin' up things. I'd work on paintin', sheet rockin', buildin' things. Puttin' in countertops, puttin' in carpet. Did some roofin' once. They had a leak up in their ceilin'. You could see this brown spot spread out wavy like. I went up in the attic and saw where it was comin' through the roof. I went 'bout fixin' it. Judy was real crazy 'bout it 'cause her paintin's were up there."

"Were any of them damaged?"

"By the water? Naw, I don't think so. They's on the other side of the attic."

"Did she do anything peculiar while you were working?"

"'Smatter of fact, she come up there and sat cross-legged by her paintin's."

"Did she talk to you while you were working?"

"Some of the time. She'd crow and laugh and say how 'bout she'd paint me fixin' the roof. That I could take off all my clothes, but leave my tool belt on, and she'd do a nudie. I remember she was coverin' that pine tree paintin' in plastic while she talked. It had a sleepin' dog in it.

Looked like a bassit hound. She worried over 'em paintin's like they was more kin to her than Pitchfork."

"Did she ever describe what that painting was about?"

"I'd ast was that her favorite. And she sayed it wasn't, that it just needed to be preserved. And I ast why, and she sayed, 'tween takin' gulps of beer, that maybe one day she'd tell everyone, but by then everyone would know. And I tole her that was a good renderin' of a dog. And she sayed she drew it from mem'ry. Use'ta be a dog like that next door that wandered over."

"Do you think Caine had anything to do with putting the body there?"

"It's what I'd guess from what Judy sayed. I don't exactly remember what all she'd sayed. After I'd get through workin', I'd start drinkin' with her. But I do remember her talkin' 'bout that paintin'."

"Do you think Reynolds had something to do with it?"

"I don't think so. His momma was ly'ble to talk like one of 'em fortune tellers at the fair. Sometimes she'd seem fake and silly. Pitchfork'd just look at her, but then go 'bout his business like it was all part of the show, part of their messed up life."

"Do you think Reynolds knew what was buried?"

"I don't know. He seemed like he knew without havin' seen it."

"Did he ever speak to you about it?"

"Naw. Not that I remember."

"Did you ever hear the bikers talk about it?"

"They'd jeer him 'bout it like some men'll get all riled up when you call 'em a pussy. Well, they'd do the same 'bout diggin' up the yard."

* * *

He'd fallen asleep then saw Cat's Paw being locked away for forty-five years. It was a sentence that would make certain Cat's Paw would either die in prison or be feebly in his eighties by the time he got out. Then he was having a conversation with Cat's Paw. Cat's Paw's hands were clasped together, interlocked through the bars of his cell. They were talking frankly to one another.

Cat's Paw stared at him hard, his face seemingly magnified in a bluish glow. He could see Cat's Paw's scars in intricate detail. The beard was longer, but through some loophole of logic, he could see through it. The face had a transfiguring feature to it that altered, but the eyes and beard remained. Then Cat's Paw growled out, "You've only been used. You've assisted him in getting away with it. You'll try to justify it a million ways for the rest of your life. But as much as you try to ignore it, I'll be in the back of your conscience, gnawing away at the façade you've built up around it, the decorations, the honors, the privileges. You'll fool yourself into thinking it's smothered, but it'll be there. Judy knew Caine had done it and buried it there. She could've dug it up, or alerted the cops, but she assisted him because she was afraid of him. The secret accelerated her self-destruction. You were like her when you could've done something. You let him bury it. You don't even have her weak defenses to justify your neglect and indifference allowing him to flee. Despite what the evidence pointed to, you told yourself you were eradicating us."

During this diatribe, Cat's Paw's voice shifted in tones and even into what sounded like his own voice at times.

The words had the edge of accusation and seemed to command more vocabulary than he'd expected of the biker, but the gestures of the dream image were of someone demanding leveling and honesty. The image's hands were thrust through the bars and folded, then open at the palms, then folded again.

Then his own voice felt-said in a defensive way, uttering a denial, "They found you guilty. You're a degenerate drain on society that deserves to be locked away because you've committed murder before. This is the one we're able to pin on you."

Then there was an internal loss of equilibrium as the image of Cat's Paw instantly let him know he could smell lies reeking even amid the pathetic, decrepit shithole he'd been sentenced to. "You've helped put others here. You'll put more here the same way you're doing me by sacrificing the politically safe. You view us as pieces of irredeemable waste. Yes, I've fought and burned things, but I paid my retribution for those things. You knew you could have me testify truthfully against Caine, but you were pushing the biker agenda to get your marks. It's your own guilt you're locking away for forty-five years. What'll eat at you is that you let something just as dangerous go. One that holds up appearances of respect and moral behavior. Seemingly everything will be fine, but one day the gears will lock up, the bolts will shear in the engineering of your mind, and the façade you helped build will come crashing down because you never took care of acting when you should've."

He watched the image of Cat's Paw flicker a smile and then back up into the cell to conduct various acts of self-mutilation. Cat's Paw spoke as he tried hanging himself with a bed sheet. When that didn't seem to work, Cat's Paw stabbed his neck with a shive, saying, "I can't be killed this way."

His own dream image had a protest stuck in its throat. He was trying to say, "At least he stood for something," but the effort seemed absorbed by the blood all over the cell. Cat's Paw's shaded eyes still stared, and the grinning image asked, "Who is more dangerous?"

He woke feeling regret and doubt about any chance of a murder case against Cat's Paw. He had a thirsty inclination to send someone to Costa Rica to chase after Caine.

* * *

He intended to subpoena Dustin even though he was uncertain what Dustin would testify to. He formulated questions based on what he hoped to hear, playing the dialogue out in his mind to anxious ends, sometimes not believing the questions and answers himself, and acknowledging the unpredictability. The refrain of his arguments replayed again and again as he went about his daily tasks. The more massive globe of the case was rising up. He had to be ready. The rest of his activities seemed only in orbit around it. He'd chase them down at their fast paces, but accomplishing these tasks only brought fleeting satisfaction.

There were several boxes of materials for the case in his office by now. He could see the case unfolding in the courtroom. He alternately relished and dreaded the images. In the competing visions, he opportunely rose to the occasion before also failing miserably, all before the public eye. It was a contest of perception, concentration, wit, tenacity, with theatrics and timing thrown in. The gravity of whether Reynolds would be sent to prison for the rest of his life undermined any minimization.

He had a sensation of enjoying attention, but at the same time he went about his work steadily. The brainless attachment of celebrity to his name annoyed him. His work was emotionally gritty and grimy at times. He dealt with hard materials, minds devoid of moral compasses, belligerent and off-kilter personalities. Being the recipient of accusatory insults and threats from multiple sources could sometimes add excitement, but it could wear on a person.

He couldn't seek public validation or he would be scattered to the public whims like scraps to town dogs. The uncertainty bent men, sending them to early graves, making them into fat gluttons, addicts to lust, hunched-shouldered, pot-bellied targets for scandal so that they carried a hunted look in their eye. Duties and self-interest could pull him in separate directions, sometimes more painful to him than any hard labor he'd done as a young man working in the summers. The duties could take him out on a precipice risking his reputation and his mental well-being.

The trial was scheduled to start in two weeks. Latanya continued handling several of his other cases. He tried to return calls in his free moments, but the preparation and gravitational pull of Reynolds's case taxed his energy. He found it difficult to get motivated to do the mindless, administrative busy work piling up.

He went over the state's witness list with Prentice. He'd met the more important ones directly. There was the county medical examiner, three different state detectives—two of which worked minimally in collecting evidence—four federal agents, and six different deputies who'd collected evidence on the site originally. A ballistics specialist would supposedly reconstruct how the bullet likely entered the body.

He was comfortable for the most part with the law enforcement witnesses. It didn't contradict the defense theory. The experts would confirm homicide, but there was no link between the bullet found in the body and any gun Reynolds owned or had history of buying. He anticipated Feld would argue a gun could have easily been acquired by one of the transients coming through and then just as easily been discarded into the river.

The state's case would include the testimony of Spring. Miller had already found her competent to testify. Both sides had subpoenaed Mantle. He wanted Mantle to testify even if the state decided not to call him. He left up in the air whether Reynolds would ultimately take the stand. Feld might drag out all sorts of unfavorable statements or could even send Reynolds's stabilization into a tailspin. He's seen the rigors of trial unsettle even fully healthy individuals.

* * *

She imagined the breaking of the news of whose body had been found traveling in tentacles of high-speed electrical pulses to the various communities where her deceased husband's once proud clan had dispersed after its head had been essentially decapitated. She, who now knew for sure she was a widow, had never been certain whether he had died, had been killed, or had abandoned them. The worst thing about it had been the open-ended nature of it. She felt in her heart that he wouldn't have abandoned them, but without conclusive proof there were always question marks when she was in a more depressed or doubtful mood. She felt an explanation of his absence deserved to be categorized better. Prior to the news, she couldn't find a satisfying way to convey that.

There'd been stressful periods when they'd gone long distances without talking. Sometimes the special fires of politics called for immediate responses. But he always returned full of love for her, both professing it, and more frequently by his manner and actions. She believed the same applied to the children, with whom he'd spent as much free time as he had.

Now Meredith had graduated from fashion design school and had moved to New York, where she struggled to pay rent. She worried her daughter might end up getting hurt if she didn't find some stability soon. Last she'd heard, Meredith made the bare minimum to support herself, working as an apprentice of sorts in a large department store where she described promotion as elusive and interactions with superiors whimsical, confusing, and frustrating. She didn't try to convince her to return to Birmingham. She intuited that whatever she implied to Meredith would be resisted. She suspected Meredith had been hurt deeply by the disappearance of her father, and that her eldest's silence, withdrawal, and lack of excitability were a front for others. But when the news reached Meredith, she'd called immediately, showing more emotion than she could remember her showing in years. Meredith even said she would plan to be present for the trial.

Her son Hugh was finishing college, where she knew he'd taken his time among the indulgences and debaucheries of his fraternity. He had political ambitions like his father and had entertained the idea of law school. At least that was what he told the girls he met and other acquaintances to capitalize however he could. His grades had suffered at times as he lost focus. She found out through mutual friends and his troubles that he concurrently drank gallons of alcohol and smoked much marijuana, while occasionally ingesting an ecstasy pill, a line of cocaine, or a hit of LSD. Some that knew him better would tell her he wore an outside mask of upbeat optimism, but that he didn't hide his anger when speaking of his missing father. She'd heard him even accuse his father for not being smart enough to avoid putting himself in a situation where he had to disappear. The fact of the absence itself seemed all that mattered to him.

When she called Hugh to inform him they'd found his father's body, he'd just gotten back the poor results of his latest taking of the law school entry exam. He began crying after she told him. He explained that he hadn't done well on the entry test, and he wasn't sure he could handle this information and stay in Tuscaloosa for the moment. He decided to take a few days off.

Corey, who she considered the brightest, had started his second year at Emory. He'd declared himself a business major, but hadn't found the classes challenging enough. He then doubled his major with philosophy. He stayed near the top of his class in both subjects. Friends described him as having an acute sense of perception that was somewhat lacking in the emotional department, even more so than Meredith. But unlike Meredith, she suspected his inclination to detach was less of a defense than something he'd been born with. His social life had always seemed anemic when compared to his siblings. She hoped Corey had enough of an extrovert in him to envision working outside the protective gates of the university.

As a boy, after the initial pain of realizing his father was gone, Corey seemed to deal with it in the shortest span of time compared to the others. The next day he went back to concentrating on long division. His father's disappearance had receded into the background for him. He didn't seem to speculate much on it, just as he didn't seem to speculate on why the earth only had one moon instead of two. Unlike her and his siblings, he seemed to have been comfortable leaving his father's disappearance as an unanswered question. It must have been one of the few questions of his existence he didn't care to know the answer.

Corey's first reaction seemed to be annoyance, which morphed into anger, then cooled into perplexity. Of late, he'd been getting into a routine that gave him a steady, satisfactory sense of accomplishment. This news must've thrown that out of whack, trivializing and minimizing it. That annoyance must've ignited into anger at whoever had extinguished his father's life. After carefully gathering information from her on the subject, a gigantic reservoir of hatred seemed to have boiled up. Then he expressed perplexity to her because of the raw violence of these emotions, which usually didn't take over his thoughts. After a few agitated days, he must've suppressed it as he would an untimely urge to vomit.

Robin was just entering her junior year. She was the most adept socially of her siblings. Perky and outgoing, she confidently expressed the whimsical and faddish remarks of teenagers. She spent more time on dress and makeup than on her studies, but by exerting her charms, she was able to cajole others to work physically or mentally for her. She had problems at times with Robin's flippant remarks.

The disappearance had occurred when Robin was so young that she seemed to have grown around the loss. It must have still been buried in her being, but she saw her youngest as a young tree that had grown around some obstruction or healed over a missing limb. Her siblings had prepared a way for Robin into the community so that others were familiar with her family and with the unexplained tragedy that hung in their background. Robin seemed less concerned about how to preserve or sustain herself than how to go about enjoying life and redeemed any untoward pity with her smiles. She tried telling Robin not to expect most of her desires to be satisfied as they occurred to her. Robin appeared naïve financially, but her spontaneity and her attention to feminine details of style, combined with a strong sense of articulating what she wanted at the moment, made her constant entertainment for the others. At times she helped her move beyond that shadow of Craig's absence.

Now the drape on the tragedy had been pulled back. He'd been brutally murdered and his strong mouth had been defiled. At this initial point of discovery, it didn't matter as much to her the exact cause of death. The fact of the warm sunshine breaking through the cold fog in that part of her mind was enough to revel in. She enjoyed a long-delayed and overwhelming sense of well-being and relief. Whenever it occurred to her, she experienced a tingly feeling, sometimes with shivers, that could cause her to weep. The weight of nearly twelve years of question marks, twelve painstaking years of raising his children, was upended into levity and lightness.

Robin, however, seemed thrown off by the resurfacing. Robin must not have the same need as she did to vindicate him. She must've just naturally assumed that no one who was similar to her would act dishonorably. Now the tragedy was being dredged out into the light again after the youngest had spent years moving past it while getting the family to look at their hope. In a childish way Robin seemed to be almost jealous of the attention the topic received.

The shock of her own initial discovery soon gave way to a blinding anger at whomever had caused the tragedy. She planned to take a leave from her job at the hotel to attend as many of the hearings as possible. She'd heard mention of the case before the body had been identified, but she'd become so detached by then from their former life that the realization it might be her husband took several weeks to even register as a possibility. Through the passing months, she came to despise the idea of Edward Reynolds, who she thought a terrible, destructive drain on society. She tried keeping an open mind about it, but she couldn't help thinking he was implicated. To what degree she wasn't certain, but she wouldn't reduce any disgust with him.

Mr. Feld had contacted her a few months after the body had been identified. She deferred to his judgment in bringing whoever was involved to answer for it. Mr. Feld had traveled to Birmingham where they'd met in the downtown lobby of the hotel where she worked.

Mr. Feld had talked to her in reassuring tones. "We've done everything possible to ensure we charged the right person."

She felt herself smiling. "I do appreciate it. Are there any other suspects? What about these stories on the Caine family?"

For a second Feld looked straight ahead, losing eye contact, and quickly said, almost in a reproachful manner, she thought, as it was so abrupt, "It's already been explored, and there's nothing more than weak circumstantial speculation, rumor, and innuendo connecting them to this."

"I just want to make sure there's no doubt and that everyone involved is prosecuted."

"The body was found in Reynolds's backyard. Where he's lived for decades in squalor. Try to look at this from a more distant standpoint. I know this is easy to say, but may be difficult to do. Even from a stranger's standpoint. For those are the persons who will make up the jury. Now think of those that make headlines as serial killer types. Those that bury their kills for some sick reason close to where they live. The evil ones outside decent society that show no semblance of communicating and interacting with others on a basic level. Then you compare that to a pillar of society, a man who spends his life bringing money and jobs into the area, who has the discipline to build a fortune, who regularly communicates with the elite leaders of the community and carries himself for the most part in a civilized manner, golfing, speaker dinners, trips out of country. When you hold these two up side by side, who do you really think is more capable of this reprehensible act?"

She paused for a second looking at him, composing her words. "But even so, I know Caine can act in a cut-throat manner in business. Won't that defense attorney be talking of the threat my husband posed to Caine's profits?"

"He may try to, but what we have is a man who acts in a civilized manner while by all accounts going through the complicated process of maintaining multi-million-dollar businesses. He pays his taxes. He has accountants, lawyers, and corporate boards to consider as he goes about his business. Now contrast that with the rash and brutal act of an intentional homicide. Would a man who travels in the elite white-collar circles be more capable of committing this, or would a man who travels in no-collar circles, basically sitting there like an isolated time bomb?

"Then consider what either of these men would have to lose. On the one hand, you've got someone in control of an empire of prestigious business connections. On the other, there's an impoverished leech living off a broken family's inheritance from a foreign state. Of those two, Caine obviously has a lot more to lose. Caine would've found a business solution no matter what legislation your husband helped pass. His family has moved capital into other industries numerous times."

"Could they have been accomplices?"

"We've found nothing to support it. It's a desperate attempt to deflect blame, Julie. They are grasping for whatever there is to grab a hold of in the long plummet to guilt and destruction. A lot of times murder doesn't make sense. It can easily occur in the warped instincts of a years-long drug addict who stumbles upon someone he doesn't recognize on his property. In Reynolds's paranoid state, he thinks this man must be scouting out his meth lab and that he probably has all kinds of information on him. He can't distinguish between someone walking along the bank of the river and someone scouting out his property. You have the bleary-eyed rage of an animal lying in wait, forming the intent to kill, and then doing it in a way that tries to hide the identity of the remains."

As Mr. Feld finished explaining, she hadn't really been hearing the last words. She'd experienced a mixture of reactions. The strongest and most dominant of which was a solid feeling of rectitude sitting like a square stone block in the forefront of her mind. It led to a surging sense of purpose, emboldening and strengthening her. Some mystery and doubt she'd carried for over a decade, that she'd been forced to adjust to but had never really accepted or been comfortable with, was becoming soluble and visible. Her usual days after the disappearance had been periods of toil and routine interrupted by mild anxious fits. She suspected that a synchronized feeling of concentrated bliss and fulfillment were somewhere in the resolution of this case, but she only seemed to catch a half glimpse of it dangling and soaring in a windy distance.

The sense of purpose felt pure. It seemed she was being drawn toward a concentrated point. The point was a certainty in the righteousness of one's beliefs and understandings.

Somewhere underneath, like a shadow to this feeling, lay the faintest suggestion that there may be some other explanation to what Mr. Feld was saying. But it was pushed away by the forcefulness of that conviction coursing through her. She had charged and quick thoughts, but she was not anxious or impatient. She was now certain that Reynolds had been the one who brutally murdered her husband in the prime of his existence, leaving her a struggling widow. All the spite and vengeance her heart could carry poured into this vessel, this container of hate, stored and directed at a creature she viewed as inhuman and grotesque. She relished the chance to label it.

She'd submitted to Mr. Feld's design. It was the first anyone had offered her on the subject. The need had been there so long that when any opportunity for fulfilling it arrived, she'd readily given into the plan, quieting any logical objections her mind might've made up about not getting the whole story. She accepted Mr. Feld's ideas just as a starving person would greedily accept a full-course meal.

Mr. Feld now pointed her hopes toward the public conviction of that man who'd robbed her of her husband and her family of a father. He put it to her in a way that made her believe it was plainly available, owed to her, and that it would be accomplished. The goal would have to be fought for. He warned her that the defense attorney Sheet was known to be an advanced and wily opponent. It would take weeks of testimony that would probably be difficult for her to hear. The media would buzz around and try to invade her privacy. She would need to ask herself whether she had the emotional reserves to sit there and watch whatever perversion the defense might throw out there to cloud the jurors' minds, to seek to deflect blame elsewhere. Her presence would encourage them to fulfill their duty and convict Reynolds.

* * *

The day before the trial was scheduled to begin, he assumed the aspect of a harried and impatient military commander. He mentally strode through the ranks and reviewed the battlefield, finding constant room for improvement as he made last-minute adjustments. Even after more than one hundred fifty such preparations and battles, from small skirmishes to large-scale campaigns, there was always the fog of uncertainty over who and what type of person would be on the jury, and what they might or might not believe. No matter what precautions or adjustments were made, there would still be that anticipatory edge of spoiling for a fight. He'd been in similar fights and had come out successfully.

He thought wryly that those no longer mattered for the moment. Once he started questioning the jurors that nervousness usually dissipated somewhat. It was an inevitable progression of building up what to expect, vying for your version of events, and then having to wait for reality to take its course. The course many times diverted from expectations, becoming a bitter razor, slicing hopes and draining them of blood.

He struggled with various internal scenarios, wrestling with them all day. Sometimes it led to extreme renunciation of what he'd accomplished, his career choice, his chances of winning, his chances of succeeding in the larger sense of the community. At the edge of these was a drastic impulse to pull out on all of it. He could go into something else, move to a different state, a different country even. Then a backlash sense of responsibility rose up to cut against the other current, pitting him against his duties and pride, torturing him. After awhile, self-destructive thoughts arose, but he had so far outlasted those.

When he got a call from Sylvia at lunch wishing him good luck, he tried his best to seem pleased. He tried laughing a little, but once they were off the phone, he couldn't help but think that he must've sounded like a gloomy whiner.

Despite his misgivings, he pointed out to himself that Reynolds seemed to be in good shape, as good as he could've hoped for given Reynolds's mental health history. Reynolds seemed eager for the trial. But even his client's equanimity bothered him at the moment. He asked himself why he should suffer during trial as much as his clients did or more so. And then he hated himself for such self-pitying thoughts. At the end of the trial, win or lose, he was most likely not the one going to jail. He also wasn't the one who had spent a year in jail waiting for trial.

His thoughts turned back to the more specific and favorable pre-trial rulings. Feld had fought him tooth and nail about bringing in evidence of Caine. In argument, he pointed out that there was a chain of circumstances connecting Caine to the murder at least as much as it did Reynolds. The evidence against Reynolds was circumstantial and so was the evidence against Caine. Then there were the comments of the dead mother implicating Caine, which, subject to hearsay, could be verified by witnesses. Miller would allow them to explore their theory.

As he proofed his motions in limine, no matter how many times he reviewed the documents, there seemed more to add to cover for some new contingency. Latanya had proofread the materials at the office and prepared his exhibit book and outline. He reviewed them an uncounted number of times making sure they were in order and the information could easily be referenced.

Dustin would be testifying against the advice of Whaley. The biker had lost between eighty and ninety pounds.

Whaley had talked to him about the number of clients who suddenly found religion behind bars. They both were skeptical of conversions under duress. After many of those had been released, they'd come back on repeat offenses or probation violations because they'd apparently lost their religious ways on the outside. Dustin's manner on the stand may be unpredictable and even dangerous, but he was after the substance behind the wild mouthpiece, however blunt, caustic, and repulsive Dustin might seem to the jurors.

The evening before trial, he left work to dine alone. He consumed no wine or alcohol, preferring not to drink anything within a couple of days of starting a high-profile trial. The twists and pressures leading up to trial were another form of intoxication. During the trial, an adverse ruling could suddenly close off a line of argument he'd been relying on. Sometimes the adjustments took all his composure to stay on track within the new parameters. Going back to the original plan could be a turbulent and unsettling grasping and discarding at what was left. This could cause long pauses, giving off the false impression that he didn't know what he was doing. Unforeseen lines of material might distract him from returning to what he wanted to get out of the witness.

The night before trial he hoped to get at least eight hours sleep. He wanted to be as rested as possible for all the attention that would be focused on the first day. As he drifted closer to the realm of full rapid eye movement, he drowsily remembered many times performing fine with much less sleep. By now he'd done all the preparation he could.

While lying in bed, he flipped over in different sleeping positions. Anxious moments from previous trials plagued his mind. His thoughts turned to the girl Spring. What sympathy would the jurors attach to her? In his vulnerable privacy, the thought of her testifying about what went on in the house caused his stomach to shrink and tighten as his confidence plummeted.

He could explain her view of the encounter between Reynolds and Dustin, but her testimony would portray Reynolds horribly. Hearing the situation recounted by an innocent child undoubtedly would influence a negative opinion of Reynolds. They could judge Reynolds as a reprehensible example of parenting rather than whether he actually murdered Spindle.

Exhausting his anxieties for the night, he reached that calm center he would need for the next several weeks. The strains of his mind relaxed and his thoughts coursed through at a slower pace, like observing the persistent triangular strain of a comet in the night sky with the naked eye, appearing delayed and slowed by a severe distance. He coasted toward highly volatile rapid eye movement. As his mind let go of his struggle with personal security and all its offshoots, he slipped into vivid dreaming.

* * *

He was below deck on a ship of some sort. His sense of its dimensions varied. For a moment he thought it was a schooner. But then it could've been a larger military vessel, maybe a destroyer. Or it might've been a cruise ship. No matter what manifestation occurred to him, the pressure of a dire event pulsated against the hull. He had a driving urge to get up top.

Some young man with a narrow head and oval face dressed as a bellhop ran past. He caught up to him. He heard words in his mind as the other's mouth contorted. There was an emergency that required the help of every hand on board. The bellhop began moving faster saying over his shoulder to go to the conference room with the others.

The bellhop disappeared through a hatch. There were levels of railed walkways under him. He could smell something acrid and smoky. The walkway curved around, ending in double doors, which he swung open. He stood in an elegant, high-ceiling room. Distinguished-looking couples in tuxedos and evening gowns were hurrying to a set of bronze-handled doors. He felt compelled to join them, but was hesitant because of his Hawaiian-style shirt and jeans.

The vessel lurched amid terrible sounds of straining. He walked into a large theatre. Hundreds of heads turned back to the entryway to look at him. Laughter burst out. The speaker on stage was bald and professorial looking. The man spoke into the microphone with a calm but demanding cadence, beckoning him forward.

When he arrived on stage, the speaker filled his vision. The audience seemed to diminish. Reminding him of some arbitrary and cruel ancient Egyptian god, the bald speaker inclined his head in a scornful expression. A sick feeling pulled whatever energy and shreds of confidence remained down with it as if his personal universe were experiencing a bending and smothering of light. Through his dream mind, he saw himself waiting for a verdict in the shape of a former case with slightly exaggerated features. He awaited feedback on what he'd argued and fought over with nothing but blasted, sweat-stained uncertainty. And they pronounced guilt. He relived the deflation, becoming small and insignificant again.

He saw a breaking husk, a locust leaving its shell and body. He felt compelled to carry on in some other form. But he hadn't learned how to accomplish this shedding. How was he to leave a mold of himself staring dead-eyed?

If he'd won, the prosecutor would've gotten the praise anyway. A self-hatred broiled up in him. He saw a bank of pinkish clouds at sunset as if they were impotently angry at the light for no longer keeping them innocently white. Only pain and torture would accompany him down to oblivion. Every material thing he'd gathered, even the attraction of a younger, beautiful woman, had depended on his consent to some unnamed, undefined indentured servitude.

He'd taken on a sliver of material as dense as materials could come. The trade-off had splintered him. The figure's face twitched with disgust and impatience as if he were dispatching putrefied refuse. He wasn't sure whether he'd inadvertently defecated himself. Through rumbling conversation, he noticed a huge exodus as the crowd hurried to side exits. He got in line with them but was ignored by anyone he tried to talk to. Through distorted time movements, he entered another metal corridor that ended in an iron ladder. The ladder smelled of sea water and wet metal as he ascended it.

He first noticed elongated, curvy pools and tiki bars. Large turrets lined the sides of the deck. What looked like an ancient cannon sat anachronistically on the prow. The massive pools were strangely empty. Guns cracked the air.

From his vantage point, he could see the ship sat surrounded by a fleet of obviously hostile vessels, destroyers, and what looked like a battleship.

The ship pitched at the sharp steering of unseen hands. The sides were stuck again by flaming lines of metal linking it to its fate. Everything was covered in a rusty light, making the scene itself bloodthirsty and giving the air a coppery taste. It was hard to breathe. He could see some men running to the turrets and the lone cannon. Smoke and waves of heat rose from the boom of weaponry.

He wondered why his unprotected eardrums hadn't exploded, but his main concern was to get off this outgunned, dying ship. A barrage lacerated the hull, tearing out holes of splintered metal, concrete, wood, and glass. He saw critical gashes dangerously close to the waterline and bodies in the water face down. He spotted an area in a corner of the ship where a group in touristy outfits was going over the edge. Once he got there, he saw they were being lowered into lifeboats through the rumble and screech. He hurried over to join the frantic rush. He was able to work his way onto one of the simple wooden crafts.

As he was quickly lowered, he looked up to see the wondrous eyes of Spring looking down at him. He felt himself shouting up in dream thoughts for her to get on board, but her expectant and curious features got farther away until she was an indistinguishable jot of fleshy yellow.

Upon hitting the water, he rowed furiously. The rowing seemed to go on for hours. He noticed a significant drop in the din and cries of the massacre he'd just left. Now an enormous expanse of ocean stretched in all directions. He began rowing again. Before he could distinguish how it happened, he was in the water swimming in a frenzy to the shore. Animal terror seized him as he thought he might already be in the process of being devoured. Oddly, he still retained the ability to swim. He reached a surf area. He could feel his skin burning as he walked through the sand toward a Tudor-style manor house.

When he got near the door, he walked up a set of recently constructed brick steps. A lacquered, ornately carved wood door was ajar. A warm light glowed inside, but it didn't reach all the corners of the expansive rooms. He noticed an elegant display of paintings on the walls along with a double winding stairwell and a marble banister. He glided up the stairwell. He recognized an extreme thirst. He followed a hallway curving to the right into a steel door. He entered darkness before grasping a lit wax candle from the wall. He was able to discern what looked like discarded theatre equipment littered about. Among sawhorses and hanging costumes, he saw historical outfits, wigs, and miscellaneous fake jewelry and weaponry.

There was a soft light coming from the center of this room. He approached and saw that the light came from a bulb of glass on a pedestal. Surrounding the pedestal was what looked like a moat with shimmering greenish water. As he got closer, he could see that the moat was actually a twisting morass of snakes and reptiles, writhing and coiled together. He heard a voice causing a terrible pain in his stomach, "C'mon now. You know this case has gone on way too long. All you have to do is get him to plead out. He'll listen to you."

He awoke with a negative stiff in his throat. The vividness of the jarring dream left him uncomfortable. The residue had him wrung up in a sickening vertigo of paranoia and disgust. He rose to address his excessive thirst.

When he lay back down, he rolled and flipped over some more. It was two a.m.

About two hours later, he drifted back into unconscious.

Part Three

The sharp intensity of the morning evaporated the ghoulish irrationality and exaggeration of the night before though a general discomfort remained. He shaved and showered. In his undershirt and suit pants, he sat down on his couch to eat a light breakfast and drink a little coffee. He remembered times when he had to force the food down on jury trial mornings due to his nerves. That'd been early on mostly when he'd first started trying cases. He could eat now, but the nerves were still present. He'd adapted to it. As he went through his normal routine, there was a constant double and triple checking of his activities to make sure everything was ready. The act of buttoning his shirt and buckling his belt had a crisp inevitability to it.

Every mundane slow dressing moment and thorough chewing of his food incongruently bore the seriousness and import of major life events. These preparations of his appearance irritated him as needlessly distracting. The details couldn't be ignored. They required strict attention even as his mind wandered through various scenarios of what he could encounter. The smallest deviation of energy required to perform a task as simple as tying his shoelace could shoot a raging, childish sensation of frustration through him.

Trying to envision what they would be like was a futile exercise. He knew, but he couldn't help it. Conglomerations of past juries, random likenesses from his personal encounters, movie, television, and book characters, shifted obtusely and in splintered flashes through already dead and non-existent conjurings of what could happen, and what they might think. It was a misshapen type of preparedness. Many of his activities demanded this type of analytical preparing. But the random selection of jurors from the community, trying to guess their predilections and prejudices, what questions they had, what comments they might make, or how they would react to him, or the prosecutor, or each other, was an unpredictable process, defying any type of nailed-down preparedness.

Sometimes he'd taken a composition of stranger judges for granted. It was a transformation that could have the ugliness of a protean, protoplasmic, multiple-eyed creature held together by unidentified forces, an unpredictable and chaotic vestige of power. Such a beast could be easily whipped into a snap judgment. Twelve random persons gathered then disappeared once their judgment had been laid. The creature's nature couldn't be easily detected.

Enthusiasts would proudly cry that it was a pinnacle of democratic achievement, an installation of rule by the people. They wouldn't see the twelve gathered in an excited, lawless exercise that might easily slip into the whimsical, exhilarating, and irresponsible cruelty of a riot. The jurors might get heated, but the process and outcome would be nothing like the spectacle of vengeance a lynch mob created, driven toward freezing vengeance in a violent symbol. That unruly progression toward violence, tripping over itself in a frenzy to snap its jaws—even ignorant to injuring itself in the process as participants would trample over one another to get at a piece of the violence, to take direct part, like a greedy, starved, and rabid pack—was the antithesis of what the enthusiasts would believe a cool-headed jury to be.

They would disagree vehemently that it was a multi-eyed beast flailing and oozing about leaving a rearranged, shifted reality in its wake, like some natural disaster convicting and killing some while showering others with gold, munificence, or pardon regardless of earned merit. They would see it as a time-honored and humane displacement of lynch mobs by a single, unifying eye of the public. Centuries of toil and wisdom went into its assembled gaze, dwarfing participants in vision and in scope. After the struggle had been put before it, the merits meted out, and the verdict determined, it often heralded some sense of pacification. Others had spilled blood to enshrine the cooler eye, the more reasonable one, the one that outlasted generations. It would outlast the cycle of a human's lifespan, and it would eventually be composed of countless communities of immigrants.

Absent the massive tensions that now came to bear on picking a segment of the community for a murder trial, portions of his mind were prone to believe in the enthusiasts, even though his body and fears slouched with the critics. Like any conversation, the dialogue with the jurors could turn on the superficial, the evanescent, the common denominator.

Before the prospective jurors entered the courtroom, the jail guards led Reynolds in from the holding cell. Miller had denied the request to remove Reynolds's leg irons during the trial, but agreed that the law required the court to minimize this emphasis. Reynolds's restraints were to be covered up during the proceedings as discreetly as possible. The guards covered Reynolds's legs with a towel. The chains were loose enough to allow Reynolds some freedom of movement. For voir dire, they were already turned around to face the prospective jurors that would sit in the gallery. The front row had been deliberately left empty to prevent a closer view.

Miller introduced what was occurring. There was an electric expectation in the air that he recognized. The media hoisted their electronic devices. Unlike the forming of the public eye, that amorphous mirage of public attentions didn't call for any deep speculation on its face. No commitments, oaths, or duties, other than to advertising. Disconnected from dollars, with a quick flash or swoop, it could lose its integrity.

His reflections along these lines began to dry up. Behind his iron blue irises he'd seen in the mirror that morning, seemingly speckled with gun metal shavings, his well-tailored gray pinstriped suit with brightly colored shirt and tie, and his hair brushed up and back and held in place, he saw his part rising. He imagined being outwardly viewed as a well-groomed man with something authoritative to say. His tanned face didn't contain many wrinkles. His imperious dark eyebrows could emphasize when needed. Trying not to wear a forced smile, he faced outward into the gallery at the people in the jury pool.

Miller asked the typical questions of whether the pool had heard about the case or knew the parties involved. His eyes followed the sea of people with their hands raised. Next to him, Latanya took notes.

Louise had bought Reynolds an older suit. He looked presentable as a man of modest means, bearing little resemblance to the wild, no-account meth head who'd entered the jail. Reynolds's demeanor had an amiable aspect, appropriately serious with no outbursts. Reynolds now appeared to have a modicum of self-control, his face as harmless as a grocery clerk's or a car washer's.

Feld smiled somewhat plastically as he stiffly arose and announced himself as a designee of the state. The smile did little to deflect the impression that Feld had the single-minded seriousness of a pallbearer carrying a coffin. The task defined him more than any of his words or features. Though striking at times, Feld was less open to chance, more conservative and down to business, less open to listening to any of what he deemed to be frivolous whispers.

He felt a swell of pride in his element. Most often, the concentration came when he began voir dire, quieting and channeling his nervous energy. The risks and doubts were still there, but there was the heightened exhilaration of being recognized as competent to attempt such a thing. He became calmly immersed in a great swathe of data, visual and auditory. He watched gestures, listened to answers, and made notes himself on occasion.

His attention was drawn to an articulate farmer. He listened to the farmer say, "I don't really believe much in lawyers. Only had one to make sure my property and will were right."

Miller asked him if the farmer could handle listening to lawyers for weeks straight. The farmer let out a whistling sound causing laughter. Miller resumed a more serious countenance. After discussing the spectacle the case had become, Miller brought everyone back to the familiar refrain of whether they could still be impartial and stick to the evidence presented in court.

Feld was known to many of them. One woman had been contacted by his office about witnessing a burglary. She was glad to help make sure the right person was caught.

There was an older teacher whose son he'd represented on a DUI. Miller asked if she could be impartial. Despite her affirmative answer, he expected Miller to strike her for cause.

Focusing on individuals seemed an overwhelming task to him when there were around a hundred. The group had to be viewed as an audience. There would be time to talk thoroughly to the ones still left after those that obviously wouldn't fit were removed. Logistically many couldn't serve because of work or childcare expense. The pool was cut almost in half, down to around sixty. Miller asked some more general questions then singled out a few others.

Miller gave Feld an hour to question. He felt the eagerness to speak, but let it lie there waiting. It was a tribal agreement that didn't have to be sophisticated, but the trust had to be there. It had to be tested and reiterated throughout the rest of the trial.

While there seemed to be no rhyme or reason to it, he believed there were consistent approaches that one could take to help relieve some of the randomness. The standard issues of the presumption of innocence, the burden of proof, and credibility would be discussed, but the exact manifestation of how was undetermined. Any number of responses could send the discussion into the unknown. It could be virtually musical with guiding posts directing the flow.

Having a jaded city cop in the pool allowed Feld to come back again and again for getting his themes across.

He looked at a myriad of different faces. If anything gave him the idea of what *the people* meant, it was during voir dire. *The people* was as fluid a concept as he could think of. It shifted, flowered, and died before his expectations. It could be harnessed for a short time, but never controlled for long.

As he stood to address after lunch, he found a highly receptive group. After he'd gone through his standard historical linking of the constitutional principles to the current proceeding, it didn't take much to get a response. He exacted a steady flow of comments. The farmer told them, "You can tell a dog's been bad by the way it carries itself. If it's slinkin' away with a hunched-over look, you can tell it's been bad by its eyes."

"What about people?"

"That might be trickier. A man could make up all sorts of things with his tongue. There are some out there that'd utter a bald-face lie and still keep a straight face. You'd have to watch 'em closer, I guess."

"What if he had a crooked back? Would you be able to believe him at all?"

"If 'twere somethin' physically wrong with him, I'd want to know. If that explaint why he was actin' unusual, then it don't necessarily mean he's lyin'. The other facts would have to line up with what he said."

He turned to the officer. "Officer, if someone was running away from you after you'd asked him to stop, would that make you think something was wrong?"

"If I see a man runnin' just 'cause I ast him to stop and I'm in uniform, I begin to wonder what he might be tryin' to run from or hide."

"What if a man or woman stands their ground? Is he more likely to be telling the truth?"

"Depends on whether he's one of those con artists that thinks he can feed you a line to get himself out of trouble. It doesn't necessarily mean I'll believe him anymore than the other. It would depend on what I seen 'em doin' and whether it matches with what they're sayin' or what others are sayin'."

"Suppose someone places a pill bottle into someone else's bag without them knowing it at the airport. They go through the airport check and they're arrested for possessing a controlled substance. Is it misleading to say that they knew about it because it was in their bag?"

Hands went up. A woman in real estate asked, "Misleading? It could just be proof. I don't know if it would be misleading."

"But it could mislead you if you were a trier of fact, and if it were up to you to determine whether the person knowingly possessed it?"

"It could mislead you into thinking that he had if he really didn't know."

"How do you determine what facts are misleading then?"

"Whether the whole story makes sense, I guess. Did he leave his bag unattended? Should he have gone through his bag?"

"Now what if the guy doesn't have a story? What if he doesn't say anything?"

"It's his bag, right? He was carrying it when he was stopped. I would want his side of the story."

"Would you be able to hold the government to its burden of proof even if the guy didn't tell you his side of the story?" There was a lull in affirmative responses.

The real estate woman volunteered again, "I guess I could, but honestly I would like to hear what the guy would say. I mean if he's got nothing to hide."

"What if he had a head injury afterwards that kept him from testifying clearly?"

"I'd want to know that."

"What if you weren't allowed to know?"

"Well then, I don't know. It may be the person's unlucky day because I would want to hear what he has to say."

"But you know everyone has a right to silence in a criminal trial?" He turned on the fuller group. "One could imagine many reasons why a person wouldn't want to testify at their trial involving serious allegations, couldn't they? What if you weren't an articulate public speaker and you felt intimated while every word you said was being recorded? What if you'd rather not be cross-examined on a subject that has caused you much anxiety and pain?"

Several raised their hands. A carpenter said, "There's a lot of reasons it'd be uncomfortable, and no one would want to do it, but to me it'd be like backing down from a job. Something makes you suspicious. Now why don't you explain yourself?"

He came to the question of how much evidence was beyond a reasonable doubt. They were to pretend they were security at a football game where possessing and drinking liquor was prohibited. "Say an honors student at the game came up to you and said that guy over there is drinking. Would that be enough evidence?"

Most everyone shook their heads no.

"Then say you go up to the patron and smell alcohol. Would that be enough?"

Still a steady shaking of heads no. The carpenter spoke up, "He could've been drinking before the game."

"Then what if the group he was standing with all had cups with liquor in them, but he had a similar empty cup. Is that enough evidence?"

Some did say that would be enough. He turned to one of these, the juror in the twenty-second position, a janitor. "What if a friend of his had handed him the cup?"

"Unh, that's awful close. He should a made a way to not get hisself there. But if he goes to explainin' hisself then I might agree. 'Em other people ought to say so too."

Feld stood up to begin a second twenty-minute round.

Why spend all this time on such a case? This question crept up occasionally, especially with the strain on his relationship with Sylvia. The question replayed her words. It seemed to buzz irritatingly over the surface of his brain like a mosquito skimming over a pond. It didn't really penetrate to the values and duties working nearer the core of his being.

Feld became a bland blur to him. When his turn arrived again to speak, he brought up abhorrence. "No one thinks that we're trying to justify it, do you?"

Some heads shook no, but there were no verbal responses.

"If you're picked for this case, would you be able to differentiate between wanting to find someone guilty and wanting to find the person in front of you guilty even if the evidence has more than one possible explanation?"

No responses.

"Would it be okay to err on the side of convicting an innocent of the charge?"

Many heads shook no.

"For those of you not shaking your heads no, if the person is bad enough, is it alright to just convict him of something?"

A good number of hands, but less than half, went up.

He turned to an accountant who'd raised his hand. "Sir, what if some of those bad people, keeping in mind that this is solely in the enforcer's opinion of who is bad or not, could be someone who they didn't get along with? What if those bad people were presumed to be guilty, would that work better for you?"

"I don't agree with that. That's not what we do."

There were some others shaking their heads. One spoke up, "No, he has to be proven guilty."

"That's right, and who has the burden in the case?"

Several answered at once, "The state."

After a few more minutes, he sat back down. Miller broke for recess and called the lawyers back to chambers to discuss challenges for cause. The woman whose son he'd represented was stricken off. When they got through, they had just over forty left.

Each side had six peremptory challenges. They began going back and forth exercising them. The farmer made it on. The officer was stricken. He'd used four of his challenges. Feld had used five.

They both hesitated on the person seated in the twenty-second position, the janitor Cleophus Snade. Feld had one peremptory left and couldn't seem to make a decision either way. After hesitating, Feld kept quiet, letting Snade stay on. While he was concerned about the way Snade had answered, he thought Snade would be fairer than the accountant. He used his fifth peremptory on the accountant.

He and Feld went back out. As Miller returned to the bench and announced who would be seated on the jury for the case, he noticed a number of smiles and relief on the faces of some and what looked like disappointment on others. Two of the women jurors leaned as if bolstering one another for what lay ahead.

Miller thanked and excused the rest. The twelve plus the two alternates were shown to the jury box and sworn in. Miller read the introductory instructions. It was three p.m. when Miller announced they were in recess until tomorrow morning at nine.

He ran through the day in his mind as the adrenaline of having started dissipated. No matter how well it went, the process was always mind bending. When he'd first started, he thought it might've been too much for him to stomach, but later he realized that he'd been discovering the amount of raw energy it took to make quick assessments and take action under scrutiny and threat to one's reputation and livelihood. After several years, he could better see where the energy was needed. There was the facile element to it. He could never be sure of what was underneath. Trying to analyze or uncover that was the weary way of paralytic depression and no way to win a trial. He had to decide he'd done enough.

He suspected he was good at it because he harbored so many doubts himself. They appeared to him in others, in himself, in his clients. But all these places of weaknesses within him, these unshored up insecurities, were soothed by his sense of pride in his work steaming up like morning mist off the earth.

Alongside that elemental ambrosia rose the brightness of Sylvia. He had an itching desire to call or text her, but he refrained. He'd asked that she leave him be for the first few days of trial. Maybe after a day or two of testimony he would call her. He would reward himself with the pleasure of confiding in her. Letting himself give into that pleasure too early may spoil what he had to do. Besides, she would have a reprieve from the tumult within him, the expansion and contraction of his hopes. He secretly expected to be rewarded for this self-denial.

The public eye had formed today, and he needed to ensure its earliest impressions were clear. The jurors' senses would likely dull as the evidentiary portions dragged on. As he lay down for sleep earlier than usual, he knew by experience that lying there trying to grasp respite that scurried away in the face of a monumental task would only frustrate him. On those early morning risings of two and three a.m., it was as if a pilot light had been turned on in the heater of his consciousness and couldn't be blown out.

He got up around three a.m., went to his living room, and began reviewing his opening statement. He would give a concise response.

* * *

After dawn, he felt drawn to a solemn occasion. It wasn't the giddy excitement of some long awaited day of reward. Yesterday signaled the beginning of completing a labor. He continued reviewing notes and exhibits over breakfast in his kitchen. He ran through his mind of how to present. He expected it would be painful to sit through Feld's damning of his client.

By the time he arrived in court that morning, there were several cameras and media persons milling about. His suit was darker than the day before, but his shirt and tie remained bright. He bypassed the media as best he could. He sat down at counsel's table and chatted with Latanya until Feld arrived shortly thereafter.

The jail guards brought Reynolds out. He watched as they placed the towel over his chained feet. Miller came out and called the case. The inertia of the moment propelled him forward. A volatility of emotion started again, exhilarating and painful by turns.

The bailiff opened the courtroom to the public. The seats in the gallery filled quickly. The jurors entered. He saw a variety of demeanors making up the personality of the public eye. Some looked gravely stoic, others smiled good-naturedly. At least one looked down after viewing the parties.

Miller announced where they were in the process and asked them to direct their attention to Mr. Feld's opening statement. Black-suited, white-shirted, and red-tied, Feld stood and walked out from behind his table.

Feld's movements seemed to be saying, here it was, a murder being pursued by law enforcement. He was a tall man. He used to be lean but had started showing some girth in his early forties. He had a full head of silver-streaked hair and wore no facial hair. Feld reached a podium set up to address the jurors. Feld's angular face jutted out prominently and, he thought, somewhat arrogantly. Everyone's attention gathered around the words flowing out of Feld's mouth, "Good morning, ladies and gentlemen. What brings us here is the tragic murder of Craig Spindle nearly a decade and a half ago. Twelve years ago, the councilman was part of a loving family which he'd left that day to walk along the river. He disappeared that day. No one knew where until last December.

"The initial search for him or his body turned up nothing. They dredged the river back then, looking for a body. Initially, there'd been a delay because Craig was a prominent man in the county. He often traveled in and outside the county."

Feld walked around the podium and faced the jury directly, gesturing with his arms slightly for emphasis. He heard Feld again, "Finding no body, the investigation ran aground. But the evidence will show that there is somebody here in the courtroom that knew where Craig Spindle's body was the whole time. The murderer hadn't disposed of it in the river, but had buried it on the property where he'd lived his whole life. That man is the defendant, Edward Reynolds, also known by his alias, Pitchfork. Mr. Reynolds thought he'd covered his tracks and buried the evidence.

"You will see through expert testimony the probable cause of death was a bullet wound. A single shot ruptured something vital in this man that had stumbled into a killer's den.

"As law-abiding citizens, you might ask what could drive a man to kill another of his own likeness? Often times there's motive for it. A spurned lover might kill out of jealousy or out of hatred for the rival. Unfortunately this still happens today, but that is not the type of murder here. Other times it's for profit. Money from the insurance company. Or it could be a more intangible gain like a status enhancement. The evidence will show that isn't what this case is about. The motive could be plain hatred and vengeance toward the person killed. An intense dislike, a family feud. Although there was some hate involved, we don't have any of those clear motives here.

"From the evidence you may not know ultimately what motive Reynolds had. One can't guess at how a sociopath views the world. His heart and mind are filled with hate or extreme indifference. This is the story of a good man stumbling into a sociopath. The sociopath is Mr. Reynolds."

Calmly watching, he teetered on objecting. Feld had left him some gaps to work with. The presentation was reminding him of a crisp and crackling news broadcast from some bygone time. Feld's hawkish features demanded attention. He was conscious of an innate and visceral opposition. He had to stifle the desire to immediately refute what'd just been said. After some time, his concentration returned to what Feld spoke, "Mr. Reynolds was reclusive on that property. He lived there with his mother before she died. Many transients passed through there over the years. Somehow the little girl Spring Brandy was conceived and abandoned there."

Looking at the jurors and answering a question by Latayna, he lost track, then heard Feld again, "When he saw there wasn't much chance anybody'd find out, he took that life. From his twisted frame of mind, a mind lacerated by meth, he saw his opportunity.

"There's the possibility Craig stumbled onto something Mr. Reynolds thought would get him in trouble, but only Mr. Reynolds knows that. Back twelve years ago, Mr. Reynolds was involved with shooting Craig once in the chest, which ruptured an artery. The evidence will show that's how Craig died. Mr. Reynolds would've had time in those moments to reflect on what he was doing.

"After Craig had been shot, Pitchfork didn't call authorities to report an accident or give any explanation. There will be no credible evidence that he did anything. But he must've thought about doing something with this body. Maybe he was cunning enough to realize the authorities would eventually be dredging the river. Craig would often go to stroll along the banks and collect his thoughts. He was a peaceful, law-abiding man and an elite community leader."

He sensed on his periphery these references had a visible affect on the three family members present. He imagined the words ricocheting within them. The widow began dabbing her eyes with a handkerchief. He heard Feld continue, "Maybe Reynolds was calculating enough to avoid that dredging. Or maybe it was more a territorial thing. He decided to bury the body on his property near a pine tree later marked by shedded locusts' exo-skeletons. He knew exactly where the manifestation of his homicidal impulse lay.

"Before or after he buried the body, he must've had an inkling of fear at being caught. So he took the shovel he buried Craig with and took it to the man's skull. He used it to sever out the man's teeth. The evidence will show Craig's remains had no dental records. An expert will testify there are shovel-like indentions in the upper jaw. Mr. Reynolds must've thought he could delay or defeat identification. Imagine the callousness it would take to defile a dead body, or, heaven forbid, a still struggling one. That is the type of barbaric disregard for society and humanity a sociopath would have.

"To show that he was protective of his kill, the girl Spring will testify. Her testimony will show she had to suffer under him. Wherever she came from, she made it out of there intact. She'll be able to give us a clear window into the guilty mind of Mr. Reynolds. She'll show the type of rage Reynolds was capable of, especially how sensitive he was to the burial area.

"Pay careful attention to the manner, the memory, the interests, and the biases of each witness testifying. The defense plans to trot a crowd of degenerates through here to try and cloud your common sense.

"You'll probably be disgusted by the end of it. The pictures and the testimony of the medical examiner may horrify you. But this has a real life and blood consequence, determining who has gotten away with this for twelve years. The only answer is plainly before your eyes. The man sitting over there is capable of murder. The body was found on his property. It was mauled in a gruesome fashion that only a sociopath could stomach.

"The state will prove he is guilty. We shouldn't have to live in a society where it's alright to let someone bury another in their yard and go on like nothing happened. Ladies and gentlemen of the jury, the evidence will show Mr. Reynolds is the man responsible."

He watched Feld pivot and swoop around the end of his table. He felt the pressure shifting to him as if somewhere inside him there was a diver going down, plummeting down, causing a tingling sensation of falling. Miller announced for the jurors to turn their attention to the defense's opening statement.

He reentered his element. "Ladies and gentlemen of the jury, you're going to hear our best two stories of how the late councilman's body arrived on the property of my client's residence. The defense isn't disputing it was buried there in a crude and horrific fashion, but we are disputing that Mr. Reynolds was the one who had anything to do with putting it there.

"The story the state will have you believe is that Mr. Reynolds committed a random act on a date uncertain, approximately twelve years ago. That he attacked someone in his territory like a wild animal. That he was on drugs, acting crazy, and that is just what you'd expect of a man like that who made poor decisions. Then to hide his crime, he buried the body on the property where he lived.

"Through the next eleven years he let the body sit there, never moving it off his property or changing anything, expecting that it was safe from ever being detected. And the state will throw in that he's the epitome of degradation, of malice, of spite, the absence of value. That only a man of his lifestyle and his proximity to the body could've done this. The prime suspect ought to be whoever lives there, right? It would be an easy equation to hold that person responsible. On the surface it has an economy to it that would make sense if we were dealing with a financial transaction.

"In choosing you as jurors, we talked about the duties of jurors to consider everything that has been presented into evidence fully and fairly. Before I introduce our theory as a much more plausible explanation of what really happened, I need to reiterate that it isn't even required for the defense to provide an alternate theory. The state has to prove that its superficial analysis is beyond a reasonable doubt. Even its best evidence will be doubtful before we show you the more plausible story.

"Mr. Feld's description of Mr. Reynolds as a sociopath could lead one to infer he would kill again and again. What would stop such sociopathic instincts? The evidence will show that the authorities combed his property and surrounding area, not finding any other bodies. The state's explanation that Reynolds is a man capable of killing given the opportunity doesn't have any other examples but the one instance it is trying to prove. The state asks you to make a leap from the superficial circumstance of where the body was located to the conclusion that Reynolds is a sociopath.

"The evidence will show that the story involves sordid details beyond the gruesome fact of homicide. There'll be evidence of a more compelling motive than what the state describes as Mr. Reynolds's animal instinct to kill when protecting his territory. The much more believable story is based on the more distinct motives of greed and pride.

"Let's talk about the first of these because it makes the most sense. At the time, around twelve years ago, the evidence will show Craig Spindle was working against industry interests by promoting tighter pollution controls, including investigations into harms on people and the environment. The river was being polluted and that was what Mr. Spindle was observing. He was in a contentious struggle with industry leaders who wanted to keep the profits rolling in.

"Mr. Spindle gathered evidence to the contrary showing how the industry leaders gained through siphoning off these profits. Those in the industrial elite became very interested in taking the thorn Mr. Spindle had become out of their side. For a while they had a majority of the council three to two, but Mr. Spindle in his persuasiveness and political skill was beginning to turn a third vote against them. His proposed legislation would directly harm their money interests."

He paused for a second thinking they may wince at the mention of his name. "Who made that decision and how was it to be executed? Boesephious Caine has a peculiar connection not only to the property where the body was found, but also to my client Mr. Reynolds. That's where the second motive ties in, but don't forget the first, which would've caused Bo Caine to suffer incalculable losses from Spindle's proposals. The second motive of familial pride confirms our best theory of who did this.

"The evidence will irrefutably show that Mr. Reynolds is Bo Caine's half-brother. Mr. Reynolds and Bo share the same father, Alcorn Caine. Alcorn had an out-of-wedlock child with one of the most ill-reputed woman in the city. Not only was Judith Reynolds from a different part of the country up north living off an inheritance, but she also wound up in jail frequently until she finally died there. Bo Caine must've hated her for entangling herself in their family's line. But they were allowed to live on the Caine land when all other lands they owned along the river were put to more profitable use.

"The Caine family name is on the deed. One can easily conclude from this that the Caines were the ones suspending family shame. They contained it on the property, but eventually Bo Caine's patience ran out in worrying the secret might leak. Bo must've been pining for a way to ensure that information never saw the light of day.

"And then the opportunity arrived for Bo Caine to take care of the problem with Spindle and shift it to Edward Reynolds and his mother. Either the family shame was safe because Edward and Judith would keep quiet under threat of blackmail with the body on their property, or, if they spoke, they would be blamed for the murder. Caine's plan would take care of the two biggest impediments to his greed and pride, the pressure of costly legislation to his money interests and recognition of his shameful half-brother. Wherever he is, he must be pleased they're canceling one another out.

"Because of Bo Caine's ties, this explanation was never investigated by the state police. The state obstinately continues to prosecute the wrong person. One of the ways we as a society have moved past lynch mobs, one of the ways we've civilized the public outrage, is through the cooler review of facts in the courtroom. We want to make sure we get it right and don't convict the wrong person based on public outrage.

"Just because the state chooses to turn a blind eye to where the evidence points in this case doesn't mean that you have to let them get away with that. Don't let your dislike of the way Mr. Reynolds lived confuse the question.

"There'll be testimony from the girl Spring, who'll say my client was making gestures open to interpretation. Mr. Reynolds had heard the story of the murder from his mother, Judith. The biker Charles Dustin had heard about it as well and used it to rile up my client. Mr. Reynolds never wanted anything to do with the body.

"And if he went to the police, what would've happened? Would Bo Caine be implicated? Or would Mr. Reynolds and his mother be? The bind Caine had put them in was working. Mr. Reynolds never dug the body up first hand. Edward wasn't even sure who committed the homicide.

"The girl Spring will be a source of great sympathy. There'll be evidence to show that despite the circumstances surrounding Mr. Reynolds and his questionable parenting skills, she still received care in that house.

"But that's not what the murder charge is about. We're not contesting what her testimony confirms. Mr. Reynolds had been told by his mother about a body near the tree line in their backyard. And the biker threatened to implicate him with it so he made a gesture toward the ground.

"Mr. Reynolds stands before your judgment as a scapegoat for a more duplicitous mind. There'll be doubt in the state's case when we're through. The right verdict will be not guilty."

He'd been able to deliver it without many references to his notes. They'd seemed attentive enough. He heard Miller's far-off voice announcing a break.

He turned to Latanya. He considered allowing her to cross one of the witnesses, but warned her not to get too excited yet. She'd handled dozens of trials by the time she'd started working for him and several since then.

Miller returned and called the jury back in. Feld announced his first witness, Detective Deputy Jared Jones. Mustached Officer Jones told the jurors of his training then described his initial response, "There'd been a fire, and the house there was destroyed. Other officers and I marked off the property as a crime scene. Most of the house and its contents had been burned to a crisp and were unrecognizable."

Feld went back, "Did you encounter any witnesses to the fire?"

"Not at the time, no. But later a survivor of the fire was interviewed after a federal investigator discovered evidence of a homicide."

"Who was the survivor?"

"The girl now known as Spring Brandy."

"Officer, after the body was discovered, did you see it?"

"Yes. We had a forensic team go in. I saw the body being exhumed. I helped cordon off the area while it was being scoured for other evidence."

"And where was the body found?"

"Near the tree line in the backyard of Reynolds's residence."

Jones identified exhibit one. "Yes. It's a shot of the tree closest to where the body was buried. A pine tree with the remnants of some seventeen-year locust shells on it."

He sat patiently as Feld methodically went through the next thirty-seven exhibits. Between markers and tape were several rectangular pits. The property had been dug up in so many gradations that it reminded him of an excavation site. In the backdrop of a few pictures, the blackened foundation could be seen. The pictures were passed around. Then they broke for lunch.

After lunch there were thirty-two more pictures of the remains.

By the time all the pictures were in, he was struggling to stay attentive. Eventually Miller announced recess for the day.

* * *

Feld took up his direct again in the morning. "Officer Jones, how did Spring describe things to you?"

"She seemed like she'd experienced more than other girls six years old had."

"And did you find her injured in any way that could've injured her mind?"

"You'd have to talk to the medics."

"Officer, did you have any concerns that she may not comprehend the full impact of what she was communicating?"

"No."

The rest of Feld's direct blurred by with little objection as Jones went back to describing his initial impressions of the crime scene. Eventually Feld resumed his seat.

He stood up. "Officer, Spring never told you she saw Mr. Reynolds ever shoot anybody?"

"No."

"Or make any admissions or confessions to it?"

"No."

"How old was she at the time?"

"I think six. I'm not sure when she was born."

"And where did you talk to her?"

"At the orphanage."

"Did she seem to remember clearly?"

"I guess so. Just off what she told me."

"And when you were bagging and collecting evidence of the fire, this wasn't a homicide investigation at the time was it?"

"No."

"Did you ever interview my client about the alleged murder?"

"No."

"When did the federal agents pull out of their investigation?"

"Shortly after they left us to collect the evidence. There was a short time when we were doing concurrent investigations."

"And did that work well?"

"It worked okay. We were both able to gather evidence."

"Did you have any disputes over who had access to what?"

"Originally they got their own search warrant. And then we got our own. They were there first. Once the body had been dug up, they took their own photos. Then we took over and used our own markers."

"Were you drawing the same conclusions?"

"Objection. Speculation."

"Sustained."

"Did you have the same suspects?"

"Objection. Speculation."

"Sustained."

"Who was your suspect?"

"Our primary suspect was Edward Reynolds. That never changed during the investigation."

"How early did you make up your minds on this?"

"Pretty early. He lived on the property. We had a body on it."

"Did your investigation lead to any evidence that might exonerate my client?"

"No, not that I know of."

"Wasn't there other persons known to be on the property during the last twelve years?"

"Yes."

"And it's possible that any one of them could've committed the act that led to the body being buried there?"

"The evidence doesn't support that. We didn't think it likely that someone would be able to shoot someone, mangle the body, and then bury it without Reynolds knowing about it. He has always been the main suspect."

"You have to admit that you don't know what his activities were on a particular day twelve years ago? He could've gone to the store? He could've been sleeping?"

"We didn't consider it plausible that he wouldn't know about it."

"And you don't know whether the body was mangled, as you said, before or after burial?"

"No."

"Besides proximity to the body, what other evidence did you have?"

"Proximity was a highly important factor. Then there was the eccentric nature of Reynolds. There was an absence linking anyone else to the area during the time the councilman went missing."

"You don't usually base your conclusions on lack of evidence, do you?"

"No."

"And there was some lack of evidence in this case?"

"There could always be more in any case, I guess."

"But you don't have a murder weapon?"

"No."

"And a bullet was determined to cause the death?"

"Yes."

"Any discovery of a gun or bullets matching anything found on the property?"

"No. By that point, the house had burned down and much time had passed. I figured he could've easily gotten rid of any gun by then."

"And there were DNA tests run on the body?"

"Yes."

"Did any of my client's DNA show up on the body?"

"Not that we could find."

"So all you have is proximity to the burial site?"

"And the eccentric behavior of Reynolds."

"Based on your experience, that seems to make my client a good target for someone trying to blame a murder on him, wouldn't you agree?"

"Objection. Speculation."

"I'll allow an answer."

"Not necessarily."

"Thank you."

He watched Feld rise to redirect. "Officer Jones, does every case have DNA evidence?"

"No."

"Why not?"

"Sometimes the perpetrators can cover themselves in a way to prevent most DNA from appearing. There may be skin or hair left over. But if there is a long passage of time, traceable amounts could disappear."

"Is there a possible explanation why Reynolds's DNA wasn't found near the body?"

"Yes. There are several possibilities. He could've put on some type of gloves."

"What about hair?"

"Yes. That could've been placed in a hairnet or tucked into a hat. And if any fell, they could've long since been carried away by worms or other creatures in the soil. Or blended into the soil with root systems."

"Officer, does every homicide case have a murder weapon in evidence?"

"No. There are quite a few cases where the murder weapon is disposed of."

"Thank you."

He stood to counter, "But you didn't find any hairs in the soil?"

"No, we didn't."

"And did you really expect a man as eccentric and spontaneous as you say Reynolds was to think of wearing a hairnet?"

"It's possible. More likely he wore a hat. It's possible he didn't lose many hairs at all during the process."

"We shed skin cells and hair constantly, correct?"

"Yes. That's true."

"Would you have expected him to think carefully on these details?"

"We thought he probably paid an inordinate attention to detail consistent with a meth high."

"And if he were separating the jaw, you think none of the perpetrator's skin or hair would've fallen off?"

"He could've been covered thoroughly."

"Did you ever find gloves or hairnets or ball caps among Reynolds's belongings?"

"Everything burned up in the fire. We didn't see any of his possessions."

Based on yawns and leaning postures, he inferred the public eye had entered a gray period listening to other officers and detectives back up Jones's version of events. Before Miller announced they would break for the day, he was able to glean from one of the veteran officers some history of acrimony between Spindle and Caine.

He drove home feeling unusually optimistic about their chances. He cautioned himself against such levity. He thought of calling Sylvia. When he got to his front door and opened it, he found a note on the floor. He picked it up then saw Sylvia's handwriting. He began reading,

Dear Mark,

I haven't heard from you in a while and I wanted to tell you things in person, but you never called to get an idea of what I'm about to say. I don't think I can live this way. There's the constant attention to work. I'm coming to realize that isn't the kind of life I want. It just isn't me. I could try and fake it for awhile, but I think it will end in unhappiness for us both later.

Every time I said I loved you, I meant it. But I can't keep saying it anymore. Something has come over me the more that you've gotten wrapped up in this case, and I've had time to sort things out and write this.

His eyes misted over as he lost his train of thought. He resumed reading the concluding remarks to make sure he didn't misunderstand the intent.

I'm so sorry!

Please don't try to contact me. You'll find my ring and my key on the counter. You can forward my things to my parents' house in Mobile.

You're an incredible man. I feel terrible, but you'll get over it.

S.

He moved to his couch to re-read. He was gripped by an overwhelming urge to vomit. He remembered that deathly sickening from before, but never to this level. An urge to lash out against something accompanied it. His eyes welled up in anger. Something indignant and white hot boiled in him. He walked around his living room shouting and cursing. Everything that brought him to this point seemed to be preparation for a huge letdown.

The physically ill sensation wouldn't leave. He sat paralyzed on the couch. He didn't care whether he got sick on himself or whether he made it to the bathroom. A string of obscenities coursed through his mind as he tried to have a discussion with her in absentia. What had he done wrong? She'd done this. She was the one who caused this. She thinks she can do better.

The self-control he exercised in the courtroom wasn't accessible. That unflappable, tight-lipped, serious, contemplating look that seemed to know how to deftly intuit when and where to exercise assertions appropriately had disappeared. That self-control tried to exercise itself over the high volatility, but he couldn't contain it. Indignation spilled over in jagged, chaotic patterns. He felt something dramatic might happen. In the seldom moments when he lost that sense of self-control, his internal life became a dizzying array of a few extreme options.

What could've caused her to mislead him? He went through several scenarios. Each quickly ended with some painful version of betrayal. He conjured up a better-suited rival, a fabricated figure on the vague, vicious outskirts of an unreasoning paranoia. There'd been earlier boyfriends mentioned. He had no frame of reference other than the infrequent words she'd spoken describing past pleasures. That'd irritated him, but he'd tolerated it. Now there was nothing to bear the brunt of his jealous delusions besides the inside of his thin-feeling skull and the suddenly inadequate material walls built up to shelter his body.

What arrogance and cowardice! Time would show she was making a huge mistake. He was sure of it.

The attacks soon subsided. His pining for her and her best interests returned, slowly coating over the vitriol. The letter seemed a weak, flimsy wisp of an intention. It was a fraudulent excuse for the pain in his innards. He'd told others about her, making himself vulnerable. Plans would have to be cancelled. The embarrassment, during one of his most publicized trials!

A more objective voice persisted within him. His self-interested core tried protesting in vain against that far-off voice. Why would she think someone could outdo him?

The pleading hope tried making its way to the top of all the clamoring hate-filled thoughts. Drawn in by the tempting impulse to roll back the hatred of her and himself, he determined to take some corrective action. He could fix it somehow. He would call her.

He shook as he scrolled to her name and pressed the call button. It went straight to voice mail. He thought of hanging up, but second-guessed that, thinking that a firm, reasonable tone needed to be taken. He left a message asking what was wrong. He was sorry. They could fix this, he told her. He could fix it. He didn't understand. At least give him a chance to talk.

Exhausted, he began going through the motions of changing out of his suit. An overwhelming flood burned close to tears, but he held them back. He wouldn't surrender to that. He had control and he'd work through it. But it was dragging him down like an undeniable weight, pulling his whole body and motivation to his feet. He had to clop along through a mind-blasted effort. The day's work combined with this unexpected personal explosion had him washing his feet then making his way to bed.

Everything seemed extremely heavy as he fell into a crooked, nightmarish sleep.

He awoke a few hours later. After the shock of obliviousness wore off, he felt the stab. He recalled in a few moments. It was as if cut or displaced nerve endings had come screaming back to life after local anesthetic had worn off. It wouldn't leave him now. As he stumbled downstairs to get some water, he barely caught himself on the banister. The shape of the letter on the coffee table confirmed his misery.

He slunk to his sofa and leaned over to double check. No messages had come. A choking nausea arose at the thought of appearing in court the next morning.

After he returned to bed, he flipped in agony, unable to really scratch the surface of sleep. Despite the despair and anguish, his normal routine began to beckon derangedly in the early morning hours. Latanya would have to handle the rest of the week.

* * *

He asked himself what day it was when the alarm went off at six a.m. in a harsh cacophony of information. The usual steady voice of the news commentator jarred on his frayed, sleep-deprived senses. It was Thursday, the voice told him, grimly announcing the start of a new ashen future devoid of the characteristics most would equate with life. No plants or animals seemed to inhabit this new world of stretching desert. It seemed the absence of his fiancée left him with nothing but the bare necessity of air. Even its intake came in cruel pinpricks, mocking his attempts to exist.

Although he woke in the surroundings of a home with central air, he imagined he was in a motel room stripped of any claim to possession. He owned nothing there where a window unit cranked along moisturizing the stale air. The hallucination passed, but he cradled the sadness. Even if he did own things, it didn't amount to anything anymore. It held no meaning, except to remind him of the pointlessness of acquisition when the poignant loss of a greater, unattainable acquisition eclipsed those things.

He struggled for an hour to get out of bed. The scratchy, irritated surface of his mind plodded him through the usual routine. He didn't eat. It wasn't just a lack of appetite; it was an inability to ingest. His stomach seemed to have shrunk into a tight, poisonous ball of steel, allowing no admittance to foreign objects. It was part of him, but seemed remote simultaneously, unnerving him. He wanted to keep it remote, for if it came to the forefront of his consciousness, he would be sick.

Realizing with a slight shock he was running behind, it occurred to him he should give Latanya a heads up. Two more days until the weekend, he thought, as a punch-drunk fighter would cling to the hope of lasting two more minutes to rest in a corner between rounds. He could hardly catch the thought to read its impression.

From a more extreme place, the idea arose of withdrawing from the case and closing his practice. He didn't really have any specific plans after that. Perhaps he could find some way to end everything quickly.

Some other impulse cut the legs out from that idea before it could mature. It was as if some bulwark had been planted in him by all the work he'd done to arrive where he was. That last remaining bulwark held against the flood of everything that threatened his sanity, his competence, his short-term health. He would let Latanya handle the next two days. He remembered and began dialing purposefully, feeling a spiky, unwieldy discomfort in taking the action.

She answered alertly. She was taken aback, but then sounded excited. When he got off the phone, it seemed something necessary had been lifted to allow the possibility of getting through the day without collapsing. He couldn't think in an orderly fashion. Grasping to remember which witness would be next, the case twirled in a meaningless parade through his jumbled mind. He hardly had the energy and wherewithal to review his case file. Through his sickened condition, he recalled it was the county medical examiner. They weren't contesting Spindle was shot, which probably caused his death.

He wouldn't disappear, but his whole confidence was on such thin foundation, he didn't want to risk speaking in public. He'd sit in a stony silence and watch matters float in and out of his vision without proper significance. He'd sit as a recording device in hopes that his mind would come back enough to coordinate events. In his fury and grief, the outside seemed to portray someone else's life.

He drove someone else's car in someone else's city as he arrived at someone else's courthouse with someone else's briefcase, walking up the steps to someone else's moment before the camera, which he ignored.

Somehow he'd groomed himself with adequate precision to keep his appearance looking nearly the same as the day before. He could hide behind the features though they felt transparent this hot morning. Even the glaring brightness of the sun didn't arouse a speck of joy within him. It seemed like everything was covered in a film of ashen dust after some violent explosion, a mind-numbing and pervasive gray. He had difficulty breathing as he approached the court doors.

He suspected others could easily see he was on the verge of crumbling. He shivered despite the heat. The echo of his shoes on the stone floor restored some ghost of his previous strength, but only in minimal shadows and vague outlines. A blurry conviction reminded him the laws could be applied and translated here into real effects on the wildly diverse, sometimes refined, often untamed, other times sloppy affairs of men and women.

He couldn't have articulated these thoughts at the moment. The source of what had given them existence in his mind remained burrowed in some safe survival haven underneath all the internal slag piles of negativity and self-destruction heaped up. The smell of such a highly vaunted place had always allured him, giving off a serious yet elegant impression. He opened the door to the courtroom. Sitting in the cushioned chair at counsel's table, hearing the crisp clack of hard-soled shoes and heels, seeing the fine aged wood of the bench and jury box meant little to him at the moment.

Once inside the trappings of the courtroom again, not just dealing with the impression of what it would be like, he felt for a moment there was a decent chance he could make it through the next two days sitting there. Dark-complected Latanya arrived dressed sharply.

Reynolds already sat next to them. The gallery was full, but it all seemed oddly inconsequential to him. The crowd seemed filled for the most part with people that had no internal purpose driving them. That lack of direction to anything of import caused him to wonder. How do they have time to come watch during daylight business hours? Didn't they have anything better to do? They, including himself, all seemed to be engines milling about in tired circles without a destination. Any communion with what he estimated the public eye was focusing on had snapped.

A mix of colognes and perfumes wafted from the audience. Ordinarily it would've raised his senses into a heightened state of arousal where transitions were easier to make, smoothing over more jagged edges of awkwardness, keeping a veneer of flow to a process that was inherently choppy, jerky, and unpredictable. Now it reminded him of untrustworthy camouflage.

Everything seemed uncoordinated. If he had the wherewithal to care about discordant impressions, then he would've done what he could to improve on them. But he only had enough to sit stiffly in his chair and keep his mouth shut. He intuited any more expenditure of energy would require him to fold his hands and lay his head down on the desk, something he couldn't tolerate no matter what internal dismantling occurred.

As the trial resumed, he leaned back in his chair and watched, barely calming himself so as not to betray containment of the loathing and fatigue that coursed from that tight knot in his center radiating outward in pulsating waves of disgust. He detachedly saw the medical examiner enter and take the stand.

He remembered that the DNA expert would testify after this. Yes, there was a dead body on the property, and yes, the body was Craig Spindle. Even in his reduced state, his mind couldn't be prevented completely from working on the progression of the trial. If they were going to testify to anything, he wanted them to testify that the body was Spindle.

The esteemed medical examiner came out in a well-worn suit. He came across as a veteran professional, decent and sincere. Through the exhibits, he showed where he'd found the bullet and how he'd estimated the death down to around a three-month range twelve years ago. More gruesome photos came in. The medical examiner kept going on about how the bullet most likely pierced an artery close to the aorta.

His attention faded in and out. The thought of sleeping on his office couch appealed heavily. He feared he might slump in his chair. When Miller broke court for lunch, he calculated he could get in a twenty-minute nap.

When he got to his office, he absently heard Louise's, "What's s'matter?"

Not responding verbally, he made an indefinite gesture. A wide array of reminders and unfinished business sat on his desk aggravating him. He ignored them in his quickly crashing consciousness. He barked at Louise to wake him up in twenty minutes. He slumped down.

He came to with Louise yelling at him, "Mark! What's wrong with you?"

"Get away." He looked at himself in the mirror, bleary eyed. His hair was slightly askew. He went to the bathroom and used water to get it back into place. His eyes seemed haggard and uneven. Brushing off Louise's imploring questioning, he put on his suit coat and moved to leave.

He returned to his cushioned seat a few minutes after the appointed time. Nobody but Latanya seemed to notice. She leaned over, "Are you okay?"

His voice sounded high-pitched to him, like a wheeze, "Fine, just keep going. Consider me immobile until the weekend."

His aching body alerted he hadn't eaten since sometime yesterday. The thought of vending machines in the lobby wasn't appetizing.

The direct examination resumed. The medical examiner went on about how the markings of the jaw, or what was left of it, were consistent with a shovel or a spade. The testimony drifted unconnected through his mind. Eventually the thought rolled around of cross-examining to take the sting out of it.

Latanya had gone over this with him previously where most of the medical examiner's anticipated testimony had been reviewed. When she stood to cross-examine, his lost focus temporarily sharpened on her words, "By the time you looked at the body it was fully decomposed. Could the bullet have moved with time?"

"Yes."

"So the cause of death becomes more uncertain the more the bullet has moved?"

"Yes. Probably true. But it was still found in a vital region of the remains. And from what was left, there was evidence an artery had been ruptured."

"So there are other possible explanations of why that artery could've ruptured?"

"Could be. But that was the most likely conclusion based on the evidence I had."

"There is no way to be highly accurate in explaining the cause of death because of the age of the body, correct?"

"The direct cause of death is accurate in my opinion. But pinning down when it occurred is more difficult. I gave a conservative range of three months."

"Is it possible the bullet could've been placed there after death occurred?"

"I suppose it's possible, but the forensic evidence doesn't support it. I found no other cause of death on a toxicology screen of what was left."

"On the matter of the jaw, is it your opinion that this occurred after death?"

"It's inconclusive from what I had to examine."

"If a person had been subjected to a shovel in the mouth while conscious, might there have been tears in tendons or other muscles in the neck as the person wrenched away to avoid it?"

"That's possible, but I'm not sure."

"But there is nothing to support that the person was still alive at this point?"

"It's inconclusive."

"Wouldn't it be reasonable for the person to block the blows with their hands?"

"I suppose so."

"And there were no signs the hands of the body were damaged?"

"None that I found."

"It's possible that the teeth removal could've been done after the body had been initially buried?"

"It's possible."

"There's no scientific evidence linking the death and the teeth removal in time?"

"It's inconclusive based on what I had. There was no way to pinpoint the exact time of death, nor the exact time when the teeth were removed."

"Thank you."

Feld's response came briefly crisp, "Did you discover anything suggesting death and the teeth removal were done at different times?"

"No. I found no evidence suggesting they were different. We analyzed the dirt around the body. If it'd been dug up, there would've been some indication of different layers. It was the same dirt."

"Thank you."

Latanya stood again. "But if the same soil was replaced, you'd have no way of knowing?"

"There could be some sign of mixing soils."

"There could be?"

"Yes."

"Your technology wasn't capable of detecting a three-month difference?"

"A conservative estimate, correct."

He lost focus again, blankly hearing a brief reiteration of questions by Feld. The medical examiner left the stand. It was three p.m. Miller wanted to begin the DNA expert testimony after the break.

He dazedly walked around the halls. Conversation seemed achingly pointless. He went to the restroom. He sat on a commode with his head in his hands.

Direct examination began of the state's DNA expert. He struggled to stay awake, positioning himself in such a way as to avoid the jury seeing him flutter his eyes or stifle a yawn. He could see they were focused on the expert.

An hour passed establishing the DNA expert's credentials and connecting that with the samples he took from the crime scene. Testimony ended for the day.

As he walked through the door of his home, he checked his cell in a hapless manner. Seeing no messages, he lay down on the couch and turned on the television. The local news mentioned the case. Acute nausea gripped him. After a frenzied run, he made it to the restroom to vomit. He went upstairs and lay down.

An erratic and miserable sleep enveloped him.

* * *

He arose excruciatingly aware of hunger. It was two a.m. He lacked the energy to fix something to eat. Recalling recent events, he couldn't get back to sleep.

When he arrived at the diner, he sat down at the counter. The overweight waitress non-judgmentally took his order of eggs, toast, bacon, and hash browns. His teeth ached and were sensitive from being sick. He stared despondently out the window. Blinking neon irradiated from an unknown source. She returned with runny eggs and greasy hash browns. He ate quickly and purposefully.

As he waited for the bill, one of the few other patrons called out to him, "You the guy on TV for the murderer, right?"

He tried ignoring him, focusing on getting his card out of his wallet.

The patron sounded heavily drunk. "Hey, buddy, what're ya, too good to talk to me? I said, you're that guy defendin' the murderer."

Since ignoring the drunk wasn't working, he turned to address him. "They haven't proven he's a murderer."

The drunk man laughed, enjoying what he must've expected to hear. "Well, how's ya gonna get him off?"

"That'll be up to the jury." The doughy, folded-faced waitress gave him a sympathetic look as she scooped up his card from the counter to run it.

The drunk continued, "How do you do it?"

"What do you mean?"

"I mean, how do you go 'bout defendin' people like that?"

He looked at the drunk clad in a sleeveless, red and black checkered, unbuttoned shirt over a grease-splattered yellowish undershirt that read *Margarita* in tall cursive green lettering bordered by some faded palm trees. He thought the drunk could just as likely be his client on any given day. Half-turned, he shrugged in annoyance.

"Hey, man, I wasn't tryin' to get under your skin or nothin'. I just wanna know how you could make a livin' that way and live with yourself?"

A wave of frustration rolled through him as he shot back, "What if the state can't prove their case? Should I encourage them to plead guilty anyway?"

"I wasn't meanin' no aggravation. A man's gotta have sense, don't he? When he sees what's plain as anything, he'd be a fool to ignore it, wouldn't he?"

"That depends what you mean by plain as anything."

"No 'fense, but who cares for someone like that methhead? He should be put away to rot anyway."

"Should he be locked away for being a methhead or a murderer?"

"Sounds like parlor tricks to me. I haul real things up and down the coasts. I don't get paid to think 'bout more than move this here to over there by then." The drunk's flabby, pink-tinged arms emphasized the tight fit of the checkered vest. The arms flexed up for a second, but then returned to gelatinous appendages. "If a no-account bastard sits 'round doin' nothin', not even pushin' paper or tinkerin' on his computer to make some money, then who cares what happens to him? He's a waste, ain't he? For all I care, throw him in the jail landfill and keep him away from pollutin' the rest of us. And if he's done worse like kill a man, then they ought to hang him. I don't mean to get into no word game with a lawyer." The drunk unfolded his arms while smiling. The drunk seemed to be enjoying this through mock anger.

He turned to avoid any more conversation. He paid his bill. It seemed the others in the diner had disappeared. As he left, he heard some sharp taunts aimed at him from the burly drunk. The drunk must've been real, not just some dreamed up poltergeist.

Drained back in bed, he seemed to lack the energy to even accomplish sleep. The ebbing of painful time stretched across a lonely, maddeningly non-descript landscape from four to seven a.m. At seven, he felt obligated to rise and make an appearance.

As he drove to court, he experienced a sudden impulse to leave for some exotic area by plane, just as Caine had done. With a stuffy feeling, he found himself resuming the same place he'd been yesterday, sitting, watching, and letting things float before his vision. The parties dug back into slow-moving direct examination.

Dividing time up didn't carry much meaning for him at the moment. The weekend loomed before him as a long, barren stretch of misery. There would be no habitual motor functions he could perform to trick his mind into thinking time had progressed faster than it had. It would be bland, clockless torture without a purpose.

There were moments when he over-imposed his problems on the faces of whoever was in his vision. Members of the jury, people in the halls and gallery, projected the face of Sylvia for split seconds. He wondered what a nervous breakdown looked like.

The trial seemed to mock him in a perversely distorted masquerade. It was reflected in Spindle's family. As his thoughts wandered in a numbing oblivion of unstructured emoting, he began to identify with them in a pathetic streak of self-pity. They'd both been meaninglessly wronged. He clicked through a series of depressing episodic memories invoking a colossal despair.

Feld spent the morning with the expert, who pointed at graphs, cited treatises, and explained how accurate the testing was within point zero one percent. He thought it must've become tiresome to the public eye. By the lunch break, he'd seen some yawns. He'd developed something akin to an appetite again.

As he strolled painfully to find a sandwich he might choke down, he thought the possible root of the problems he suffered was the initial decision to go into the law. But even in his sleep-deprived and anxiety-ridden state, he couldn't fully accept that premise. There'd been too much contradicting evidence by this point. Then the flourishing flood of accolades and grateful clients evaporated quickly in the heat of more blinding anger. There seemed only to be a skimmed skin left of the hopes he had with her. He was sounding a slow retreat back to where he'd been before he met her. That place seemed exquisitely inadequate, something that should be granted him as a matter of natural right.

The so-called profession seemed to blend into a molten mass of inconsequence, which he half desired to be consumed by. It could be seen as a worthless bantering about of lofty notions that a clunker salesman could do just as well with. Or he could be seen as a gutless opportunist of grievous situations with no real hand in the ultimate outcome. It could all be determined by chance and posturing. He swallowed what felt like blocks of wetted sandpaper as thoughts crashed into caustic words in his mind. Before being uttered, they returned to their less distinct states. He couldn't finish the sandwich he'd ordered. He ate some chips, washing them down with some acidy soft drink. The rush of sugar crept into his tired derangement.

The DNA expert was up for cross. For the first time in the last day and a half, he instructed Latanya by telling her to go slowly and thoroughly. He didn't really track what was being said but appreciated the number of questions going off again and again. An hour and a half elapsed before redirect came back on.

The redirect ended. To his first small enjoyment in nearly two days, court adjourned for the weekend. When he got back to his home, he was tempted to drink himself into oblivion. Instead, he went to bed.

* * *

The next morning, he couldn't raise himself.

Latanya called him midday inquiring what to expect Monday. The neighbor who'd seen Spindle walking along the river was up next. He remembered a trestle about a mile or two from the properties that allowed limited public access to the river. That's the path Spindle would've taken. Would she need to be prepared to cross again? She received dead air from the other end. He heard her distant voice asking what was wrong.

He told her of the pending cancellation of his marriage and that he needed a few days to recover. He wanted her to prepare in case it took him longer.

* * *

On Sunday afternoon, he propelled himself back into reviewing his notes.

As he mentally prepared, the anticipation and nervousness of performing returned. Like numb limbs, his faculties awoke slowly. After a somber meal, he went to bed early.

* * *

Sleeping most the way through the night, he rose in time with the prior routine. He was able to hold down breakfast. When he arrived at court, he didn't feel as thin-skinned and rigid. The self-piteous morass he'd been wading through had faded.

The neighboring property owner took the stand. The neighbor came across as a straight-forward, rural country-man who'd seen the councilman walk the river around the time he disappeared.

"Could you point out exactly how often you saw Mr. Spindle do this?"

"Can't say specific on that day or not. But I seen him walk the river. More than once up till 'round he disappeart."

"Did you see him ever enter your neighbor's property?"

"Not directly."

"Did you ever see anyone attack Mr. Spindle?"

"I didn't see no one attack him."

"Did you ever hear any gunshots in connection with seeing Mr. Spindle walk the river?"

"Don't remember specific. Gunfire goes off from time to time where I live. There's huntin'."

By the end of his cross, he estimated the public eye had stopped paying much attention. The morning had invigorated him, but he still felt weakness at lunch. The federal agent would be up next. He needed to be sharpest there. Then he would have to use a careful touch crossing the priest and the girl.

His thoughts shifted back to Sylvia. He considered the unlikely chance of procreating in a timely fashion. He doubted he'd find someone less weighted down with baggage. He recalled a parade of women already married once or multiple times, women raising kids out of wedlock, women with alcohol problems, women with controlling tendencies susceptible to dramatic blowups. Then there were wildly promiscuous women. Some had drug habits. Others had eating disorders. All manner of bad combinations occurred to him, leading to let downs, break ups, disastrous losses of emotional investment, fortune, and prestige.

She'd been the exception, the beam of redemption he'd been holding out for. He mulled it over as he ate a tasteless sandwich, an annoying requisite to keep his energy. By the end of forcing it down, a childish impulse struck him to not show up.

When he returned to the courtroom, he made light conversation with Latanya until Miller came back out. He'd been in this position many times before, not wanting to begin the prickly task of cross-examining an officer, but knowing with a nauseating certainty he had to. Feld had Mantle recount finding the body. The agent vaguely referenced investigation of Dustin's activities.

Mantle's testimony took the rest of the afternoon. He made several hearsay objections, but most of the damaging testimony, specifically the child's implication of Reynolds having knowledge of the burial site, came in. The outline was there for the priest and girl to fill in.

When direct was over, Miller broke for the day. A line of questioning nagged at him, but in his reduced state, he blindly groped to remember what it was.

After falling asleep, he awoke to the fear of some missed point rankling in his mind. He contemplated whether he was losing his sanity and whether he should take some action against himself.

* * *

By morning, he'd shaken off the brunt of those thoughts. In eating his breakfast, it came to him. He was going to question Mantle on the resistance to getting back on the property.

He clearly saw where he wanted to end up with Mantle. The earlier questions flitted up to it, "In your report, there was a delay in time before you were allowed on the property?"

"Yes, there was."

"Why was there a delay?"

"There was a security guard who wouldn't let me in."

"Did you inform him you were a federal agent in search of evidence?"

"I did, but he wouldn't allow me on."

"Did you show him your credentials?"

"Yes."

"Was there anything valuable on the property at that point?"

"Only construction equipment and a scorched foundation."

"How did you overcome this resistance to your entry?"

"I went back to my vehicle and made a phone call to get a warrant and had it printed. I showed him while he was talking on his cell. After he got off the phone, he let me go about my business."

"And do you know who the legal owner of the property is?"

"Yes, it is Boesephius Caine."

"Did it seem like the security guard was unusually resistant to your entry?"

"Most times people comply. He eventually backed down."

"Agent, at anytime have you contemplated others to be involved with Craig Spindle's death other than my client?"

"Objection."

"Overruled."

"Yes. The biker that goes by the alias Cat's Paw."

"Do you think they acted together on this?"

"The evidence seemed to show that both were aware of the body."

"Did you ever investigate the actual owner of the property, Boesephius Caine?"

"He wasn't available. Our focus was to find evidence on the biker. The state investigators were more focused on the homicide."

"Do you personally suspect Caine?"

"Objection!"

"Overruled."

He watched Mantle hesitate slightly before answering, "It was the state's job. I'm not equipped to answer that. I haven't collected evidence other than on Cat's Paw. To hazard a guess would go against my training."

"So you're saying you think Bo Caine could've been involved, but you weren't able to gather enough evidence to support the theory?"

"No solid opinion either way."

"Did you rule Caine out as a potential suspect?"

"We don't claim responsibility for anything beyond collecting evidence on the bikers."

"Agent, do you now suspect Caine as being involved?"

"I'm not personally aware."

"As a professional investigator, do you think he was involved?"

"I don't have any hard evidence."

"Any circumstantial?"

"None that I'm aware of."

"What about his fleeing the country, does that cause you concern?"

"Objection, Your Honor, relevancy."

"Overruled."

"Yes, it does cause me concern, but he was not the focus of my investigation."

"What evidence did you collect of my client implicating him in the homicide?"

"The state focused on that."

"So you didn't collect any evidence on my client?"

"Some samples from the body were processed through the federal labs."

"Besides what was sent to the labs, the other evidence amounted to the incident in the backyard described by Spring?"

"Yes. That was the main evidence."

"And in summary, it amounts to gestures and words seen and heard behind a screen door over two hundred feet away?"

"I'm not sure of the exact distance, but she didn't see them point blank, no."

"Thank you."

He heard Feld resume, "Did the girl ever say she saw a body?"

"No."

"How were you led to where the body was?"

"She'd shown us the pine tree where she'd seen the two, Reynolds and Cat's Paw, arguing. We dug and discovered the remains near there."

"Thank you."

He stood again. "Did you ask her if she'd seen anybody else attaching significance to that pine tree?"

"I'm not sure I asked her that exact question."

"And did she tell you that was the only time she'd seen someone near the location where you eventually dug?"

"Not that I remember."

"So you can't rule out that there may've been other events that caused that location to be significant to the girl?"

"No."

"Thank you."

After Mantle had stepped down from the stand, other detectives had taken it to no substantial effect. He went home that night recognizing some rhythm. It was coming back to a barely tolerable situation he could control. He found his judgment and stamina returning by degrees.

Trying to keep Sylvia off his mind, he turned on the evening news. He focused with an urge to criticize. While it ran, he prepared himself a frozen dinner in the kitchen. He thought he heard something from the front of the house.

He saw the black clad figure entering with his back turned into the dining room. The intruder's head was covered. There was a pistol drawn. Recoiling a second in shock, he pulled his cell out and dialed emergency. He set the open phone at his feet as he edged up behind the diminishing wall created by the stairs. As he got up against the wall, he could see the edge of the figure whirling around.

He was about ten feet from the intruder as two shots rang out wildly. One bullet missed and sank into the banister. He felt a bright solid stinging shock through his leg.

He'd been lunging toward the figure as the bullet entered his leg. Sweating profusely, adrenaline and instinct drove him. While they wrestled on the ground, another shot went off simultaneously creating a sharp shock in his chest and arm. Despite the pain, he found himself holding the gun in a dizzying moment.

The intruder scurried out the front door. He saw the man must've punched through the side glass to unlock the deadbolt. He heard someone on his cell yelling, "Is everything alright?"

He lay down on his carpeted floor with blood pooling underneath him. He examined his chest. The blood seemed to be coming from farther up near his shoulder. He couldn't tell for sure. He thought of the shock of death. Unexpected, unwanted, but inevitable. Kind of like what she did. He willed himself to the cell and whispered his address then lay his head down. By the time the sirens were wailing on his block, he only faintly heard them.

* * *

When he awoke, the hospital bedside clock displayed Wednesday morning. Something was very much out of control. He was going to be late for something. He sank back for a second hoping against the real gravity of his concern that he was on vacation or in a dream state. Within moments, the responsibility bleeped madly. Today was a trial weekday. A panicky compulsion ran through him.

He attempted to rise up, but an excruciating pain demanded he lay back down. The pain had a leaden, non-negotiable quality to it that switched his mindset to one of an invalid required to take a sick day. There seemed no possibility of functioning through that disorienting feeling.

He relented back into a hazy unconsciousness. Vivid action scenarios occurred to him. Life-threatening agility feats cluttered his dreams. He left a platform to catch a moving vehicle to get away from some unspecified danger. He climbed high peaks where crevasses opened up. He jumped out of flying aircraft. The conclusion of these attempts to avoid injury or death was continually postponed.

He fell in and out of awareness. At times he sensed an IV in his arm. Then he was aware of another human's hands checking bandages on his leg and upper chest. This red-tinged, unreal passage of unproductiveness continued indefinitely.

The next time he woke, it was Thursday morning. He called for the nurse, who in turn called for the doctor.

The gray-bearded doctor had full, thick, black eyebrows. He guessed the doctor to be in his fifties. The doctor's eyes were dark. He couldn't distinguish the doctor's pupils from where he lay. The doctor reassured him, "The gunshot wound through the clavicle is fine. It's healing properly. But the one in the leg is nastier. The bullet just missed the femoral artery and caused a great deal of blood loss."

"When can I return to the trial?"

"I don't see how there's any safe way for you to return to work before two weeks pass. There's a chance of infection. You might tear some of the internal sutures we've made."

"That's not soon enough."

"I understand you have the murder case. It's been all over the news. The hospital prevented the media from getting information about you."

"Could you get me a phone? Where is my cell?"

"Certainly. I'm not sure where your cell phone is. I'll have the nurse bring you a phone."

After dialing a couple of numbers, he got through to Latanya. "What's the status with the trial?"

"Miller delayed proceedings and is considering declaring a mistrial."

"No. Keep going. I expect to be back there Monday."

He checked the clock. A quarter to noon. He'd have three full days to recover.

* * *

She'd been at dinner with her husband. A neighbor of M.L.'s was friends with his secretary, Louise Merrywater's family. The neighbor had seen the commotion outside M.L.'s house and called Louise. There'd been a break-in and someone had been seriously injured. The news crews arrived that night. Louise told her M.L. had been taken to the hospital.

Wednesday morning, she'd gone to get the files and notebooks she expected to need. At court, she'd informed Miller she would be taking over the case until further notice.

Miller had been inclined to declare a mistrial. In chambers, Feld had been opposed. Apparently Feld saw this turn of events as beneficial. Maybe Feld didn't want to repeat the last week and a half of testimony.

She'd told Miller she'd yet to have a chance to talk with M.L. Both parties had been prepared to continue. Miller had reserved his decision and ordered the trial to resume Thursday morning.

On Thursday, she watched Feld call Father McGowan next. Feld went into the priest's observations of the girl initially. The girl didn't eat much, wouldn't talk, wouldn't leave her room.

"Objection."

Objection overruled. The priest thought she was in shock from the fire still. Then they'd brought her kitten in.

He looked so rigidly starched up there in his black garment and stiff collar. In the muggy air outside, it had to be hot in that outfit. He said the girl had screaming fits. Well, why didn't you perform an exorcism? Hush now. This doesn't necessarily hurt us. Yes, she eventually started talking. It's the insects again. Wait now.

"Objection, hearsay."

Objection overruled. But then she gets to talk about the conversation with Mantle. She's going to say it anyway. And then Reynolds had pointed to where the girl pointed later.

She watched Feld use the rest of direct to confirm what had already been testified to by Mantle. By the time of cross-examination, it was almost eleven thirty a.m. Miller called recess for lunch.

She remembered what M.L had said about the heart of the state's case being the girl's testimony. They couldn't be overly aggressive with such a sympathetic witness.

When she returned from lunch and stood to address the priest, she wanted to know whether Spring spoke badly of Reynolds. No, she did not. And no, she was not afraid of him either. Since the fire, the girl often wondered how Reynolds was doing. And would it have been reasonable for her to be afraid?

"Objection."

Sustained for speculation. Not important. Already got what I needed. Did she say anything about seeing him dig near the locust tree? No, she didn't. Thank you, Father McGowan.

The two nuns would be next. She expected they would take up the rest of the afternoon and perhaps part of the next day. Then there would the child psychological expert. She looked over at Reynolds. He'd maintained calmness despite the absence of M.L. He'd watched the proceedings with an eerily objective interest as if he were watching a documentary on someone else's fate. The first nun shuffled in toward the witness stand.

Reynolds would most likely be sentenced to life if they lost, but she couldn't dwell on that. It would throw her off. Maybe that was why she'd blocked Reynolds out. She knew M.L. had spent several hours with him answering questions on what it would be like.

The unyielding timeline of the trial didn't allow ample time to address every angle or thought unless they were specifically carved out in space ahead of time. Sometimes good thoughts had to be sacrificed in order to keep tempo and not seem utterly lost by the unfolding of events. She returned to active listening. Her lines weren't scripted in advance and could be improvised at any moment. Words should be spoken carefully and precisely, without idleness or meaninglessness.

She listened as the nun gave more detail on the reticence of the girl initially. The girl had screamed at night as she adjusted. By the end of the nun's direct examination in later afternoon, Miller adjourned court for the day.

No word from the hospital. She drove to the hospital herself. The desk told her M.L. wasn't available to see anyone. She returned to the office to prepare for the child psychologist. A blurring period of wakefulness then eating passed by before she lay on her comfortable bed.

* * *

The next morning, the second nun described the girl as traumatized though she gradually opened up. Had Spring spoken in a derogatory manner about Reynolds? No, she hadn't. And she had wanted to know how he was faring? Yes, she had.

Near the end of the second nun's testimony, her cell vibrated quickly. At the conclusion of the clergy's testimony, Miller granted a short recess.

Outside, she was put in contact with M.L. She understood there was to be no mistrial. Because who knows how long Dustin and Screed would be on board? Understood. He would be back Monday for the girl's testimony. But if the expert finished early? She could review M.L.'s notes.

She flipped her phone shut and walked back into court.

* * *

After he hung up the beige, anonymously functional bedside phone, he went through a twenty-minute period of useless anxiety to the point that beads of sweat formed on his forehead. Under the squawk of the mounted television, he conducted mental scenarios. But he had no way to do anything with this bear clamp on his leg.

He had a desire to tear the man down who'd done this, as compelling as the desire to itch his mending flesh around the excruciatingly sore bullet holes. After this surge of impotent rage spent itself, he turned to more practical terms. The way to attack was with exoneration, but he couldn't litigate from bed. He slipped back into sleep.

* * *

She returned to counsel's table. She wasn't looking forward to possibly cross-examining the girl. Any novelty in defending a murder case had worn off. It was now about questions and answers, the nuts and bolts of legal structure.

The expert took the stand. The man struck her initially as somewhat pompous, but he handled the material adeptly, explaining with examples of traumatized children, referencing the shock of abuse.

She cringed internally during some of it. She fought back the unrealistic desire to wipe away testimony with bad connotations. No evidence of abuse was coming in, but she worried what the jurors might improperly assume from the symptoms the girl had exhibited. She'd reviewed the expert materials the night before, but she couldn't be expected to digest it all. Exasperation began creeping in, causing an intolerable burning in her face and chest.

She tried delving into one treatise the expert cited. But it was too much information. She put it aside for a second and tried to concentrate. Should she have even moved to the defense side? As the expert went on in a now almost charming manner, deep frustrations welled up within her from some unidentified area full of episodic memories of inadequacy. She looked on veiled behind a blank stare.

At lunch, she ruminated over a cup of vegetable soup, spiteful of her body's stubborn animal will to live despite whatever beatings her mind took. As she ate, her cell vibrated. M.L. wanted to speak to her. She fought back an urge to lash out. She yelled how horrible it was. She heard him tell her to calm down a second. Then he coughed and cleared his throat. He said he knew what she was going through. Being pushed into a corner where it doesn't seem there's any way to win. He'd been there plenty. And so had she. She was just forgetting it or it hadn't been this intense yet. He coughed again. Don't let it buckle her, he told her. The expert can't put words in the girl's mouth.

She flipped her phone shut. She finished her soup and went back to looking over the expert materials. She skimmed topics on memory and perception. It was too much to get through over lunch.

Back in court, she crossed on the accuracy of his opinions. A child's behavior isn't always rational and easily categorized? There could be certain consistencies in traumatic situations. Had he done statistical analysis? The book and charts talk about the numbers. But the studies weren't a hundred percent certain? They were done with methods to reduce error to insubstantial margins. How big was the pool of children studied? Which specific study? Her questions seemed only to emphasize the expert's points. The clock read three thirty p.m. After Feld covered twenty minutes on redirect, Miller broke court for the weekend.

Hearing this, she became much less anxious than she'd been the day before. Some pride even glowed in her chest. But when she couldn't reach M.L. by phone, something sank again in the pit of her stomach. Coming in, she'd expected maybe one or two crosses. What if it came to opening their case? In the beginning, she'd wanted some, but not all of the glory weight. She threw back her slumping shoulders into better posture.

* * *

He woozily awoke Saturday morning. He called for the nurse. She was younger and not bad looking, thin with black hair, but for some reason he wasn't attracted at the moment. He asked her to take him outside. She refused him, "No, you have to stay in bed, the doctor won't allow it. It's too hot out there anyway."

"I'm going to have to get used to it if I'm going to leave."

"You're going to be here at least another week."

"I'm not."

"Whatever." He thought she smiled somewhat flirtatiously with him.

By the time the doctor checked in on him at noon, Louise had already brought in a couple of binders. Looking toward the binders on his lap, the doctor assumed a stern expression. He meant to respond to the doctor's glare with a look of calm inquiry.

The doctor spoke first, "The nurse tells me you want to leave Monday morning?"

"That's almost right. I'll be gone by Monday morning. It's not a question of whether I want to."

"Mark, you can't do that to yourself. I won't be held responsible. Your body needs at least another week. And then another week after that of light duty. I know you want to be at that trial. I understand. I have patients that I can't stop thinking about sometimes, looking for another angle to save their lives. But I can't be held responsible for it. You know about liability."

"I'll sign away your liability. Don't worry about it. Just get it documented that I left against your direct recommendation. You can't force me to stay here. Don't suppose you know any dealers of wheelchairs open on the weekends?"

"Your body needs time. The blood is still replenishing itself. There could be leakage from the leg wound. You're going to be weak and liable to dizziness, even fainting spells, if you engage in strenuous activity."

"Could I borrow one from the hospital?"

The doctor showed a frustrated grimace then turned to leave with the air of a parent futilely trying to admonish a recalcitrant troublemaker. He called Louise to look up all the wheelchair dealers within a fifty-mile radius.

That night, she and Prentice delivered one. They helped him get out of bed into it. He unplugged his interferon IV and began wheeling around the room. He went wheeling down the halls in his hospital gown. The chair seemed a little big, but was a comfortable enough fit, like trying on a new pair of shoes. Turning in it hurt his upper arm, which was still in a sling. He gingerly used some of his muscles there to control the chair. He wanted the sling off by Monday.

The nurse that'd attended to him earlier was working extra shifts that weekend. After being called by an orderly, she ran up the stairs from the floor below. He was already in the elevator pressing buttons. She called out, "Stop! Mr. Sheet! Please stop."

He kept the door open and then wheeled toward her. "See how my recovery is progressing." As he said this, he grabbed a wheel with his good left arm to bring himself to an abrupt stop near her. He was perspiring.

She admonished him, "You shouldn't be taking the IV out on your own. You look paler than when you were lying in your bed." She got behind and started pushing him back toward his room. Once back in the room, she helped get him into bed. She returned the IV to his arm, telling him half-heartedly, "You're not to leave bed without my permission." In a more conciliatory tone she added, "Maybe tomorrow we can have you wheeled outside."

"My persistence is starting to work on you?"

She turned away with a smile seeming to ask what would drive a man who'd suffered two gunshots wounds and surgery to want to leave the hospital so quickly. He perceived her attraction to him, even if she might be unaware of it registering within her. He was tired from the first exercise he'd gotten since being admitted and fell asleep.

* * *

The next morning he was up early. Groggily, as he got his bearings, he remembered. Through an orderly that served him breakfast, he found out the nurse from yesterday wouldn't be back on shift until the afternoon. He began reviewing his binders to prepare for the girl's testimony. Though he had lingering doubts, a firmness in his mental state was slowly returning. He'd have to cross her gently anyway. He didn't see any benefit to being sharp, hanging on her every word.

By two p.m. on Sunday, the black-haired nurse's shift began. She smiled at him as she unhooked the interferon IV.

"That's the last of that I'll need."

She shook her dark, straight hair. "Mr. Sheet, you know you shouldn't be leaving for another week."

He immediately perspired in the heat outside. She wheeled him through a plant-filled common area. He insisted on pushing himself to get used to it. She walked alongside. They began talking about her as he wheeled back and forth in between the planters. He admired her slender body and curves. He found out where she'd gone to high school, where she'd gone to nursing school. "By now you have a boyfriend or husband?"

He noticed her blush. "I've been seeing someone, but I don't know."

He stopped the wheelchair a little abruptly. Then he wheeled around again in silence. He stayed out there for about fifteen minutes working on it before he came back to her. "Can we go back in?"

She walked with him as he rolled back. At the sliding doors, she saw the red streak in his gown. He caught the concerned glance. "Nothing to worry about. Just a little run-off." She pointed to the trail running all the way to his puffy hospital slipper. She grabbed the handles on the back of his chair. He gave in to her pushing him.

When he got back in bed, she inspected the surgery site for infection or a loose stitch, but didn't see anything obvious. He grabbed hold of her arm tight. "Now I don't want you going to the doctor with this. I've got a trial I can't be missing."

About thirty minutes later, the doctor appeared. He viewed the wound then announced detachedly, "I'm going to unsew some of the external stitches to see if the internal sutures are slipping to cause the blood loss. Mostly pus seems to be draining, which is normal, but we must be sure. Mark, you must abandon any daydreams of leaving by tomorrow morning."

He meant to look quizzically at the doctor without saying anything. The nurse hung back looking like a morose traitor. After they left, he called Prentice and Louise.

If he needed more surgery, it would have to be after the trial. Maybe it was a delirium, but he had a gripping clarity of what he was about. His near-term purpose required him to be at that trial. If ever he thought he was being called to do something, which his analytical mind was always skeptical of, returning immediately to the trial was part of it. He'd been dreaming about it, sometimes in twisted difficulties restructured from images of his work. The underlying point of completing the tasks was the same.

He went to bed early around eight. Before he fell asleep, he called the nurse back for a final request. "Could you explain to the night shift that I need to be wheeled around this morning at four a.m. sharp?"

* * *

After he woke to his alarm at four, a half-cognizant orderly wheeled him down to the outside. The nurse wasn't on shift any longer. While Prentice engaged the lethargic employee in a conversation over smokes, Louise wheeled him to a rental van equipped with a wheelchair lift.

The orderly must've heard the lift from across the common area. He could hear the orderly's voice through the muggy, empty night air, "Wait! You can't leave yet, sir! You haven't checked out properly!"

Louise swung the van around to the street behind the hospital to pick up Prentice. He instructed Louise to stop by his house. He had to get changed into a suit eventually. He heard Louise expected a large bonus this year.

They entered his home through the back porch. Louise wheeled him into his den. There was still blood on the carpet, but the crime scene investigation had been cleared. Prentice helped him change into a suit. In taking off the hospital garb, Prentice pointed out, "Hey, man, you're leaking. You sure you want to put on your slacks yet? Let me see if I can dress it up a little." Prentice returned with a cloth and began wiping his leg, then wrapped fresh gauze around the stitched-up wound. After getting cleaned and dressed, he worked on maneuvering the chair around in his driveway. After a half hour, he went back inside to review the materials.

At eight-thirty, he roused Louise from the couch to drive him to court. After being lowered slowly by the mechanized platform, he wheeled himself up the handicap ramp. This accommodation had been appropriate to him before in a detached sort of way, but now he appreciated its concrete usefulness. Likewise, the button to automatically open the door was more than a gratuitous luxury.

The media gorged on his situation, floating around him in a dust cloud of questions, none of which found purchase. The cloud seemed to grow hazier by the moment as more of the buzzards arrived. Cell phones and video must be spreading the visuals. He wheeled himself into the courtroom and resumed his place behind counsel's table next to Latanya. Reynolds was smiling at him and stuttered something unintelligible, to which he winked. He leaned over to whisper about his recent health setbacks. Listening intently, Reynolds seemed oblivious to the fact that his life in prison was at stake in the unpredictable mechanisms of the court he was caught in.

He noticed Feld eyeballing the two of them as if he were viewing some type of inappropriate joke unfolding. He came over to inquire what was going on.

He greeted Feld, "You didn't think I'd lie down entirely, did you?"

"You were released?"

"I'm here."

"Are you fit enough? Be straight with me, Sheet. I don't want him getting a retrial because you were out of your skull representing him."

"Go ahead. I'm in wherever it leads."

"I don't care either way. Whoever's doing it, they need to be fit."

"You seem rather uptight, Feld. Don't worry about me. I'm fit as an Arabian steed."

Miller appeared from chambers. A slight moment of startled realization flashed across his countenance, but he quickly adjusted. "So you're able to rejoin us?"

"I'm able, Your Honor, with the temporary aid of this mechanical chair."

"I would like to see you both in chambers."

After he was through the door, Miller abruptly stopped them in the hallway. "What's going on here? I thought you were bedridden for another week at least?"

"Judge, I had a remarkable recovery. I'm ready to continue."

"You're okay with trying it from your chair?"

"I may have to adjust my cadence, but I've been working on maneuvering."

Miller looked over at Feld. "What do you think?"

"I would object that this is prejudicial. It could evoke sympathy. It needs to be shown Mr. Sheet is fit to handle the case."

Miller looked at him. "Are you fit?"

"As a marathon runner. And my arm will be healing soon. Should have the sling off within the week so I can regain full pointing ability."

"On any pain meds?"

"Nothing but over-the-counter pain relief."

"As long as he's fit, I don't see a basis to prevent him from taking over his own case. You can note your objection on the record."

He turned to wheel himself back in. As he rolled back behind counsel's table, he noticed Brandy the firefighter and his family amongst the crowded rows in the gallery. He sought out the girl but couldn't see her.

Latanya let him know she'd seen Spring outside. The state's paralegal and witness coordinator had been trying to coax or calm the girl even though she didn't seem to need it. Latanya mimicked what she'd overheard them repeating, "Now honey, be sure you remember what happened before the house burned down."

At ten a.m., the state called Spring. He perceived attention wrap tighter around the proceedings thick and stuffy as a winter coat indoors. He imagined the media wanted to transform the telegenic six-year-old into a beatific, thin, and ethereal creature, which had some truth to it, but not in the way they imagined. The state groomers would no doubt hope for her to be an incarnation of innocence that the collective public will would coalesce around to protect. He speculated Feld wanted the jurors to ask themselves, if this here isn't protected and sacrificed for, what else then could be sacred?

Spring looked far away on the witness chair. A special seat had been pre-arranged so that she could reach the recording microphone. Her voice was a high-pitched alto with a soft, honest wonder at the edge of it.

He'd been full of brash confidence on his return, but the effect of the image she was presenting was half enthralling him and half turning his stomach in painful knots. She hadn't been free to leave the house. Most times it sounded like she stayed isolated in her room while the others caroused. His attention refocused as he heard Feld asking, "How did they take their medicine?"

"Objection, relevance."

"Overruled. Go ahead and answer."

"They would sniff it up their nose. Or smoke it. Sometimes people stuck needles in their arms."

"Who were they?"

"Uncle Rey-Rey sittin' over there. And Chris's dad. And the uncles with motorcycles. Sometimes there were ugly people with sores on their arms who smelled bad."

The depravity, the unkempt house, the derelicts sleeping in their own waste became vivid through the girl's testimony. The state was using her angelic voice. Her simple descriptions only amplified his imagination and fears. He fired off a few objections from his chair, but quickly saw them become impotent as flares, only shining more light in their flight.

The drunken matriarch was paraded through the public eye. An inebriated hag with an exaggerated sense of importance was all she seemed, cut off from any semblance of nurturing. He listened to the lithe descriptions, "Grammie threw up on the couch and it was in her hair."

"Did Grammie ever hit you?"

"Grammie didn't hit me, no. I would go in my room when Grammie got real sick. Aunt Cherie would talk to me sometimes to keep her away. Sometimes Grammie would stay away for a long time."

"Would Uncle Rey-Rey ever hit you?"

"Objection."

"Overruled."

"No, Uncle Rey-Rey wouldn't hit me. We would play board games sometimes. Or do puzzles. Most times I played with the aunts. When Uncle Rey-Rey was takin' his medicine, he'd sometimes mess up and move the wrong way. I'd have to show him what he did wrong."

He lost concentration to a throbbing soreness as Feld went on about John and Chris Screed. He refocused when Feld asked, "What was Chris's daddy like?"

"Chris's daddy wore a big belt with lots of tools. He built things."

"Did you see him build things?"

"He built onto the buildin' out back. And he worked on our roof."

"What was the building out back?"

"It was a place where Uncle Rey-Rey and Chris's daddy kept tools. When Uncle Cat Paw and Uncle Muffler would come over, they'd pull evarthin out and sleep on beds without legs."

"Did the motorcycle uncles stay there a long time?"

"They'd stay for a while and come in and share Uncle Rey-Rey's medicine. Uncle Cat Paw would pick me up so I could walk on the ceilin'."

"Did the uncles ever make you feel uncomfortable?"

"They were fun and laughed real loud. They had hairy beards and were big, but I didn't get scared after I got to know 'em."

"Did you ever see them get mad at each other?"

"All the time. Uncle Rey-Rey would yell at 'em, and they'd holler back."

"Did you ever see them get in a fight?"

"Sometimes."

"What would they do?"

"They'd hit on each other. I'd watch 'em from the back porch."

"Was Uncle Rey-Rey like that too?"

"I saw Uncle Rey-Rey get mad at Uncle Cat Paw one time. Those ladies that work for you tole me to remember it real good."

He smiled as Feld hesitated just a slight moment. Then Feld resumed, "What happened then?"

"Uncle Rey-Rey was real mad and he yelled at Uncle Cat Paw that he was goin'ta put him under the locust tree."

"What do you mean?"

"He was goin'ta put him dead in the ground. Where I showed the police officer."

"When did you show the police officer?"

"When he came to the priest's and nuns' house and ast me questions. Then we went to where our backyard use'ta be."

"Now what exactly did your Uncle Rey-Rey say that day?"

"I heard him yell he'd put Uncle Cat Paw in the ground if he didn't shut up."

"Where did he point?"

"Near the locust tree."

"What's the locust tree?"

"It's a pinecone tree with some shells on it. Chris's daddy tole me those were seventeen-year-old locusts. They come up out the ground when they get ready as grown-up locusts."

"Did you ever see Uncle Rey-Rey dig there?"

"Ont-anh. I just saw him point there."

"Do you know if he put the skeleton there?"

"I don't know where it came from."

"Do you know if Uncle Rey-Rey knew it was there?"

"Objection, speculation."

"Overruled, go ahead and answer."

"I don't know. He pointed to it."

"What did he say as he was pointing?"

"That he'll put Uncle Cat Paw there too."

"So do you think he knew about it then?"

"Knew 'bout what?"

"Knew about the skeleton already down there?"

"Sort of, but I don't know how much."

"What do you mean?"

"He might know there was a skeleton 'cause other people tole him even though he might not have seen it."

"But you are sure he said too?"

"Un-hunh. He did say that."

"What did Uncle Cat Paw do when he yelled like that and pointed at the ground?"

"He was laughin' at Uncle Rey-Rey. He wanted to fight him I think."

"Did he say anything?"

"Not that I could hear. He just laughed real loud."

"Did they do anything else?"

"Uncle Cat Paw went back toward the buildin' out back and Uncle Rey-Rey kept on starin' and shakin'. He'd taken a lot of medicine earlier. Then he started comin' back to the house. I ran back to my room, but not all the way. I stayed in the hall. I's use'ta doin' that when there were just grown-ups 'round and they didn't want to play with me. I stayed in the hall and watched him sniff a bunch more medicine up his nose. Then he went back outside."

"You ever see him dig around the locust tree?"

"Not that I remember."

"Anything else you remember about the locust tree?"

"Me and Chris use'ta play hide n' seek and we made the locust tree home base. Chris was faster than me and he could find me easier than I could find him. One time when I's countin' with my head on the tree, not peekin' or nothin', Uncle Rey-Rey scared me 'cause he come up and poked me on the shoulder. I thought Chris was teasin' me, but I turnt 'round and seen Uncle Rey-Rey. He yelled at me askin' why I's playin' 'round the tree? I tole him me and Chris wanted to use the locust tree for home base. And he sayed he don't want us usin' that tree for nothin', no playin' atall. And I sayed okay. And then he went and found

Chris behind some other tree and tole him to stop. He tole us to pick 'nother tree for home base."

"Did he ever say why?"

"Not really. We'd get in trouble if we'd play 'round it. So I would walk away from it and always go 'nother way when we went to the river."

He shook off being slightly mesmerized. The public eye of the jury seemed enraptured, many of them leaning forward seemingly trying to physically absorb what she had to say. In his periphery, he noticed Reynolds making gestures toward his face. He looked back to the girl. Miller was staring down at him. "Anything by way of cross-examination?"

Even though he'd been startled, he composed himself. Being confined to a chair made it easier to cover loss of balance. He wheeled out and around counsel table, placing himself in full view of the jury, angled toward the witness stand. "Good morning, how are you today?"

"I'm okay. Maybe sad a little."

"Why is that?"

"'Cause I haven't seen Uncle Rey-Rey in a while and he's in trouble."

"Do you think he deserves to be in trouble?"

"Objection."

"Overruled."

"You mean, did he do bad things?"

"Do you think that he should be in trouble for putting the skeleton in the ground?"

"I don't know."

"You don't know who put the skeleton there, do you?"

"Ont-anh."

"And you never saw Uncle Rey-Rey put the skeleton there."

"Ont-anh."

"Or see him dig around the locust tree?"

"Ont-anh."

"Did Uncle Rey-Rey ever talk about putting the skeleton there?"

"Ont-anh. But he talked 'bout puttin' Uncle Cat Paw there."

"Did Grammie ever talk to you about putting a skeleton there?"

"Not really."

"Did she ever say anything about the locust tree?"

"Grammie had this paintin'. I ast her why was there a dog sittin' near the locust tree. I ast her did they used to have a dog like the one in the picture, one that had long ears? And she sayed there was no dog no more, honey."

"What was the painting of again?"

"A dog with long ears layin' down in front of where the locust tree was."

"When was the last time you saw Grammie?"

"'Fore she died when I's four."

He fought an urge to roll back and forth to reflect how he sometimes paced. Given the sling on his arm and the cumbersomeness of the chair, he refrained. "When you saw Uncle Rey-Rey point where the skeleton turned out to be later, how far away were you?"

"I's on the back porch lookin' through the screen."

"And could you see through the screen good?"

"There was a hole in part of it that I's lookin' through."

"How big was the hole?"

"Big enough for my eye."

"Just one eye?"

"Un-hunh."

"And do you know how far away the locust tree was from the house?"

"It's one of the first trees 'fore the woods that go to the river."

"Do you know how many feet?"

"A bunch."

"What if I wheeled back some? Say from me to you. Was it that far?"

"It was further than that."

He then backed up to the gate to the gallery and rolled midway back through the aisle and raised his voice, "How about here?"

"Further."

He wheeled back to the doors to the courtroom and yelled, "About right here?"

"Even further."

He rolled forward. "And from there could you really tell where he was pointing?"

"Un-hunh. Uncle Rey-Rey was pointin' at the ground."

"How's your hearing?"

"I hear good."

"And from that far back, could you hear exactly what they were saying?"

"I couldn't hear all they sayed 'cause they was talkin' low. But when they started yellin', I could hear Uncle Rey-Rey."

"Did you hear what Uncle Cat Paw said before Uncle Rey-Rey yelled at him?"

"I just remember him laughin' real loud. I couldn't hear what he sayed."

"That was the only time you saw Uncle Rey-Rey pointing at the ground there?"

"That I can remember."

"Did you see where exactly he was pointing?"

"Near the locust tree."

"Was he pointing exactly where the skeleton was found?"

"It was close to where they found it."

"And you wanted to see Uncle Rey-Rey after you went to the orphanage?"

"Objection."

"Overruled."

"Un-hunh. I missed him."

"Was he ever nice to you?"

"Un-hunh. He gave me toys and could be nice most times."

"Did you watch a lot of TV in the house?"

"Un-hunh. I watched cartoons and lots of TV shows. Sometimes the shows were for grown-ups. I'd get bored. But sometimes I'd watch 'em anyway."

"How often did you watch TV?"

"I watched it all times of day. Whenever."

"When you remember things, do you sometimes think of the TV shows?"

"Sometimes."

"Can you tell the difference between what really happens and what happens on TV?"

"Sometimes it seems like the TV was really happenin'. I'd be real scared at some of the night time shows' music. But then the aunts would tell me it wasn't real."

"How were you feeling while watching Uncle Rey-Rey and Uncle Cat Paw yell?"

"I's scared. I run away when I saw him comin' toward the house."

"What time of day was it?"

"In the afternoon. 'Cause it was hot."

"What were you doing right before the yelling happened?"

"Cartoons had just ended."

"Are you sure what you remember wasn't mixed up with what was on TV?"

"Un-hunh. Uncle Rey-Rey was yellin'."

"When you left from the screen door and were in the hallway, did he say anything to you?"

"No. He went back outside."

"Let's talk about Grammie a second. Did they have any type of service once you found out she'd died?"

"Uncle Rey-Rey sayed she was goin'ta be creamed and turnt to ashes. Her skeleton wasn't goin' in the ground."

"Did Grammie ever talk about someone else putting a skeleton in the ground?"

"Don't remember her talkin' 'bout it."

"Did she ever make you scared?"

"Sometimes. She drank a bunch. She'd come in my room and talk 'bout things."

"Anything you remember for sure?"

"She sayed if anythin' ever happens to her, I'll know why one day."

"Did she ever complain about people?"

"Grammie complained a lot. Then she would drink and laugh a lot. Her words sometimes come out mushy. I couldn't hear what she sayed so good."

"Let's talk about Chris's dad a second. Did Chris's dad ever say anything about a skeleton in the ground?"

"Don't remember. But when he was on the roof once and drinkin' beer, he sayed he was ly'ble to fall down and be a skeleton a buzzard wouldn't touch 'cause of the heat up there."

"Did he ever talk to Grammie?"

"Un-hunh. They both like drinkin' beer."

"Thank you." He wheeled back behind his table.

Miller looked up at the jury. "We're going to take a fifteen-minute break now."

It was getting closer to lunch. He took out his handkerchief and wiped off his forehead. He felt lightheaded. His suit pants were stuck to the inside of his leg. He saw a wet, dark red bloodstain showing through.

It'd gone quicker than he'd expected. He waited to go to the restroom on account of his leg. He was able to conceal it sitting down. He'd have to cover it some way as he moved. He leaned over to tell Latanya to get a doctor to his house that afternoon after five. Then he closed his eyes. When she patted him on the shoulder, he reopened them. Ten minutes had passed.

His eyes glazed over as Feld rehashed what was already out there. The courtroom became somewhat of a blur, but he had his ears attuned for any discordant material.

After Miller called lunch recess, he waited for the crowd to disperse. With his briefcase over his lap, he made his way to the small cafeteria in the hallway. Latanya brought him a sandwich, which he ate quickly. When they returned to the courtroom, he had the bailiff call in the transport request for Screed the next morning and to have Dustin on standby.

When testimony started up again, he felt visibly weakened. He passed the recross to Latanya. He listened to her ask more about the Screeds. Feld asked exceedingly redundant questions. As the girl was getting down from the witness stand, he watched her start to walk over toward Reynolds, who was wiping his eyes. She was smiling. The bailiff steered her back to the central flapping aisle door.

Feld rested the state's case at three thirty. Miller excused the jurors. Once the courtroom cleared, they discussed transporting the federal prisoners. Screed would take the stand in the morning, followed by Prentice, the DNA expert, then Dustin. They would finish with Reynolds, should he take the stand.

He left the courtroom with his briefcase over his leg to hide the blood. Back at the house, he was pushed into his living room. He felt overexerted and sick. An elderly, thin doctor arrived. Louise had described the doctor as respectfully entering the twilight years of his career. The doctor had time to make house visits. The doctor undressed the wound saying in a hoarse voice, "Not the artery. Otherwise there'd be a lot more blood. You need to be careful, son. Infection could set in."

The doctor shot the area up with anesthetic. He cut some of the external stitches to take a look. After an inspection, he sewed the wound back up. "Here's some antibiotics. If you start running a fever, call me or go back to the hospital. The thing will keep draining. You may want to wear older suits." The doctor wrapped gauze around the wound before leaving.

Louise fixed him something to eat. He'd instructed her to have everything ready by eight tomorrow. He went to sleep in the dining room where the bed had been moved to avoid him having to go up and down the stairs. Through the window he saw a patrol car. The city police had been driving by every thirty minutes or so.

* * *

Prentice got him up the next morning to help him get dressed and into his chair. He ate a light breakfast of melons and toast. They arrived at court just after eight. He expected Screed by eight thirty. Prentice assured him in advance that Screed had something more respectable to wear than the grimy construction overalls he'd been arrested in. Prentice had purchased a pair of used slacks and a button-down shirt from the donation store.

Screed took the stand at nine. He gestured toward Reynolds, "How do you know him?"

"I knew his momma first. She'd come over to Miss'sippi where I's from. Ran into her at a bar. She was older than I. That was before I had my boy. She'd invited me over to stay whenever I felt like. Me and Pitch started tyin' one on together years ago. I'd pass through when I could. After I had my boy, we'd both come through."

"About how often?"

"It varied. Sometimes I'd get work lined up in Florida. I'd stop back through on the way to my hometown. All that development kept goin'. Then after the hurricane I'd go to N'awlins. Didn't make it through as much for a while."

"What type of work would you do?"

"All types of construction. Carpentry, paintin', roofin', anythin' needs mendin'."

"How often did you talk to Judith Reynolds?"

"Evar so often when I's there."

"What type of relationship did you have with her?"

"I wouldn't call us lovers ness'sarily, but sometimes we woke up in the sack naked together after we had too much Natch. I feel bad admittin' it, seein' she was a bit older than me, but it's true."

"Did you ever see any bikers around there?"

"I'd seen Cat's Paw and Muffler. Don't even know their real lass names."

"Who were they to you?"

"They were acquainted with Pitch and his momma."

"Did you interact with them?"

"Sometimes we tied one on together."

"Were you friends?"

"Don't know that I'd call us that. We had some wild times together, but they was always a little separate. In their own world, I guess."

"Did you ever get in a fight with them?"

He paused a second. "We exchanged words sometimes, but I don't remember it comin' to blows."

"How about between Cat's Paw and Mr. Reynolds?"

"I seen 'em argue."

"Did you ever hear Mr. Reynolds make any threats to Cat's Paw?"

"Yeah, I seen him make threats, but that was just talkin', you know."

"Did you ever witness him carry out threats?"

"Naw. It was just talk. They'd try to get on each other's nerves. Nothin' come of it."

"Did you ever hear anything about a body in his backyard?"

"Yes, I did."

"Who'd you hear it from?"

"His momma. Judy."

"When did she tell you?"

"It'd have to be two or three years ago, gettin' close to when she died. She took me upstairs and showed me this picture she painted with a hound sleepin' in front of a pine tree. Looked like a renderin' of her words."

"What did she say about it?"

"She started talkin' funny like she was lettin' me on a big secret. Then she says the man who owned her land made her life miserable. She sayed Bo Caine was the one that hid somethin' there. And I ast her what she was tryin' to tell me. And she sayed…"

"Objection, hearsay."

"Overruled. Continue with your answer, Mr. Screed."

"She sayed Caine tole her she was to guard it and if she turnt on him nobody'd believe her anyway. And I ast her why she was tellin' me. She sayed 'cause she was drunk. And then she started tryin' to get on me. But I pushed her off. I wasn't drunk. And she sayed I can't tell no one. She sayed she wouldn't own it."

"What did you do next?"

"Went downstairs and left her up there. Didn't think much on it till I started readin' in the papers later. Didn't make much sense at the time."

"Did you talk with Mr. Reynolds about it?"

"Yeah. I talked to him 'bout it once. I's tellin' him how crazy his momma was gettin'. He sayed she'd probably picked up all kinds of stories in jail."

"Thank you."

He wheeled back. Before Feld could begin cross, Miller signaled for a break and sent the jurors out. Feld began arguing for what could come in to impeach Screed. They'd discussed this earlier, but it took an hour of wrangling to come to the same conclusions.

After lunch, Feld launched into it. "So, sir, you hail from Mississippi?"

"That's right."

"But you've never really had much of a home in Mississippi?"

"Use'ta have a trailer there that run in the family, but it got ruint."

"Did you sell it?"

"Yes, sir. I'm still 'llowed to sleep on the property. Built a little shanty on it."

"So you've been homeless for most of your adult life?"

"I wouldn't say so. I usually find some wood and shingles 'tween me and the elements. Most times a pilla too. I worked my whole life. I ain't one of those beggin' at busy intersections."

"But you've stolen from people before?"

"What you referrin' to?"

"You've taken from people without providing them services?"

"Oh, you mean in Florida. That was a misunderstandin'."

"It's a guilty on your record, isn't it?"

"Yeah. I pleaded guilty to it. It was a misunderstandin'. That was the quickest way to get it over with."

"How is it a misunderstanding to tell people you're a licensed contractor when you're not?"

"What I'd agreed to do for 'em people was things I'd been doin' my whole life. The gov'mint regs were different down in Florida."

"But the regulations didn't cause you to skip out on a job before finishing and to keep the money?"

"Those people had broke they contract."

"Let's talk about your drinking. Did you drink most times when you were over there at Pitchfork's place?"

"Yes, sir."

"And what would you say the average amount was that you drank?"

"I don't know. Pitch's momma had case after case of beer. Probably 'bout a twelver a day."

"You mean a twelve-pack of beer a day?"

"Give or take. Yeah."

"You can't say for sure because you can't remember?"

"Well, I don't remember evar day. It weren't like I's keepin' notes. There were some days I didn't drink."

"All that drinking would affect your memory, wouldn't it?"

"Could sometimes, but I got a high tolerance."

"When you were talking to Judy Reynolds that time in the attic, you'd been drinking, right?"

"Yes, sir. But not as much as she. I wasn't that drunk."

"How about meth? Were you doing some meth too?"

"I'd been drinking, but I wasn't doin' no meth."

"And Judy Reynolds was drinking too?"

"Yeah, she was. All the time."

"Are you sure you remember what she said?"

"Yeah, it stood out. After I seen what happened with the body bein' found, it made more sense."

"Now you don't remember exactly when she said it, do you?"

"No, sir."

"Could've been two or three years ago you said, and you never thought of telling anyone?"

"I remember tellin' Pitch 'bout it. He sayed he'd heard that rumor from Cat's Paw, but didn't believe none of it."

"Did Reynolds ever threaten you in connection with the body?"

"No, sir. We didn't evar talk 'bout it much after he tole me his momma was half crazy on Natch."

"And you were good friends with Pitchfork, and still are?"

"Yes, sir."

"You'd probably remember things in a way that'd help him out, wouldn't you?"

"I remember 'em the way I remember 'em."

"You'd be willing to tell this jury whatever sounded good about him because you wouldn't want him to get in trouble, right?"

"No sir. I tole you what I remember. I ain't makin' it up."

"How can one tell with your record of dishonesty?"

"That deal in Florida was different. It was a bad deal. I got no business makin' somethin' like this up."

Feld turned for his seat. He wheeled back out. "Now Mr. Screed, you've been trying to explain yourself for the time when you pleaded guilty to theft involving your services. Could you explain it to the jury?"

He watched Screed look over at the jury with eyes that fluttered a little. "It was a misunderstandin'. I'd gone down to Florida on a tip from a cousin of mine 'bout some people needin' their roof fixed. I got there and gave 'em an estimate. Chris, my son, was with me. We'd rented a cheap motel room while I worked days there. They'd given me a draw down on half the work upfront.

"After I started, others 'round seen how good I's, and I started gettin' other work offers. Then I got payment for 'nother roof job to start once I finished the one I's on. It was 'bout a grand. I's gettin' through the first job when I noticed a weak spot on the frame of the house. There were rotted two-by-four studs evarwhere. The new roof I's layin' would've caved in under it. The people I's workin' for were gone on vacation. So I went 'bout fixin' that too. The job ended up runnin' over two weeks 'cause of that.

"When I ast for compensation the first owner tole me naw, he didn't authorize no overruns. He wouldn't even pay me for the roofin' job 'cause it run late. Weese got into it and I stormt off. That thousand-dollar draw down from his neighbor slipped my mind 'cause I'd already used it to pay for the motel. I's clear out of town 'fore I cooled off and remembered. I did wrong in not turnin' 'round, but I felt I'd been done wrong too.

"'Bout nine years later, I's passin' through the Florida county. Got stopped for a bad blinker and found out I'd a war-rant 'cause of that time. They halled me off to jail. I pled guilty 'cause I didn't have no money to post bail and 'cause I made the mistake of never sendin' the money back to the other guy. That unlicensed contractor stuff is just gov'mint redtape tryin' to keep me from makin' a livin' at what I'm good at."

"Did you know the girl Spring at Mr. Reynolds's resi-dence?"

"Yeah. She and my son were friends."

"As far as being friends with Mr. Reynolds, would you make up a story like this to protect him?"

"No, sir. I know this here is serious, clean truth business. I took an oath and such and they got me on record. I ain't gettin' tangled up in any lie. I'm just tellin' these people how I seen it and heard it from his momma and him. I never seen no body. We only talked 'bout what his momma sayed."

"Thank you."

Feld strode out. "It's easy for you to claim honesty when the only witness you remember telling you those things about the body is dead, isn't it?"

"I ain't lookin' to quarr'l none. I ain't lyin' if that's what you're gettin' at."

He watched Feld continue to try to squeeze something out of Screed. By the end of Screed's testimony it was late afternoon. Miller called a recess. They'd start tomorrow with Prentice then the DNA expert.

He'd bled again. When he got back to his house, Prentice helped him change the gauze. The old gauze was soaked and crisp from dried blood and pus. He thought he might have to give his close from the chair. At least his sling would be off by then.

* * *

The next morning, he felt better after a full night's rest. That concrete firmness was returning in his head, catching fire in his chest, and coursing through his limbs.

When he arrived to court, he rolled to counsel's table, opened his briefcase, and began reviewing his notes. To the side of the jury box, he saw the white projection canvas where the slideshow would display.

Prentice testified how he obtained the sample. He showed the jury pictures of the monogrammed golf tees in the meticulously preserved bags.

The DNA expert arrived just after ten. He wheeled himself out and asked background questions to qualify her as an expert. After showing a good number of slides, the discussion switched to how the samples were matched. There were a few moments of readjustment as she sometimes continued giving an explanation that anticipated several questions. She'd analyzed the sample. There was the preservation of it, the identification of it, the mapping of its alleles, and then the comparison to the target.

Laying out the background and foundation took most of the morning. After lunch, she went into the comparison. The sample collected from the golf tees was highly similar to Reynolds. It wasn't a full sibling match, but the samples were nearly ninety percent the same. She related how a subsequent test on Alcorn Caine confirmed with above ninety-nine percent accuracy that Alcorn was Reynolds's father.

On cross, Feld tried attacking the process. "How large were the samples you used?"

"I had a large enough sample from the golf tees. It's the residue of sweat and body fluids on it that we used. Too small a sample would've been inconclusive. We wouldn't get a clear picture of alleles. That wasn't a problem with these samples."

"What if the defense investigator had picked up another's tee from the foursome?"

"The confirmation of the connection with Alcorn Caine's DNA confirmed the earlier conclusion of a connection between the sample collected on the golf tee and Boesephius Caine."

"There's a margin of error with these machines interpreting the samples?"

"The chances of that were calculated at less than one percent."

Feld's questions glanced off. Miller recessed court for the evening.

Back on his couch, he winced as Prentice changed his bandages. He wished the pale, black-haired nurse was here to do it, but then the thought took on a sickly tint. It had a guilty aura to it that must've been connected to the loss of his fiancée. Although some part of his mind allowed him these new luxuries and urged him to move on, his gut still clung to a misplaced loyalty.

His wound had drained significantly. Despite the soreness, sensitivity, and irritation, his body was healing itself. Lying in bed, he contemplated with a tender sense of well-being the power of nature to repair itself, realigning channels that had been broken or ruptured to once again carry blood through him, mending torn muscle and flesh. He thought of the pain as payment for the healing, evidence work was being done.

His sentience ebbed away. A swift swirling of images, a cacophony if they'd been in audio, caused him distress in a semi-conscious bubble of anxiety. Some images from the courtroom's earlier events arose while other images were anticipations of what was to play out. Then there was darkness before he submerged into distorted, abstract, and puzzling dreams.

* * *

Upon awakening, the soreness pinned him to the bed. He fought off the sluggishness of wanting to lie there soaking up more blue-lighted early morning sleep before returning to the demands of the oxygen-filled world of robust activity.

Prentice arrived at the appointed time. He painfully acclimated back to the realistic time-constrained world of linear schedules, rules that attempted to restrain the chaotic night atmosphere. A semblance of structured daily events hovered on his backbrain as Prentice helped him prepare. By the time the van arrived, he was reviewing documents in his wheelchair.

Dustin was scheduled to arrive at ten. The expert retook the stand at nine, and she went over the numbers again, reiterating the miniscule chance of error. The familial connection was a real fact now.

Miller called recess until ten thirty. Latanya leaned over to let him know Dustin was in the holding cell. When he entered, Whaley was trying to avert his client from testifying.

He heard Dustin protest, "I'm not pleading the fifth to anything. What else can they do to me?"

Because of his leg irons, Miller ordered that Dustin was to come in before the jury came out. Although Prentice had tried to arrange more formal clothes, Dustin insisted on the black T-shirt and blue jeans he'd been apprehended in. He saw a Bible sitting next to Dustin on the wooden wall bench. He let Dustin know, "The prosecutor may go into unexpected details of what went down on the property."

He watched Dustin look at Whaley, who was shaking his head while saying, "You know I think you're making a mistake in doing this?"

Dustin's face became tense and gnarled. Then he watched Dustin's eyes loosen, become more jocular, as Dustin laughed briefly. "Grow some balls."

He heard Whaley. "I've got to look out for your interests, even if you don't want to. So I'm going to try to prevent you from destroying yourself legally. But if you're hell-bent on it, it's your choice. Just remember, you can always plead the fifth."

"I won't be needing the fifth."

He and Whaley left back into the courtroom. Whaley took a seat in the first row behind his table.

As Dustin entered the courtroom led by the guards, he imagined a shock-proof barrier between Dustin's eyes and Dustin's mind. Outward reality seemed to have lost the ability to surprise or alarm Dustin. The biker's weight loss and beard growth supported the impression of detachment. Strength projected out from bundled muscle in Dustin's folded, uncovered, hairy arms, like a pair of vibrating pistons with cords of veins slightly straining to keep them fed and in place. His black T-shirt hung loosely over what'd hardened from fat. On his shoulder from under the shirt sleeve, part of the claw of his namesake tattoo stuck out in a slant.

He saw a glistening shine in Dustin's dark eyes. Dustin's gaze seemed to convey knowledge of numbered days.

Going past accepting that, they seemed committed to a course of action based on a limited probability of life left. The eyes brought Dustin's face into stark relief as though the globes themselves stood out beyond expected proportion, making the man's head a confluence of vibrant expansion.

He watched two guards walk Dustin over to the witness stand. Dustin seemed as if he were approaching a scaffold unrepentantly. He approached the stand from the side with those eyes peering forward seeing only the purpose that must've been wrought by disciplined hours of physical and mental exercise.

He watched Dustin eye Miller. Turning outward toward the filling gallery, Dustin's eyes shone like glazed dark metal focused on the back wall of the courtroom. The two guards stationed themselves strategically in case of any sudden movements. Miller had the jury brought out.

Dustin stood to take the oath of honesty then sat back down. He wheeled out. "Sir, could you state your name for the record?"

"Birthname is Charles Dustin."

"How did you come to know Mr. Reynolds?"

"We knew him as Pitchfork. Through the man's mother."

"How did you meet her?"

"She'd been drinking at a tavern I stopped by passing through town."

"Did you drink together?"

"Yes, we did. And she took us back to her place when she found out we didn't have a place to stay."

"Who was we?"

"Muffler, my friend and fellow biker."

"And did you stay at the house then?"

"Yes. We stayed there about a week the first time."

"Did you meet Mr. Reynolds then?"

"Yes. He was young then. Probably twenty years ago. He was a teenager."

"Did you see him frequently after that?"

"Probably twice, maybe three times a year."

"How long would you see him during those visits?"

"We'd stay there a couple of weeks, maybe a month depending on where we were going next."

"So you got to know them pretty well?"

"I knew their habits. Yeah, you could say I knew 'em."

"Would you stay in their home?"

"Sometimes. More often we sat around drinking beer with 'em."

"With Mr. Reynolds?"

"More often with his mother. She was the drinker. Reynolds drank sometimes too, but he was more into other things."

He thought Dustin might turn on Reynolds for a moment. He waved it off. They knew about the meth use anyway. "How often did you drink with the mother?"

"About everytime we seen her. She always had beer or some liquor."

"Did she ever talk about Mr. Reynolds murdering someone?"

"No, she didn't."

"Did you know anyone else that was living there more permanently?"

"People'd stop by. The only regular ones were Pitchfork, his momma, and the girl. For a while a couple of women stayed around to help take care of the girl."

"Did you ever talk to the girl?"

"I did."

"Did she ever say anything about Mr. Reynolds injuring someone?"

"No, she didn't."

"Did you ever come across a body on that property?"

"Never saw one with my own eyes."

"Did you ever see anyone killed on that property?"

"No, I didn't."

"Do you know a man named John Screed?"

"Yes, I know him. He'd stay there for stretches of time until he found work closer to the coast."

"Did he ever talk to you about a murder in relation to the property?"

"Yes, he did."

"Could you describe what he told you?"

"Objection."

"Overruled, go ahead."

"He told me that Pitchfork's momma took him up into the attic and showed him a painting. She told him that a man had been buried on the property."

"When did John Screed tell you this?"

"I don't remember exactly. We were buzzed most times we talked. But I remember him telling me this."

"Did you verify whether it was true or not?"

"You mean dig?"

"Or any other way?"

"I talked to Pitchfork's momma one night when we were drinking. She told me the owner of the property, Caine, had killed Spindle and then buried him on her property—"

He heard some sighs in the courtroom. Feld stood up yelling, "Move to strike, Your Honor! Objection! That is hearsay!"

From his wheelchair, he trained an incredulous look at Feld. They'd handled this earlier in pre-trial motions.

"Overruled, continue."

"No, I didn't ever dig or see the body myself. For all I knew at the time it was a spook story from a worn-out drunk."

"Did she say when this had happened?"

"She wasn't exact."

"Did she say how the body got there?"

"She said he'd been shot and then the body was brought out. And that Caine threatened her to keep her mouth shut or they'd blame her and her son. She'd refer to a pine near the tree line."

"Did you ever have any encounters with Reynolds around that pine tree?"

"Yes. One time he snapped off at me near there."

"How did he do it?"

"I told him I wanted a better deal on an arrangement we had. He got mad about it. He yelled that he'd put me in the ground."

"Did you tell him about what his mother told you before this?"

"Yeah, I'd mentioned it. I thought he already knew about it."

"When did you tell him?"

"Not sure exactly. Within about a year after I heard it. He was high one night and I asked him if it ever unnerved him knowing there was a body in his backyard."

"What did he say?"

"Objection."

"Overruled."

"He asked what I was talking about and I described what his momma told me."

"What was his reaction?"

"He had a stunned look on his face. He said something like quit bullshitting me."

"Did you talk about it again before he got angry with you that day?"

"Yeah. I could tell it irritated him. I'd use it to get him riled up."

"How did you react when he yelled at you that day?"

"I laughed."

"Why?"

"'Cause I'd gotten under his skin and I didn't think he could do it anyway."

"Do you know him to be involved with causing the death of Craig Spindle?"

"No, I do not."

"Thank you."

He wheeled back to his table. Miller called recess for lunch.

After they resumed, he watched Dustin being led back in. Feld began, "You have a biker name you go by, don't you?

"Yes. Cat's Paw."

"What type of business were you and Muffler conducting with Pitchfork?"

"We exchanged money for drugs."

From the barely audible gasp behind him, he sensed Whaley. He turned around quickly to see Whaley putting his head down, shaking it, pinching it with his thumb on one temple and his pointer finger on the other temple like a vice grip.

"Really? And what type of business would have you living part-time in a house of some drunkard you met at the bar?"

"Same answer I just gave."

Feld seemed to have stumbled at having braced himself for nothing. "So you're in the business of selling and buying drugs? Did you carry weapons with you?"

"Objection."

"Overruled, answer it."

"Yes."

"And did Mr. Reynolds have guns?"

"I'm not sure. I think there may've been one in the house, but I never saw it."

"When you say you drank a lot with his now deceased mother, how much would you drink on average?"

"I don't know. Maybe a case of beer a day."

"A case of beer a day?"

"That's what I said."

"That could cause some memory problems, couldn't it?"

"It could, depending on what you're trying to remember. I remember the things I've testified to."

"And what you heard about this explanation for the body on the property, it came from a drunk storyteller?"

"Yeah. She was always drunk."

"So how well do you remember what was said?"

"Pretty well. It wasn't a normal conversation topic."

"And tell the jury why we should believe you?"

"They can believe what they want. That's how it happened."

"Isn't it true that you've been convicted of theft before?"

"That's true."

"And that was an instance of you being dishonest?"

"It was more a matter of getting food at the time."

"At the time you were thieving, that's when you heard the story and had the encounter with Pitchfork threatening to put you in the ground as well?"

"I wasn't thieving on a regular basis. I took some food a couple of times to eat."

"But part of the reason you had no money was that you were traipsing about the country using and selling drugs?"

"Objection."

"Sustained."

"You're friends with Pitchfork, aren't you?"

"I guess you could call us that."

"You wouldn't want to see him come to harm here in court, would you?"

"Punishment will be meted out according to what has already been ordained."

"Bible quotes?"

"I didn't come here to convince anybody of anything, but what you're trying to prove isn't true. Pitchfork didn't murder that body as far as I know. And I don't care if he rots just the same as me."

"You mentioned earlier that Reynolds was into other things, what type of other things?"

"He was into methamphetamine. You know, ice, speed."

"Did you ever see him lose his temper?"

"Yes. Sometimes I got under his skin."

"Why didn't you go to the police after finding out about a buried body on the property?"

"I didn't see it with my own eyes. It wasn't my business. I couldn't tell whether his momma was making it up."

"So you covered up for them. What would prevent you from covering up for them now?"

"I didn't cover up. It wasn't verified."

"Is anyone paying you to keep it quiet?"

"Nope."

"In your previous line of illegal work, you'd be the type someone would go to for a contract killing?"

"I've been approached before."

"And did you take the contract?"

He felt Whaley poking him in the ribs, telling him to call a break so he could talk to his client. He turned around to see Whaley splayed over the gallery wall. He asked for a side bar. Miller granted it to talk to all three lawyers and called a recess to allow Whaley to talk to his client briefly.

After the courtroom had been cleared, Dustin was led to the holding cell where Whaley went in behind him.

When they resumed, Feld asked, "Have you taken contracts to harm people?"

"Yes."

"And did you take one regarding the dead councilman, Mr. Spindle?"

"No."

"Now a person who is an admitted drug dealer thief who has taken contracts to harm people, why should the jury believe his denials of being involved in this murder?"

"Because I wasn't and that's how Caine's manipulating it."

"Fine conspiracy story from someone facing prison time. Wouldn't you want to avoid any connection with this murder to avoid being confined?"

"I'm most likely spending the remainder of my life in prison no matter what you say. I accept that. That doesn't change my position one way or another. You're working for Caine to get him off for murder."

"The main source you're relying on was constantly drunk, you said?"

"Yes she was, but—"

"But she was telling the truth just this once while she was in her right mind?"

"She went on about many things, but she only focused on this a few times."

"So that means she was telling the truth?"

"The way she said it, I believed her."

He watched Feld stare at Dustin disdainfully before sitting down.

Miller called an afternoon break. When they came back at three thirty, he rolled forward with trying to rehabilitate Dustin. "Did you ever take a contract involving Craig Spindle?"

"No, hadn't even really heard of him until Judy mentioned him."

"And how long ago were your shoplifting cases?"

"They were nine years ago."

"How much was taken?"

"Less than twenty dollars everytime. I took a box of fried chicken once and some potato salad. Things from the deli. Muffler had a steak stuffed down his pants."

"Does that have any bearing at all on whether you'd tell the jury the truth today about what you heard and what you witnessed in regards to this case?"

"No, it doesn't at all. Seems like a phony distraction to me. I came here to tell what I know against the advice of my counsel. That food run has nothing to do with it."

"You're not gaining anything if Reynolds is not guilty of this?"

"Nope. If anything, it increases chances the feds will look at me funny. If I was gonna go about it that way, then I'd try to get time off by squealing on him."

"And you've no qualms telling everyone in open court today what you've been involved with and what you haven't?"

"That's right."

"Was Reynolds part of your motorcycle club?"

"No. You need a bike, first of all. Then you need to be able to ride it well. Pitchfork wasn't a rider."

"Do you know where exactly he was pointing to when he yelled at you?"

"Don't really remember. It could've been at straight soil for all I know."

"Have you made a substantial change of yourself in the past several months?"

"That's right."

"Could you explain?"

"I began a regimen of working out and reading the Bible. I limited meals so I lost weight. All the toxins started leaving my system and I dropped a bunch of fat and I gained a bunch of muscle."

He listened distractedly as Feld reemphasized Dustin's reckless lifestyle and prior thefts before sitting down again. After Feld was done, Miller called an end to the day.

He left exhausted. When he got home, he barely had enough energy to eat. Prentice washed and redressed the wound. The effort anticipating Dustin's testimony had drained him. He fell unconscious at seven p.m.

* * *

Upon awakening, his internal tempo quickened. Despite Reynolds's checkered past, Reynolds would be taking the stand. He believed most jurors wanted to hear from the defendant, especially when the evidence begged for some type of concrete explanation. Reynolds was a borderline call.

After Reynolds had been placed in the witness stand and the crowd had been let back in, he saw Feld talking to the Spindles. He'd noticed the look of scorn on the respectable-looking widow's face had changed by slight degrees through the trial. The state's victim advocate came over to join Feld in talking to the family. He sensed that the widow didn't seem pleased with whatever Feld was telling her.

The image of her disagreeing with Feld relieved something. He couldn't deny that being pitted against an unpopular public outcry didn't appeal to him. Being the recipient of displeased, accusatory stares from respectable persons wasn't something he enjoyed. His in court persona could shrug this off effortlessly, grinning at the hatred, but in his more private moments he sometimes had a hard time digesting it while maintaining a non-critical, upbeat opinion of himself.

The disagreement he thought he perceived gave him a swell of hope that the widow was beginning to doubt what they were trying to label her hatred with. He didn't permit himself the luxury of the comfort this brought for very long.

Reynolds seemed calm and had a receptive, non-confrontational, and contemplative look. As Reynolds sat waiting on the witness stand, the now docile, short-haired man looked engaged and concentrated. The jury leaned forward, heavily focused on the man charged.

Reynolds introduced himself with a high-pitched and shaky voice. He heard the stutter. The background that had already been established by the other witnesses was reiterated. He brought up the topic of the body. "Did you ever have any conversations regarding the burial of someone at your residence?"

"P-people tole me."

"Who?"

"M-my momma tole me that Ca-Caine had killed someone and buried h-him in our backyard.

"Did you believe her?"

"Wasn't sure at first, th-then I started to believe h-her."

"Did anyone else talk about a body on the property?"

"Y-yes. Cat's Paw and J-John Screed."

"Did you ever see the body firsthand?"

"N-not in p-person."

"When did you first find out about the body?"

"The detectives. Th-they showed me pictures."

"How did the girl Spring come to live with you?"

"Sh-she was abandoned by a w-woman that stayed with us."

"When did this happen?"

"Her momma left about s-six months after sh-she was born."

"Who took care of her?"

"I tried to. I got h-her things to pla-play with. If anybody was rowdy w-we'd make sure she was safe in h-her room. Most times it was one of two w-women 'round that would sp-spend more time with h-her."

"And how do you know John Screed?"

"Through m-my momma. He'd been comin' over for years."

"How often would he stay?"

"Va-varied. Sometimes a couple of w-weeks or even a few m-months."

"Did he bring anyone with him?"

"After his son was b-born, he'd bring his son Chris."

"What games would they play?"

"Th-they'd run 'round the yard mostly and out t-toward the river."

"Did you ever admonish them for playing too hard or inappropriately?"

"Y-yeah, sometimes Chris would play too rough with h-her. I'd get on h-him or tell John. Then that time she m-mentioned 'bout playin' h-hide n' seek. I t-tole 'em to stay away from 'round that pine tr-tree. L-like I sayed, I'd n-never seen no body. I didn't want 'em diggin' up s-somethin' on 'count of what M-momma sayed."

"Did the owner of the property ever visit?"

"I seen the property ma-manager Ca-Caine sent. H-he'd come to co-collect."

"Did the property manager talk to you?"

"N-not really. I mean he sayed words to me, b-but it was l-like they didn't mean n-nothin'. L-like he was talkin' to a bl-block of wood."

"Did he ever tell you to change something?"

"H-he come out to get the water pipes f-fixed once. W-we had to live off bottled water a few months. H-he was slow 'bout fixin' things. Usually l-left it to us."

"Did he have any other criticisms?"

"N-not really. H-he'd let M-momma know he was comin' and all the beer ca-cans would get piled up and w-we'd have someone put 'em in the cr-crusher John made. We'd try to clean up the pla-place."

"Did he ever threaten to evict you?"

"N-not that I remember. M-momma'd be late with the rent. Sometimes for m-months when she was l-locked up. I'd send m-money when I c-could."

"Did he ever raise the rent?"

"N-not that I remember."

"What was the rent?"

"Five hundred a m-month."

"And what did that include?"

"A h-house and a property to the water. 'Bout f-five acres. Before I's born, I think it used to be two fifty. It must've got raised by the time I's gr-grown."

"How do you know Charles Dustin?"

"H-he was a friend of ours that would v-visit. H-he and Muffler."

"Did you ever have any disagreements with them?"

"Sure w-we did. They could be trouble sometimes. We'd get heated up and y-yell at one 'nother."

"Was Spring ever around when that happened?"

"I'd try to keep h-her away from it."

"Do you recall the situation she described earlier about you yelling at Cat's Paw?"

"Y-yes."

"What do you recall of the event?"

"I remember wakin' up and d-doin' some m-meth and then goin' out ba-back. They's makin' some racket in the sha-shack with a buzzsaw and I just wanted some quiet near the r-river. They'd extension c-cords all the way from the h-house. So I unplugged one. Then Cat's Pa-Paw come up out of there. He caught up with me near the l-locust tree. Then he said how 'bout l-lowerin' the ra-rates or I'm a'start diggin'. I flew off the ha-handle. T-tole him h-he'd end up in the gr-ground too. I's p-pointin' n-near the tree where they d-dug the body. I's only pointin' off wha-what I'd heard."

"How did he react?"

"He just l-let out one of his big belly laughs. H-he sayed he didn't b-believe I could take him."

"How far away were you from the house at this time?"

"It's 'bout two h-hundred feet."

"Did you know if anyone else was watching you?"

"N-not at the t-time."

"Did you ever try to dig up the area to check?"

"No."

"Did your mother tell you anything about the body?"

"Sh-she mumbled things that make more sense n-now."

"Did you hear anything about a burial?"

"J-John Screed tole me what she'd sayed 'bout the p-paintin' with the d-dog and the l-locust tree."

"Did you ever check after that?"

"No. I never d-dug up 'round that tr-tree."

He wheeled back behind his table as Feld stood. "Mr. Reynolds, you did methamphetamine for over a decade every day?"

"N-not evarda-day. I took some da-days off."

"And that has caused you some permanent mental health problems?"

"I take m-medications to calm me down."

"And you drank for years as well?"

"Y-yes. I drank since I's tw-twelve, but not all the t-time."

"And during the periods we've been talking about in this trial, you were drinking or using meth or using both?"

"What t-time periods?"

"Approximately twelve years ago when the councilman disappeared, to when you say you heard from your mother and associates about a body being buried in your back yard, to when you threatened to put your biker friend in the ground too."

"I ca-can't remember what I's doin' da-day to day twelve years ago. N-not sure I's usin' m-meth all the time then. I never seen Sp-Spindle then or evar. I don't remember bein' h-high when I heard the stories of the b-body. Y-yes, I's high when I y-yelled at Cat's Paw."

"Let's talk about your mother for a moment. She wasn't the warmest mother to you, was she?"

"N-no, sir. She was wild. Unpredictable. She was very c-cold sometimes."

"And she drank about anytime she could?"

"Y-yes, sir."

"What was her usual?"

"She drank 'bout a b-bottle of liquor a day or sometimes a ca-case of beer."

"And it has been testified that she'd been in jail. Was that on account of her drinking?"

"Most times. Y-yes, sir."

"So how did you believe what she'd say when she was drunk?"

"She was drunk m-most times. You c-could tell. She'd mumbled 'bout somethin' buried m-more than once."

"Would she mumble about other things too?"

"Sure."

"And did she slur her words?"

"Y-yes, sir."

"And did she sometimes say things that didn't turn out to be realistic?"

"Sometimes, yes."

"How could you tell whether what she said was accurate or not?"

"The way she kept r-referrin' to somethin' b-buried, and then 'em findin' it."

"But you couldn't tell what she was saying most of the time, could you?"

"S-sometimes no, sir."

"And it's convenient for you now that you're charged with this crime that the one with whom this story originates is dead?"

"I don't see nothin' c-convenient 'bout this, sir."

"It would be easy for you to concoct this story and have your mother take the blame for knowing about it because she's dead, right?"

"She l-liked to drink, but I wouldn't say things 'bout h-her that didn't happen."

"And the fact that the others, Cat's Paw and John Screed, riled you up was because you had something to do with this no matter what your mother said?"

"That ain't tr-true. I didn't evar see any b-body."

"How is one to believe that you wouldn't have noticed someone coming onto your property into your backyard about two hundred feet from your back porch and bury a man without you knowing about it?"

"I don't know h-how the body g-got there."

"You never did leave the house much, did you?"

"N-not much. No, sir."

"But yet you never noticed anyone coming on the property to dig a hole deep enough to bury someone?"

"N-no, sir."

"You're lying to the jury now, aren't you?"

"N-no, sir. I didn't see anything l-like that."

"You know how far down the body was buried, don't you?"

"Th-they sayed four feet earlier."

"And how long do you think it'd take someone to dig a hole like that by themselves?"

"A c-couple of hours, I guess."

"And you're telling the jury that neither you nor anyone in household would've heard anyone digging for a couple of hours?"

"I can't speak for others, but I d-didn't."

"Are you suggesting that your dead mother may've been in on the digging?"

"I d-don't know. She's the one that sta-started bringin' it up."

"It would be easy for the three of you to agree after your mother's death, if anything ever came up about the body, to blame it on your dead mother?"

"We never had a c-conversation like that. I don't remember the la-lass time it came up with Cat's Paw or Scr-Screed."

"But you do remember the incident Spring described watching from the screen door?"

"Y-yes. I remember y-yellin' and pointin'."

"So you knew where the body was then?"

"I g-guessed based on what I'd h-heard."

"Did it ever occur to you to alert the authorities that there may be a body in the yard?"

"I never seen it f-firsthand. I figured I'd get in trouble just for m-mentionin' it."

"But you could've explained to the authorities what you're trying to explain now?"

"I f-figured they wouldn't believe me. Ca-Caine kn-knew 'em."

"Well, why would you figure anyone would believe you now with the consequences you're facing that would give you more incentive to lie?"

"B-because that's how it wa-was."

"And that's the easiest explanation. You never saw the body in your backyard, but you heard about it and your dead mother knew why it was there?"

"Tha-that's right."

"And Spring, who testified that she was afraid of you when you yelled at Cat's Paw, didn't she look frightened that day?"

"I don't remember when I seen h-her after that."

"Didn't she go back into her room because she was scared of you?"

"She stayed in h-her r-room alot."

"And that was because you forbade her to leave the house?"

"She wasn't 'llowed to l-leave 'cause she was young. I ha-hardly evar l-left either."

"And when you were high it wasn't uncommon for you to get angry and then forget the details later?"

"I got angry sometimes, y-yes. B-but more often I'd k-keep to myself."

"You lost your temper that day talking to Cat's Paw, didn't you?"

"Y-yes. I loss my t-temper."

"And for you to kill a person would only take one flare-up of that temper, only one burst of rage to carry out a threat like the one you made to Cat's Paw?"

"I didn't do no rage k-killin'."

"Did Spindle meet you on the river and confront you about the squalor of your property?"

"N-no. That never happened."

"Did you see someone in your territory and have a rush of adrenaline combined with the meth high and saw an opportunity no one would find out about?"

"Nothin' evar happened that way."

"Were you paid by someone to do it? To finance your drug habit and to keep from being evicted?"

"N-never happened."

"But the body turned up on the property where you've lived all your life?"

"It did, but I didn't s-see it until I saw those p-pictures."

"And you have no other explanation?"

"N-no."

"What type of work did you say John Screed did for you around the house?"

"H-he fixed our roof. H-he put a can crusher on the back p-porch. He was always b-buildin' and repairin'."

"And he was drunk pretty much the whole time you knew him?"

"Y-yes."

"Does two drunks mumbling to each other sound like a place where much credible information would come from?"

"I d-don't know. I wasn't s-sure."

"So out of this house full of drifters, the people around most were John Screed, the two bikers, and those aunt characters?"

"Y-yes."

"And do you know where the so-called aunts are?"

"N-no."

"But they lived with you for about a year or two and helped raise Spring?"

"Y-yes, they did. Linda stayed 'bout four years."

"Did they ever talk about the body?"

"N-no. Not that I remember."

"But they would've talked to your mother, correct?"

"Y-yes."

"And no teasing came from them about the body?"

"N-not that I remember."

"Your mother talked to a lot of people, didn't she?"

"I guess s-so."

"And wouldn't you have expected her to talk to persons in jail?"

"I guess sh-she would've."

"And not a word of your story spread to the rest of the community?"

"N-not that I know of."

"Nobody else knew about it except you four?"

"N-not that I know of."

"And your mother kept that information to herself except when these particular transients, Cat's Paw and John Screed, came through?"

"H-her and John sometimes slept together. Th-they was closer than most. And Cat's Paw had b-been comin' 'round for years."

"But no one else ever heard enough to try and blackmail you or spread the information to anyone else?"

"I don't know who else might've known. N-none of us talked 'bout it m-much."

He watched Feld exhibit an incredulous stare on the jury before sitting down. He wheeled out carefully. "Did you know Caine was your half-brother before the body was found?"

"N-not until this ca-case."

"Did your mother mention his name?"

"Y-yes, she did. She talked 'bout h-him in a hateful way."

410

"And your mother wasn't always in the house when people were staying there?"

"N-no. Sometimes she'd be in ja-jail or just r-roamin' 'round."

"So she may not have interacted much with many of the people that came through there?"

"She was gone a good b-bit. She wasn't always talkative when p-people were over. She'd keep to h-herself. G-go to the attic with her pa-paintin's."

"And Caine's property manager was paid rent every month since you remember?"

"Y-yes."

He wheeled around back to his table. He watched Feld stand. "And you never noticed Caine come on the property at all?"

"N-no."

"And you don't ever remember seeing someone digging in the backyard?"

"N-no."

"And you never noticed a freshly dug area?"

"I don't remember it. No. That area near the p-pine was mostly d-dirt anyhow."

"You expect the jury to believe that you never noticed a freshly dug area right out in your backyard near a well-worn path to the river?"

"I didn't n-notice any."

Feld flashed his incredulous look again before sitting. He didn't wheel out this time. "How often would you inspect the grounds?"

"N-not really regularly."

"And did you spend more time inside or outside?"

"M-mostly stayed in. Spesh-specially durin' summer."

"How often did you go to the river?"

"Ma-maybe once evar two months. Can't say for sure. It va-varied."

After Reynolds's testimony, Miller released the jurors to be back after the weekend. The lawyers were to stay to finalize jury instructions. They would close on Monday.

He determined to be walking by the time he delivered it. There'd be a couple of visuals he'd use, overarching timelines on placards, including the gaps of time, to emphasize uncertainties. There was also the lack of particularity in the number of persons passing through the house at crucial times.

After Prentice cleaned his wound, he went to bed.

* * *

After nine Sunday night, he thought he heard something outside. Prentice's German shepherd, Tecumseh, went out and barked for a while. Prentice had let Tecumseh stay as an additional alarm besides the ongoing patrol. He went to the backdoor with the aid of his cane. It wasn't his normal gait, but he thought it would suffice. He saw in the glare of the back floodlight a pair of eyes that he figured must be a raccoon or a possum. He worked an hour more before getting into bed.

* * *

The next morning, Louise and Prentice picked him up. He insisted on using the cane to and from the van to the court. He strode stiffly past the cameras into the court-room. Through a rustling of papers, he made last-minute adjustments. He explained to Latanya where to put the visual displays. He saw Feld studying his notes. Miller came out and read the instructions to the jurors.

He knew he would have to endure an hour or so of hearing the opposite of what he wanted to hear. He'd grown used to enduring it, but it'd never been completely comfortable.

They glided into Feld's airtime. After Miller announced the state's closing argument, Feld strode out to the podium. "I come before you as a representative of the state to prove the charge of murder committed by Mr. Reynolds some twelve years ago. The evidence has shown Mr. Reynolds was an anti-social outcast, that he lived a dysfunctional lifestyle, that he had a drug problem, and that he is callous enough to murder a man and bury him on his property. He expects the rest of the world to blindly accept his crude attempt to cover the act up, to blindly accept that he had no idea that this had occurred, to blindly accept that other motives were at work, and that he didn't have as much motive as others to do this. But I will ask each of you not to lose your focus as the defense tries to distract it.

"The defense is going to say that so much time has gone by, who knows what could have happened? Just because Mr. Reynolds buried this heinous crime that deprived a family of a prominent and productive member of society doesn't mean that he should be able to use the delay to evade the truth.

"The question is not as much why, but how? How could he do this? Whatever murky motive, whether he did it slowly or quickly, he formed the intent to kill. The forensic evidence shows he tried to cover up the identity of the body by smashing out and removing evidence of the man's dental records. This crude attempt failed to take into account the advancement of DNA identification. It was just the type of crudeness to expect from an anti-social man like Mr. Reynolds, behind the times, stuck in his depravity. The man struck out at whatever prey happened onto his property. You can't ignore the connections the evidence presents. Don't let Mr. Reynolds continue to cover up the murder."

He watched Feld move closer to a display set up. "The body was found approximately two hundred feet from the back porch near one of the first pine trees before the land turned into a wooded area. The grave was approximately four feet in depth. The age of the body at the time was about eleven years give or take three months. How is it possible that one wouldn't notice that a grave had been dug in this area within open view and near a well-worn path toward the river? That is not credible.

"First, the man also known as Pitchfork asks us to believe that he didn't hear or notice the grave digging, that he didn't notice the movement of the body into his back yard. Even less credible is his explanation that it was sparsely grassed over there. Even if it were so, he would've been able to tell for weeks at the very least that the ground had been disturbed there. His sudden discovery of the approximate location some ten years later when he was pointing at the general area and threatening another shows his knowledge. That wasn't the sudden second-hand knowledge from his rambling drunk mother. It was first-hand knowledge of where he'd killed and buried Craig Spindle. He knew then and knows now how it occurred and why he did it. Now all he's trying to do is cloak himself in a garment of reformation and mental absence."

He sat watching Feld, tempering the annoyance he felt listening to him. The jury did seem to be engaged with Feld. Several minutes passed by before he started actively listening again. "The state's DNA expert revealed the identity of Craig Spindle. He was known to walk along the river. Whether Reynolds lay in wait for him or reacted like a startled predatory animal, he had time to form the intent to kill. Reynolds had time to reflect on what he was doing and to avoid the temptation to kill another man gratuitously, for the sake of fulfilling some anti-social compulsion to tear away at whatever positive fabric of society he could. Not only did he take the action to kill, he compounded it afterwards, showing a plan to hide the murder. He didn't stop in horror after spilling the man's blood by shooting him. He deliberately tried to conceal the body's identity by taking a shovel to the man's jaw. This grotesque fact demonstrates the cold, calculating callousness of what he's capable of.

"The expert testified that the destruction to the jaw was likely done by a shovel. How would there've been time for some interloper to attempt to accomplish this undetected? To carry in the corpse would've taken at least two men based on Spindle's size. How could the residents not see or hear the activity needed to get the body there?

415

"There was testimony from the investigators on how it was discovered, beginning with the girl Spring at the orphanage who'd been forced to live in squalor with Pitchfork. Isolating her to a transient bunch of seedy, low-life characters, Pitchfork left her to TV and toys. This innocent amongst the outlaws led the way to the body. She has shown another day when Reynolds's rage boiled over. He acknowledged the gravesite of his guilt. With sick pride in having the capacity to kill, he pointed to it and held the deed up as a testament and threat to what he'd done and what he would do to Cat's Paw.

"If anyone is credible of those from the house, it would be this young, innocent girl who somehow survived. She spoke to you about the everyday drug abuse and debauchery she witnessed from these characters who've concocted a story to try and shield Pitchfork from guilt. She tried to put things in a way that minimized the terrible behavior, saying he was taking his medicine. But her actions speak louder. She was scared of him after she witnessed his harsh words that day and she ran back into the hallway. She could see where he'd been pointing when he yelled out he'd put Cat's Paw there too. She remembered it because he wouldn't let them use that pine tree as home base for hide n' seek. That area was off limits. It was more than a suggestion from others. It was first-hand knowledge that he didn't want anyone else to discover. After she recovered from the fire on the property, she led the investigators there. Despite her attachment to the killer, she pointed him out.

"The defense has picked a few transients to back up Pitchfork's story. Two derelicts, both convicted of crimes of dishonesty before, they are the witnesses they bring to defend this notion that Mr. Reynolds didn't know about the body firsthand.

"The first one, this Screed character, was a shiftless carpenter that's been in trouble before for not doing what he promised and said he was going to do. How are you going to trust him when he comes in now to say he heard it from Pitchfork's mother? He chases work from Florida to New Orleans to everywhere between with his son tagging along. Conning his way when there's not enough work. He says Pitchfork's mother told him the story of Caine's stranglehold on their family. So why would she suddenly tell this outsider about it so that he could use it for leverage? Why would they stop with having their house rent low? Why not truly blackmail the wealthy Caines?

"But they were too afraid, the defense will say. Paralyzed at being made a scapegoat. Why would Reynolds's mother care about that? With the fool she made of herself on a regular basis in being dragged off to jail? If it were so important a secret, why tell this shiftless contractor? It's far easier not to believe a word he says. Then there's the point that he's a friend of Pitchfork. He wants him to get away with this. Most of the time or all the time he was drunk there. He wouldn't know the difference if Pitchfork or Pitchfork's mother told him. Given his constant consumption of alcohol and drugs, how accurate can he be? He is completely unreliable.

"Then there's the biker, Cat's Paw. He has also been convicted of crimes of dishonesty that make him unbelievable. He was inebriated as well on a constant basis at the defendant's residence. What memory problems can you expect with his voracious appetite for alcohol and drugs?

Now he says he heard the same story, from the same drunk mother, but is it clear who told whom first? No. Pitchfork says she used to mutter hints of it to him and then his two associates confirmed it.

"How are these people to be believed? They aren't telling the truth. They're interested in getting their friend Pitchfork off with no responsibility even though the body was found on the property he was living on and has been living on his whole life. He pointed at it in reference while threatening the biker. They don't deny the threat and the reference.

"Mr. Reynolds himself speaks of his own inebriation, high on meth. What type of rational behavior would you expect from the man? He can't be expected to have acted rationally. He behaved more like the animal he'd become. He's not clear when he first heard the story through his mother or through his alcohol- and drug-laced buddies. How good is his memory? But he says his mother mumbled about it, muttered under her breath about it. If she spilled secrets, why didn't she mutter that his father was Caine's father?

"Mr. Reynolds has everything to lose here. And that is why he is interested in concocting anything he can to avoid conviction. But you will see through this. You can tell who to believe and which story makes sense. We have a substantial amount of forensic evidence here locating the body, identifying it, estimating the time and cause of death. Mr. Reynolds is a self-admitted drug addict, an anti-social outcast. He was given a chance to lash out, and he took it. There's the convincing testimony of Spring that solidifies the intent and knowledge of Mr. Reynolds. He knew about this. Why else would he care where the children played hide n' seek? Why would he threaten another pointing to the same location the body was found?

"The intent is also shown by the marks on the skull. That evidence shows a design to hide it. The intent is shown by the grave dug on his own property. Why would someone else bury a body in a place they couldn't watch over closely? The intent is shown by his threatening another with the same fate.

"Ladies and gentlemen, there is no way to doubt the evidence. He's been caught with a body in his backyard. Mr. Reynolds did this and Mr. Reynolds needs to be convicted of this. Don't let him dodge the evidence. Don't let him walk away after having torn a tremendous hole in your society, in a family. Don't let Craig Spindle's killer go free."

Several jury members had been leaning forward while Feld spoke. He watched them settle back. Some adjusted themselves. After a few moments, he heard Miller announcing the defense's closing argument.

He rose stiff-legged with his cane and made his way slowly out into space in front of his table, facing the jury. The onlookers leaned forward. Their attention seemed drawn into his figure as if he were beyond them but part of them at the same time, a possible mouthpiece of some disembodied explanation that hadn't yet been verbalized within them. From his slightly bent figure, he heard his own loud baritone voice firmly shoot up through the musk and perfume in the air, accentuating the wood and ink and cleaning detergent beneath. He spoke as if he were in his own dwelling.

"The state has put before you a compelling case for the murder of Craig Spindle. But the man sitting there," he pointed at Reynolds, "was not the one who committed it. You likely know who the real murderer is. You already do. Now it is only a question of whether to blame someone innocent of the crime charged, as the real murderer would have you do. The murder was the culmination of a plan to get rid of a political enemy and to make his shameful half-brother the scapegoat. It is a matter of courage to look at the evidence fully, carefully, and honestly to see how the setup occurred around twelve years ago and how it is now snapping shut on the neck of Mr. Reynolds. It's a trap that he didn't have the knowledge or rearing to figure out how to combat.

"Over two hundred years ago, the founders of our country got together to write a document containing principles of holding the government accountable to its people that are still alive today. Two important ones in any criminal trial are the presumption of innocence and the burden the state has of proving their case beyond a reasonable doubt.

"Applying those principles to this case starts with Judith Reynolds and her son Edward living on a property that was cheaply rented to them by Bo Caine's father, Alcorn Caine. They were given a break on the rent to this parcel of land that abutted the river. Was this aimless generosity? No. The evidence has shown this was minimal hush money to keep the connection hid. Why would his mother care to squeeze more out of them? She didn't really need to. She was content to live her renegade and artistic lifestyle, content to drink herself into oblivion, which she eventually did. But the truth of what happened regarding Craig

420

Spindle skewed within Judith all through those years she tried keeping it bottled up.

"It's unclear when she knew and how much of a role she directly played in Spindle's burial, but knowledge of the body buried put a buffer between the other secret, the original shame of a bastard born that the Caines wanted hidden. She stored away both, the former secret closer to the surface. Eventually it bubbled up and popped whatever lid in her it was under, and spilled over into those close enough to hear it, other renegades, many of whom you may have trouble identifying with. It tried to be revealed in other ways, through symbols or references in her oil painting, but it eventually clawed and garbled its way out of her throat.

"Those that were near included a construction worker on the move who sometimes shared her bed. She took John Screed upstairs in a drunken spree and spread the word to him about what the painting with the pine tree signified. Screed would come and stay with them on his way through, fixing what he could, drinking their beer. He was the first to find out. And he's come before you, honest enough about his faults and deficiencies, his flying hither, his drinking, and his unsteady work history. Not an upstanding citizen, you might conclude, but does his testimony line up with the rest of the evidence? Would he lie for the defendant for no perceivable benefit to himself?

"His story does make sense and reiterates what's been shown by science, the hidden familial connection. What does Screed have to gain in seeing Mr. Reynolds exonerated of murder? If the prosecution is painting him as a self-interested opportunist, he's more likely to lie the other way to make sure he isn't implicated in this at all, so that all the blame goes on Mr. Reynolds. The truth of what he knew came out in his testimony. Judith told him and he conveyed the information without inspecting for himself. If he were having a hard time with it, his testimony would've shown less consistency.

"The same story boiled over into the biker Charles Dustin's mind. He'd stay up drinking with Judith too. In a drunken moment she let it spill again. She could afford to let that secret closer to the surface spill. Remember the manner in which Mr. Dustin testified? There was complete disclosure. He said things against his interest. Why would he say things to exonerate Reynolds when he is being closely scrutinized himself? He told you the truth. He repeated what he'd heard to see if he could get a rise out of Reynolds. He used it to irritate him. And when they had a disagreement, Reynolds yelled back with it at him. Mr. Dustin testified he never thought Edward was capable of going through with his threat. That's why he laughed in his face.

"Where was Mr. Reynolds's motive? The state has repeatedly referred to my client's rash predatory tendencies. But where is the evidence of this? That is the speculation the state needs to connect to the goal of pinning it on Reynolds. That isn't motive. That is the absence of motive. Reynolds is painted as some kind of modern day mythical monster that takes his toll on whoever comes on the property.

"How much more believable is the interest of the Caines? You heard from the testimony that Spindle was an active opponent of the industry the Caines relied on for their wealth and power. The vote on the city council was being turned against Bo Caine's interests. Caine was the one with the motive to resort to violence. And he devised this plot to pin it on his half-brother, a source of shame and fear, emotions a man like Bo Caine must not have been able to tolerate very long. Bo didn't want to mix blood with this embarrassment. The two secrets checked one another, canceling one another out. He got an edge over the latent threat that had held his family's pride hostage for years, and he got rid of a thorn in the side of his business. These blatant motives are real. The one the state has been trying to grasp at is not."

He motioned for the display to come out. He pointed at the outline of Bo Caine's motives. "In contrast, the motive of Mr. Reynolds is absent, vague, and mysterious. Is that the kind of evidence you should be comfortable with in convicting someone?"

Turning to the next page on the display, "The state's case is vague in terms of when or how this occurred. The medical examiner estimates the time of death within a range of three months sometime twelve years ago. How can you be sure what time of day or night the burial occurred? Isn't it possible that two people carrying the body, either from an adjacent property or from the river, could've done so at night? Couldn't they have dug a shallow grave and laid the dirt back on top?

"Then there's the matter of the bullet. No gun was found matching what was estimated to be the likely cause of death. The way the state describes it, Mr. Reynolds acted as an animal burst out of its cage. Wouldn't such an animal normally kill with blunt force trauma? But then the state's own expert says the death was caused by a bullet from an unknown gun. Doesn't match any guns Reynolds owns or once owned. You might surmise he could've thrown the weapon in the river, but it still doesn't match any guns ever registered to him. That's because they can't link that bullet to Reynolds. The science couldn't bend that in their favor. The evidence equally supports that Caine or one of his men killed Craig Spindle off the property and then had his body carried in to be buried, probably at night. Extra steps were taken to disfigure the jaw either to hide the identity for a while longer or to make it look like someone less sophisticated had done it.

"Why would the supposed killer, who didn't involve himself in politics, who supposedly committed a gratuitous murder because he had the opportunity, care about covering up an identity he didn't know the significance of? If it was just a murder of anti-social opportunity, why would identification of the body make a difference in that type of killer's mind? Why would such a person care about delaying or possibly defeating identification altogether?

"Caine had the body on the property giving him leverage and security on the family secret. An unidentified body works better for him in this regard. It's less likely to link a motive related to profit. And if it is discovered, it more likely crushes those embodying the shame he was also trying to bury.

"Even though Mr. Reynolds grew up in a household where his mother stayed drunk around the clock and lived a lifestyle beyond anything you might consider within acceptable norms, there was one redeeming relationship he had. That was with the girl Spring.

"You might skeptically ask, redeemable? Yes. He did his best to shield her from the other undesirable elements around her. Some of that he caused himself, but he's not on trial for his parenting skills. The way in which he tried to keep her free from the scourge he was born into could be seen by the gratitude and care in her voice. She has a genuine concern for him.

"The main evidence the state would have you rely on so heavily can be interpreted different ways. What the state relies on are the words and gestures observed by Spring through a screen door over two hundred feet away. You need to consider her opportunity and ability to observe what she was testifying to. Not the best vantage point, but we're not disputing what direction Reynolds was pointing in, whether he was making a sweeping gesture or not. Three witnesses testified he blew up that day, including himself. But the pointing and threat can be squared easily with what has been said the whole time. He was referring and acting on what he'd heard. What she saw is evidence that Reynolds had been told of a body buried on the property.

"Mr. Dustin told you that he laughed because he knew Reynolds didn't have it in him to carry out such a threat. He told you he was unaware that Reynolds knew anything more than what he and John Screed had passed on to him. The fact that Reynolds told the kids not to play around the tree where he'd been led to believe a body might be buried doesn't make Mr. Reynolds guilty of murder. His knowledge wasn't firsthand knowledge, it was unverified knowledge at best.

"Our constitution and laws have long since put the burden on the government to establish a citizen has committed a crime. When you look at the evidence before you, Reynolds is presumed innocent. The defense has shown a reasonable doubt as to whether Mr. Reynolds committed murder with intent to kill. Nor did he have any part in causing the death of Craig Spindle. Even though the defense has no burden to do so, we've shown you who had the real motive to kill the legislator. It's Bo Caine's property. Even if you go so far as to think the evidence supports that one of them had to have done it, then the state hasn't proven their case beyond a reasonable doubt as to Edward Reynolds. Craig Spindle's death was a twisted plan of Reynolds's half-brother Bo Caine to try and kill or ruin them both in one action.

"Consistent with your oath, when you begin deliberating, don't forget to discuss the absence of motive of Mr. Reynolds and the presence of motive in Bo Caine. Don't forget that nothing links Mr. Reynolds to the bullet in the man's chest. Don't ignore that Bo Caine has absconded to Costa Rica. Remember that the gestures the state places so much significance on can be explained consistently with our version of events. Convicting an innocent man won't avenge Craig Spindle. Don't rush to judgment in an attempt to remedy the family's deep pain if you have the wrong culprit before you. This isn't the man. The verdict should read not guilty of murder and any lesser includeds."

He eased back to sit down. He watched Miller turn back to the jurors to announce the state's rebuttal.

Feld walked directly to the front of the jury box. "The defense asks you to abandon your common sense and to consider what ifs when the evidence is clearly in the man's yard. The right man is on trial. There was no evidence presented of men sneaking onto the property to bury the body. This stork-dropped-the-baby-off story should be ignored for the ludicrous attempt to cover up guilt that it is. It insults one's common sense. The body didn't just suddenly appear in Reynolds's yard. He put it there and referenced it as shown by the testimony of Spring and himself.

"The defense cries there's no gun linking him to it. Well, how easy would it have been to throw the gun in the river or pass it along to another transient? It has been over twelve years. Reynolds certainly has had ample time to find a way to get rid of a gun by now.

"One main witness the defense relies on in its cockamamie story is the defendant's mother who is no longer alive. We don't get to hear what she would say. Not that she would necessarily be helpful from what we've heard. By all accounts she was a rambling drunk. We've heard second-hand testimony of her muttering. How believable are the people that she told? They all are inherently unreliable. When you add in their inebriation, you've the ingredients of a tall tale, a fabulous story for drug addicts and drunks to entertain their warped, addled, and enfeebled minds. This hearing isn't about entertaining drunks and addicts, it's about reality. The reality that Pitchfork killed Craig Spindle.

"The discovery of the murder of an innocent is a deplorable and disgusting event. Killing opportunely, because Reynolds thought he could get away with it, shows that callous, inhumane streak in him that is capable of such indifference to life. The defense has concocted and cobbled together a story based on Caine and Reynolds sharing the same father and that Caine's business stood to gain something. Remember that these men he is accusing are reasonable men, prominent citizens with much to lose in getting entangled in such repugnant business.

"A choice has to be made over who is more credible. Reynolds with his years of drug abuse and his fractured mind is not credible. He is interested in testifying falsely as he has everything to gain by making up a story or by feigning he didn't know anything.

"The state can't and doesn't have to explain why Reynolds acted irrationally. It's not the state's job to speculate on what makes him completely tick. But we've explained how he acted. The irrationality of murder often times doesn't make sense. He could've been following some subhuman instinct to cover his tracks even if it was a futile or nonsensical act when the greater evidence of the body remained, which, if ever found, he'd still have to explain.

"You needn't probe the depths of his twisted perceptions and anti-social reasoning, if it can even be called that. As far as you need to go has been provided for overwhelmingly. His intent to kill another and his action of doing so were buried in his yard. His defense is a sideshow to distract and to morbidly entertain, to spin the evidence in a way that covers up irrefutable facts. The body was in his yard. He pointed to it later and referenced it to his cronies and then Spring.

"These characters the defense has brought in to support their theory are shady and not credible. The believable ones are the investigators, the officers, and the scientists. The only correct verdict is guilty of the crime of murder in the first degree. Reynolds knew what he was doing and he was methodical about it afterwards in removing the teeth. He has lied to you about it. Don't let him walk."

He still had to concentrate to keep from slumping. After he'd finished closing, he'd become strangely relaxed even though he paid attention for objections. It seemed to be some otherworldly relaxation extending beyond himself in a confident radius. He wasn't on edge at hearing his theories attacked in rebuttal. It hadn't been as flashy or technically impressive as other closings he'd made. Whatever the result, the public eye couldn't dodge his points in its deliberations. On any assigned case, the chances were abysmally low that it would even go to jury trial. Even less that the jury would acquit.

After the jurors were excused to deliberate, he disregarded the cameras. He left his team to celebrate on their own in their own way, explaining that he was weak from the expenditure of energy. He went back to the house to rest.

That evening as he foraged for some leftovers to eat, he didn't notice their car. The city officers that had been patrolling his street must've let up now that trial testimony had concluded. Tecumseh stood watch in the backyard so he wasn't concerned. He returned to bed.

* * *

While waiting to see the widow, she thought back on what had transpired. M.L.'s trajectory the day after closing had placed him on a collision course with the chaotic, zigzag meanderings of Estoniaz, whose earlier failed attempt had led him to Florida, then to Atlanta, and then back again to the sleepy street where M.L. resided and lay in bed. She thought of the assassin moving around haphazardly, like a swatted wasp or insect with a broken antenna but still retaining a stinger. A jangled nerve on Caine's executive body.

Piecing together from the aftermath, Estoniaz had made his way to the woods behind M.L.'s house again. A tranquilizer dart quelled any potential noise from Tecumseh. Despite the basic, fanatical quality of Estoniaz's life, what was found on the former paramilitary guerilla showed a sophisticated knowledge of how to inflict death with a cadre of weapons.

When Estoniaz entered the dwelling for a second time, he must've found M.L. asleep on his bed in the dining room. The intruder must've had no problem slitting M.L.'s throat. There was no evidence of a struggle. She imagined M.L. jerking awake and struggling to breathe. Estoniaz must've waited to make sure the job was complete so he could collect the other ten thousand dollars.

Another trajectory had brought Prentice to the residence. Prentice had left celebratory drinks to check on M.L. Estoniaz must've seen headlights pull quickly in the driveway. There'd been a curtain in the makeshift bedroom pulled open slightly. The assassin must've seen the shadow of Prentice moving toward the front door.

As Prentice approached the front door, he'd told her he noticed the absence of Tecumseh's barking. Instead of knocking, he'd gone around the side.

Prentice told her he'd heard the dull grinding slide of the glass door. Seeing Tecumseh lying immobile in the middle of the yard had confirmed his suspicions. It had been a rush from then. Prentice had seen a darkened figure slinking away, scurrying back into the shadow at the back of the yard toward the fence. He'd made up ground at an angle. He'd sprinted as fast as his lungs and muscular legs could take him.

Prentice told her just as the figure put one leg up on top of the chain link fence to launch himself over into the woods, he got hold of the man's clothing, a light-weight, dark-colored mesh material. He said the man reeked something horrid. He'd wrapped his arm around the man's chest. Estoniaz was about two-thirds the size of Prentice. As Estoniaz fell, he'd knocked Estoniaz's skull with a forearm.

Prentice told her Estoniaz was unconscious. He'd dragged Estoniaz back to the house and the light. Estoniaz had roused himself, struggling a bit against a stronger hand. Prentice had asked what he was doing there but had received no response.

Prentice told her he saw some orange electrical cord on the kitchen floor near the sliding glass door. Holding Estoniaz tight, he'd reached for it and then sat the man down and tied him to a kitchen chair. Estoniaz had still squirmed. Prentice had punched him a few times, which bloodied his nose until he quit squirming.

Prentice told her he'd yelled for M.L. but got no response. He'd described a wet, coppery smell in the air. As Prentice yelled again for M.L., he'd flipped open his phone to call emergency. Dragging the chair behind him, scratching the linoleum, then scraping across the carpet, Prentice had entered the dining room. He'd seen blood all over the bed. The nearly decapitated head of M.L. had been unnaturally turned too far away from its former connection with his body. Prentice told her he'd turned to vomit.

Prentice told her panic had run through him as he got sick. He told her he had the irrational urge to go and hold him, tell him it'd be alright, the doctors were on the way. But he'd seen there was nothing he could do. He retched and vomited.

After, he'd focused on what to do. He sat watching Estoniaz squirm against the cord. He'd described the slick-skinned, sweat-stinking murderer snorting and sputtering in between short snickers, mumbling about *la familia*. Prentice had told her it seemed like a circuit had burnt out in the man's mind.

The police and medics arrived. M.L. had been pronounced dead from loss of blood hemorrhaging through his sliced jugular. Prentice had told her he was led away to be questioned about what happened. The man later identified as Estoniaz had been taken into custody.

Within hours, federal investigators became involved. Mantle had identified and gathered evidence against Estoniaz, who was on suicide watch in the county jail. Based on Mantle's familiarity with the Spindle murder investigation, he'd sought and secured immediate transfer of Estoniaz to federal custody.

The jury had been sequestered at a local hotel because of the media attention and the violence revolving around the case. The next morning before they continued deliberating, she'd detachedly listened as Miller warned them again of reading or watching any news.

After the jurors had left that next day to deliberate, Miller called her and Feld into chambers to discuss what would be newly discovered evidence if Caine was shown to be involved in M.L.'s death. She'd been disconsolate and somewhat disconnected, not as sharp as she usually was, but she hadn't let anything major slip away. She hadn't pushed for or agreed to a mistrial. Why would she at this point when all the evidence had been heard? She didn't want to risk aborting an acquittal.

For the next three days, the sequestered jurors had continued to meet during business hours to deliberate. At the beginning of Friday morning, Miller had called her and Feld back to inform them that at the end of the day yesterday, the jurors had been discussing the possibility of being deadlocked. Miller had given the jurors the rest of the morning before going on the record.

After lunch, she'd returned and the jurors had been brought back in. She'd listened as Miller asked the foreman if further deliberations would be fruitful in changing anyone's positions. The farmer had expressed that they'd reached a verdict on the charge of first-degree murder. The farmer said he didn't think more time would change their positions on the lesser includeds.

Upon hearing this, Miller called a quick sidebar. After which the clerk read into the record the verdict, "We the jury find Edward Reynolds not guilty to the charge of murder in the first degree."

She remembered a rising of gasps in the courtroom. She and Reynolds had been preoccupied with thoughts of M.L. The jury had been unable to reach unanimous verdicts on the lesser includeds of second-degree murder or manslaughter in the first or second degree. She'd watched Feld summarily exit after hearing the outcome.

She'd talked with some of the jurors who'd voted to acquit on the lesser includeds. They'd told her the jury had been deadlocked six to six on murder in the second degree, eight to four to convict on manslaughter in the first degree, and eleven to one to convict on manslaughter in the second degree. They'd gone back and forth over the three days and were sick of it. She'd excused herself. They would've found out soon enough about M.L.'s murder and perhaps now understood her abrupt departure.

Although Feld had avoided talking to the jurors, she'd seen him on the front steps of the courthouse, addressing the news cameras. Feld had promised to the cameras that the second-degree murder charge would be filed again immediately. Feld had said he hoped that the next jury would be better able to reach the right decision.

The media had gorged again on the outcome. M.L.'s murder had spurred a federal investigation into county law enforcement. Later she'd seen three of the jurors who'd voted guilty televised saying that the attempted murder and murder of M.L. would've changed their vote on the lesser includeds.

Any admonishment she believed Feld should've received for disrespecting jurors in the media appeared slight in retrospect once the corruption investigation had targeted him. Feld had been paid over the years by Caine with various favors and bribes. It was revealed that the mortgage on Feld's extravagant house had been paid down by affiliates traced to Caine. Third-party text messages had been discovered, believed to be from Caine, asking for updates on the trial against Reynolds. Not only would Feld be disbarred and lose his job, but based on what she'd heard from her former office in Montgomery, she expected Feld would eventually be entering guilty pleas, probably to obstruction and bribery.

While she took over M.L.'s practice, she'd observed the federal investigation cause an implosion within the structure of the local county prosecutor. Feld had been their lead trial attorney. The head county prosecutor, Sticklett, was implicated in the corruption charges as well. Although it was well understood that Caine had gotten Sticklett elected, the evidence of bribery was less direct. Sticklett escaped with a forced resignation and pending disbarment.

The change of leadership in the county prosecutor's office occurred before the office was able to refile the second-degree murder charge against Reynolds as Feld had promised. Interim county prosecutor Fry had been named two months after the mistrials had been declared on the lesser includeds. Fry had informed her he'd decided not to refile and would let the feds handle it now. There'd been local and even regional outrage calling for a manhunt to bring Caine back from wherever his money was shielding him. The latest rumor she'd heard put Caine in a remote area of Brazil near the rainforest.

On hearing that the county wouldn't refile, she'd scheduled a jail visit. She informed Reynolds that it looked like they'd succeeded. She warned that the state could still refile on the second-degree murder charge because there was no statute of limitations. However, if there ever was another jury, they could possibly hear about how M.L. had been murdered by someone paid by Caine.

Reynolds was still in custody on the manufacturing charge. Over the next few weeks, she and Fry reached a

plea agreement for Reynolds to one count of class B manufacturing for five years in prison. With good time, that
would leave Reynolds about two years. He was transported
to Atmore about a month later. After Reynolds had been
transported, she'd received the phone call from the councilman's widow wanting to meet in person.

In M.L.'s former office, she watched the widow arrive
to sit on the other side of her desk. Julie said during the
trial, it'd shocked her to begin to believe in M.L. despite
her anger. Julie said Feld had convinced her Reynolds was
the one behind their loss. She and her children had been
ready to latch the hate onto anyone he suggested. Julie told
her for most of the trial that is what she did. Some of her
children hadn't stop believing Reynolds had done it until
Feld had been indicted.

Julie said the proceeding was supposed to get to the
heart of that large hole in their lives left by their missing
family member. She began to have doubts when M.L. continued from his wheelchair. Julie said she'd thought to
herself, was this some type of gimmick? Had M.L. orches-
trated some injury in hopes of distracting the jurors with
sympathy? Julie said she then started to wonder at the certainty with which M.L. kept on. Julie told her Feld seemed
to become craftier and more smug. By the time Reynolds
reached the stand, Julie said she was beginning to believe
that Caine had something to do with it.

Julie said she'd been sitting there as if at the foot of
a scaffold waiting for the spectacle of a public sacrifice
to atone for the memory of Craig. But then the evidence
caused her to question if M.L. was right about Caine. Julie
had begun imagining how her husband would've looked

at the evidence, at the familial relationship, and at how Caine had left the country. Julie began to believe they'd targeted a man they could easily crush and no one would know the difference. Julie said all her stored up outrage began to turn against the perverse way they'd been going about it.

Julie told her before Reynolds was transported to prison that she'd gone to meet with him face to face and apologized to him for not standing up more to Feld. Julie explained Feld had taken advantage of them on a subject they'd still been vulnerable on.

Julie told her based on what she'd heard, she thought Reynolds was really much more calm and decent than she expected. Reynolds had put her at ease by saying that if he were looking at it from another life, he would've probably suspected himself the same as Julie had. Julie said Reynolds had let her know how heavy the weight was when the charge against him seemed to be what everyone wanted to believe. He told Julie giving into the lie seemed at times to be easier.

Julie said her family had healed somewhat, but there was still a deep scar where Craig used to be. Sometimes it was as if the wound there would fester up. Julie said she at least knew now she could identify who had caused it. Julie told her she knew Craig hadn't been a coward who had abandoned his family. She knew he'd been an upright man. She listened to Julie thank her.

She leaned back in M.L.'s chair, her chair now. Given the rush in business, she was swamped. Normally she would've rushed the person to get to the point and move on as she had to catch up. But what Julie spoke resonated soothingly. The scorn she'd perceived from that corner of the court, where the widow and her family had been behind Feld, had annoyed her, even if it had only been her own self-consciousness.

Now she leaned back farther, her mind seemingly somewhere absent but still looking on her guest. She was uninhibited to a degree that anything she said seemed right. Somehow she was taken back to working outside raking in the first touch of autumn among the smell of dead leaves.

She thanked Julie for coming. As they were getting up, she let Julie know it meant a great deal considering. They hugged and then the widow left.

She continued to work for a while with a quickened mind. Her tasks seemed delineated and accomplishable. After a few hours, she took a break. She got up and walked lackadaisically to the window of the office where she looked out on the modest downtown. She could see the river steady as a slate-colored engine.